Hoch's Ladies

Hoch's Ladies

By

EDWARD D. HOCH

Introduction by Michael Dirda

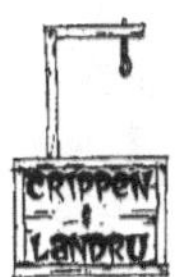

Crippen & Landru Publishers
Cincinnati, Ohio
2019

ISBN (Clothbound edition): 978-1-936363-41-4
ISBN (Paperback edition): 978-1-936363-42-1

FIRST EDITION

*Printed in the United States of America
on recycled acid-free paper*

Jeffrey A. Marks, Publisher
Douglas G. Greene, Senior editor

Crippen & Landru Publishers
PO Box 532057
Cincinnati, OH 45253
USA

Email: info@crippenlandru.com
Web: www.crippenlandru.com

CONTENTS

INTRODUCTION BY MICHAEL DIRDA

Francis Bacon famously observed that "Some books are to be tasted, others to be swallowed, and some few to be chewed and digested." Edward D. Hoch's work, however, doesn't fit any of Bacon's categories. His stories are meant to be savored. A collection like *Hoch's Ladies* resembles those tasting menus at classy restaurants: Each story is expertly prepared, beautifully presented, at once light and delicious. There's no fat or gooey sauce in Hoch's fiction. Every ingredient is there for a reason.

And what is that reason? Quite simply, it's the creation of a plot, almost always involving a murder, that will keep a reader turning the pages to find out who done it, and why, and how. In the past, Hoch has been rightly labeled a consummate puzzle-master and even likened to Will Shortz, the celebrated creator of crosswords. Today, though, we might view him as the Marie Kondo of the mystery. His fairplay stories emphasize a clean, uncluttered narrative line, just a handful of characters, and solutions that are logical and satisfying. Each one sparks joy.

And there's a lot of that joy to go around. After all, Edward D. Hoch (1930-2008) wrote nearly a thousand short stories. *Ellery Queen's Mystery Magazine* ran a Hoch contribution in every issue for 34 straight years. That's mind-boggling just on its own, even without taking into account the steady excellence of the work itself. As Jacques Barzun and Wendell Hertig Taylor noted in their magisterial *Catalogue of Crime*, Hoch stories "should be turned to first in any issue of *EQMM*" adding that their ingenious denouements never "hinge on a single trifling detail. The plots are lifelike and reasonably complex and the situations are inventive." His who-and-howdunits are, in short, perfect light entertainments.

Over the years, Hoch developed more than two dozen recurring characters, including a spy and code-expert named Rand; the contract thief Nick Velvet, who only steals oddball items, such as the water from a swimming pool or the contents of an empty room; Captain Leopold, an American analogue to Georges Simenon's Inspector Maigret; and even an occult detective named Simon Ark, who claims to be a 2,000-year-old Copt. In Hoch's very first published story, "Village of the Dead" (1955), Ark must figure out why 73 people—all the men, women and children in an isolated small town—suddenly flung themselves from a cliff in an apparent mass suicide.

For many readers, Hoch's best detective—and certainly his most endearing—is Dr. Sam Hawthorne, a general practitioner in a small New England town but a specialist in solving uncanny, miraculous-seeming crimes. In the very first Hawthorne "problem," a horse-drawn sleigh enters one end of a covered bridge and never emerges. In another, a trapeze artist disappears before the eyes of a packed audience. Hoch even reworks the hoariest of all impossible crime set-ups: A man is stabbed to death in an isolated cabin surrounded by freshly fallen snow in which there are no footprints.

Over the years Crippen & Landru have issued several Hoch collections, including the entire Sam Hawthorne series in five volumes. All are must-haves for any aficionado of the classic mystery. *Hoch's Ladies* adds one more essential volume, for it gathers together the adventures of Hoch's three female investigators: Libby Knowles, who works as a bodyguard; Susan Holt, the promotions director for a huge department store who possesses a knack for seeing what others have overlooked; and Annie Sears, a homicide detective who moves from El Paso to San Diego.

In some ways, these three women may seem roughly alike: They are young, attractive and ultra-competent, as well as regularly subject to heavy-handed passes and bedroom invitations from the various men they encounter. This sexual attention is nearly always unwelcome, another one of those tiresome things a twenty-something woman was forced to put up with in the 1980s and 90s (when most of these stories first appeared). Libby and Annie do count avuncular older police officers as mentors or colleagues. Susan, however, must deal on her own with a persistent and obnoxious male co-worker.

While Hoch's stories are invariably clever, often culminating in a double-whammy ending, they draw considerable energy and inspiration from unusual backgrounds, places and occupations. For example, the plots in *Hoch's Ladies* turn on weather prediction, race track construction, deerstalker caps, elite security systems, a Southwestern town's cactus festival, Iceland's use of steam heat, Christmas decorations in Japan, and an inexplicable stabbing death in a shower. Sometimes the fairplay merges into the truly far-fetched, but that only adds to a story's surprise-quotient. There's always pleasure in learning the secret pattern linking seemingly disparate elements, no matter how improbable the actual murder method might be. For instance, "The Cactus Killer"—featuring Annie Sears—is simultaneously hackneyed and deeply bizarre. Reading Hoch, though, you quickly learn to pay close attention, recognizing that every detail, even the most trivial—especially the most trivial—is there for a reason: You can shake any of his stories and nothing extraneous will fall out.

Still, Hoch can be more than a mere technician, frequently adding small humanizing touches to his characters. For instance, Libby Knowles started her protection agency after resigning from the police force: She did so because the man she loved, another cop, turned out to be a crook, eventually killed in a high-speed chase. Susan Holt slowly ages through her 11 adventures in various parts of the world, while also gradually climbing the corporate ladder at Mayfield's department store. Annie Sears wants desperately to prove herself on her new job with San Diego's homicide department. As for suspects: Either the least likely or the most likeable may turn out to be a cold-blooded killer. Some stories end with a real emotional wallop. In "A Traffic in Webs," Susan Holt's visit to Japan—to acquire a unique Christmas display—inadvertently causes two murders. In "The Invisible Intruder" Libby Knowles unearths enough tragic family backstory for an entire Ross Macdonald novel.

So uniformly smooth and expertly wrought are the stories in *Hoch's Ladies* that it's almost impossible to pick a favorite, let alone the best. Being a member of the Baker Street Irregulars, I did find "A Parcel of Deerstalkers," set in Meiringen, where Sherlock Holmes grappled with Professor Moriarty at the Reichenbach Falls, to be especially dazzling. But then, as a John Dickson Carr fan, I was also wowed by what one might call the locked-bathroom murder in "A Shower of Daggers." Still, there's no need to choose. Just buy *Hoch's Ladies*. To paraphrase a certain insurance company's catchy slogan: You're always in good hands with Ed Hoch.

Michael Dirda is a Pulitzer Prize-winning critic for The Washington Post *and the author of several books about books, including* On Conan Doyle, *which received a 2012 Edgar Award.*

It was during her college days that Susan Holt first encountered Walter Pater's essay on Leonardo da Vinci with its celebrated evocation of the Mona Lisa. One phrase read: *She . . . has been a diver in deep seas, and keeps their fallen day about her; and trafficked for strange webs with Eastern merchants.* That last part especially stuck in her mind. She did not know exactly what it meant but she knew, like Mona Lisa, that it was something she wanted to do—to traffic for strange webs with Eastern merchants.

Careers often move in strange directions after graduation, and for Susan her course in art appreciation led somehow to a job in retailing, in the promotions section of Manhattan's most famous department store. She'd been there seven years, handling a good bit of the Christmas promotions and the displays that went with them, when Saul Marx, the head of the department, entered the office on the first working day after Christmas.

"Time to get started on next year's planning," he said, as he always did right after Christmas. "We've got to top this year."

"That'll take some doing," Mike Brentnor said from his desk opposite Susan's. "Got any ideas?"

Saul Marx always had ideas. That was why he was head of the department. "I've been reading about something really spectacular in Tokyo this Christmas. One of their big stores has a display of spider webs that—"

This was too much even for Brentnor. "Spider webs! I can find some up at our country place if you really want them."

"I'm serious," Marx assured him. "In fact, I want you to fly over there while the display is still in place. These aren't your ordinary spider webs. They're said to be bizarrely beautiful, almost like works of art. Once you see them I want you to phone me. If they're as wonderful as I've heard, we'll make the artist an offer to show them here next Christmas."

"The artist?" Mike Brentnor scoffed. "You mean the spider who wove them? What would I offer him—ten thousand flies?"

"There's a Japanese professor who creates them by feeding various drugs to the spiders—LSD, pot, that sort of thing."

"My God! We'd have the SPCA on our necks!"

Strange webs, Susan thought, and suddenly remembered that phrase from her college reading of Walter Pater: *. . . trafficked for strange webs with Eastern merchants.* "I'll go," she said almost without thinking. "Let me go to Tokyo."

Saul Marx turned to stare at her, as if only then remembering she was in the room. "You, Susan? Do you think you could handle something like this?"

"I arranged last year's spring show of exotic flowers, and I handled negotiations for the Best of Britain promotion two years ago," she reminded him. "You sent me to London for that."

He thought about it, but not for long. It was obvious Mike Brentnor wasn't enthused with the idea, and the only other person to send was on vacation till after New Year's. "I want someone to see these webs on display in the Tokyo store," Saul said. "They come down after New Year's, so it has to be this week. Are you up to that, Susan?"

She glanced at Brentnor, who was sinking into his pouting mode. "You bet I am!"

"Very well. See me in my office at two and we'll go over the details."

That evening she broke the news to Russell, an off-and-on live-in boyfriend who was rehearsing for a play down in SoHo. Arriving at the loft where the actors were just finishing their run-through, she got him aside. "Bad news, Russell. I can't make Nell's New Year's party. I have to fly to Tokyo for the store."

"What? Tokyo?" His face showed disappointment and the beginning of anger. "I was counting on it, Susan. What happened?"

"Brentnor doesn't want to do it and I'm next in line. I have to catch a display while it's up and negotiate to bring it to New York for next Christmas."

"Tokyo, for God's sake! There's no chance you can get back in time?"

"Today's the twenty-seventh already. I'm flying over Wednesday but it'll be late Thursday their time when I get in. That gives me Friday to see the display and that's New Year's Eve. Even if every-thing went perfectly, it would be Saturday night or Sunday before I could get back. You can tell Nell how sorry I am."

"I don't know that I want to go alone."

"Why not? You know everyone."

"It's not the same going alone on New Year's Eve."

My God, she thought, he's pouting just like Mike Brentnor at the store. "I'm sorry," she said firmly. "It can't be helped. It's my job." He turned to walk away and she added, "What about tonight?"

He gestured toward the others. "I'm rehearsing. That's my job."

She nodded. "You can use the apartment while I'm gone if you wish. You still have the key, don't you?"

"It's around somewhere."

She turned away, trying to mask her annoyance. "I'll be back next week. You can call me."

"Sure."

Susan caught the Wednesday morning flight to Tokyo, settling in with her laptop computer for the long journey ahead. The trip took about fourteen hours, and Tokyo was fourteen hours ahead of New York time. Her eleven a.m. flight from New York would land her at Tokyo's Haneda Airport at three o'clock Thursday afternoon. It was a day lost to her, and there was little consolation in the fact that part of it would be regained on the return flight.

The airport was on the southern fringes of the city and the newer Narita Airport was even farther away. Something she noticed in the terminal after landing was that she was taller than most of the Japanese men. Back in New York she rarely thought about her height. Suddenly one of these Japanese men was right in front of her, bowing from the waist. "Miss Susan Holt?" he asked in perfect English.

"I—Yes, that's me."

"I am Takeo Keio, manager of Fuji Star. I have come to meet you and guide you around our city."

"How nice!" She shook his hand. "This is my first visit to Tokyo. I was worried about finding my way around."

"We will claim your luggage and pass through customs. Then I will deliver you to your hotel."

"Thank you, Mr. Keio."

His limousine was long and white, like one that might be rented for a wedding back home. She settled into the plush leather seat, anxious for her first glimpse of the sprawling city. "Tokyo extends over nine hundred and thirty square miles," Mr. Keio explained as they headed away from the airport on the expressway into the central city. "Yet everything is crowded. It is a very confusing city to a visitor."

"New York is crowded too," she assured him.

"Ah, but not like Tokyo. I have been to New York many times. Your stores are always a great inspiration to us."

"I understand Mr. Marx spoke to you on the phone about our interest in the webs display."

"Yes, yes! Professor Hiraoka has performed a miracle. Wait until you see his webs!"

"I'm anxious to get a look at them."

"Fuji Star is open late tonight if you care to—"

Susan glanced at her watch. It was after four already and she wanted nothing so much as a warm shower and a bed. "I'd better wait till morning," she pleaded. "The long flight really exhausted me."

"Very well." He spent the rest of the drive pointing out the sights to her, and when she remarked on a large structure that looked like the Eiffel Tower he announced proudly, "It is fifty-nine feet higher than the Eiffel. Our Tokyo Tower is for radio and television transmission. We have four major commercial rivals here—Fuji TV, which has no connection with our store, Nippon TV, Tokyo Broadcasting System, and TV Asahi. You may view them all on the set in your room. And that large building just ahead is your hotel. It is across the square, only a five-minute walk from Fuji Star."

"Thank you so much for the tour, Mr. Keio."

"I will look for you in the morning, then? We will be closing early for the New Year's holiday, so I suggest you arrive before noon."

"I'll be in your office by ten," she promised.

Susan knew virtually no Japanese, so she spent little time with the network stations on her TV. She ordered dinner in her room and relaxed with a channel showing English-language news. Presently she stretched out on the bed to get more comfortable and fell asleep almost at once. When she awoke it was dark outside. She turned off the television and noted that the time was just after midnight. Then she took the shower she'd promised herself and went back to bed sleeping restlessly until around five in the morning.

Looking out at the wakening city, Susan was surprised at the amount of early-morning activity. By the time she went down to breakfast at seven, the streets resembled a New York rush hour. The hotel restaurant served a passable Western breakfast. Back in her room she wrapped a small gift she'd brought for Keio, remembering that unwrapped gifts were considered rude in Japan. When she left the hotel just after nine, she noticed a Japanese youth follow her out.

As she waited for the traffic light to change, she suddenly had the impression of being shoved in the small of her back, but it happened so quickly she couldn't call it a deliberate act. Then she was falling, her leather briefcase flying from her grasp, just as a speeding taxi bore down on her. She landed on her hands and knees, feeling the pain, bracing for the instant impact of the taxi. Then a dozen hands were on her, yanking her out of harm's way as the driver slammed on his brakes.

"I— thank you," Susan managed to gasp, looking down at her skinned and bleeding knees.

"Here, let me help you," a kindly British voice said. She looked up to see a slim man in a gray topcoat reaching out his hand to help steady her. "Are you staying at the hotel?"

"Yes." She grimaced in pain.

"I'll help you back inside and we'll see about those knees. You almost got yourself killed."

"The crowd just seemed to push me—"

Inside the lobby the Englishman issued a quick command in Japanese. "It doesn't look serious but you should get it cleaned off. I've asked that someone escort you to your room."

She flexed her knees and both of them seemed to work properly despite the pain. "Thanks so much."

He presented his card. "I'm Geoffrey Peters, Miss Holt. With the British Trade Delegation. Please call me if I can be of further service."

She smiled at him, brushing the loose grime from her hands. "I will. Thanks again."

Upstairs she bathed her sore knees and put on a fresh pair of pantyhose. Luckily she still had time to reach the store by ten. It was not until she was halfway across the street, remembering the kindness of Geoffrey Peters, that she wondered how he had known her name.

Takeo Keio was awaiting her in his office on the seventh floor of Fuji Star, a massive department store filled with wonders Susan could barely imagine. After exchanging traditional gifts and sipping tea served by Rumiko, his pretty secretary, they set off to tour the store together.

"Did you take the escalator to my office?" Takeo asked.

"I was running a little late," she admitted. "I took the elevator." She told him about falling in the street.

"That is terrible! You could have been seriously injured or even killed! People here are so thoughtless at times with their pushing. You must avoid our subway tubes at all costs, especially during the rush hour when people are jammed together like cattle." He took her arm gently, as if to protect her. "But come—the first wonder of Fuji Star is at our escalators."

As they approached she saw a small Japanese woman dressed in a traditional kimono standing next to the moving staircase. The woman bowed politely and said something in Japanese. Only then did Susan realize she was looking at a robot, an automaton equipped with an audiotape to supply information. "What did she say?"

Keio smiled proudly. "The ones at the escalators warn women to lift their kimono sleeves so as not to get them caught. Others around the store inform shoppers of special products and sales. I will admit we borrowed the idea of the automatons from Mitsukoshi, our largest competitor."

"It's wonderful!"

"Something for New York, perhaps?"

"Well—the bowing is what gives them charm, and that wouldn't be suitable in American stores."

"Ah yes!" Takeo Keio said. "A different culture."

It was obvious he was withholding the webs for the tour's finale, and they finally reached a small softly lit gallery on the top floor, not far from Keio's office. The sign next to the entrance was in both Japanese and English: *The Strange Webs of Professor Hiraoka.*

Susan entered slowly, seeing at first only a dozen glass-covered cases positioned on the walls, their contents shrouded in shadow. Then the spotlights went on, all at once, and she stood stock-still, frozen by the beauty and wonderment of what she saw. "These are exquisite," she said softly, as one might speak in church. Each of the cases held a single large spider web, its strands glistening with something like dew. The first web seemed perfect in all respects, the second off-center a bit. They seemed to grow more bizarre, of wilder formation, as she moved around the gallery. Here was one with two centers, and another with a dead fly caught at the end of a funnel-shaped tunnel. All of them glistened in the spotlights, shimmering magically. Susan stood for a moment at each one, even the most outrageous, as if expecting the web's maker to appear in one corner, carefully inching its way toward that dead fly.

"You are impressed?" the Japanese asked her with a proud smile.

"I must have these for New York. They are works of art."

"I cannot negotiate for America. You must speak directly with Professor Hiraoka. I know the prime minister himself has promised to come if he shows the webs in Tokyo next Christmas."

"Where can I find him?" she asked, unable to shift her gaze from the mesmerizing webs.

"He has been coming in every few days to tend to the webs, but tomorrow is the final day of the exhibit. The webs will be packaged carefully and returned to him."

"What tending do they need?"

"These glass fronts lift open and the professor sprays a special moisturizer on the webs. That accounts for their shimmer and dewlike effect."

"Where does he live?"

"Professor Hiraoka teaches at Waseda University here in Tokyo and lives near the campus with his wife and family. If you wish to arrange an appointment it would be my pleasure to place my limousine and driver at your disposal."

"That's very kind of you," Susan replied. "I hate to bother him over the holiday weekend. Do you think it would be all right?"

"Certainly. For most of our people New Year's is a more important holiday than Christmas, but Professor Hiraoka is a Christian. I expect he will spend tomorrow working in his study like any other day."

"I'm surprised you celebrate Christmas at all in a Shintoist and Buddhist country."

He smiled slightly. "It is a secular holiday here. We have a place for Santa Claus if he helps to sell merchandise."

"Fuji Star has other stores around the country, do they not?"

He nodded. "Twenty-seven in all, although this is the largest. It is a publicly held corporation. I manage only this store, which has enough problems for me these days."

Susan glanced at her watch and did some quick mental arithmetic. Noon in Tokyo meant that it was ten p.m. the previous night in New York. Saul Marx had told her to phone him at home after she'd seen the webs, but it might be a bit late. Better to wait till later and call him at the office. By that time she would have spoken to Professor Hiraoka. "If you would give me the professor's phone number, I could call him for an appointment now."

"Certainly. I have it in my office."

Keio placed the call for her and said a few words in Japanese to the professor. Then he turned the telephone over to her. "Hello, Professor Hiraoka. My name is Susan Holt. I'm from America."

The voice on the other end was strong, with a good command of English. "Miss Holt, it's my pleasure! Takeo has told me about you and your interest in my webs. I feel honored that a great New York store would send someone over here to see them."

"I'd like to speak to you about them, Professor. I know it's the New Year's weekend—"

"Would you be free to come out here this afternoon?"

"Well—yes, of course. Mr. Keio has loaned me his car and driver, so I should have no trouble finding the place."

"Very good. About three o'clock?"

"Perfect. I'll be there."

Professor Hiraoka lived on the outskirts of the city, in a pleasant area where the crush of people and places, railways and highways finally began to abate. Keio's driver pulled up in front of the house and said he would wait for her. The residence itself was modest, and the door was answered by a young man of around twenty who seemed vaguely familiar. He ushered her into a small study where Professor Hiraoka awaited her.

He was tall for a Japanese, taller than Susan, and wore a black silk kimono that was tied loosely in front, revealing pants and a dress shirt beneath it. He bowed slightly and accepted the wrapped gift she'd brought along. "How kind of you," he told her. "This is my son, Yoichi."

Yoichi bowed too, and in that instant Susan remembered where she had seen him before. He was the young Japanese in her hotel lobby that morning, the one who had followed her outside just before she was pushed into the street.

Yoichi left them and Professor Hiraoka settled down behind his desk. He was nearly bald and wore tinted glasses that lent a scholarly yet mysterious look to his face. "I consider it a great honor that you have come here to my home."

"Your webs are creations of real beauty. How do you achieve it?"

He smiled. "By trial and error. I read of some experiments in which LSD was given to spiders and caused them to spin fantastic webs. I experimented in my basement workroom with all sorts of drugs and over time worked out the correct combinations for maximum results. I am aware that some people have an intense dislike for spiders, but no one can fail to appreciate the beauty of a magnificent web. Come, I will show you my workroom."

She followed him out to the kitchen where his wife was beginning to prepare dinner. She was a small, pretty woman who hardly looked old enough to have a son of Yoichi's age. "Beware of the spiders," she cautioned Susan as they started down the cellar steps. Obviously her husband's work was something of a family joke.

The Hiraoka's home was one of the rare Tokyo houses with a basement. Professor Hiraoka switched on the lights and Susan found herself surrounded by more of the glass wall cabinets she'd seen at the store. "You'll notice we have air holes and little pegs along the sides to encourage the spiders to start their webs. The pegs can be placed closer together if necessary, though naturally I like the webs to be as large as possible. Once they are spun I spray them with this special solution which causes them to glisten in the light and also strengthens the web somewhat."

"Could they be flown to America in these display cases?"

He hesitated for a moment. "I believe so, if they were well padded and insulated against the cold. A ship might be a bit smoother but it has the disadvantage of taking much longer. The webs should be inspected and sprayed every few days."

"Do the spiders accompany them?"

"No, no," he said with a chuckle. "Their work is finished. But I should go with them. Would this be a problem?"

"Of course not. We were planning on it. Certainly we'd want you to supervise their installation and lighting, just as any artist would."

"The spiders are the artists. You might say I am merely their manager."

She turned from the webs and inspected the rest of the basement. On one wall was a locked cabinet and he opened it for her. "I obtain the hallucinogens through the university. When I am away I return them. I take no chances on a burglary."

They discussed financial considerations and Professor Hiraoka was quite reasonable. "How long would you want to show my webs at your New York store?"

She took a small calendar from her briefcase. "In our country the Christmas shopping season really starts the day after Thanksgiving, Naturally we have decorations in place before that, but Friday, November twenty-fifth would be the opening day for the display. It would remain in place until Christmas, which is one month. Of course you would need time on both ends to prepare the display and then dismantle it. I would guess six weeks in all. In addition to your fee for the display we would pay living expenses for you and your wife in New York during that time. Would your son be coming too?"

"No, he has other interests."

"This evening I'll phone New York and have them fax me the agreement. I'm sure there'll be no problem over the terms."

They returned to his study. "I will look forward to this. My wife and I have been to New York only once before, many years ago, when I spoke at Columbia University."

Susan was warming to the whole idea. "I'm certain we can get you on some of the television talk shows. You must have humorous stories about spiders getting loose in the house."

"A few," he admitted with a smile.

"You said you read something about spiders on LSD. Is it possible that you also read the English writer Walter Pater? He wrote an essay on the Mona Lisa in which he mentioned trafficking for strange webs, and that's exactly what I'm doing."

"I never read Pater," he admitted, going to a section of his bookcase containing English-language volumes. "But I did read another Englishman, Jonathan Swift. Are you familiar with *Gulliver's Travels?*"

"Of course," answered Susan, who hadn't read it since freshman year in college.

"You may remember here in the third part when Gulliver visits the Academy of Lagado he encounters a professor who fills his room with cobwebs of various hues, achieved by feeding colored flies to the spiders that spin them. He also feeds them gums and oils to strengthen the webs. The professor's object is to replace silkworms with spiders capable of producing colored silk strands strong enough to be made into clothing." He handed her the open volume.

The book was an 1865 edition of *Gulliver's Travels* with illustrations by Thomas Morten. It had been published by Cassell, Petter, and Galpin in London. The illustration did indeed show a man with sparse long hair, a beard, and glasses, wearing a ragged kimono, greeting visitors to his cobweb-covered room. Spiders could be seen in many of the webs. The man seemed to be oriental and looked a bit like Professor Hiraoka.

"I'm surprised Swift's satire would be of interest to you."

Professor Hiraoka smiled at her. "And why shouldn't it be? After all, the only nonmythical country visited by Gulliver was Japan."

Susan phoned the store from her hotel room just before midnight. "It's almost the new year here," she told Saul Marx. "I'm celebrating all alone with a glass of champagne."

"Good for you," he grumbled. "We've got another fourteen hours to go. How are you doing with the webs?"

"Perfect! They're really beautiful things. We'll have pictures in every New York newspaper and half a dozen national magazines."

"You met the man who produces them?"

"Professor Hiraoka, yes. He's very nice and most cooperative. He and his wife are looking forward to visiting New York." Quickly she ran over the terms of the financial agreement. "Does that sound reasonable from your end?"

"What about the shipping expenses for the webs? You'd better check into that from your end."

"I already have." She gave him the figures. "And I assume our standard liability policy will cover insurance."

"We usually add a rider for special exhibitions like this."

"Fine. Could you type up the necessary agreement and fax it to me here at the hotel? I'll get Professor Hiraoka's signature on it tomorrow." She gave him the number of the fax machine in her room.

"It'll be waiting for you when you wake up in the morning. You've done a fine job with this, Susan."

"Thanks. I appreciate that. And Happy New Year."

"Happy New Year to you too."

She glanced at the bedside clock as she hung up the phone. It was still ten minutes before midnight. Suddenly the phone rang and her first thought was that Saul Marx was calling her back about something.

"Hello?"

"Miss Susan Holt?" asked a male voice with a British accent. "Yes?"

"I wonder if you remember me. We met outside your hotel this morning. My name is Geoffrey Peters."

"Oh yes."

"I know it's very late, but I assumed no young American woman would retire before seeing in the new year. I'm downstairs in the bar and I wonder if I might buy you a drink."

"I was just getting ready for bed," Susan replied, "but I appreciate the invitation. Thank you. Perhaps another time."

His voice dropped slightly and the tone changed. "It's very important I speak with you about what happened this morning. It was not an accident but a deliberate attempt to kill you."

"I'm sure you must be mistaken," she said, but an image of Professor Hiraoka's son following her out of the hotel loomed large.

"Your life is in danger, Miss Holt. We must talk."

For a split second she considered inviting him up to her room, but immediately dismissed the thought. For all she knew the debonair Geoffrey Peters could be a robber or a rapist. "I'll be down in fifteen minutes," she decided, "but only for one drink."

He was waiting in the bar, seated alone in a corner booth. The television set had finished proclaiming the new year and the bar's few customers were beginning to settle down. Most seemed to be Europeans, though there were a few Americans too. Peters wore a gray suit with a brightly striped vest. Earlier she'd only had the impression of a slim British gentleman. Now she saw that he was probably in his late thirties, with a bit of a twinkle in his eye. Seeing that, she wondered if this was all an elaborate ploy to get her into bed with him.

"So glad you could come," he said loudly enough for anyone who might be interested. "Would you join me in a champagne toast to the new year?"

She saw the open bottle with two glasses. "I just had one in my room, but I suppose another wouldn't harm me."

He agreed and poured her a glass. "As I told you on the phone, I'm sorry to disturb you so late. But I believe it is vital that you know your life is in danger." His voice had dropped much lower.

"I hope you're just exaggerating."

"I wish I were. You were pushed in front of that taxi this morning by a young Japanese man. I believe he did it deliberately."

She took a sip of the champagne. "Let's start at the beginning, Mr. Peters."

"Please call me Geoffrey."

"All right, Geoffrey. Why were you watching me this morning?"

"I didn't say I was."

"You knew my name. You were watching me just as he was. How do I know it wasn't you who gave me a push?"

He ignored her question and said, "The young man who pushed you is Yoichi Hiraoka, the professor's son."

"I suspected as much," she admitted. "I recognized him when I visited their house today. But why? He didn't even know me."

"Japan has many of the same problems as Germany these days—a resurgence of the kind of right-wing factions that helped bring on the Second World War. Hiraoka's son is active in such a group."

She remembered his father saying simply that he had other interests. "But why would he try to kill me? He'd never even met me. And what business is it of yours?"

The Englishman said quietly, "We were advised of your mission. So was Yoichi's group."

"Mission? What mission?" Susan was growing angry now. "I'm over here to arrange an exhibition of Professor Hiraoka's webs for next Christmas, back in New York."

"How long are you staying?"

"The store is faxing me the agreement overnight. If I can obtain Professor Hiraoka's signature tomorrow I'll take a plane out of here the next day."

"They don't want that agreement signed. That's why an attempt was made on your life."

"What you're saying doesn't make any sense," she argued. "Why should a rightist group care about those webs and what happens to them?"

"We don't know. The only thing certain is that Fuji Star department store has become a focus of their activities. Group members under surveillance are often seen to enter the store and browse around, though they rarely buy anything."

"Are they shoplifting?"

"No. They've been watched very carefully and they do nothing suspicious."

"Do you work for the Japanese government?"

He smiled slightly. "I'm doing some antiterrorist work for them under contract. That's all you need to know."

Susan finished her champagne. "Thank you for warning me about Yoichi. I'll be on my guard. Good night, Mr. Peters."

He stood up as she left the table. "Happy New Year, Miss Holt."

She slept a bit later the following morning and when she awoke she was surprised to see so many people on the street, even on New Year's morning. Many of the stores appeared to be open. On her way down to breakfast she picked up the contract that had been faxed to her room and reviewed it while she ate. When she was satisfied it was in order she used her fax machine to make several more copies.

Susan could see the Mitsukoshi department store from her hotel and she decided to visit it. Tokyo's largest, it boasted a multistoried entrance hall and a grand staircase with a huge sculpture representing the goddess of sincerity. The escalators, as in Fuji Star, had bowing automatons warning about kimono sleeves. She bought a small gift, a blue cotton *yukata*—a loose-fitting garment that went over the head and tied around the waist, to be worn after bathing or at the beach. It would look good on Russell, if he'd gotten over his anger at her sudden business trip.

On the street Susan was very careful not to stand too near the curb and she kept an eye out for Professor Hiraoka's son, but there was no sign of the young man. With some time to kill before she returned to the professor's home for his signature on the contracts, she decided to return to Fuji Star on the off-chance that Takeo Keio might be at work, even on a Saturday that was New Year's Day. Japanese managers, after all, were notorious for hard work and long hours.

The store was about as crowded as Mitsukoshi's had been, and she was sorry now that she hadn't bought her gift here. She made her way to Keio's office on the top floor and asked his secretary, Rumiko, if he was in.

"Yes," she replied with a smile. "He had a visitor who'd brought him a New Year's gift, but I believe he's free now. Let me see."

She went to the door of his office, knocked, and opened it. Her short, startled cry brought Susan to her side at once. Takeo Keio was slumped over his desk, his head resting in a pool of blood. He'd been shot through the left temple.

The police took charge quickly. Rumiko, sobbing at her desk, told them what little she knew. A young Japanese man had arrived to see Takeo Keio at eleven that morning, saying he had a New Year's gift for him. There was indeed a gift, a small hand-carved Buddha that sat on the desk just at the edge of the blood from Keio's fatal wound. Rumiko had heard nothing unusual from the office, indicating that a silenced pistol had probably been used.

"They were together about ten minutes," Rumiko said. "Then I went over to the files. As I returned to my desk I saw the young man walking away toward the elevator."

Susan watched while the police searched the office carefully. "A silenced pistol is usually an automatic," the detective in charge explained to her. "We want to find the ejected cartridge case, if the killer didn't take it with him."

He spoke good English and smiled to put her at ease. Only his eyes were cold. He'd said his name was Sergeant Shimane.

There was nothing on the desk top except the Buddha and a few of Keio's papers. The wastebasket was empty this early in the day. They went over the carpeted floor and found nothing at first, until one detective felt around the leg of a chair and came up with the cartridge case. Sergeant Shimane examined it carefully and dropped it into a plastic evidence bag.

"Now tell me what you were doing here, Miss Holt," he said.

"I had business with Mr. Keio. I'd seen him yesterday, and I returned to speak with him again today."

"On New Year's?"

"I took a chance he'd be here since the store was open."

The detectives had finished their examination of the office without finding anything else the killer might have left. Photographers and fingerprint men moved in and Sergeant Shimane escorted her outside. Rumiko had recovered enough to telephone the store's main office with news of the killing. Shimane questioned Susan some more, noted the hotel where she was staying, and advised her to contact him before she left the country. Then she was free to go.

With Keio's limousine no longer available, Susan took a taxi out to Professor Hiraoka's residence. The professor's wife answered the door and Yoichi was nowhere to be seen. The professor came out of his study to greet her. "I have been looking forward to your arrival," he said, seeming genuinely pleased.

"Before you sign the agreement I'm afraid I must tell you some bad news. I've just come from Fuji Star. Takeo Keio has been shot to death in his office."

"What? What's this you're saying?" He seemed startled by the news. "Who could do such a thing?"

"The police are looking for a young man. I know nothing more about it."

He shook his head. "Terrible, terrible—"

Susan removed the contract from her briefcase. "Professor, there are one or two questions I must ask you."

"Go ahead."

"Have you received any recent threats regarding the display of your webs? Is there anyone who didn't want them shown in America?"

"There've certainly been no threats. Are you implying that Keio's murder is somehow connected with my webs?"

"I don't know. It's a possibility."

"The only one opposed to showing the webs in America is my son Yoichi, who has strange nationalistic ideas at times."

"Is Yoichi here now? I'd like to see him."

"He left early this morning to meet friends."

The professor's wife had been hovering near the study door. Now she entered, to his great displeasure. "Naomi—do not interfere in this!"

But she wouldn't be silenced. "What is this about my son?" she asked. "What has he done?"

"I don't know," Susan said. "I just want to talk to him."

"Those people," she muttered, then switched to Japanese.

They talked, or argued, for some minutes. Finally Naomi left the room and Susan turned to the professor. "What is the trouble?"

"She fears Yoichi is a member of a militant group bent on violence."

"Do you think it is true?"

"I know it is true," he said with a deep sigh.

"I hope we won't have any trouble in New York," Susan said. She produced the contract. "Please sign these. I'll explain anything you don't understand."

He started reading the contract, pausing now and again for the meaning of some word or phrase. Finally satisfied, he affixed his signature to three copies just as they heard the front door open. "Whose taxi waits outside?" a voice yelled. She knew it was Yoichi.

He entered the room and saw her, throwing down the heavy jacket he'd been wearing. His face twisted with fury as Professor Hiraoka tried to calm him. "You have signed the contract, Father! You have signed my death warrant!"

Naomi Hiraoka appeared behind him, trying to grab her son's shoulders. He fought her off and the professor shouted something in Japanese. It was an angry scene, and Susan wished she was out of there. She felt like one of those helpless flies, trapped in a web she couldn't comprehend.

Yoichi broke free of his mother's grasping hands and ran out of the house with his father's voice shouting after him. He'd left his heavy jacket on the floor and Susan picked it up without thinking. She felt the weight in the pocket and immediately imagined a small gun, the weapon that had killed Takeo Keio. It was not a gun but some sort of remote-control device.

"What's this?" she asked the parents. "Is it for a garage door?"

But Professor Hiraoka and his wife continued arguing, ignoring her for the moment. She dropped the gadget into her purse.

"I must go," she told them, scooping up the signed contracts.

They ceased their argument and Professor Hiraoka tried to regain his composure. "You must excuse us. Being the parents of a rebellious son is not always easy in today's Japan."

"Nor in today's America," Susan sympathized. "Did he know Takeo Keio?"

"He'd met him at the opening of my webs exhibit, of course. Yoichi is often at Fuji Star, for whatever reason."

"Has he been in trouble with the police?"

"I fear so. He has been arrested in demonstrations at the airport and the university."

"What did he mean about this contract being his death warrant?"

"I do not know. He wished me to exhibit the webs at a celebration next December marking the hundredth anniversary of our victory in the Sino-Japanese War, but I was against the idea from the beginning. My webs are works of art, not militaristic celebrations."

Susan stuffed the contracts into her briefcase. "My taxi is waiting. I must be on my way. A copy of the contract will be returned to you together with the advance payment agreed upon. We will be in touch about the shipping dates for the webs."

"I would like to travel with them, on the same plane if possible."

"I think we can arrange that. I'll look forward to greeting you and Mrs. Hiraoka in New York next November. And I hope your personal problems are resolved."

He bowed. "Thank you, Miss Holt."

Susan went back to her hotel and ordered a sandwich from room service. The contracts were signed, her job was done. She could be on a flight to New York in the morning. The murder of Takeo Keio was no concern of hers, whether or not Yoichi Hiraoka had pulled the trigger. Still. . .

She opened her purse for a tip when the room-service waiter arrived and saw Yoichi's remote-control device resting there. She'd forgotten all about it. Pointing it toward the window, she pressed the button on top.

Nothing happened.

She pointed it toward the room's television set and nothing happened.

She sat down and ate her sandwich.

Was it something connected with Fuji Star? Yoichi frequented the store, and Geoffrey Peters had told her that other members of the rightist group did too. Susan walked to the window and stared across the square at it.

One last time, one last visit, she decided. She left the briefcase and contracts in the room but took the remote-control unit with her. Nervously crossing the wide street, expecting to see Yoichi lunging toward her at any moment, she made it to the store without incident. As she entered a greeter was telling customers in Japanese and English, "We will be closing in thirty minutes because of the holiday."

She took the escalator up to the top floor and noticed that a police officer stood guard at the door to Keio's office. Walking down the aisle toward the furniture department, she pressed the remote-control gadget in her pocket. Nothing happened.

This is foolish, she decided. If the purpose of the device was to set off some sort of explosive, she might blow herself up by accident. She headed for the down escalator. The waiting automaton bowed and the mouth on the white doll-like face began voicing a warning about kimono sleeves. She pressed the button in her pocket as if to zap it.

Instantly the voice was cut off, overridden by another message in Japanese. Strange.

Customers were beginning to leave the store, streaming down the escalators with their bags. Clerks were cashing up for the day. She waited until no one was near and approached the bowing figure again, activating the remote control in her pocket. Once again the substitute message came from the bowing figure.

"We are closing now," an employee told her, hurrying past.

"Thank you."

She turned, not knowing what to do, when suddenly she saw the Englishman, Geoffrey Peters, coming from the direction of the furniture department. "What are you doing here?" she asked.

"I heard about Keio's death and came as soon as I could. I understand you found his body, along with his secretary?"

"That's right, and I may have discovered why he was killed. You told me this store seemed to be a focal point for activity by young rightists."

"Yes," he agreed, staring at the remote-control gadget she produced from her pocket. "What's that?"

"I found it in the pocket of Yoichi Hiraoka's coat. Watch this!"

The bowing figure voiced her special message and Peters was taken aback. "This unit overrides the standard taped message with a special message. These rightist youths have been coming here for instructions, triggering this device when no one else was within earshot." He took the gadget and tried it himself.

"Keio was seen doing this and someone killed him."

"Perhaps," Peters said a bit uncertainly.

"What does the message say?"

"Meet me in the gallery after the store closes."

"That's now!"

"I just came from that area and I saw no one."

"Come on," she urged.

He followed her back to the furniture department, to the gallery entrance, and the spotlights came on as they walked past the sign announcing Professor Hiraoka's wonderful webs. Stretched out on the floor beneath the first case was the body of Yoichi Hiraoka.

"He's been shot," Geoffrey Peters told her, kneeling to examine the body. "We're too late."

"The killer can't be far."

It was clear to her now. She knew what had to be done. "I'll get the police," Peters said, leaving her for a moment.

Susan walked past a white-faced automaton that bowed in her kimono and announced a sale on the second floor. She hurried on, ignoring it. Another blocked her path, bowing, starting to speak as she came out of her bow, and Susan saw the silenced pistol slide from the sleeve of her kimono, coming up fast toward Susan's face.

Then she heard a deafening gunshot behind her as Peters fired and the figure toppled backwards, blood gushing from her shoulder.

"My God!" Susan gasped, frozen with fright.

"It's all right," Peters said, kicking the gun away from the traumatized fingers. "I'll get some of this paint off the face and we'll see who it is."

"I already know who it is," Susan managed to tell him. "It's Takeo Keio's secretary, Rumiko."

Sergeant Shimane and his men were still in Keio's office when they heard the shot and came running. Susan's legs were a bit wobbly as she sat down on one of the chairs. "Call an ambulance!" Shimane ordered one of his men. "What happened here?"

"She killed Yoichi Hiraoka," Peters said, "and she tried to kill Miss Holt here. Yoichi's body is in the gallery."

"Keio's secretary?" the detective asked, unable to believe it. "I just finished questioning her an hour ago!"

"She killed Keio too," Susan assured them. "No doubt with this same gun. We should have known her story about the young visitor with the gift for Keio was a lie. The little Buddha was sitting alone on the desk. When you searched for the cartridge you found nothing else on the floor and the wastebasket was empty." Shimane and Peters both looked blank. "Don't you see? There was no wrapping for the gift! In Japan gifts are always wrapped—it's rude not to! If the killer bothered to bring a gift at all, it would have been wrapped. If he took the wrapping with him he'd have taken the gift too. Rumiko lied about the visitor. After she killed Keio she left the Buddha on his desk to bolster her story, forgetting that she should have left a wrapping too. She's the one who's been doctoring these automatons so they'd deliver special messages to members of the youth group. It was a perfect method of getting instructions to them quickly without the danger of using a tapped telephone."

"And Keio discovered what she was doing?" Sergeant Shimane asked.

"Of course. That's why she had to kill him. The group wanted Professor Hiraoka's webs to be displayed in Tokyo next year because—" Even as she spoke, the whole plot was unfolding in her mind. "—because the prime minister himself had promised to visit them. There would be an assassination attempt, a bomb planted by Yoichi in one of his father's wooden frames, a signal for an uprising. When the contract was signed and Yoichi knew he had failed, he came here to report to Rumiko. He knew even without his remote-control unit that she'd be waiting in the gallery. She figured his death would be blamed on the stranger who shot Keio, so she used the opportunity to kill him. As Yoichi must have feared, the organization had no further need for him once he'd failed in his mission to win his father's exhibit for the Sino-Japanese centennial. Rather than a co-conspirator, he had become a danger to them."

"She was clever," Peters agreed. "The kimono and the face paint allowed her to pose as one of the automatons if someone came along while she was waiting for a meeting. When she recovers from her wound I think she'll be ready to talk about the others involved."

Susan felt suddenly tired. She'd run down at last. At that moment she only wanted to be out of there and on her way home. As it turned out, she stayed on for Yoichi's funeral service and helped to comfort his parents. Geoffrey Peters was there too, perhaps to comfort her. Trafficking with Eastern merchants hadn't been at all what she'd expected.

"Hurry up!" Mike Brentnor shouted as soon as he spotted Susan Holt alighting from the cab at Kennedy Airport. "We're supposed to be checked in by now!"

Whatever had possessed her to agree to a three-day trip to Iceland with Brentnor, she'd asked herself time and again during the past week. "It's part of the job," her boss Saul Marx had told her. "The best way to publicize a new line is to be in at the beginning. I want you to go to Reykjavik with the buyer and get a look at this entire line of Icelandic woolens." Saul was vice president of promotions for Manhattan's largest department store, and when Mike Brentnor moved out to become a dry goods buyer Susan had become Marx's chief assistant. It was a relief not to be working with snide, sexist Brentnor any longer, but the relief was short-lived that day in April when Marx told her she'd be traveling to Reykjavik with him. "He's the buyer now, Susan. And you're promotions manager. I want you working as a team on this."

So here she was at the airport at seven in the morning, ready for an eight o'clock flight to Reykjavik. The time in Iceland was four hours ahead of New York, so it would be six in the evening by the time they landed after their six-hour flight. She'd had a recent flight to Tokyo more than twice as long, but that didn't make it any more inviting, especially sharing a seat with Mike Brentnor.

"I was going to call your apartment," he said with his sickly grin. "I thought maybe you and the boyfriend overslept."

"Russell doesn't live with me," she said coldly, "if that's what you're implying. Where do I check in?"

"International departures. Our seats are in business class."

"Well, that's something." She was traveling light, with only one medium-sized suitcase on wheels. It should be enough for a three-day stay. She checked it through quickly and found Brentnor waiting for her at the other side of the metal detector.

"Had breakfast?"

"A glass of orange juice. They'll give us something on the plane."

They boarded together and took their seats up front. Susan unzipped her briefcase and removed the color photographs of the items the store would be buying—quality woolen garments with new designs and colors. Brentnor hoped to have them in the store by September, or October at the latest. "They're offering us an exclusive on their full line of sweaters, jackets, scarves, gloves, leg warmers, socks, and blankets."

"I see lots of competition out there, Mike, and at lower prices than these."

"Wait till you see the quality and you'll change your mind. I have a blanket in the office that's unbelievable. They say Iceland has more sheep than people."

Breakfast was served soon after their Icelandair flight's departure. Susan dozed through the movie and lunch that followed, and awoke as they started their descent into Reykjavik. It was a small place by American standards, Brentnor told her, with a population of less than 100,000. "Look at all those brightly colored roofs on the houses!" Susan said, her forehead pressed against the plane's window as it circled south over the city.

"That would be the Old Town. See that big modern church with the statue out front? That's Leifur Eiriksson, the Viking."

"What religion are the people?"

"Mostly Lutheran, a few Catholic, even some pagan believers in Thor."

"My! You do read the guidebooks."

It was a bit after six when the plane touched down at Keflavik, thirty miles southwest of the city, and taxied to the terminal. "The Leifur Eiriksson Terminal, of course," he told her with a chuckle. "That's a big name around here."

They were staying at the Hotel Loftleidir and a hotel bus delivered them to the door. "Let's unpack, have dinner and a good night's sleep," he suggested. "We'll be meeting with Bjorn Arnarson first thing in the morning."

"By the time I unpack I think I'll be ready for bed, Mike. I'm really not too hungry. Maybe I'll just order a snack from room service."

"Sounds good to me. We could order together in your room or mine." He glanced sideways at her. "This doesn't have to be all business, you know."

His bold proposition startled her and she tried not to show it. Her reactions to Mike Brentnor had been varied but mostly negative. She'd never once imagined him in a romantic context of any kind.

"Please, Mike," she replied with a sigh. "I'm tired."

He shrugged, as if it were her loss. "See you in the morning, then."

They arrived at the Yggdrasill Mills before ten o'clock, following a taxi ride past a huge outdoor swimming pool from which steam seemed to be rising continuously. "The whole city's heated by steam," their Irish cabdriver explained. "There are hot springs all over the island. They swim outdoors in the middle of winter. One of the springs, Geysir, is the origin of the English word 'geyser.'" He turned off the main road. "They just opened a big new geothermal plant here a few weeks ago. Biggest of its kind in the world, I guess. Keeps the downtown sidewalks clear of snow in the winter."

Off in the distance, beyond the woolen mill that was their destination, she could see towers of steam gushing from the earth. "Is this place safe?"

The driver laughed. "The people who live here love it, and I got to admit, on a midwinter night even I can develop a certain fondness for steam. Here's my card. Name's Patrick Culhane. Give me a call when you're ready to go back."

Mike Brentnor led the way into the big white building that was their destination. Bjorn Arnarson, the president of Yggdrasill, proved to be a sober-faced man in his fifties who greeted them in an office dominated by a large wooden plaque with a carving of a great tree. "Welcome to Iceland," he said in passable English. Then, noticing that Susan's attention was attracted to the plaque, he explained.

"It is Yggdrasill, the world-tree whose branches stretch out over heaven and earth, a bit of Scandinavian mythology which supplied our company with its name."

"Your woolens are fantastic," Mike Brentnor said, cutting through the small talk to get down to business. "We are prepared to make you an offer for the entire line."

Arnarson motioned them to chairs and took out a large cigar, offering one to Brentnor, who declined. "You don't mind, Miss Holt?"

"Of course not," Susan answered bravely, not about to challenge a man's right to smoke in his own office.

"What quantities did you have in mind?" he asked Brentnor.

Before he could answer they were interrupted by the ringing telephone. Arnarson answered with a single word Susan didn't understand. He spoke a few more words of Icelandic before hanging up, his expression grimmer than before. "You must excuse the interruption. This is a sad morning for us. One of our female employees was brutally murdered overnight. It is a great shock to us all. Here in Iceland crimes like that are rare."

"I'm so sorry," Susan told him. "Was it one of the knitting-machine operators?"

He shook his head, putting down the cigar. "A young woman named Sjofn Kristjan. She worked in the payroll department, a lovely young thing. They found her near one of the city's swimming pools."

"How was she killed?" Brentnor asked.

"With a hammer. The police believe it was a sex crime."

"Terrible!"

Arnarson nodded. "I'm afraid my mind is on her instead of business today. I've always thought of my employees as one big family."

"Of course," Susan said quickly, before Mike could pull out his calculator and get back to business. "We'd planned to be here three days. Would you feel better about talking business some other time—perhaps tomorrow?"

He seemed relieved by her suggestion. "Actually, I would. There's a police sergeant on his way to see me about Sjofn's death, and I fear he'll arrive before we could complete our business. Suppose I have someone show you around the plant, which you'd want to see in any event, and tomorrow morning we'll talk business."

Mike Brentnor looked unhappy, but he could hardly raise an objection. "Fine. We'll look the place over and be back at the same time tomorrow."

The man chosen to show them the plant was a young vice president named Jon Jonsson. He had longish brown hair that he wore parted in the middle, and Susan found him quite attractive. But it soon became apparent that this was not an ordinary workday at the Yggdrasill Mills. Everywhere they went small groups of employees stood in clusters, talking glumly and sometimes whispering when they noticed Jonsson's approach. A middle-aged woman was actually crying as they entered the payroll department.

"I'm terribly sorry, Mrs. Schwartz," Jonsson told her. He introduced the American visitors and the woman made an effort to recover her composure.

"She worked right at the next desk. It's a terrible thing," the woman told them. "I moved here to escape the violence back home, and now this happens."

Susan gathered that "back home" meant Germany, but she didn't inquire into the nature of the violence. She could see Jon Jonsson was anxious to move on, and the local murder needn't concern them, tragic as it might be. Jonsson led them next into the mill itself, explaining that most of their woolen products were now produced by machine, although a few of the finer pieces were still handmade. The plant foreman, a bearded man named Hermann Steingrim, spent a great deal of time with them, pointing out the entire process by which a skein of wool became a fine, stylish sweater. Susan had to admit that their products were superior to anything she'd seen in Manhattan stores, with the world-tree symbol linking items as different as gloves and blankets into a single fashion statement.

"I think we've got a winner if the prices aren't too steep," she told Brentnor as they followed Jonsson to the next point on the tour.

"I told you they were neat. If the cost is a little high that'll just make them all the more exclusive."

At the conclusion of the tour they phoned for the taxi and waited with the vice president until it arrived. Susan couldn't help noticing the two police cars parked at the plant's main entrance. The cabdriver, Culhane, noticed them too. "What's going on with the police cars?" he asked as they climbed in.

"One of their employees got killed last night," Brentnor told him. "We'll be going back to the Loftleidir now."

He swung the cab around in the parking lot and headed back toward the city center. "That must be the girl they found by the big Laugardalur swimming pool. I just heard about it." He was one of those drivers intent on showing off the city, even though it was not his own. They detoured so he could point out the university, then took a drive through the Old Town section while Mike Brentnor grew increasingly impatient.

Finally, when the driver asked if they wanted to visit the swimming pool where the girl's body had been found, Brentnor barked out, "No! Take us to the hotel!"

As he was getting out of the taxi at their destination, Susan decided on a sudden impulse, "I think I'll see the sights, Mike. I'll be back in time for dinner."

"Suit yourself," he told her, tossing a few kronurs onto the seat.

Patrick Culhane whistled. "He doesn't like sightseeing."

"Well, I do. Drive me around for an hour. Then you can bring me back here." She peered out at the landscape. "Why aren't there any trees in this part of town?"

"The Old Town has trees, and they are planting them elsewhere. It's a long process. Almost nothing is left of Iceland's forests." He turned down a side street. "They say that during World War II the Yank soldiers were told that Iceland had a virgin under every tree, just waiting for them. They got here and there were no trees."

"Is that true?"

"About the trees or the virgins?"

She laughed in spite of herself. "What's an Irishman doing in Iceland?"

"It seemed like a good idea at the time. I'll probably go back someday. Hey, do you want to look at the murder scene?"

"Why not?"

He drove through the busy streets until they came to what appeared to be a modern stadium. "It is a stadium," the driver said in answer to her question. "They often have swimming meets here. There's an Olympic-sized pool with lanes marked off, and a slightly smaller free-form pool connected to it. The public can continue swimming even while competitions are in progress."

"Isn't the water too hot with all this steam rising from it?"

"That's really caused by the temperature difference between the water and the air. The pool is a perfect temperature for swimming. If it gets too hot the water is cooled. This is a popular place, especially in the summer. There's a campsite and a youth hostel nearby."

As they left the taxi and strolled toward the pool, she saw a figure emerge from the steamy mist, striding toward them like a ghost. At her side Patrick Culhane tensed and then relaxed. "It's only one of the police," he told her. "Hello, Sergeant."

"What are you doing here, Pat? This is a crime scene."

"Just showing an American the sights. This is Sergeant Oxara, Miss—" He glanced at her inquiringly.

"Susan Holt." Oxara was a big man whose ruddy complexion went well with his occupation. Maybe police looked somewhat alike all over the world. "You have a lovely country here, Sergeant."

"We think so. What happened last night is not typical. The streets are perfectly safe, at least on weekdays. The men like to drink on Friday and Saturday, but mostly they behave themselves."

"Who was the victim?" Culhane asked.

"Her name was Sjofn Kristjan. She worked out at the mill. Someone killed her with a single blow from a hammer."

"The hammer of Thor."

Sergeant Oxara allowed himself the hint of a smile. "No, just a plain hammer for driving nails. He threw it into the water after he killed her."

Susan glanced around. "Where was the body?"

"Over there by the bridge."

There was indeed a gracious curving arc of a footbridge at the spot where the two large pools merged. From the top of it one would have a perfect view of both. "She was killed during the night? I wonder what she was doing here."

"Young people like to sneak in for a midnight swim, even though it closes at five-thirty on weeknights. I suppose the steam attracts some folks."

"Had she been assaulted?"

"Her undergarments were ripped, but we don't think she was molested. You'll have to read the papers for anything else you want to know, miss." He walked away from them, and almost at once he'd vanished from view in the rising mist.

"A strange place," Susan commented.

"Good place for a murder," the driver said. "No one could see what was happening."

"I suppose not." When they'd returned to the cab she decided, "Let's go back. I've seen enough for one day."

"We just began!" he protested.

"We began at the wrong place."

Susan took pity on Mike Brentnor and joined him for dinner in the hotel dining room. They ordered an Icelandic dish called graflax which sounded something like a camera but proved to be a pickled, salt-cured salmon served with a special sauce. "I guess when you're in Iceland you eat fish," Brentnor grumbled.

"There were meat dishes on the menu. Besides, this isn't half bad."

"Where did the taxi driver take you?" he asked, managing to make it sound like an assignation.

"To look at the murder scene. We met a policeman."

"That must have been exciting."

"Apparently it's an unusual occurrence here. I heard people talking about it when I got back to the hotel."

He finished up the last of his salmon. "I sent my wife a postcard. Did you know the stamps say 'Island' on them?"

"It's Icelandic for 'Iceland', Mike."

"Oh." He pushed his plate away. "How about some dessert?"

She was already sorry she'd agreed to dine with him, and after dinner he suggested a walk around the block. The night was chilly and they hurried to get back inside. "I think I'll turn in early, Mike. My body's not adjusted to the time difference yet."

"I know how both of our bodies could get adjusted together."

Susan sighed and pushed him gently on the chest. "Look, Mike, you've got a wife back home and I've got Russell. I have no intention of getting involved with anyone else. You've tried this two nights in a row. Don't try it a third time."

She turned and entered the elevator alone, not waiting for him. Later, after she'd slipped into her nightclothes, she went to the window to peer out at the traffic. Mike Brentnor was just crossing the street, walking quickly away from the hotel. She wondered where he was going.

Susan had arranged for the taxi to pick them up at the same time the following morning. Mike Brentnor seemed tired and subdued, and she made no comment on the previous night's events. "Sleep good?" he asked once they were under way.

"Not bad. It's certainly quiet around here."

The driver, who seemed to consider himself one of the party by now, chimed in. "This is Friday. It'll be noisier tonight. Reykjavik is a two-night town—Friday and Saturday."

"So I've heard," she answered. She stared out at the bleak countryside, wishing there were more trees. Soon the mill came into view as it had the previous morning. Happily, there were no police cars in view.

"We'll phone you when we're ready to come back," Brentnor told the driver.

"I'll hang around," Culhane offered. "It's a slow morning."

They had to wait only a few minutes before being ushered up to Bjorn Arnarson's office. He seemed better in all ways than he had the previous morning. Shaking hands with them both, he asked, "Have you been enjoying your visit to Reykjavik?"

"It's very nice," Susan told him. "It could be a little warmer, though."

He nodded. "We still have snow to the north. It will stay till summer. Have you seen any of our nightlife?"

"I saw a little," Brentnor admitted. "I tried one of the discotheques last night. It was pretty tame."

The older man chuckled. "What do you expect from a country that had no alcoholic beer until 1989?" He opened the folder on his desk. "But now, down to business. What are your needs for the Christmas season?"

Brentnor opened his own briefcase and extracted a typed proposal. He passed the original to Arnarson with a copy to Susan. She saw the figures for each item in the company line, some of them running to twelve gross. It was a large order. "Could you deliver these in New York by September?"

"I believe so, but the prices you offer are too low for some items. You know, Mr. Brentnor, that our top-quality sweaters could bring more than two hundred dollars each in Manhattan. I have been there. I know the prices at Christmas time."

"The economy—"

The company president wrote down a few quick figures on his pad. "For delivery on or before September thirtieth, these would be the prices. I could make some concessions, of course, for a two-year contract."

The dickering went on like that for another twenty minutes before a compromise of sorts was arrived at. Arnarson called in his secretary and told her to type up the formal agreement. "Two years," Brentnor grumbled. "You drive a hard bargain."

"I have confidence in you, and in Miss Holt here. You will make Yggdrasill the toast of New York."

He offered them a bit of sherry to seal the bargain, and each drank a polite sip. Then they departed with handshakes all around. "You will have our chairman's signature on the agreement within a week," Brentnor promised, zipping the papers into his briefcase. It was a minute after eleven by the reception-room clock as they left the building and started across the lot to where the taxi waited.

But something was wrong. Culhane was out of his cab, head down, running toward them. For an instant Susan thought the man must be out of his mind as he hit them at full speed and dragged them to the pavement. Then she heard the single crack that sounded like a pistol.

"I know shooting when I hear it!" he shouted. "Keep your heads down!"

"What's happening?" Mike Brentnor demanded. "Who's shooting?"

"Damned if I know." He covered them with his body.

Susan lifted her head enough to see three figures wearing ski masks run from the office next to the mill's main entrance. "What is it—a robbery?"

One of the masked men, holding a pistol and a large plastic sack, seemed to look their way but kept on running toward a small car that had suddenly appeared, driving fast to meet up with them.

"It's Friday. They were after the payroll." Culhane rolled off them as the masked men jumped into the car and drove away at high speed.

"It looks like they got it," Susan said, breathing hard as she got to her knees and tried to brush off her coat. "This is peaceful Iceland?"

"If that was the payroll, they'd better start paying by check," Brentnor said. He scrambled to his feet as if about to give chase but the getaway car had already vanished from sight.

It was Jon Jonsson, the company vice president, who was the first out of the building. "My God, did they get away? They have the payroll!"

"You still pay in cash?" Susan asked.

Distracted, he seemed barely to hear her. Culhane supplied the answer. "The hourly workers are paid in cash. Salaried employees get checks."

Bjorn Arnarson himself had appeared in the main doorway. "Jon," he shouted, "what is it?"

"They escaped with the payroll. Three masked men."

"A fourth was driving the getaway car," Culhane corrected.

"Is anyone hurt?"

Jonsson had no answer to that question, so he and Arnarson hurried together toward the payroll department with Susan and Mike Brentnor trailing behind. "I heard a shot and looked out to see them running toward a car," Jonsson said. "One was carrying a plastic bag."

Inside, Mrs. Schwartz was close to hysterics. "They had guns," she cried. "I couldn't stop them. I called the police as soon as they were out the door."

Some of the other women were trying to comfort her, but the company president insisted on hearing the whole story. "Tell me exactly what happened."

"I think they had the ski masks rolled up to look like caps. They pulled them over their faces as they came through the door. For an instant I thought they were machine operators coming for their pay, but then I saw the masks." Her voice cracked. "And the guns! One man fired a shot at the ceiling. I left Germany to get away from this!"

Jon Jonsson tried to comfort her while in the distance Susan heard the first sound of a police siren. "Did you recognize any of them?" he asked.

"I barely saw them before they pulled down the masks. I couldn't describe any of them."

"How much did they get?" the president asked.

"All the cash. They knew right where to look."

Sergeant Oxara himself arrived in the first police car. He issued an immediate command for road blocks as soon as Brentnor and their cabdriver had given a description of the getaway car, then listened quietly to Mrs. Schwartz's account of the robbery, confirmed by another woman who'd been working in the department.

"The first one through the door fired the only shot," Mrs. Schwartz told Oxara. "He seemed to be in charge. We both just froze and he directed the other two behind the counter to scoop up the trays of payroll envelopes. Then one of them went to the cash drawer and took all the big bills that were still in it. They even looked in the safe where we keep extra cash for emergencies."

Oxara turned to Bjorn Arnarson. "How much would that be?"

"If they got everything it could have been around 95,000 kronurs," the president replied. "We won't know until we do an inventory."

"Is it covered by insurance?"

"Of course."

Mike Brentnor, calculating quickly, whispered to Susan, "That's more than one hundred and forty thousand dollars."

Sergeant Oxara glanced around at them, then back to the president. "How many people knew the money would be here?"

"Just about everyone in the city, I imagine. We pay our hourly workers every second Friday. There are nearly two hundred of them on the various shifts."

Others from the mill, including the manager, Hermann Steingrim, had crowded into the payroll department, and the sergeant finally ordered everyone out so fingerprints and photographs could be taken. "They won't find anything," Mike Brentnor predicted. "Those guys were wearing gloves."

Susan turned to their driver. "You may have saved our lives, Patrick. Thank you for the fast action."

"It was nothing, ma'am." He gave her a smile. "Just part of my service."

They shook hands again with Yggdrasill's president, and expressed proper outrage at the robbery. "It has been a bad week for us," Arnarson agreed. "First the Kristjan woman's murder and now this!"

Suddenly it occurred to Susan that the two crimes might well be related.

On the way back to the hotel she pursued her theory with Mike. "Don't you see? Sjofn Kristjan worked in the payroll department with Mrs. Schwartz. Oxara told me it didn't appear to be a sex crime, even though her underwear had been ripped. Someone wanted it to appear like a sex crime, but it was something else entirely. Mrs. Schwartz said the robbers knew right where to look. They knew because the dead girl told them. Then, with the actual armed robbery approaching, she either got cold feet or they were afraid she'd talk about it afterward. So they killed her Wednesday night."

"Since you're not with the Reykjavik Police Department, what difference does it make? We'll be flying home tomorrow afternoon."

"Maybe I should speak to Sergeant Oxara about it."

"And maybe you shouldn't. Suppose they make you stay here as a witness of some sort?"

"But I think—"

"Oxara seemed fairly intelligent. I'm sure he'll come up with the same theories as you."

"I suppose so," she admitted.

But back in her room she started expanding on her original thought. If Sjofn Kristjan had been involved in planning the robbery or supplying information to the gang, it seemed most likely it would be through someone with whom she was romantically linked. A boyfriend. That sort of thing happened all the time. It was not something she'd discuss with her family, but someone she worked with might remember a key fact—a phone call, perhaps, or even a handsome young man who picked her up one day after work.

That afternoon, when she thought the police would have gone, Susan called the payroll department at the mill and asked for Mrs. Schwartz. When she heard the familiar German accent she explained who she was. "I was wondering if we could meet after work. I wanted to ask you about the girl who was killed."

"Not the robbery?"

"Well, that too," Susan admitted. "I'm at the Hotel Loftleidir. Would that be a convenient meeting place?"

"Yes, I suppose so." Her voice was tentative. "This won't get me into trouble, will it?"

"Of course not. I just have a few questions."

"I finish up here at four-thirty. I could be there fifteen minutes later."

"I'll meet you in the lobby," Susan said.

Mike rang her in the early afternoon to suggest some sightseeing but she put him off. "I've got a headache from this morning. I guess I'm not used to being thrown to the ground while gunmen run by."

"Take a couple aspirin. I'll check with you later."

She left her room by midafternoon to avoid another call from him, and spent an hour exploring the small shops near the hotel. In one she purchased a pair of bookends made from the island's lava. The clerk told her that ten percent of Iceland's total land mass was made up of lava, and Susan found herself thankful that none was flowing at the moment. A volcano eruption on top of a murder, a robbery, and Mike's unwanted advances would just about finish her.

She returned to the hotel lobby at twenty to five to find Mrs. Schwartz waiting for her. "Mr. Jonsson told me to leave early because of what happened," she explained. "He's a nice man, very considerate of the employees."

"Would you like some tea or a bit of wine?" Susan asked.

"Some sherry would be nice."

When they were settled in the hotel's lounge with their glasses, Susan worked into her questions slowly. "I gather things were unpleasant for you back in Germany."

"That's true enough. I've only been here five years. I could see when the wall came down there would be trouble. All the poor from the east pouring into the west, and immigrants from Eastern Europe as well. In my town they killed a Gypsy family and I decided it was time to leave. I had a sister in Reykjavik so I came here. A year later she married the captain of a fishing boat and they moved to Nova Scotia. I'm still here."

"But you're Mrs. Schwartz. Where is your husband?"

"In prison back home. He was one of those who killed that Gypsy family."

"I see."

She took a sip of her sherry. "But you don't want to talk about me. You were asking about Sjofn." Away from the mill she seemed younger, more relaxed, even after what she'd been through that day. "What did you want to know?"

"Did she have boyfriends?"

"Of course. She was an attractive twenty-four-year-old woman. Why wouldn't she have boyfriends?"

"Did any of them ever come around to the mill?"

She looked away, as if uncertain how to answer that. "For a while there was someone at work."

"Who was that?"

"Steingrim, the plant foreman."

"The bearded man. He took us on part of our tour yesterday." Susan wondered what to do with this information. "Did you tell the police?"

"Not yet. They didn't really ask, and I didn't want to get him in trouble. He has a wife and family. Besides, it's been over for some time."

"Who had she been seeing lately?"

"I think there was someone but I don't know who."

"Someone at Yggdrasill?"

She shrugged. "Sjofn didn't talk about it."

"Did you like her?"

"She was friendly. I enjoyed working with her. We didn't see each other outside of work."

"Could she have tipped off someone about the payroll money? From what you told the police it sounded as if they knew just where to look for the money."

"I can't believe it was Sjofn."

They chatted a bit more about the city while she finished her sherry. Then Mrs. Schwartz said she really must be going. "I don't even know your first name," Susan suddenly realized.

The woman smiled sadly. "It's Myra."

"That's a pretty name. You should use it more often."

She smiled. "My divorce will be final soon. Then I'll feel like a woman again." Myra Schwartz got up to leave, then remembered something else. "Sjofn's new boyfriend might have been someone at the mill too."

"Why do you say that?"

"I asked her once how she'd met him and she said he gave her a ride home one night."

When she returned to her room Susan found a message from Mike suggesting dinner at a nearby restaurant. She phoned his room and agreed to meet him in the lobby at seven. It was, after all, their final night in Iceland. "Is your headache better?" he asked as they met.

"Much better, thanks."

They walked to the restaurant and ordered drinks. Mike Brentnor frowned at her across the table and said, "You're playing detective again, aren't you?"

"What do you mean?"

"I saw you in the lounge with Mrs. Schwartz."

"She seemed like a nice woman. I wanted to get to know her better before we went home."

"Do you think she's involved in the murder and robbery?"

"I doubt it. She seems quite nice." Susan didn't intend to share what little she knew with Mike.

"Of course that girl's killing might have nothing to do with the robbery. She might have been attacked by some man on the prowl for a woman."

"Like you, Mike?"

He almost spilled his drink. "What in hell are you talking about?"

"You saw me with Mrs. Schwartz and I saw you sneaking out of the hotel last night."

"I went to a disco. Anything wrong with that? You can't seriously believe I'd attack someone on the street. My God, Susan!"

"I'm sorry, Mike, but you see how these things can look. I turned you down so you went out on the prowl. But Sjofn Kristjan hadn't been sexually molested, and her death wasn't a spur of the moment murder brought about by resisting a man's advances. The killer brought a hammer to the scene, probably from his car. He meant to silence her, and chose the swimming pool because the night mists from the water helped obscure the scene."

"You should tell that to Sergeant Oxara," he said, settling down a bit.

"Perhaps I'll tell the killer instead."

The food was good and when they'd lingered over dessert and coffee long enough, Susan said, "I have to get back to the hotel. There's someone I have to call."

"Susan, don't do anything foolish."

"I won't."

She found Patrick Culhane waiting for customers outside the hotel. "Patrick, we're leaving tomorrow but there's something I need to do tonight. I want to call someone and then go to meet him. Will you take me?"

"Glad to," he said with a smile.

"I'll be back in a few minutes."

She went up to her room and looked up the number in the phone book. When he came on the line she identified herself and said, "I have some-thing very interesting to tell you. Can you meet me in a half-hour out at the Laugardalur pool?"

"Where Sjofn Kristjan was killed."

"That's right."

"I'll be there," he said and hung up.

She sat on the bed for a moment, hoping she was doing the right thing. Then she hurried downstairs to the waiting taxi.

As they drove toward her destination, Culhane said, "It's a cold night. There'll be lots of steam coming off that pool tonight. Who are you meeting there?"

"A man. It's just something I have to do."

"Want me to wait?"

"Yes."

A heavy mist hung over the entire pool area when they reached it, and Susan hurried from the taxi toward the open gate. She could not see if anyone was there before her and she moved cautiously through the mist. It was a foolish thing to be doing, she told herself, feeling a bit like Nancy Drew in some of those books she'd read as a child. Alone in the dark with a murderer—that was some brilliant idea!

She circled the big pool once and began to suspect he wasn't coming at all. Then she heard a sound and saw a figure looming up ahead of her. "Here I am," she called out. "Looking for me?"

Patrick Culhane stepped forward. "I was worried about you. Thought I should make sure you were all right."

"I'm fine."

"No one here yet?"

"I don't see anyone, but the gate was open."

"Sometimes kids break the lock to get in for a late swim." He moved a bit closer.

"I wanted to ask you about something strange at the mill this morning, during the robbery. You pushed Mike and me to the ground and said you knew shooting when you heard it, but the only shot wasn't fired till an instant later, when we were already down."

"What do you mean?"

"Sjofn had a new boyfriend, one she met when he gave her a ride home. Isn't that what cabdrivers do—give people rides home?"

His hand came up, and there was enough moonlight for her to see the knife. "I threw away the hammer," he said quietly. "It'll have to be a blade this time."

Trembling, Susan backed toward the edge of the pool. "You won't use that. You went to a lot of trouble to save us from harm this morning. You waited at the mill because you were afraid we might come out just when we did, while your friends were stealing the payroll. You didn't want American visitors killed, and you don't want to kill me now."

"It would be bad publicity for our cause," he admitted, and in that instant Susan understood.

"You came here from Ireland. The robbery was to raise money for the IRA, wasn't it?"

He lunged at her then and she went backward into the warm water. There were shouts and indistinct visions of running men, and suddenly hands were reaching for her, pulling her out soaked but alive.

"Sorry I waited so long," Sergeant Oxara told her, "but we had to hear it all."

At the airport the following afternoon the sergeant was there to see them off. He shook hands with Mike Brentnor and told him, "This is a brave lady, brave and smart both. She phoned last night and asked me to meet her at the swimming pool. I never dreamed she was going to deliver the killer of Sjofn Kristjan and solve the payroll robbery for us too."

"What about the other four who actually pulled off the robbery?" Susan asked.

"Culhane is talking. We rounded them up this morning and recovered the money. Your guess was a good one. They all have IRA connections. It appears the Irish Republican Army would have profited to some extent from the robbery."

"He did try to protect us from harm," Mike said. "Do you really think he would have killed you last night?"

Susan didn't know. She didn't want to think about it. It would be a long time before she'd forget that nightmare of Culhane coming at her through the mist. He was different from her in many ways, but in one way there could be no doubt. She would never have his fondness for steam.

A PARCEL OF DEERSTALKERS

For Susan Holt, it all began the morning her assistant Emmy Spring gasped and fainted in the outer office. Susan heard the thump of her body hitting the floor and came running, along with a half a dozen others in Mayfield's promotions department. Emmy was a dark-haired young woman in her mid-twenties, pretty in a delicate way, who'd been working there about a year. She had a desk in the outer office, and Susan saw at once that she'd been opening the morning mail.

While the others crowded around the fallen young woman, trying to revive her, Susan glanced at the open parcel, about the size of a breadbox. She was not particularly surprised to see that it was filled with deerstalker hunting caps with their visors in front and back. The Sherlock Holmes promotion, of course. They'd been expecting the parcel for a week. What they hadn't been expecting was the small, pale object that lay on top of the caps. It was a severed human ear, and when she saw it Susan felt a bit faint herself.

It was Mike Brentnor, who had an answer for everything, who first suggested a Sherlock Holmes story. "It's 'The Cardboard Box,'" he told them. They were seated in Susan Holt's office an hour later, trying to explain it to Detective Sergeant Mulligan of the NYPD. He was one of those types who take copious notes, writing all the time, asking questions without ever looking up at the speakers.

"What about 'The Cardboard Box'? I haven't read Sherlock Holmes since I was a kid with the chicken pox."

"Well, this woman receives two freshly severed ears in a cardboard box. I think her name was Susan in the story. Maybe the ear was meant for you, Susan."

Susan Holt blushed slightly, as Brentnor would have expected. Though they no longer worked in the same office, he never missed an opportunity to chide her, to remind her he was still around even after her rejection of him. "No," she corrected immediately. "The parcel was addressed to Emmy, wasn't it?"

Emmy Spring was quick to agree, having recovered from her fright. "I was expecting it. When I was in Meiringen last month I arranged to have a dozen of the Sherlock Holmes caps sent to us for promotional purposes. We planned to use them for photographs and displays."

Sergeant Mulligan glanced up briefly from his notebook. "You're promoting Sherlock Holmes at Mayfield's?" Somehow the idea of Manhattan's largest department store planning a promotion around a fictional character amused him.

"Why not?" Susan countered. Holmes has been used in advertising at least since nineteen-oh-four and probably before that. We intend to feature a storewide promotion with Holmes using his magnifying glass to seek out special bargains. I know that's hardly original, but we will supplement it with Holmes memorabilia. Emmy was in Meiringen, Switzerland, last month arranging for us to duplicate the reconstruction of Holmes's cluttered sitting room that they have in the basement of their Sherlock Holmes Museum. We'll also be importing some of the pipes and magnifying glasses and deer-stalkers they sell there. It hasn't decided whether or not we should include the T-shirts and postcards too. That may be a bit tacky for Mayfield's image."

"The ear is real, Miss Holt. It's not part of any promotion. We'll photograph it and send a copy to the Swiss police along with all relevant data. I suspect they have a body to match it."

"Why would anyone send the ear to us?" Mike Brentnor wanted to know. "Are they warning us not to do the promotion? Are we being threatened by some sort of Sherlockian psychopath?"

"Hardly," Susan answered drily, refusing to be caught up in any hysteria. "I'm sure the Swiss authorities will come up with a very mundane explanation. Perhaps there was an accident in the mailing room." The words lacked conviction even to her own ears, but she wanted Brentnor out of there. Whatever it was, she could handle it better on her own.

Sergeant Mulligan asked a few more questions and then closed his notebook. "Well, if there's a crime, it's out of my jurisdiction anyhow. Let the Swiss handle it."

After he'd gone Brentnor asked Emmy how she felt. "Maybe you should take the rest of the day off."

"I'm all right," the young woman insisted, glancing in Susan's direction. "It was just the shock of opening the lid and seeing that—ear!"

Brentnor drifted away and Susan got down to business. "We've got a lot riding on this promotion, Emmy. I don't have to tell you that. I need to know who you saw in Switzerland, what and who might be behind this thing."

The younger woman smiled. "You don't believe it was an accident in the mailing room?"

"Hardly!"

"Well, I rented a car at Zurich airport and drove down to Meiringen, which is just a short walk from Reichenbach Falls. The place is brimming with Sherlockiana—is that the right word?—centered around the Sherlock Holmes Museum, which is housed in a former Anglican church. The people at the museum were very helpful, especially in allowing us to duplicate their reconstruction of the sitting room. The deerstalker caps are manufactured and sold at a nearby shop by a man named Bernard Wor. I took back samples to show Mike, since he's the buyer for special promotions now. After he agreed to order a few gross I phoned Wor in Switzerland and had him dispatch a dozen deerstalkers for photography and promotional purposes. It might be cute to have some of the salesgirls wearing them too."

"Could the ear have belonged to this man Wor?"

"I have no idea." Emmy Spring frowned in concentration, as if summoning up his image. "I think he was a larger man, though. That awful ear seemed smaller more delicate."

Susan nodded. "A woman's ear. Or a child's. Look, Emmy, give me a list of all the people you saw in Meiringen. I have to get on the phone and see what I can learn."

She reached Bernard Wor first, his voice clear and Germanic on the overseas line. "Yes, I sent the parcel of deerstalkers," he quickly agreed. "What is wrong? Are they not satisfactory?" she told him about the human ear and h scoffed. "Surely you must be joking, Miss Holt. They were packed and shipped from this very building."

"Have you had any—" she hated to use the word. "—accidents lately? Could someone have placed that ear in the parcel as a joke?"

"Certainly not!"

"There's a Holmes story where a pair of ears—"

"I know. I have read the entire saga more than once. Be assured, Miss Holt, your ear was no publicity stunt. I knew nothing about it."

"Could I speak with the person who actually wrapped the parcel?"

"Whoever it was, she is gone for the day. You realize it's after five o'clock here."

"Of course. I'm sorry. I just wanted to alert you to the problem. I expect your local police will be contacting you in the morning."

"I will tend to them when they call."

"I hope this won't affect your shipment of the remaining caps. I know our buyer is still quite interested in them."

"I understand. They will be shipped air express within a fortnight."

"Thank you, Mr. Wor."

"How is Miss Emmy Spring?"

"Fine, after the shock of opening that parcel."

"Give her my best wishes, please."

"I'll do that."

Susan hung up and checked off his name on the list. She called the number Emmy had given her for the Sherlock Holmes Museum but got only a recording in four languages listing their hours. She decided the rest of her calls would have to wait until morning.

But by morning it was too late. She walked into her office at 9.30 to find Emmy Spring frantically reporting to Mike Brentnor. "They're talking about canceling everything—your product orders, the promotion, everything!"

"What's this?" Susan asked, slipping out of the raincoat she'd worn against the threat of leaden spring skies. "What's going on?"

"Rima Fredericks, an Englishwoman at the Sherlock Holmes Museum, just phoned to say they're rethinking their commitments."

Susan cursed silently. "What did Wor give you?"

"I have a letter of intent, not a real contract." She passed over a letter signed by Wor in Meiringen on April fifth.

"We don't need them," Brentnor point out. "There are other Holmes sitting rooms we can duplicate. The Sherlock Holmes Pub in London has a nice one. And we can get other caps too."

Susan Holt sighed. "But this is Reichenbach Falls, Mike—the place where Holmes and Moriarty supposedly plunged to their death! We want to be able to say *Direct from Reichenbach Falls* on our displays and merchandise. What's the trouble with them, anyway?"

"Apparently the police have been causing an uproar ever since Mulligan contacted them," Emmy told her.

"Do they have a body to go with the ear?"

"I don't know, but they've managed to frighten the people we're dealing with over there pretty badly."

Susan debated her options, then said suddenly, "I'm flying to Switzerland, Emmy. See if you can get me a reservation on a flight to Zurich overnight. I'll rent a car there."

Mike Brentnor immediately brightened at the prospect. "I'd be happy to come along and help. You might need a man."

She glanced at him distastefully. "No thanks, Mike. Not this time."

"But I could—"

"I'll phone you if I need anything."

She left the office early that afternoon and went home to pack enough clothes for a three-day trip. She hoped it would be shorter than that. Russell was just making breakfast when she reached the apartment. His current off-Broadway play kept him on a crazy schedule that played havoc with their social and love life. By the time he got home most nights, after twelve, she was fast asleep.

"You're not going off again!" he grumbled, his unkempt blond hair catching the afternoon sunlight through the southern window.

"Just for a couple of days. We have an emergency with our Sherlock Holmes promotion."

"Where are you going this time? London?"

"Reichenbach Falls, actually. It's in Switzerland."

"God, you're crazy! Brentnor going with you again?"

"Hardly! I wouldn't trust him within fifty feet of me outside the office."

He grunted. "Want a piece of toast?"

"Thanks." She wolfed it down, suddenly remembering she hadn't taken time for lunch.

"Does this have to do with the ear?" he asked, remembering what she'd told him the previous night.

"Yes. Apparently it's caused quite an uproar over here."

He bent to lightly kiss her own ear. "Be careful. I want you back intact."

The distance from Zurich to Meiringen was only about fifty miles, although it was much farther over the curving mounting highways. Susan's little rental car was a joy to drive, but it still took her better than two hours to make the trip. Driving into the quaint little town at high noon she suddenly felt as if she had stepped back a full century in time. Men and women wearing Victorian clothes and carrying walking sticks and open parasols strolled along the street in groups.

Susan had chosen to stay in the new Sherlock Holmes Hotel rather than in the nineteenth-century Park Hotel du Sauvage, which served as a model for the hotel where Conan Doyle had Holmes spend his last night. She asked the desk clerk about the people in Victorian dress and he beamed. "We hope it'll become an annual custom on the fourth of May. It's the anniversary of Holmes's plunge into the falls, and a number Sherlockians dress up to honor the event."

The date had meant nothing to Susan, whose knowledge of the stories was confined to a few of the most popular tales. "This is the fourth of May," she agreed. "Which way is the Sherlock Holmes Museum from here?"

"The old church at the center of town. It's a cream-and-ochre building with a rose window and a tin roof with a turret. You can't miss it. There's a bronze statue of Holmes out front."

She quickly unpacked in a modern hotel room that offered a breathtaking view of the snow-capped mountains. It would be a wonderful place for a relaxing vacation but she was here on business. The museum was easy to find when she stepped out again into the May sunshine. Outside she paused to admire the seated bronze Holmes, by a British sculptor named John Doubleday.

The first person to greet her inside the remodelled church was Rima Fredericks, the Englishwoman who'd phoned Emmy. "So nice to meet you, Miss Holt. I'm sorry this business caused you to come all the way over here."

She was a woman in her forties, still fairly attractive though she dressed plainly and wore her dark hair in an unbecoming bun. "Are you in charge here?" Susan asked.

"No, no. I'm only an employee. The director of the museum is away at the moment and Mr. Eiger is in charge. He made the decision to cancel the events at your store."

"I guess he's the one I should see."

Rima Fredericks went off to find him, leaving Susan alone among the facsimiles of Conan Doyle manuscripts and other Sherlockian treasures. There was a portrait of Doyle himself, along with an etching of Stoneyhurst, the school he attended. She was just starting to read about it when a gruff Germanic gentleman joined her. "I am Fritz Eiger. I understand you have flown from New York to see me."

She handed him her business card. "Susan Holt from Mayfield's. You and Bernard Wor both indicated your willingness to help us in our promotion. We are planning to construct a duplicate of your Sherlock Holmes sitting room, clearly labeled as being identical with the one here at Reichenbach Falls."

"I'm afraid we can't allow that at the present time." His lips had curved into a sad smile.

"Why not, may I ask?"

"The police are investigating the possibility that a serious crime has been committed. The director would never forgive me for allowing the museum's name to become linked with anything scandalous."

"What crime is that?"

He stared at her through his wire-rimmed glasses. "I believe a human ear was sent to you. As in the story of 'The Cardboard Box,' we can assume it came from a dead body."

"Is anyone missing in the town?"

"I cannot answer for the police."

"Will you reconsider your decision?"

"Not unless this matter is cleared up. It's not just me. Bernard Wor feels the same way, for whatever that's worth."

"I'm on my way to see Mr. Wor next."

"You will find him at the Sherlock Shoppe," he said with some distaste. "Just down the street."

"I still hope I can change your mind," she said as she departed.

A man and woman in Victorian costume were just leaving the Sherlock Shoppe as she approached. "Fine deerstalkers," the man commented. "The best quality I've seen." He was an American, something that surprised Susan. With those costumes she'd somehow assumed they were all British.

She knew Wor the instant she saw him behind the counter. He exactly fitted Emmy Spring's description of him. His accent was thickly Germanic, as it had been on the phone. Whereas Fritz Eiger had seemed dull and studious, this man looked her over as if he might invite her into bed at any moment. "Miss Holt, all the way from America! You are even more charming in person than on the telephone."

She smiled, deciding to go along with his game. He was fairly handsome, maybe still in his late thirties. "I've come to charm you out of a few gross of deerstalkers, with special Reichenbach Falls labels sewn in."

"The police believe someone has been murdered."

"I know that. If true it's too bad, but commerce must go on. Why would you cancel an order because of a possible murder that doesn't concern you?"

"It may concern the shop. The parcel of deerstalkers was mailed from here."

"You told me on the phone it was packed by one of your women. May I speak with her?"

"That would be Bruni Zandt. She's ill today."

"I would think this is one of your busiest days, with all those Sherlockians about."

"I know. The rest of us have been very busy."

As they spoke, more costumed visitors entered the shop. Bernard Wor's two clerks were both working the cash registers and he went off to summon more help from the workroom out back. When he returned he said apologetically, "I'm sorry, but we must continue this in the morning. We're just too busy today."

"I understand."

In truth Susan was beginning to feel some jet lag after her all-night flight from New York. She'd never been great at sleeping on planes, and this time she hadn't slept at all. She left the Shoppe intending to return to her hotel room, but when she saw a group of Victorian-clad tourists heading toward the falls a short walk away she decided to join them. It was, after all, the Reichenbach Falls that had inspired Conan Doyle to set his story in this beautiful place. All else had come from that fact.

The falls were an awesome spectacle. They were really a cascade of five consecutive waterfalls, narrow and thundering through a cleft in the Alpine rock. A woman's voice behind Susan spoke into her ear above the roar. "This is the best time of year to see them, when the melting snows from up the mountain make them a real torrent."

She turned and saw that it was the British woman, Rima Fredericks, from the Holmes Museum. "Hello there! I wanted a look at them before I turned in early. Has the museum closed?"

"I was on the early shift today. How long will you be in town?"

"A day or two, depending on how long it takes me to straighten out this business." She put a hand on the railing to steady herself.

"Fritz was a fool to cancel the agreement. It's good publicity for us. I'm sure when the director returns he'll straighten things out."

"Bernard Wor canceled too," she told the woman. "I think he fears one of his employees is involved in this ear business."

"Which one? I often visit them in the workroom."

"He said Bruni Zandt sent the package, but she seems unavailable for questioning."

They'd stepped back from the edge of the falls, the better to converse, and the others had wandered up ahead of them. Some appeared awed to be standing on the ledge where Holmes and Moriarty had engaged in their final struggle. For the first time, Susan became aware of a funicular with a red gondola that ran down the side of the cliff, providing a better view of the falls. "That only operates in the summer," Rima Fredericks said, following her gaze. "But you might be here till then if you're waiting to see Bruni."

"What do you mean?"

"She took off last month. The rumor is she embezzled money from Mr. Wor."

"I wonder why he didn't tell me that."

"He doesn't talk about his business affairs. When he first opened that place some of the residents thought he was cheapening our town. They said a name like Sherlock Shoppe sounded too commercial, too American."

"Your whole town is commercial, in case you haven't noticed it. You've built an industry around Holmes's plunge into the falls."

The Englishwoman gestured around her. "Obviously it's what the tourists want. They travel here as an homage to Sherlock Holmes and they want to see the memorial tablets, statues, and museum. They want to take back a deerstalker and a magnifying glass as souvenirs.

"I suppose you're right," Susan replied, too tired by now to argue about it. She took one last look over the ledge at the cascading white water and said, "I really have to get some sleep. Jet lag, you know."

"Come by the museum in the morning. I want to help. I still see that poor Emmy opening the box and finding the ear on top of the caps."

Susan promised to be there, remembering she had more questions for Fritz Eiger too. She walked back alone to the Sherlock Holmes Hotel with every intention of going straight to bed. But it was dinnertime and she decided she was hungry. After that, finally in her room, she remembered the time difference and decided to phone Sergeant Mulligan back in New York.

She recognized his voice immediately. "Mulligan here."

"Sergeant, this is Susan Holt from Mayfield's. I'm phoning from Switzerland."

"Doing a little mountain climbing, Miss Holt?"

I'm trying to keep our promotion plans alive. Your police are apparently a bit heavy-handed over here."

"To the best of my knowledge I have no authority over the Swiss police."

"I'm calling about the ear."

"Have you found a body to go with it?"

"Not yet, but I'm looking. Has your lab examined it?"

"Of course."

"What did they find?"

"It was hacked off, not cleanly removed. We believe it came from an adult woman, but we can't be sure."

"Why a woman?"

"The size, for one thing. And the lobe is pierced for an earring. Of course that's not conclusive. It could be from a man or boy."

"How recent was it?"

"Hard to tell for sure. There's evidence it was preserved in rough salt and possibly frozen for a time. It could be weeks or months old. Of course the whole thing still could be a publicity stunt. The ears of that Holmes story were preserved in salt."

"Yes, but—" she began and then left it hanging.

"You might suggest the police there check back a bit if they've got no recent killings."

"Thank you, Sergeant. I'll let you know if they find anything here."

"I'm sure they'll advise me, Miss Holt," he answered drily.

After that she slept.

By morning the tourists had put away their Victorian costumes and the crowds had thinned out. Refreshed after a good night's sleep, Susan ate breakfast at the hotel and then went off to see Bernard Wor once again. He smiled as she entered, and came around the counter to greet her. "I am so pleased that you could return, Miss Holt. Yesterday was too busy for a proper conversation. Let me show you around."

His hand rested lightly on her shoulder as he guided her into the work-room at the rear of the shop. She managed to edge casually away and asked, "Do you make the caps back here?"

"We do the final sewing and assembly. Most of the other items, like the magnifying glasses, are purchased at wholesale, though we affix our Sherlock Shoppe sticker to them."

Susan glanced at the mailing table. "Is this where the parcel would have been wrapped for us?"

"Right here," he confirmed.

"How is it possible that a human ear could have been added to the package without anyone noticing?"

He shrugged. "It's a small thing, easily concealed in the hand. Then too, Bruni often works late getting out overseas shipments."

"I was told that Bruni Zandt has been gone for some weeks."

He peered at her and said, without changing expression, "Did I say Bruni? I meant Eva, the woman who took Bruni's place. I haven't gotten used to the change yet."

"Could I speak with Eva?"

"Certainly. She's right over here."

Eva was very young, probably still in her late teens, and she spoke no English. Bernard Wor stood by to translate, but there was no way she could question the girl about the missing Bruni or anything else. She turned back to Wor. "Do you have an office where we could talk?"

He led her up a flight of stairs to the second floor above the Sherlock Shoppe. The office had windows looking down on the workroom and others at the front of the building looking out on the Holmes Museum in the old church. Susan gestured out the window and said, "If you were to change your mind and join in our promotion, I believe Mr. Eiger would too. The other shops we need would fall in line as well."

"The police have been here already about the ear," he said.

"The ear's not going to disappear just because you back off on your commitments. In fact, the police might decide you have something to hide."

He seemed to grow pale at her words. "If Eiger goes along with you, I will too," he decided.

"I'm on my way to speak to him now." She took some papers from her big purse and ran over the terms of the agreement again. "I'm authorized to increase our order for deerstalkers by three gross, in assorted sizes, if you sign a contract today."

"See me after you have Eiger's signature."

"I want yours first, to use as a bargaining chip."

"Increase your order by five gross and I'll sign."

"That's more than we can sell."

"Nonsense! You'll sell out in a week with that publicity about the severed ear. I might even suggest including a nice Swiss chocolate ear with each cap. White chocolate, of course, since I understand the ear was white."

She couldn't believe he was serious. "Mayfield's would never do anything like that."

"More's the pity."

Susan gathered up her papers. "Emmy Spring said you could be difficult."

He smiled and said, "Give my regards to Emmy."

As she was leaving the office she noticed some boxes of lethal-looking objects. "What do these axes have to do with Holmes?"

"Nothing. I have a second shop down the street that sells mountain climbing equipment. These are a new type of ice axe. Man cannot live by Sherlock alone, even in Meiringen."

She picked one up and hefted it. "You could kill somebody with one of these. Or tear an ear off."

"Maybe you could. Not me."

She dropped it back in the box. "I'll return when I have Eiger's agreement. Can I at least tell him he can call you?"

"Of course."

She left the Sherlock Shoppe and walked down the street to the museum. There was still a chill in the air, but she couldn't expect much better for the first week in May. A few tourists went in just ahead of her and she waited till they cleared the front desk before approaching Rima Fredericks.

"Hello again," the Englishwoman said with a smile.

"Is Mr. Eiger in?"

The dark-haired woman hesitated. "He is, but the police are with him now. Just a moment while I ring his office."

Susan waited with growing apprehension while she spoke a few quiet words into the phone and listened to the response. "You can go in," the woman told her. "They wish to speak with you too."

She took a deep breath and entered the indicated door. Two beefy men in open trench coats sat across the desk from Fritz Eiger. One of them rose and introduced himself in heavily accented English. "I am Captain Altdorf of the Swiss police. You are the American who discovered the severed ear in the parcel of deerstalker caps?"

"I'm Susan Holt. I work at Mayfield's in New York with Emmy Spring, the woman who actually found the ear."

"Ah, yes. but you were present at the time?"

"I was."

"It was a left ear?"

She had to think for an instant. "Yes, the left." The vision of it was still there, unwanted, in her memory.

"A body was found two weeks ago along the banks of the Aar River north of here. It was badly battered and decomposed and we have only now been able to identify it through dental records. It was the body of Bruni Zandt, a young woman employed at the Sherlock Shoppe here in town. She had been missing for about a month. As you may know, the Reichenbach is a tributary of the Aar River. If a body went over the falls here it might come to rest on the banks of the Aar."

"Her ear—".

"The body was missing its left ear. We thought nothing of it at first, because of the condition of the corpse. But when we received the report from the New York police, someone remembered the woman on the riverbank. We retraced her possible route back up to the falls and started checking on missing persons in this area. The dental records identified her."

"But the ear wasn't lost when she went over the falls," Susan insisted. "It would have been more damaged than it was. And it would probably have vanished somewhere in the river, eaten by predators."

"Exactly, Miss Holt. The existence of the ear tells us two things. Bruni Zandt was murdered, and it was her killer who mailed the ear to your office."

"The parcel came from the Sherlock Shoppe, as you know. Perhaps Mr. Wor can tell you something."

"I have men questioning him at this moment. I am going there myself now. What brings you to Meiringen, Miss Holt?"

She explained about the store's promotion plans and the problems that had arisen. "Some believe that the dead woman fled after embezzling money from Wor's shop," she told them.

"We are aware of that."

"I can't imagine there was very much money involved."

Captain Altdorf smiled. "Mr. Wor has foreign business connections. The amount could have been sizeable."

"I'd like to get to the bottom of this before I return to America."

The stocky man kept smiling, but his tone was icy. "I notice you have the same initials as the great detective, Miss Holt. Do not try to emulate him. We don't want another body going over Reichenbach Falls."

Susan waited until the police finished questioning Wor, then entered the Sherlock Shoppe. She purchased a Holmes-style pipe for Russell and was charging it on her credit when Bernard Wor came down from his office, looking a bit haggard. "The situation has changed since our talk, Miss Holt."

"I know. Your police have identified Bruni Zandt's body."

He glanced at the sales clerks on duty. "Come up to my office, please."

Once upstairs, he seated himself behind the desk. "How much do you know?"

"Some people think she embezzled money from you, possibly a large amount of money."

"I have various investors in other countries. A large amount of money was delivered to me in cash, in Italian lira. I foolishly thought it could remain in my safe overnight, until I took it to a bank in Zurich the following day."

"This Bruni had the combination?"

"Yes."

"When did it happen?"

"Just a month ago today." He got up and walked over to the windows that looked down on the workroom. "You can see the safe from here, under the table at the far end of the room."

"How much money did she take?"

"In your currency, it would be about eighty-five thousand dollars."

"It must be insured."

Bernard Wor smiled sadly. "There is only my word that it was ever here, or that she took it."

"Look, I have to clear up this matter of the store promotion. Can you come with me right now to see Fritz Eiger? Maybe then I can help you with your problem."

Rima Fredericks directed them to the museum basement, where Eiger was busy arranging the various components of the Holmes sitting room. "We have signs telling them not to touch anything, but they do, of course. Sometimes, when no one's on duty down here, they even steal something— Holmes's jackknife that skewers the mail to the mantel, for instance. Boys like to take those. Once one of Dr. Watson's scimitars was missing from between the windows."

Susan gazed at it all, imagining it reproduced on the fourth floor of Mayfield's: the furniture, the Victorian wallpaper, the *Times of London*, the bullet marks in the wall, even teacups and plates on the table. "When was the scimitar taken?" she asked.

"Oh, I don't know. Back in the winter sometime. But we keep extras of everything."

"Look, I've got you both together and I'd like to resolve this business. The police have a body to go with that severed ear now. no one things it's a publicity stunt any longer. There'll be money and publicity for both of you if you stick with your original agreements, and I'm sure other local merchants would join in. You'd be putting Meiringen right on Fifth Avenue!"

It took another twenty minutes of discussion, and a slight sweetening of the original terms, but in the end she had them. At least the problem that had brought her there was solved. When she left the museum she went at once to her hotel room and placed a call to the store. Emmy had taken the day off to move to a larger apartment, so she was forced to give the good news to Mike Brentnor.

"They've both signed," she told him. "We're set. I've increased your order for deerstalkers by five gross."

"Five—"

"It was that or nothing. I'm going to meet with the manager of Sherlock Holmes Hotel before I fly back tomorrow. He might be interested in a tie-in of some sort."

"That's fine. You'll be back tomorrow, then?"

"My plane's due at JFK at two thirty-five. I should be in the office before four."

After speaking with the hotel manager and a couple of other local merchants, Susan was convinced she'd done all she could for the store's promotion. She stopped back at the museum just as Rima Fredericks was leaving for the day.

"Which way are you going?" Susan asked. "I'll walk with you."

"I live quite close-by, but we can walk up to the falls again if you wish."

"Fine."

The Englishwoman set a good pace, and the usual ten-minute walk to the lower falls was completed in less than that. "You haven't seen the good view from farther up," she told Susan. "The central falls is only fifteen minutes higher and quite impressive."

"Isn't it dangerous?"

"It was to Moriarty, but all the ledges have these metal railings. They're quite safe."

"They weren't safe enough for Bruni Zandt."

Rima Fredericks turned sharply to stare at her. "What do you mean? Do the police believe she was killed here?"

All around them the roar of the falls filled the air, making talking difficult. A spray of water dampened their clothes as the wind shifted. "You know she was killed here, Miss Fredericks."

"We're getting wet," she told Susan. "We'd better go back."

"You were often in the workroom at the Sherlock Shoppe. It was easy for you to distract that girl Eva and slip the ear into the parcel of deerstalkers."

"You think I did that?"

"I'm sure of it. You commented earlier on what a shock it must have been for Emmy to open the parcel and find an ear lying on top of the deerstalkers. I doubt if the police supplied the detail that it was on top of the caps rather than under them. You knew it because that's where you placed the ear."

"Why would I–?" She had edged closer to Susan, perhaps to hear better above the roar, but the result was to force her closer to the railing over the falls.

"Don't!" Susan shouted, pushing back, struggling. The wet rocks beneath her feet were slippery and slimy. Her face hit the railing.

They wrestled there, locked in each other's arms, just as Holmes and Moriarty might have struggled more than a century earlier. Susan felt herself slip, her right foot going over the edge, as she clung desperately to the railing.

Then suddenly Captain Altdorf was there, yanking the Fredericks woman away, hauling Susan back from the brink. "Thank God!" she gasped. "She's the one. She sent the ear!"

Emmy Spring met her at Kennedy Airport the following afternoon. "What's the bruise?" she asked, horrified at the sight of Susan's face.

"It's a long story. I was wrestling at the edge of Reichenbach Falls, trying to be Sherlock Holmes."

"It's a wonder you weren't killed!"

They went down to the baggage claim while Susan waited for her suitcase to appear. "At least I found out who put the ear in that parcel, and where it came from."

"Tell me!"

"Wait till we get this bag to the car."

"Are you going home or to the store?"

"To the store, briefly. I've been up forever, but I guess I can last for a few more hours."

Once in the car Emmy deluged her with questions about the trip. "So who sent that ear?"

"Rima Fredericks, the Englishwoman who works at the Sherlock Holmes Museum. She phoned you the other day."

"But whose ear was it and why did she send it?"

"It belonged to a young woman named Bruni Zandt who worked in the Sherlock Shoppe."

"I don't believe I met her."

"I think you did, just once—when you killed her, Emmy."

As Sergeant Mulligan told her later, accusing someone of murder while she was driving a car out of Kennedy Airport wasn't the wisest thing Susan ever did. It was lucky that they only ended up off the road in a ditch, with Emmy Spring sobbing out the whole story that Susan had already figured out.

She'd been standing in Bernard Wor's upstairs office, examining that box of ice axes while he stepped out for a moment. Looking down through the windows at the workroom, she noticed a young woman employee make her way to the safe beneath the table at the far end of the room. She was furtive about it, glancing over her shoulder to make certain the workroom remained empty. But as she unlocked the safe and removed a thick white envelope from it, she never thought to look up at Wor's office windows. Emmy didn't even know the young woman, but she realized she was witnessing a crime. She didn't wait for Wor to return. She ran down the steps after the fleeing woman, still clutching an ice axe in her hand.

Outside it was almost dark—the first week in April—and still chillingly cold. Perhaps sensing she was being followed, Bruni Zandt ran up toward the falls. Emmy caught up with her at the first overlook. They struggled, Bruni pushed her, and Emmy swung the ice axe with all her might. It took off Bruni's left ear with a horrible spurt of blood. Terrified by what she had done, Emmy grabbed the wounded woman's purse and shoved her over the railing to the falls.

She claimed she still planned to report it to the police, but when she opened the envelope and saw a small fortune in Italian lira she changed her mind. The deed was done. She could not bring this unknown woman back to life. The money had not been hers, and it had already been stolen from Bernard Wor. It was as much Emmy's as anyone's. That was the story she told Susan by the side of the road as they waited for the police, and that was the story she would tell the Swiss courts later when they extradited her and tried her for murder.

"How did you ever tumble to such a thing?" Sergeant Mulligan asked Susan the following morning, as she made her statement in his office downtown.

"First it was the ear. I asked myself why it had been sent. Was it a tasteless publicity stunt suggested by Doyle's story 'The Cardboard Box'? I doubted it, because there were two ears in that story. Why not two ears here, if that was the sender's purpose? Obtained from a medical school, two would be as easy as one. No, the ear was sent for a different reason entirely. It was sent as an act of blackmail, undeniable proof that a dark deed had been witnessed. The parcel of deerstalker caps was addressed not to the store, nor to me, remember, but to Emmy Spring, who'd been over there just a month earlier."

At first Mulligan needed convincing. "You need more than that to tie her to the killing. Was she over there at the right time?"

"At exactly the right time. Even before her confession and the statement from Rima Fredericks, I could place her in Wor's upper office, with a perfect view of the safe, on the day of the robbery. She brought back with her a letter of agreement, signed by Wor on April fifth. I arrived here on May fourth, the Holmes anniversary, and the following day Wor told me the embezzlement occurred exactly one month earlier—April fifth, the very date Emmy got his signature on the letter. He discussed all business matters in his office and certainly the letter would have been signed there. Add to that the presence of those ice axes as a possible weapon—"

"You mentioned a missing scimitar from the Holmes sitting room."

"A scimitar would have made a cleaner cut, not the hacked-off wound you reported to me. The pointed ice axe seemed a much more likely weapon. And is there any evidence that Emmy Spring might have smuggled that stolen money back into this country? In a way, there is. She just moved into a larger apartment, which in New York almost certainly means a more expensive apartment." She took a deep breath. "I placed her at the scene, with an available weapon, and evidence of a recent improvement in her finances. We had the human ear addressed to her, and the highly emotional reaction it brought. When it turned out the ear came from a woman killed a month ago, I just couldn't overlook the possibility of Emmy's involvement. When I learned the Fredericks woman sometimes visited the Sherlock Shoppe workroom, it seemed likely she saw the crime and was blackmailing Emmy, sending the ear as proof of what she knew. She might even have demanded the money when she phoned Emmy about the possible cancellation. She'd been above Emmy and Bruni Zandt on one of the ledges that evening and saw the whole thing. She retrieved the severed ear after Emmy fled the scene and kept it in her freezer."

"Where did this money come from in the first place?"

Susan shrugged. "Somewhere in Italy. Perhaps it was Italian Mafia money, on its roundabout way to a Swiss numbered account."

Sergeant Mulligan smiled. "Sherlock Holmes would have been proud of you."

"I thought of him when I was struggling on that ledge. But I knew I wouldn't die because he didn't, did he?"

AN ABUNDANCE OF AIRBAGS

The first thing Susan Holt saw as her rented car topped the rise in the area south of Des Moines was a field of huge multicolored balloons swaying gently in the afternoon breeze. Somehow she hadn't expected so many, even though she knew it was ballooning country, with the National Balloon Museum not far away. At the car rental place they'd thought she was bound for the Madison County covered bridges like most of the other summer tourists in the area.

"Warren County is right here," the perky attendant had pointed out on the map, "but are you sure it's not Madison County you want?"

"Balloons, not bridges," Susan had insisted.

And here they were, spread out before her, their big colorful bags painted with basic stripes and elaborate designs, familiar corporate logos and rare mythological creatures. One was even a pretty good replica of the Montgolfiers' classic design from 1783.

Susan had flown and driven here from Manhattan because Mayfield's department store was planning a fall promotion built around the theme of ballooning—"Values Up, Prices Down"—and it was her job to organize and promote the event. They needed blown-up photographs, personal appearances by balloonists, and even, if possible, one of the more colorful balloons itself. She had written and spoken to a balloon enthusiast named Duncan Rowe, and this was the man she'd come to see.

She guessed there were more than twenty balloons in the open field, all inflated and ready to be released from their tethers. Along the far end of the field were two rows of parked cars and Susan pulled in beside the last one. A blond man in his twenties, wearing khaki pants and a Balloon Federation of America T-shirt, was standing by a white convertible with the top down. "You chasing?" he asked.

"Pardon me?"

"Are you a chase car for one of the balloons?" He smiled, showing perfect white teeth.

"No, I'm looking for Duncan Rowe."

"You came to the right person. He's my uncle."

"Really?"

"Come on, I'll introduce you. He's right over here."

"I'm Susan Holt, from New York. I've spoken to him on the phone."

"Philip Rowe. Glad to meet you."

She couldn't help noticing his muscular arms and body as she followed him across the grass to a red-and-white-striped balloon. The girls in her office would have called him a hunk. The slender gray-haired man in the basket of the balloon had the same smile and she knew at once that this was Duncan Rowe, Philip's uncle.

"We've talked so many times, I feel I know you," she told him when Philip had introduced them.

Duncan Rowe's smile widened. "You're even more charming in person. May I call you Susan?"

"Certainly. And this is Daisy?"

Duncan Rowe chuckled. "My nephew tells me only eccentric old men name their balloons after women, but I think of her as a Daisy." As he spoke he was feeding propane from one of the cylinders to the overhead burner coil that heated the air inside the bag. To Susan's eyes, it seemed fully inflated already.

"I'd love to go up in one of these sometime," she told him.

"No time like the present! Hop aboard!"

"No, no—I'm not dressed for it," she insisted, glancing down at the skirt she'd worn on the plane.

"I can probably find you a pair of jeans," Philip volunteered.

"No. Another time." The inflated balloons were beginning to bump each other as they prepared to ascend. "When can I speak with you about the Mayfield's promotion?"

"It's now or never," he told her with a grin. "Come on! I need a passenger to balance the basket."

"Your nephew—"

"He's chasing in the car."

Susan Holt sighed. He didn't really need her, she knew, but if she was going to make friends with the man, this was the easiest way to do it. "All right, give me five minutes. I have a pair of slacks in my garment bag."

"Five minutes, lads!" Duncan Rowe shouted to the ground crew as they tugged at the basket to hold it down. He turned down the fuel valve as she sprinted toward her car, feeling just a bit foolish.

She unzipped the garment bag, pulled the slacks from their hanger, and slouched down in the backseat while she pulled them on over her pantyhose. The wraparound skirt was quickly unsnapped and discarded. She was out of the car and on her way back in three minutes.

Philip Rowe handed her a yellow crash helmet. "Here—wear this."

"Your uncle's not wearing one."

"He thinks he's indestructible."

She buckled the helmet under her chin and accepted Philip's hand as he helped her into the woven wooden basket. Duncan Rowe immediately turned the fuel valve and the burner above their heads gave a deep-throated roar. The basket lurched as the ground crew relaxed their hold. "Have a good flight!" Philip shouted above the roar.

"How much does that airbag hold?" Susan shouted into Duncan Rowe's ear as they rose quickly off the ground. Learning the mechanics of something had always been her method of calming fear.

"First off, young lady, they're no longer called airbags. Those are found in automobiles these days. This is simply a bag, or more properly an envelope. Large ones can hold nearly a quarter-million cubic feet of air. This is only about half that size. As the air is heated it expands, and the upthrust lifts the balloon. I control it by means of vents near the top which can be opened and closed. Also, of course, more fuel will send us higher and less fuel will bring us down."

Susan had overcome her initial fright and took time now to inspect the interior of the basket. It held cylinders of propane fuel for the burner in three of the corners, connected in series so they could be consumed one after the other. There was also a small fire extinguisher attached to the bottom of the thick gauge box containing an altimeter, compass, and other dials. Two straps to control the envelope flaps hung down from overhead. There were gauges on each of the fuel cylinders as well, and a dropline for help in landing.

"Hold on tight with both hands," Rowe warned her as they rose past the treetops. "If we hit those you don't want to be thrown out!"

"Is it a dangerous sport?"

"One of our people was killed last week," he answered grimly.

"Really?"

"A good friend named Bruce Manchester. He'd been ballooning for twenty years without a mishap. He went up alone and somewhere above the treetops he simply fell out. He was dead the instant he hit the ground."

"Suicide?"

Duncan Rowe shook his head. "I can't believe it. He was happily married, in perfect health. His insurance business was thriving."

"A heart attack?"

"The autopsy showed nothing. And no injuries except those caused by the fall."

They glided past the final treetop and she relaxed her grip on the basket. Rowe turned off the burner and they drifted along in silence, enjoying the panorama of the countryside. "How high are we?" she asked, gazing down at a dozen colorful balloons below them.

He consulted the altimeter. "Close to two thousand feet." He flicked on a switch and the burner roared above her head, sending them higher. She was glad the helmet helped shield her hair from the heat. "We have to stay below the commercial airlanes but we can go up to five thousand feet in this area."

The wicker basket was four feet square and could probably have held two more passengers. In her mind she pictured kids climbing over it at Mayfield's. "Could we have this basket and balloon for our fall promotion at the store?"

"You mean inflated?"

"No, no—our ceilings aren't high enough. But this basket is pretty neat and the deflated balloon could be draped above it."

"Why my balloon?" He gestured below them, where the others seemed to play tag with a passing cloud. "Kevin Nova has a Pegasus graphic on his. Mine's just stripes."

"People can see Pegasus at their gas station. And the more elaborate designs don't show up well when the balloon's deflated. We could use blown-up photographs of them around the store, though."

"What would you pay for all this?" he asked, cutting off the fuel again.

"I have a contract in my car."

He looked down over the side. "There's Philip and his girl, following us in the chase car. Perhaps it's time we took Daisy down."

"How do you land this thing?"

"Downwind, using the burner and maneuvering vent. If I can't land it without help I'll deploy the dropline for Philip and Rita. Once on the ground the fuel system is shut off and the deflation port is opened to release the remaining hot air. The balloon collapses and we gather it into a long cylinder for packing into the envelope carry sack."

While he spoke he'd decreased the amount of fuel to the burner and the balloon began losing altitude. Susan watched the needle on the altimeter as it sank below a thousand feet. "What are these other gauges?"

"The variometer measures the rate of climb and the pyrometer indicates the temperature of the air in our envelope. This one is a compass, of course."

The ground was coming up fast and she took a firm grip on the basket, bracing for the shock. The basket bumped once as it hit and then toppled over on its side. She was bounced around but climbed out gamely as Philip and his girl came running up.

"Are you all right?" Duncan Rowe's nephew asked.

"I'll survive."

"This is Rita Bloom. Susan Holt."

Rita was in her early twenties, a fresh-faced young woman with hair the color of Iowa corn tassels. It wasn't until she opened her mouth that Susan recognized the unmistakable New York accent. "I came out here to attend Drake University and after graduation I just stayed," she explained when Susan questioned her. She had a way of gesturing as she spoke. "It's so much more open than Manhattan."

Looking around at the cornfields, Susan had to agree with her. "You ever been up in one of those?" she asked, gesturing toward the rapidly deflating balloon after removing her helmet.

"Oh, sure! Philip took me up a couple of times. It's not so bad after your first flight."

A red pickup truck had turned off the road and was bumping across the field toward them. The side of the door read Glen's Auto Repair, and Rowe identified the man who jumped out as Glen Leavor. "Glen picks up all the pieces for us, transports the baskets and bags back home."

Leavor was around thirty, dark-haired and with a shadow of beard on his chin. Susan imagined he was quite the hit with local ladies who might find Philip Rowe beyond their reach. "Pleased to meet you," he said, making a halfhearted effort to tip his baseball cap. "Want to give me a hand with this basket, Phil?"

The two of them lifted the wicker carriage by carrying handles near the bottom and hoisted it onto the truck. Glen helped gather the collapsed balloon into a cylinder and pack it into its carry sack.

"We're having drinks at our place for the balloonists," Duncan Rowe told him. "When you deliver that stuff come in for some refreshments."

"I'll do that," Leavor said. "See you!"

"He's a big help," Philip said as the truck pulled away, heading for a big green balloon that was just landing nearby. "We all chip in to pay him."

"Do you always have a party after flights?" Susan asked.

Duncan Rowe smiled. "Sometimes. This one's partly for your benefit, so you can meet some of the people. They're a great bunch. Most would do better than me in New York."

The Rowe house was situated on a small rise at the end of an impressive driveway. Despite some colonial touches, it was a modern home with spacious rooms and a state-of-the-art kitchen. "Duncan's wife Diana passed away last summer," Rita Bloom explained as she and Susan entered through the kitchen door. "It was a great shock to everyone."

"Had she been ill?"

"Not ill. She was—"

Duncan entered just behind them, ending the conversation. It was obvious that he took great pride in the house and he insisted on giving Susan a tour while they waited for the others to arrive. "I hope I can lure you away from all this for our fall promotion," Susan told him. "It's beautiful country here."

"Especially beautiful seen from the air." He showed her his oak-paneled den, where posters and photos of balloons in flight dominated the room. There were shelves of books on the sport, too, and a few gold trophies Duncan had won. Susan paused over a framed picture of Duncan and a handsome middle-aged woman holding one of them. There were other pictures of her on the walls.

"Your wife?" Susan asked.

"Yes." He said nothing more on the subject.

They returned from the tour to find the house filling up with men and women, mostly in their thirties and forties. They were handsome, athletic people with the money to buy, maintain, and fly the balloons she'd admired earlier. Duncan introduced her to a few of them before his nephew called him out to the kitchen where there was a problem with the hors d'oeuvres.

She found herself finally with a slender, bearded young man with the appearance of a sea captain. His name was Kevin Nova and she immediately recognized it. "You're Pegasus! I mean you have it on your balloon!"

"That's right," he confirmed with a smile. "How'd you know?"

"I was up with Duncan today and he pointed it out. I remembered your name. That's quite a balloon!"

"Thank you. It always attracts attention at the races. And you must be the lady from the New York store that's going to fill the place with our balloons."

"Well, pictures mostly. But we do hope to have one or two deflated bags, along with their baskets and accessories. I think it would be a great attraction."

"Do you want Pegasus?"

Susan made a snap decision. "I do, if I can think of a way to display it. Our ceilings—"

"I was in Mayfield's once on a trip to New York. Isn't there an area between the first-floor escalators that's quite high and open?"

He was right, of course. "We have about fifty feet there," she agreed. "But your balloons are higher than that when inflated."

"We could partially inflate them, enough to show the design, and hold them up with wires. It's got to be faked somehow anyway, since I doubt that you want the burners going to heat the air."

"How else can you keep them inflated?"

"With gas. Some European balloonists still use hydrogen or helium, though hydrogen is very dangerous. You don't want a fire. A small amount of helium would do the job. We don't have to fly off anywhere."

"We certainly don't want a fire," she agreed. 'This is a fairly dangerous sport, isn't it?"

Kevin Nova smiled down at her. He was half a head taller than she and when he stood this close she was quite aware of having to look up at him. "Why do you say that?"

"Duncan mentioned a Bruce Manchester who fell out of his balloon last week."

"Yes. A terrible tragedy, but it was no accident. I was right below him when it happened. Just before he fell I'll swear I heard a loud crack like a gunshot. Then his body came hurtling past me."

"You're saying he was shot?"

"I don't know. The autopsy found no bullet wound. But that's what I heard."

"You think he shot himself?"

"Or someone else shot him."

Susan shook her head, trying to grasp it. "But he was alone, wasn't he?"

"He was alone," Nova agreed. "The balloon got tangled in the treetops and had to be hauled out by Leavor and some others. It was a mess. But then Manchester was something of a mess too after falling a couple of thousand feet. Of course, when there was no bullet wound, no one believed my story of hearing a shot."

"It must have been something else. His foot might have hit something in the basket as he fell."

"Nothing would make that noise. Besides, he wasn't the first accident."

"He wasn't?" She had the feeling she was about to learn something she'd rather not know. "Duncan's wife Diana died the same way last summer."

Glen Leavor and some others had arrived while she talked with Nova, and the repairman announced that everyone's balloon had been safely recovered and delivered. Apparently some of the group kept their equipment at home in the garage while those cramped for space rented storage sheds nearby. Susan spotted Rita Bloom just handing Leavor a drink and went to join them. He was the sort who kept his baseball cap on in the house but he seemed pleasant enough as he conversed with Rita.

"Listen, Glen," she was saying, "if I can go up in one of those things anyone can. I'll get Philip to take us both up next week."

He held up his free hand in mock alarm. "No, I feel safer on the ground. Sometimes when I pick up the bags after an accident they're punctured and shredded. I don't want to be in one if that happens."

"I hear there was an accident just last week," Susan interjected. "Manchester's balloon was punctured."

"It ran into a tree," Leavor said, taking a sip of his drink.

"Could something have punctured the bag before Manchester fell?"

Rita smiled at her. "You've been listening to Kevin and his story about hearing a shot. When they couldn't find a bullet in Manchester, Kevin decided it must have punctured the envelope and the sudden deflation threw Bruce out of the basket. But it couldn't have happened that way. First of all, he wouldn't have heard a distant shot so clearly. Whatever he heard, he thought it came from right above them, where Manchester's basket was. Second, a tiny bullet hole wouldn't have deflated that huge envelope so quickly. It would have been more like a slow leak."

"The balloon drifted on for several minutes after Manchester fell," Glen Leavor confirmed. "I was watching it from the ground with the others in their chase cars. The burner was off and it just gradually drifted lower until it got snagged in the trees."

"Someone told me Mrs. Rowe died the same way last summer."

Rita seemed to pale a bit at the words, but she was quick to correct them. "No, Diana's death was entirely different. It was a terrible blow to Duncan."

"Didn't she fall from a balloon?"

It was Leavor who answered. "That was suicide. She left a note for Duncan. He has it framed. She'd flown with him and knew how to handle the balloon. That day she took it up without any chase car. She knew she wouldn't need one."

"It was terrible for him," Rita confirmed. "He was a wreck for months."

"I'm glad to see he seems to have recovered," Susan said.

"He's getting there, slowly."

Duncan Rowe joined them at that point and the conversation ceased. He'd had a few drinks and Susan could see it was no time to talk business. "Could we get together tomorrow," she asked, "and go over the contract?"

"Contract? Sure, anything for you. Want to go for another ride with me?"

"I don't think so. Tomorrow I'll stay on firm ground."

He let his eyes wander over the other guests, finally settling on Nova. "Kevin, are you going up tomorrow?"

"I wasn't planning on it," the bearded man replied.

"I'll race you, one on one."

"Ah, Duncan—"

"I'd lay money on that race!" Leavor announced. "Five hundred on Duncan to win!" Within minutes his bet was covered by the others. They agreed on a ten A.M. race, weather permitting.

"I never thought balloon racing was a gambling sport," Susan remarked to Duncan Rowe. "I'll see you tomorrow." It was time to call it a day.

She was up early and left her motel by nine, hoping she could catch Duncan at home before the race. But when she reached the house only Rita Bloom was there, loading the dishwasher with breakfast things. "You just missed him. Philip is driving him over to the launching field where we were yesterday."

"I'm sorry," Susan admitted. "If there's going to be another champagne celebration after this one I'll never get my contracts signed."

"We'll try to keep him under control." There was something grim about her tone of voice that Susan couldn't help noticing. "What's the matter?"

"Oh, nothing. Philip says it's foolish, that I read too many detective stories."

"Why's that?"

"I'm worried about this race. I keep thinking there might be another accident, like what happened to Mr. Manchester last week."

"Why should there be another?"

"Well, that's the part Philip says is foolish. You see, Duncan was supposed to take that balloon up. It was called the Star-burst, with a dark blue envelope and random white spots for stars. At the last minute Mr. Manchester wanted it so they switched and Duncan took Daisy like he usually does. If someone did kill Mr. Manchester, maybe they were after Duncan."

It sounded crazy, but Susan had learned that the truth was often crazy. "Come on," she said. "Let's get over there."

The field, when they reached it, presented a quite different sight from the previous day. There were almost as many cars and onlookers, but now only two of the hot-air balloons were in position and fully inflated. "Pegasus and Daisy," Rita observed. "There they are."

Susan drove past the waiting Pegasus, barely acknowledging Kevin's wave from the basket. She parked up close to Daisy and darted across the trampled grass to the big red-and-white-striped balloon. "Duncan! Wait!"

"Wait for what?" he asked, turning the fuel valve up a bit. "You can't join me today, Susan, much as I'd like you to."

She gripped the edge of the basket from the outside, examining every inch of it, searching for anything out of the ordinary, but it was exactly as it had been the previous day. Certainly there was no danger there, no frayed ropes or loosened fastenings.

"We have to release it," Philip shouted. "Kevin is taking off."

"All right," she said with a sigh, letting go of the basket, smothering her fears with a smile and wave to Duncan. "Good luck!"

Daisy was off the ground only seconds after Pegasus, rising straight up into the clear morning sky. "Come on, if you want to chase it," Philip yelled to Rita and Susan. They piled into his white convertible and took off. The course was to be ten kilometers—six miles—across the open countryside over flat farmlands with a minimum of trees, he explained as he drove. It was a short race as races go, but the one-on-one challenge had been more sport than serious competition.

Susan glanced back to see a line of cars following them. She recognized Glen Leavor's red truck and the chase car for Kevin's balloon. Most of the others had been at Duncan's house the previous night. High above them, the colorful balloons had drifted far apart. It was difficult from this angle to tell which was in the lead.

Philip turned onto a side road to better follow his uncle's route, and then it happened without warning. Suddenly a tiny speck was falling from the basket of the red and white balloon.

It took Susan just an instant to realize that the speck was a man and the man must be Duncan Rowe.

They found his body in the center of a cornfield, after searching the lanes of knee-high stalks until they spotted him sprawled on his back staring at the cloudless sky. Rita screamed and tried to run to him, but Philip held her back. Susan, seeing there was nothing she could do here, glanced back at the road where Leavor's truck had just pulled up.

She ran back to him and said, "Duncan's dead. Let's go after that balloon."

"What for?" he asked blankly.

"Something killed him. I want to know what."

Leavor headed back onto the main road and sped toward the area where the red and white balloon was beginning to lose altitude. Kevin's Pegasus balloon had continued on course. Apparently he was unaware of what had happened. "These things need radios," Susan said.

"They use cellular phones to communicate during formal events, but this was just fooling around."

"It wasn't fooling around for Duncan," she reminded him grimly.

"I know. I didn't mean—"

"There was his wife last summer and Bruce Manchester just last week. They have to be connected."

The balloon Daisy was losing altitude at a faster rate. It just missed a stand of trees and bounced across a dirty road into a ditch. They reached it within minutes. Susan and Leavor were both out of the truck, running toward it as the red and white envelope settled down around it.

"Looks all right," Leavor announced, pushing some of the deflated fabric out of the basket. "I can't see what went wrong."

"Neither can I," Susan admitted, "but if he jumped, something made him do it."

"Here come some of the others. We'll get this onto my truck. I'm sure the police will want to examine it."

With a little help Leavor quickly loaded the basket into his truck and collected the envelope into its cylinder. Susan rode back with him and they encountered Kevin Nova on the way, flagging them down from his chase car. "What happened?" Nova asked Susan, the blood drained from his face. "I heard—"

She nodded. "Duncan is dead. He jumped or fell from his balloon. We don't know what happened."

"Just like Manchester."

"It appears so."

"Are Philip and Rita back at the house?"

"They're with his body," Leavor told him. "It's in a cornfield about a mile back along this road."

"Go on. We'll follow you."

Someone had called an ambulance and it arrived just as they did. Rita was sobbing now, with Philip trying to comfort her. A state police car had arrived on the scene and Philip asked Susan if she could drive Rita back to Duncan's house in the convertible. It was no time to explain that New Yorkers rarely drive even if they have a license, so she agreed. It was like another rental car.

Once they were under way, the blond young woman stopped crying and settled down. "Philip was very close to his uncle," she explained. "I feel very sad for him."

"Have you known Philip long?"

"Since last summer. We met in Des Moines just after I graduated from Drake. He's been wonderful to me."

"Did Duncan have any enemies? Is there anyone who would want to kill him?"

"No one. He was very popular, especially among the balloonists."

"Yet I feel that someone or something forced him to jump. Manchester's death the week before is too much of a coincidence, especially since he went up in the balloon Duncan was planning to pilot."

"You know, they used to write mysteries like this, with locked rooms and impossible crimes. They don't do it so much anymore." She began warming to the subject as Susan drove. "I've read some stories about killing somebody like this."

"In a balloon?"

"No, no, I don't remember one of those. But there was a young woman on a balcony once who fell to her death. It turned out the killer, on another balcony, used a bullwhip to yank her off and send her falling. He wrapped it around her neck and pulled."

Susan nodded. "Kevin Nova was right below Manchester's balloon, and claims to have heard a shot. It could have been the crack of a bullwhip."

"Except he wouldn't have said that if he did it. And besides, he was far away from Duncan's balloon today. Bullwhips and lassos just wouldn't have worked. If it's murder it has to be some other method."

"What other method is there?"

"Well, John Dickson Carr once had a novel where the killer introduced carbon dioxide gas into a tower room. The victim jumped from the window to avoid suffocation as the gas displaced the oxygen in the room."

"That wouldn't work in an open-air balloon basket," Susan pointed out.

"Then maybe something else made him jump. A writer named C. Daly King wrote a story about the crew of a motor-boat who jumped overboard and drowned for no reason. It turned out there were giant wolf-spiders hiding on board that came out when the boat's motor heated up."

"No wolf-spiders," Susan insisted with a firm shake of her head as she pulled into the Rowe driveway.

"Maybe a giant bird of some sort, a vulture or an eagle—"

"You read too many mysteries, Rita."

"Then you think he just jumped?"

Susan didn't answer till Rita let them into the house. Then she said, "I don't know. The answer may lie in the first death, a year ago. When we were talking last night, Leavor mentioned that Diana Rowe had left a suicide note for Duncan, and that he still had it. Do you think I could see it?"

She hesitated a moment, then said, "I suppose so. He had it framed with her picture and hung it in his den."

"He framed her suicide note?" Leavor had mentioned that too.

"He always considered it more of a love letter."

Susan followed her into the den and stood before a large color photograph of a strikingly handsome woman, her lips curled into a slight enigmatic smile. Beneath it a rectangle had been cut in the mat to show a brief handwritten note: *I'm leaving our vacant existence yet our unique grand love endures nobly.*

Susan reread the words with their seeming contradiction. She was still staring at them when Philip Rowe came in a few minutes later. "That was Diana's suicide note," he said quietly. "Now my uncle is with her."

"You think he killed himself too?"

"There's no other explanation. The state police agree."

"No other explanation," Susan agreed reluctantly.

"You'll be returning to New York now?"

"I still have a store promotion to plan. I'll have to speak with Kevin now."

It was sometime after one when Kevin Nova arrived at the house with some of the others to offer their sympathies. She got Kevin aside and asked him about taking Pegasus to New York in the fall. "I can't think about it today," he told her. "After what happened to Duncan I don't feel like ever going near a balloon again."

"What happened wasn't your fault."

"He wouldn't have been up there if I hadn't accepted his challenge to the race."

"You weren't racing Manchester last week, were you?"

"No," he admitted, but that didn't seem to make him feel any better.

Leavor had brought the downed balloon to the state police substation for examination, but they'd been unable to find anything out of the ordinary. Philip spoke to them on the phone and then came to announce that the death would probably be classified as an accident, as had Manchester's the week before. There was no evidence of suicide, and murder seemed out of the question.

"No one would have a motive for killing Duncan," Kevin Nova agreed.

No motive, no means. Susan thought about it. Was it only her past experience with crime that made her see something here that didn't really exist?

She decided to stay one more night and speak with Nova again in the morning.

Susan awoke in the morning knowing who killed Duncan Rowe and Bruce Manchester. She knew who'd killed them and how it had been done. Perhaps her subconscious mind had been working on it while she slept.

After breakfast she drove over to Duncan Rowe's home, hoping they'd all be there prior to visiting the funeral parlor. Philip and Rita were serving bacon and eggs to some of the usual crowd, and she saw Nova and Leavor at once. She walked into the living room as if she owned the place and went right to the den.

"Susan," Rita called, "do you want some breakfast?"

"I've had it, thanks." She lifted the picture of Diana Rowe—the one with the suicide note—off the wall and walked back through the living room with it.

Philip interrupted her. "Where are you going with that?"

"To the police. It's evidence in a murder case."

After two deaths, the killer was beyond bluffing it out. He leaped from the sofa and tried to grab it from her. For an instant no one seemed to know what was going on. Finally they held him down while Philip demanded an explanation from her.

"He was Diana's lover," she said simply. "She couldn't break away from Duncan and she couldn't give up the affair, so she went up in the balloon and found another way out. Even with her suicide note she found a way to communicate with each of them. You all looked at it for a year and no one ever saw it. Perhaps you just needed a fresh set of eyes."

"Saw what?" Rita asked, staring at the note below the photograph.

"Read it: *I'm leaving our vacant existence yet our unique grand love endures nobly.* That was the message for Duncan. Now read the first letter of each word and get a quite different message: *I love you Glen.*"

Glen Leavor glared at her and said nothing. The men holding him tightened their grip.

"He felt that Duncan had driven her to suicide, and he spent a year devising the proper vengeance. He failed last week when Duncan and Manchester switched balloons at the last minute. The innocent Manchester died in place of Duncan. Yesterday Leavor was more successful."

"But how?' Philip demanded. "How could he have forced my uncle to jump to his death from that balloon?"

Susan was staring at Glen Leavor, whose expression of controlled anger hadn't softened. "Duncan didn't jump, he was pushed. You might say a blow from a giant boxing glove knocked him out of that basket. He was killed by an air-bag—an automobile airbag."

It wasn't until Glen Leavor confessed to the police many hours later that Susan and the others learned the full story. It was Nova's report of hearing a shot just before Manchester fell that had made her think of an airbag. "It's like a shot when they go off," she explained. "The igniter squib detonates with a bang, just like a gunshot, and the airbag is inflated with nitrogen gas in something like fifty milliseconds. I'd guess it was hidden in the box behind the control panel. What I took to be a fire extinguisher attached to a bracket on the bottom of that box was really the small tank for the compressed nitrogen gas."

"But you and Leavor reached the downed balloon together," Philip said. "Why didn't you notice the deflated airbag?"

"Because Leavor painted it the same colors as the balloon's envelope. I did notice him pushing some of the deflated fabric out of the basket, but I thought it was part of the envelope. Naturally he removed the entire gadget while he was bringing the basket back in his truck. Leavor's in the auto repair business, remember. And he encouraged the race by immediately betting on Duncan to win. He probably stocks airbag kits as replacements after accidents. He no doubt inflated it with an air pump, spray-painted it to match the envelope, and then replaced it and reattached it to the pressurized tank of nitrogen gas. Getting it into that gauge box would have been easy."

Susan's deductions had been correct so far as they went. Leavor revealed he'd added a device like a kitchen timer to the box so it would buzz after a certain number of minutes. When Manchester and Duncan Rowe lifted the lid to find the cause of the buzzing they activated the airbag. Angled slightly upward, it hit them with the force of—yes, a boxing glove. Without an automobile seat behind them they were thrown backward, over the edge of the basket to their deaths.

"I suppose they were the first victims murdered with automobile airbags," Susan told Rita as she prepared to leave the next day, but she wished somehow she could have changed that to "almost" murdered in the case of Duncan Rowe. She'd liked the man, and she would have liked having him at Mayfield's fall promotion. As it was, Kevin Nova had agreed to take part, with his balloon.

She knew every time she looked at it she'd remember Duncan's body falling through space.

From his office above the entrance to the main building of the state prison, Warden Chester Coyne could always hear the demonstrators on an execution night. They started early, before nightfall, with their chants and songs and speeches, and kept it up until confirmation came that the execution by lethal injection had been carried out, usually sometime after midnight.

On this night in late November he'd been deluding himself that the turnout might be smaller than usual. The condemned man was white and middle-class, with a particularly brutal murder on his record. He wasn't some disadvantaged youth from the inner city, lured into violence by the easy money of drugs. But by six o'clock they were out there, lighting little bonfires against the night chill, settling in for another countdown.

There was a knock on the warden's door and Captain DeMarco, in command of death-row guards, entered without waiting for the standard invitation. DeMarco was like that, and sometimes it annoyed Chester Coyne. "What is it, Captain?"

"I asked Feltzer what he wanted for his last meal. He says Chinese food."

Warden Coyne sighed. They couldn't prepare that in the prison kitchen. "All right. Send out for it."

"Which place?"

"Whatever is closest. Make sure there's tight security when they deliver it." Chinese food!

When he was alone again Coyne stared at the telephone on his desk. The red phone was a direct line to the governor's office, but he knew there'd be no pardon tonight. The death penalty had been one of several issues in the recent election campaign, and the governor's support of it had been one of the factors in his reelection.

Coyne glanced at the typewritten schedule on his desk. David Feltzer was scheduled for his last meal at eight-thirty p.m. He had requested a visit from his wife and his brother at ten o'clock, and at eleven he would be visited by the Catholic chaplain of the prison. Shortly after midnight, pursuant to the warrant for his execution, he would be taken from his cell to the death chamber, strapped to a gurney, and fitted with an intravenous tube that would introduce a sedative into his body. At some point in the proceedings, after the condemned man was asleep, the designated executioner would add a lethal dosage to the tube. Death would be quick and painless.

The warden turned and stared out at the growing crowd beyond the prison gates. All those who opposed capital punishment should be able to die so peacefully!

Shortly after eight o'clock Captain DeMarco returned, giving his usual perfunctory knock. "The Chinese food is here. Want to come with me?"

"Sure," Chester Coyne said. It would be the last time the warden would see Feltzer until he was led into the execution chamber. This was the part he hated, seeing and comforting a man who would soon be dead, but he viewed it as part of his duty. Capital punishment was easy to support in the abstract, a bit more difficult when you were speaking to the condemned man from just a few feet away.

David Feltzer was forty-five years old now, though he'd been only thirty-three at the time of the murder. He'd been unemployed and desperate when he passed a note to a bank teller and took the packet of money she handed him. It was an exploding dye-pack, and it had gone off moments later as he reached the bank parking lot. Enraged and desperate, and covered with red ink, he'd seized a young high-school girl named Meagan Brady and dragged her into his car as a hostage. The only witnesses had been across the street, unable to help, but one of them did get his license number.

The girl's body had been found a few hours later in a country ditch. She'd been shot in the head. Feltzer was apprehended by state police that night, fleeing through the southern part of the state. He offered no resistance and, in fact, signed a confession, claiming the police had deprived him of sleep during twelve hours of questioning. It had taken the jury only half that long to find him guilty and recommend the death penalty.

Feltzer's wife and brother had stuck with him through a number of hearings and appeals. He'd admitted the robbery but insisted he'd dropped the girl off unharmed. No one really believed him, least of all Warden Coyne. As he entered the condemned cell now with Captain DeMarco he still harbored a distaste for the man.

"We've brought your Chinese dinner as you requested, Feltzer," he said, stepping out of the way as DeMarco placed the containers of food on the small table a guard had brought in. The guard would remain with him while he ate.

David Feltzer had grown thin and pale during his twelve years of imprisonment. He looked especially bad this night, which was to be expected. They
never looked good during these final hours. "Thanks, Warden," he muttered
without meeting their eyes. He stared at the plastic knife and fork the prison
had provided, then at the wooden chopsticks that had come with the food.

"Your wife and brother will be here at ten," Coyne told him. "The chaplain will come at eleven. You'll have an hour with him."

The prisoner nodded, apparently deciding to use the chopsticks. "It'll be
good to see them." He emptied the containers onto paper plates.

"Is there anything else you'd like with your meal?" DeMarco asked.

"This is fine." He took a bit of food and seemed to grimace slightly. He
took another portion between the chopsticks and brought it to his mouth.
Coyne decided he was probably out of practice with the chopsticks. The third
portion got away from him, falling to the floor.

"Never mind," the warden told him. "We'll get it."

David Feltzer raised his eyes to Coyne for the first time. "I think I'm going
to—"

Then he slumped over the table, knocking the paper plate to the floor.

Captain DeMarco was at his side, trying to lift him. After a moment he
gave up and looked at Chester Coyne. "He's dead, Warden. I think he's
taken poison."

It was Susan Holt's bad luck to arrive in West Caroline two days after the
death of David Feltzer. She'd flown there because her employer, Mayfield's
of Manhattan, had just completed an agreement to purchase Brookline, a
chain of department stores headquartered in West Caroline. She and Mike
Brentnor had come down from New York to help plan the special store promotions to be held when Brookline changed its name to Mayfield's in six
months.

"We'd like to have the new name in place for the Easter selling season,"
Brentnor had explained to Brookline's top executive, a gray-haired man
named Ziegler. "But that would only give us four months."

"Not enough time," Ziegler decreed. Susan had already decided he was
not the sort one argued with. "We need at least six months. Call it the end
of May."

"That would be satisfactory," Susan said quickly, before Mike could dis-
agree. "We'll want to meet with your promotions manager for some preliminary planning."

"That would be Simon Feltzer, but you'll have to wait till tomorrow. Simon buried his brother this morning."

"I'm sorry to hear that. Was it sudden?"

"Well, yes and no. He was awaiting execution for murder and he killed himself a few hours earlier."

"My God!" Mike Brentnor said. "How—?"

Ziegler cut further questions short with a wave of his hand. "You can read about it in the morning paper. We have business to discuss here."

As they drove back to their hotel, Susan grumbled, "What a cold fish! Simon Feltzer must have a great time working for him."

"We'll have to pick up a paper and read about it." Susan shrugged. "We've got nothing better to do till tomorrow morning." She was dreading the evening with Mike Brentnor, remembering a previous occasion when she'd been forced to fight off his unwanted advances. He'd behaved himself around the office since then, but here they were on a trip together and the memory of last time was all too clear. She decided to check the newspaper for a nearby movie.

The newspaper account of David Feltzer's death was hardly satisfactory. It hinted that police were still investigating the circumstances, trying to determine how the condemned man had gotten the poison. There had been no ruling of suicide as yet.

"Why would he commit suicide when the state was going to kill him in a few hours anyway?" Brentnor asked as they relaxed over a cocktail in the hotel bar.

"Some people have," Susan pointed out. "Goering did."

"Who?"

"Hermann Goering, Hitler's right-hand man during World War Two, commander in chief of the German air force. He swallowed a poison pill a few hours before he was to be hanged as a war criminal. Don't you know your history?"

"I have a tough enough time with modern stuff." He chewed on a lemon slice that had come with his drink. "What's on the schedule for tonight?"

"I think I'll look for a nearby movie I haven't seen."

"Hey, this isn't Manhattan! In these burgs the movies are all out at the malls."

He was right, of course, as she discovered when she glanced through the entertainment pages. They ended up having dinner together and then she made a hasty escape to her room.

In the morning they showed up at Simon Feltzer's office at the Brookline store. The appointment had been set for ten o'clock, but when they got there they discovered Feltzer was in a meeting with a detective investigating his brother's death.

Simon Feltzer himself was a rumpled man of about forty, with thinning hair and thick glasses. He didn't look like any sort of department-store executive, but then Susan was probably judging him in New York terms. He met them at the door with a beefy man who was introduced as Detective Sergeant Green. The sergeant nodded to Susan and said, "Sorry to delay your meeting like this. I have to check in with headquarters and then I'll be back for just a minute."

"We can start our meeting in the meantime," Simon Feltzer assured them. "Come on in."

The blond wood furniture in the little office seemed a holdover from a few decades back. Susan sat across the desk from Feltzer and immediately began to remove schedules and ad layouts from her attaché case. "I was sorry to hear about your brother," she said sympathetically. "It must have been a terrible shock."

"Well, not really," the man said. "Mildred and I have been expecting it for twelve years, so to speak."

"He was on death row that long?"

"Counting the trial and everything. Let's see—I'm thirty-nine now. I was a callow youth of twenty-seven at the time, bumming around without a job. David was my older brother, driving a newspaper delivery truck until he got laid off. Mildred was pregnant and he was desperate for money. That's what made him do it."

"The paper said he'd killed a girl," Mike Brentnor said without feeling. He might have been discussing the weather.

"I still can't understand that part. He must have gone a little crazy."

"Mildred was his wife?" Susan asked.

Simon Feltzer nodded. "She stuck by him all these years, never remarried. A nice woman. The shock of David's arrest caused her to lose the child."

Before Susan could say anything else there was a tap on the door and Sergeant Green returned. "Sorry to interrupt. I just wanted to tell you, Mr. Feltzer, that they've reviewed the results of the autopsy and the preliminary investigation. Your brother's death is being listed as a homicide. Somebody poisoned that Chinese dinner."

The news had left Simon Feltzer speechless, and when Sergeant Green departed Susan Holt was the first to speak. "Why would anyone poison a man about to be executed?" she wondered. "I suppose there's some slight rationale for suicide—a desire to control one's own destiny, to cheat the executioner as Goering did—but what would be the motive in murdering someone about to die after twelve years in prison?"

"I wish I knew," Feltzer said softly, barely breathing the words.

"It doesn't really concern us," Mike Brentnor decided, trying to steer the conversation back to business. "Now about the opening promotion, I was thinking of a tropical-bird motif—"

"I—I'm sorry," Feltzer said. "This has been quite a shock."

It wasn't the first time Susan's job had involved her in a murder case. "I might be able to help if you told me something of the circumstances," she offered. "I could try, anyway." Brentnor shot her a look which she chose to ignore. Certainly Simon Feltzer was no good to them in his present state of mind.

"I've told the police what little I could," he said. "I visited my brother frequently during his imprisonment, but it wasn't as if he was free. I suppose his fellow inmates had become his friends."

"On death row they're pretty well segregated from the rest of the prison population," Susan said. Then she thought about it and asked, "Could you give me the name and address of his wife? Maybe if I went to see her I could learn something."

Mike Brentnor objected. "Susan, we're here to plan the merger promotion—"

"You two can get started on it while I talk to her."

Feltzer seemed to agree. "At the funeral yesterday she told me she'd help in any way she could. I don't think she ever believed it could have been suicide." He checked his Rolodex and wrote down an address and phone number for Susan. "She's still Mildred Feltzer. She never went back to her maiden name."

Susan took the slip of paper and gave Mike a wave. "I'll see you back at the hotel later."

Mildred Feltzer had an apartment in a middle-class neighborhood of West Caroline. Susan phoned first and asked if she could come over. It was something about her late husband, she said, not giving details.

"Are you a reporter?" Mildred asked suspiciously.

"No. I'm working with David's brother. He gave me your address."

"All right," she agreed after the briefest of hesitations. "I'll be expecting you."

Mildred was a stout woman with a lined face that must have been very pretty twelve years earlier. Now, with ageing and the weight gain, she was sinking into unattractive middle age. "Hello, Mrs. Feltzer. I'm Susan Holt."

"Come in and sit down, and please, call me Millie. I'm Millie to my friends. My husband was always Dave. Simon's the only one who ever called us David and Mildred."

"Thank you," Susan responded, taking a seat on a worn sofa. "This must have been a difficult twelve years for you."

"It's been a difficult lifetime. I'm used to it by now. I can never forgive Dave for what he did, to the poor girl and to me, but I've lived through it."

"The police are convinced now that he was deliberately poisoned."

"I know. Sergeant Green stopped by to tell me a short time ago."

"Why would anyone kill Dave at such a time, just before his execution?"

"I think it was some sort of horrible accident. I told the sergeant he should be investigating that Chinese restaurant."

"Did your husband like Chinese food?"

"Sure. He often told me that was one of the things he missed in prison."

"You stuck by him through the trial and everything even though you knew he was guilty of this terrible crime?"

Millie Feltzer frowned, perhaps considering how to answer the question. "At first I thought he was innocent. I thought the whole thing was some horrible mistake that would be cleared up in a few days. I even started keeping a scrapbook of the newspaper articles so we'd have a record of the wrong Dave had suffered."

"A scrapbook? I'd like to see that if I could."

"I suppose it would be all right now. It's history of a sort, now that he's dead." She went over to a bookcase that held a couple of scrapbooks along with a few paperback volumes. At least one was an astrology guide. Susan wondered whether a better day was coming soon for Millie Feltzer.

She opened the first scrapbook and saw the headline: "Girl Taken Hostage by Bank Robber." Then, "Missing Girl Found Dead; Suspect Apprehended." The following day there was a typical newspaper photograph of the accused man in handcuffs being hustled into the courthouse for arraignment, his face partly hidden. "Tell me about it," Susan requested.

"I was pregnant at the time and it was my last week at the bakery. In those days there wasn't any pregnancy leave, at least not where I worked. Dave had lost his job delivering papers and he was pretty depressed about it. Everything was coming apart at the worst possible time. When I told him we needed some money he said he'd get some. He stopped by the bakery in the early afternoon and that's the last I ever saw of him as a free man." She was staring at the floor, remembering it.

"When did you learn of the robbery?"

"That was a funny thing. I was listening to the radio news while I was driving home around four. They reported a bank robbery across town—a masked gunman who escaped in a Toyota. About a half-hour later two police officers came to the door. They were investigating a bank robbery and asked about Dave's car. A witness had spotted the license number. Right away I remembered the news report and said it couldn't be his car because his was a Chevy, not a Toyota. But this was a different bank robbery, and a teenage girl had been taken as a hostage." She broke down in tears then, and Susan turned to the scrapbooks for what happened next.

The girl, Meagan Brady, had been found shot to death in a ditch that evening. A few hours later state police had spotted David Feltzer's Chevy at a truck stop and arrested him without incident. The murder weapon was not recovered, although the dye-stained money was. At first Feltzer admitted the bank robbery but denied killing the girl, saying he'd let her out alive, along the road. The following day, under intensive police questioning, he signed a statement admitting he'd shot her when she started yelling for help. He later tried to recant the statement but it was used in evidence at his trial.

While Millie was recovering her composure Susan Holt glanced through the second scrapbook, taking in the long sad story of endless appeals and attempts to gain a new trial. Finally the state supreme court had ruled there were no grounds for a stay of execution, and the governor had made it clear there would be no clemency. That was where the second scrapbook ended.

"Suicide?" Millie repeated in answer to Susan's next question. "No, he never mentioned suicide. I think he always expected the governor would relent at the last minute and commute his sentence to life in prison. I knew it wouldn't happen, but I didn't expect this."

"Did he have a favorite Chinese restaurant?"

She shrugged. "That was more than twelve years ago. The one we went to most often closed long ago."

Susan could think of no more questions. She rose and shook hands with Millie Feltzer. "Thank you for what you've told me, Millie. Could I borrow these scrapbooks till tomorrow?"

"Sure, but what are you looking for?" she asked. Susan paused at the door, but she couldn't answer that. She didn't know herself.

Her rented car was parked on the street, and she knew she should be getting back to the hotel where Brentnor would be waiting. But her plans suddenly changed when she saw Sergeant Green walk across the street to intercept her. He must have remained in his unmarked car after telling Millie the verdict on her husband's death. He'd witnessed Susan's arrival and awaited her departure.

"May I speak with you, Miss Holt?"

"I suppose so."

He came around to the passenger side and got in next to her. "You seem unduly interested in the death of David Feltzer. Might I ask why?" His stocky body filled the seat but somehow he seemed more friendly than frightening.

"I handle promotions for Mayfield's of Manhattan. We've recently merged with your local Brookline chain and I'm here to work with Simon Feltzer for a few days on our joint promotion plans. Naturally he's very upset about the circumstances of his brother's death. I thought I might help by trying to find some answers."

"What did you learn from Mildred Feltzer?"

"That she likes to be called Millie."

His eyes narrowed just a bit and she regretted her flippancy immediately. He was a man who took his job seriously. "What did she say about her husband?"

"Only that he wouldn't have committed suicide. What makes you think he was murdered?"

"The warden and the captain of the guard were with him all the time he was eating. They saw nothing unusual. And an examination of the Chinese dinner shows that the poison, a cyanide compound, was all through the food. David Feltzer didn't swallow a capsule of it, nor did he manage to sprinkle a little on top of his egg foo yung."

"So someone at the restaurant must have done it."

"So it seems. Though Captain DeMarco, who ordered the meal, swears he never mentioned it was for the condemned man. It might have been for the warden."

"Which restaurant prepared it?"

"The Lucky Dragon. It's about a half-mile from the prison. DeMarco says he chose that one because it was closest. The state prison is actually outside the city."

"I was wondering about that," Susan said. "Bank robbery is a federal crime. Why was Feltzer in a state rather than a federal prison? And why are you investigating a murder outside the city limits?"

"We have a metropolitan government in West Caroline, and the state specifically asked our help on this case. As for the federal charges, a judge ruled twelve years ago that since the kidnapping took place outside the bank, the two crimes were separate. The federal authorities allowed us to try Feltzer first on the more serious murder charge and we obtained a conviction." He smiled a bit. "Does that answer all your questions, Miss Holt?"

"You've questioned the people at the Lucky Dragon?"

"Of course."

"Could the poison have been added at the prison?"

Green shook his head. "The food was in closed containers delivered directly to the captain of the guard. He got the warden and they delivered the dinner to the condemned man together. I don't see how it could have been tampered with."

"Who else would have visited David Feltzer that night, before his execution?"

"His wife and brother, and the Catholic chaplain. Of course he was dead before they saw him."

"I'll let you know if I find anything," Susan promised, hoping he would take the hint and leave her car.

"That's generous of you." His voice carried more than a trace of irony. "But I can't have you impeding our investigation. This is no place for amateurs."

"I'll stay out of your way," Susan promised.

"Good. We understand each other." He got out of the car, but as she drove away she could see him in the rearview mirror, watching her.

Susan phoned the hotel and told Mike Brentnor she'd been delayed. "How'd you make out with Feltzer?"

"Not bad. He settled down after a while. I think he likes the tropical-bird idea. When will you be back?"

"I want to make one more stop."

"Maybe we could have lunch together."

"I don't think so, Mike."

"You're being a detective again, aren't you?"

"Just a bit."

She hung up and found the address of the Lucky Dragon in the phone book. The restaurant did a fair lunch business, which surprised Susan. She'd always thought of Chinese food as a dinnertime option. The manager was a neatly dressed man named Charlie Osko, and he spoke with her as he folded boxes for takeout orders. "What is it you wish to know?" he asked.

"It's about the death at the state prison the other night. I understand the condemned man ate a meal prepared here."

"I can tell you nothing I have not already told the police."

"Did you work that night?"

Osko was growing nervous. 'Yes, I was here as you see me now, handling takeouts."

"Then you packaged the prison order."

"Yes, just like any other."

"Who delivered it?"

"We employ two part-time drivers for delivery. The prison run was made by Nieh Yuan."

"Is he here now?" Susan asked.

The man smiled about something and replied, "Making deliveries to office buildings. He'll be back soon."

Susan stood to one side, watching the manager's routine. As the takeout orders came out of the kitchen, he checked them against his list and placed them in white paper bags, writing the destination in pencil on a slip of paper he clipped to the top of each bag. Then he divided them carefully into two groups, according to location. After a few minutes, a Chinese-American youth came in from a delivery. "Got the next batch ready, Pop?" he asked.

"Right here."

Susan took a step forward but Charlie Osko shook his head. "Not Yuan. This is my son, learning the business."

The son departed with four orders and Osko was distracted by the ringing telephone. While he took down the information for a reservation, Susan went up and checked the bags behind his back. Today there were none for the state prison.

A young woman of about twenty entered, a high-cheekboned beauty who hurried to the counter and grabbed up the remaining bags. Nieh Yuan had returned.

"Miss Yuan?" Susan asked.

"That's me. What can I do for you?"

"I'm interested in the dinner you delivered to the state prison earlier this week."

"I told the police nobody stopped me, nobody poisoned it while it was in my car."

"Did you have any other deliveries on the same trip?"

"Just one. Most of the others had been earlier. I delivered the food to the prison first because Mr. Osko said it was important."

"What did you do with it at the prison?"

"Captain DeMarco was waiting for me at the gate. He took it."

"Do you know him personally?"

"He calls about once a month, usually when he's on the night shift."

"Did he get any food that night?"

"There was only one meal. I didn't know who it was for until later."

Susan could see that a visit to the prison was unavoidable. She called first and asked to speak with Captain DeMarco. Explaining that she was working with Simon Feltzer, she requested a brief meeting with the captain. Perhaps he thought she was a lawyer. In any event, he agreed to give her fifteen minutes if she could come out right away.

A guard took her to DeMarco's office on the second floor of the prison's administration building. DeMarco was a tall, muscular man with a square jaw and hard eyes. She decided he'd found the right line of work. "I'll only take a few minutes of your time," she promised. "I need to know what happened to that Chinese dinner after it arrived here."

"Is Feltzer's brother thinking of suing the state?"

"I can't comment on that."

DeMarco took out a stick of gum and popped it into his mouth. "Nothing happened to it. I took it from this Chinese girl who delivered it and went up to the warden's office. We never opened it until we were in the cell with the condemned man."

"And no one could have tampered with the food during that time?"

"Certainly not!"

"Do you still think he killed himself?"

"I suppose he must have."

"The police are saying it was murder."

"I heard that. I don't believe it."

"Who decided to get the Chinese dinner from the Lucky Dragon?" Susan asked.

"Warden Coyne told me to order it from the closest place. I'd had Chinese sent in from the Lucky Dragon and I knew that was closest."

"Tell me, was David Feltzer ever in any trouble during his stay here?"

"No more so than any death-row prisoner. They think they can get away with anything, but we soon straighten them out here."

Susan remembered something else. "While I'm here I'd like to speak with the chaplain if I could."

"Well, I don't know about that. Let me ring up Warden Coyne."

Five minutes later, Susan met the warden. He was a bit older than DeMarco, and possibly a bit more intelligent. "I understand you're a lawyer, Miss Holt."

"No, I never said that. I said I was working with Simon Feltzer. Actually, I'm in promotions."

DeMarco's face reddened. "Then you can just promote yourself out of here, young lady! What's your game, anyway?"

"The truth. That's never a game."

Warden Coyne removed his glasses and rubbed his eyes. "Why do you want to see Father McGee?"

"Whether it was suicide or murder, there has to be a motive. The chaplain might be able to suggest one."

The warden turned to Captain DeMarco. "See if Father McGee is available. She can speak with him here, in your presence." He started for the door, then remembered to say, "I hope that will be satisfactory, Miss Holt."

"Perfectly."

DeMarco made the call and went back to his paperwork. Presently Father McGee appeared, a small white-haired man who spoke with a trace of an Irish accent.

"It's a pleasure to meet you, Miss Holt," he told her. "I understand that you know David's brother."

"I'm working with him. I came in from New York to help with the merger plans."

"Yes, the merger. It's big news here in West Caroline. I hope it doesn't hurt employment."

"I'm sure it will benefit the entire region," she answered diplomatically. "I was wondering if you could tell me anything about David's last days. What was his mood like?"

"Are you hoping to comfort his brother?"

"Perhaps. Do you know Simon?"

The priest shook his head. "Nor David's wife. I never met either one. He talked of them, of course."

"Did he ever talk of the crime, of this girl Meagan Brady whom he kidnapped and killed? I'm not asking you to violate the seal of the confessional—"

"David Feltzer never confessed to me. He was not a Catholic, though I think I was able to offer him some spiritual guidance. He told me he wanted to write out a statement when I visited him for the final time, in case he didn't survive his execution."

"Didn't survive—?"

"David was not an educated man. He had an idea that if he took some sort of antidote before his execution it would counteract the effects of the lethal injection. He'd seen an old movie once on late-night television about a man who was revived after being put to death in the electric chair. I assured him the doctor would have to certify his death before his body was removed."

"So he was finally prepared to die?"

"I think so." Father McGee hesitated. "Comforting men like David Feltzer is a very difficult part of my job here. Like my Church, I am opposed to capital punishment."

"Would you have sanctioned his suicide?"

"No, of course not."

Captain DeMarco stood up. "I think that's all the time we can grant you, Miss Holt."

"I'm finished. Thank you, Father McGee."

"It was a pleasure speaking with you."

A guard escorted Susan to the front gate.

By the time she returned to their hotel, Mike Brentnor had gone out again, leaving her a message that he was over at the Brookline store with Feltzer. It was getting past midafternoon and Susan opted to wait until morning for another business session. Instead she turned her attention to the scrapbooks she'd borrowed from Millie Feltzer.

The first day's reports of the bank robbery and kidnapping were sketchy. It wasn't until the second day, when the press focused on the shocking nature of the crime and started more extensive coverage, that the paper ran a sidebar interview with the bank teller. The man had handed her a note saying he had a bomb and would blow them both up unless she gave him all her hundred dollar bills. She handed over a dye-pack triggered to explode in two minutes.

He'd made it to the parking lot when it went off, enveloping him in red dye and smoke. Teenaged Meagan Brady, on her way into the bank, had been grabbed as a shield by the robber and forced into his car. When the state police apprehended David Feltzer that night, he still had stains from the dye on his hands and face and clothing.

Susan turned over several pages quickly, until she came to the accounts of Feltzer's trial. No bomb was ever found, nor was the murder weapon located, and Feltzer recanted his confession to the girl's murder. But the evidence was overwhelming. The teller identified him as the bank robber, and the bank's security cameras had caught him as well. Several witnesses across the street had seen him force the girl into the car, and one of her shoes had been found in the backseat. The dye-stained money was recovered from his car, and from the beginning he had admitted the robbery. He only denied that he had killed Meagan Brady after first admitting it. As the District Attorney commented at the time, he changed his story when he realized he could get the death penalty.

She turned to the final pages of the second scrapbook, but there were no clippings about David Feltzer's death. The ending of the story, for her, remained a blank.

Susan puzzled over it and went back through the pages again. She was convinced the motive for David Feltzer's murder lay deep in the past. But what motive? Could a relative of the murdered girl be so obsessed with revenge that he was not content with capital punishment administered by the state? That seemed doubtful. Such a person would want to kill Feltzer with his bare hands, or with a gun, not with a quick-acting poison he could not even watch.

Or could he watch it? Warden Coyne and Captain DeMarco had been in the cell at the time. Might one of them—?

No, if they wanted vengeance the death chamber was only hours away, with no risk to them.

Then she remembered something the priest had said. She backtracked through the conversations in her mind, saw again the Lucky Dragon restaurant where the food had been prepared, and considered the possibilities. An idea began to form itself in her mind. No evidence, nothing but an idea.

She opened drawers in the hotel room until she found one containing envelopes and writing paper. Did people still write letters from hotel rooms? Apparently some did. She folded the sheet of paper and slid it into an envelope which she sealed.

There was a knock on the door. She looked through the peephole and saw Simon Feltzer. "Just a minute!" she called. Then, after a pause, "Come in, Mr. Feltzer. I was just thinking about you."

He settled down in one of the chairs, tossing his blue trenchcoat on the bed. "I finished up with Mike and thought I'd see if you were back."

"I just got in," she told him. "I was out at the prison talking to the warden and the chaplain." She picked up the sealed envelope, careful not to show the back with its hotel logo on the flap. "Father McGee says your brother left him this envelope for the police. I'm to give it to Sergeant Green."

"I'll take it," Feltzer said, reaching for the envelope.

"No, his instructions were to give it only to the police."

"Then why would he give it to you, a woman he doesn't even know?"

"I have no idea."

Simon Feltzer didn't fully believe her, but he couldn't take any chances. He went over to the bed and yanked the belt from his trenchcoat with one quick motion. Susan was on her feet, running for the door, when he grabbed her arm and whirled her around, the belt looping easily around her neck. "You meddled in this too much," he growled, and pulled the belt tight.

"Don't—!"

There was a pounding on the door and the grip on her throat loosened for a split second. Then it tightened again as the door burst open and two burly men pulled him away from her. She coughed, gasping for breath, and finally managed to speak. "I called hotel security before I opened the door, Mr. Feltzer. If you killed Meagan Brady and your own brother, I figured you wouldn't hesitate with me."

Later they met in Mr. Ziegler's office, with Sergeant Green and Mike Brentnor both in attendance. "I only want to tell it once," Susan said, "so I figured we should all be here. The whole thing hinged on motive, of course. Why would anyone poison a condemned man about to be executed by lethal injection? It couldn't have been an accident, not with that much cyanide spread throughout the Chinese meal. Suicide was also out of the question. He had no opportunity to poison the food with the warden and captain of the guard watching him. So it was murder. In revenge for killing the girl? Why take the risk when the state was doing the job? In revenge for something that happened in prison? Same objection. Financial gain? All the killer had to do was wait till midnight. The risk involved in poisoning the food—and I'll explain that in a minute—meant that it had to be done. It was no mere whim."

"Why did it have to be done?" Sergeant Green asked.

"What was David Feltzer going to do before he died? Meet with his brother and his wife, and the prison chaplain. My first thought was that he was going to make a dying confession to another murder. It's not that unusual among condemned prisoners. And Father McGee confirmed that David Feltzer wanted to leave a statement with him. I assumed it was for the police, and that was what I faked in my hotel room. Simon Feltzer took the bait too well, and tried to kill me. It confirmed what I'd suspected—that David was killed because someone feared a last-minute confession."

"A confession that he killed someone else?"

"No," Susan said softly. "A confession that he never killed anyone. Think about it. Is there the slightest confirmation of this in the facts of the Meagan Brady case? Yes, there is. No one doubts that David Feltzer panicked after robbing the bank and kidnapped the girl. But did he kill her? Feltzer's note to the bank teller threatened a bomb, not a gun. No gun was mentioned, no gun was seen. Why would Feltzer threaten to explode a bomb, a far-fetched threat at best, when he could mention the very real gun, and even show it? Was the answer that he had no gun? Surely his story of letting the girl out of the car alive could not be believed. Even in her frightened state she'd have taken her shoe for the long hike ahead. She died in Feltzer's presence, but if he didn't shoot her, who did? He was alone in the bank, apparently alone in the car. If he had an accomplice, what would that accomplice have been doing while he robbed the bank?"

"What?" Mike Brentnor asked.

"Robbing another bank!"

"Another—"

"Millie Feltzer told me there was another bank robbery at the same time, carried out by a masked gunman. There was the gun, the missing gun! The two bank robbers met as planned after the robberies, probably to divide the loot. The second robber, the gunman, hadn't expected the girl. She'd seen too much, so he shot her. Who was this second gunman? Someone very close to David Feltzer, because he confessed to the killing at first. Even after changing his mind, he never implicated this person. He was going to the death chamber this week without revealing that name. For twelve years he'd kept the secret. Only two people in the world were that close to him—his brother Simon and his wife Millie. Would Millie, quite pregnant at the time, have murdered Meagan Brady in cold blood? Of course not! And she was working at her bakery job at the time of both robberies. Millie could not have done it, either physically or psychologically. Then how about Simon? Twelve years ago he was bumming around without a job, to use his own words."

Sergeant Green shook his head uncertainly. "You still have to tie him in to the poisoning and tell me how he did it."

Susan thought she could do just that. "Consider this. If Simon or any outsider poisoned the food, it had to be done at the Chinese restaurant. The delivery girl had no way of knowing it was for the condemned man. Who would David have told in advance that he had a craving for Chinese food at his last meal? Again, either his brother or his wife. Simon could easily have known the request would be made, and that it would be phoned to the only Chinese restaurant anywhere near the prison. He went to the Lucky Dragon that night, ordered a meal of egg foo yung to go, and added poison in the parking lot. Then he went back inside, as if waiting for someone, until he saw a bag addressed to the state prison lined up to be delivered. While the owner was on the phone or otherwise diverted, Simon switched bags, clipping the state prison note to his poisoned meal. I tried it myself, going up to the bags while the owner was taking a reservation. He never noticed me."

"I'd never believe it if he hadn't tried to kill you," the detective said. "As it is, we might just get a confession out of him. I can't believe, though, that David Feltzer would keep quiet about this for twelve years, taking the blame for his brother."

"What would it have gotten him to tell the truth?" Susan pointed out. "He was still an accessory to a felony murder, still facing a death penalty. I doubt if he would have told the priest anything, in the end. I think he would have protected Simon right into the death chamber. But Simon wasn't willing to risk that."

After they arranged to start over again with Ziegler the following morning, Mike Brentnor said, "I hope we can get through this merger without your finding any more mysteries to solve."

"I'll try," Susan told him.

"How about dinner tonight?"

"You know, you might tempt me with some Chinese food."

A PARLIAMENT OF PEACOCKS

Susan Holt was dining with two executives from Harrods department store, at one of London's most fashionable restaurants. The appetizer was delicious and the music sublime. She was enjoying the stimulating conversation about the world of international retailing, and only wished she could stop yawning.

The middle-aged man seated next to her, a store manager from Istanbul, had joined their party at the last minute. He smiled sympathetically and said in a low voice, "Did you fly in last night from New York?"

"How did you guess?"

"You'll feel better after a good night's sleep."

His name was Abidine Tekin, and his silvery hair and moustache gave him the appearance of an exotic movie star. She guessed him to be in his mid forties, and, like herself, he was in London to learn the techniques Harrods and other stores used for their promotions.

"We are much impressed by the way you handle these things at Mayfield's," one of the Harrods people was saying to her, yanking her mind back to the business at hand. "Was yours the first store in Manhattan to use a fully painted city bus to carry your advertising message?"

"Mayfield's was the first department store. The technique had been used previously to promote a TV series and individual products."

The restaurant was located on the top floor of one of the city's newer hotels, the Princess of Wales. Its windows commanded a breathtaking view of London by night, with tables running along three walls. The fourth wall, backing up to the kitchen, was given over to a small bandstand where a quartet of piano, drums, bass fiddle, and saxophone played show tunes and songs from the sixties while a young blond singer named Yolanda filled the room with her strong but subtle voice.

Susan guessed her to be around thirty, with a slender figure that showed to effect beneath her blue satin gown. Straight blond hair, ending just above her shoulders, fell in front of her face as she sang, with the microphone held almost to her lips. She was not really attractive, but her voice gave her a certain charm.

The group played for almost an hour, then took a fifteen-minute break while Susan's party waited for its main course. It seemed the perfect opportunity to slip off to the ladies' room and Susan did just that. "Hurry back," Abidine Tekin urged, obviously enjoying her company more than that of the Harrods executives.

Susan glanced at her watch and subtracted the five-hour time difference with New York City. It would be five o'clock there now and her boyfriend Russell should be at their apartment. She'd promised to phone if she had an opportunity. When she left the ladies' room she slipped into one of the glass-enclosed booths and inserted her phone card in the slot. Almost at once she heard a woman's voice from the booth to her right and realized that the soundproofing was none too good. "I got your page. What is it? I'm working." Susan Holt recognized the blue dress and blond hair. It was the singer, Yolanda, on her break. After listening for a moment she continued, "No, I told you last time I was out of the business. I'm singing regularly now. I don't need anything else." Another brief silence and then, I know the money is good, but I'm steering clear of the peacocks. It's too dangerous."

Under ordinary circumstances Susan would never have eavesdropped on a private conversation, but she'd just heard the woman singing and was fascinated by this sudden revelation of her private self. Then, as if sensing she might be overheard, Yolanda dropped her voice and the rest of the conversation was lost.

Susan quickly dialed her Manhattan number and was disappointed when she got the answering machine. She left a brief message for Russell and then returned to her table. The three men politely stood up as she slid into her chair. "Does Mayfield's have dining facilities on the premises?" one of the men asked.

"We have a coffee shop in the basement, near the entrance to the subway—"

"She means the underground," the Turk translated for the Harrods people, a bit to Susan's annoyance.

"—and a larger restaurant upstairs that serves beer and wine."

The older of the two Englishmen nodded. "We find customers linger longer if there is some nourishment available."

Susan was quick to agree. "In the States even large bookstores and some libraries now have coffee bars and cafes."

Their main courses arrived as the music resumed with a lively rendition of "The Girl from Ipanema." Susan remembered from her previous London trip that it was a perennial favorite in restaurants and clubs. They were finishing dessert after a leisurely meal when the band took its eleven o'clock break.

As one of the Harrods executives was paying the check, Abidine Tekin smiled and invited her for an after-dinner drink. I'm afraid I couldn't keep my eyes open another ten minutes," Susan answered honestly. "Perhaps another time."

"How long will you be here?"

The waiter arrived with a long-stemmed rose for Susan, the only woman in the party. She took it and said, "Just three days. I fly back to New York on Friday."

Abidine smiled. "Perhaps I will phone your hotel."

The singer Yolanda was wearing a glittery gold gown as the band began its final set. Susan gave the Turkish gentleman a smile without really answering, then followed the others toward the elevator. But Abidine was persistent. "Which hotel are you at?"

She glanced at her watch and saw that it was 11:30. Tired as she was, it might be better to have a drink with the man now than be pestered with calls for three days. "May I change my mind about that drink?" she asked. "It would have to be a quick one."

His smile broadened. "We can stop in the lobby." He excused himself to go to the men's room, meeting her five minutes later at the dimly lit lobby bar.

They spent a pleasant hour over liqueurs, discussing their dinner hosts and the city in general. "They are so geared to the international community," Susan observed, sipping her drink. "Harrods even has machines for currency exchange, right in the store! You put in your dollars or francs or marks and the correct number of pounds is delivered automatically."

"At a small profit, I'm sure." He lit a dark Turkish cigarette and offered her one but she declined. "You don't smoke?"

"I stopped a few years ago."

"Married, engaged?"

She held up the bare fingers of her left hand. "There is a boyfriend, though, back in New York. We live together off and on."

Abidine brushed at the tip of his moustache as if curling it like an old rogue. "London can be a very romantic city."

"I thought that was Paris. Sorry, Abidine, but it's time I said good night before I fall asleep."

"Surely I can walk you back to your hotel."

She gave him a tired smile. "That won't be necessary. It's only a block away." She rose and held out her hand. "Thank you for the drink. Perhaps well see each other again at Marks & Spencer or one of the other stores."

He knew enough not to press it. "I certainly hope so."

Susan left him there in the lobby bar and hurried outside. It was shortly after midnight and a light drizzle had set the streets glowing with reflected light. She was staying at the Grosvenor House, more than a block away but not far. As she circled around the rear of the Princess of Wales she heard a sound like a muffled scream. A short man with close-cropped white hair was tussling with a woman against the wall of the hotel. His right hand came up and Susan saw the blade of a knife catch the glow of a street light. Suddenly she was wide awake and running toward them, unmindful of the danger.

"Let her go!" she shouted. "Help! Police!"

Susan grabbed for the man's upraised arm, yanking it away from the woman. He dropped the knife and broke free, dashing away down the slick narrow street. Only then did she turn toward the woman and realize for the first time that it was Yolanda, the singer from the restaurant upstairs.

"Not the police," the woman sobbed. "Don't call them."

Susan retrieved the fallen jackknife, snapped it shut, and dropped it into her raincoat pocket without thinking. She tried to help Yolanda to a taxi, but the woman was trembling with fear. "Where do you live?" she asked. "I'll take you home."

"N-no! He'll be waiting there too!"

"Who will?" When she didn't answer, Susan asked, "What about your musicians? Can one of them help?"

The woman looked up through her tears. "You know me?"

"I was upstairs for dinner. I heard you sing. Who's trying to kill you?"

But Yolanda only shook her head. "It doesn't concern you."

"It does now," Susan told her. She introduced herself and explained that she was in London on business. 'You can't go home and I certainly can't leave you in the street. You can spend the night in my hotel room. I've an extra bed that's not being used."

"No—"

"It's that or I call the police. Take your choice."

"Not the police," she said again.

Susan hurried her along the narrow street until they reached the courtyard that was the hotel's entrance. Once safely in the room, Yolanda began to relax for the first time. Her makeup was streaked and tears had washed the mascara from her eyelids. "He was trying to cut my face," she told Susan.

"Do you know him?"

She nodded. "They call him Cargo. He used to be a merchant seaman."

"Why would he want to injure you?"

Yolanda fell silent. After a moment she asked, "Do you have anything to drink?"

Susan glanced around the room. "I suppose there's something in the mini-bar. I haven't really looked." She opened the small refrigerator and glanced inside. "Here we go—whiskey, gin, vodka. Also beer and soft drinks. And champagne!"

"A whiskey and water will do nicely, thanks."

Susan didn't think she could handle one herself and chose a Coke instead. "Now tell me what this is all about."

"It's nothing you want to hear. I appreciate your coming to my rescue like that and offering me a bed for the night, but I can't involve you in my troubles." For the first time Susan caught a touch of an accent in her voice. It wasn't British but she couldn't quite place it.

"Are you American?" she asked.

"I was brought up in New York, but my parents are Spanish. I use Yolanda as my stage name but my full name is Yolanda Delgado."

Aware that she was getting herself more deeply involved than might be wise, Susan said, "I have to tell you I overheard part of a telephone call you made during your ten o'clock break. I was in the next booth, calling New York. I didn't mean to eavesdrop."

The young woman seemed startled. "What did you hear?"

Susan shrugged. "Some business about peacocks. You were refusing to do something for the person on the other end."

The singer shook her head as if to clear it of memories. "I did some foolish things when I first came to London. I needed the money but that's no excuse."

"Do you want to talk about it?"

"I was just calling back someone who'd paged me. He offered me a job but I turned it down."

"You wear a pager while you're singing?"

Yolanda lifted her skirt and revealed a small plastic box strapped to her thigh. "It doesn't beep. It just vibrates against my skin. Then when I get a chance I return the call."

Susan determined not to press her. She didn't want to know any more. "I have to get to sleep, and I'll probably sleep late in the morning. If you have to leave, just let yourself out."

"Thank you. You're very kind."

Susan went into the bathroom to undress, leaving the door partly open. In the mirror she saw Yolanda dip her right hand into her purse for a pen and write a few words on a slip of paper. She came out wearing a robe and offered an extra nightgown to the singer. "I think we're about the same size. This should fit you."

While Yolanda was undressing in the bathroom, Susan's curiosity got the better of her and she peeked into the woman's purse to see what she had written. There was a loose sheet of Princess of Wales notepaper with Y 11 written in purple ink, and then Susan's name and room number in black ink.

She awoke from a dreamless sleep feeling refreshed. There was sunlight visible at the edges of the drapes and she knew it was late. Rolling over to look at her watch on the bedside table, she saw that it was nearly eleven o'clock. She'd made up nicely for that missed night's sleep on the plane coming over.

Suddenly Susan remembered the previous night's adventure and sat up, staring at the other bed. It was empty and unmade, though the sheets and blankets had been straightened somewhat. In the bathroom she found her nightgown, washed out and hung up to dry. A note on the sink said simply, "Thank you for saving my life!" It was unsigned.

Luckily Susan had left the morning free to recover from her trip. Her first appointment wasn't till after lunch. She'd have something to eat at the hotel and walk around London for a bit. At least with the sun shining she wouldn't need her raincoat. It was at a newsstand on Piccadilly an hour later that she saw the headline on an afternoon tabloid: Gov't Aide Slain in Hotel Love Nest.

She was not a reader of tabloid journalism and would have ignored it except for the photograph of the Princess of Wales Hotel beneath the headline. She bought a paper and skimmed the article. A young parliamentary aide named Jonathan Ellis had been found stabbed to death in a room at the hotel. Indications were that the room was being used for some sort of sexual activity and the leadership of the House of Commons was already taking steps to hush up the affair. The body of Ellis, married but separated from his wife, had been found by the chambermaid around nine that morning. The condition of the body and a broken wristwatch the victim was wearing placed the time of death around eleven-thirty the previous night. The murder weapon had not been found.

Suddenly Susan Holt remembered the knife she'd picked up in the street after knocking it from the hand of Yolanda's attacker. What time had that been? After midnight, surely. Yolanda's group had returned for their final set at eleven-fifteen, just as her party was leaving. She'd stopped for a drink in the lobby bar with Abidine and been there about an hour. She must have left the hotel around twelve-fifteen and come upon that man Cargo attacking Yolanda. That timing made sense, because the band's final set would have ended at midnight or a few minutes after. If Cargo had stabbed this man Ellis at eleven-thirty, he could have gotten downstairs and waited for Yolanda to emerge from the hotel forty-five minutes later.

And the murder weapon might be resting in Susan's raincoat pocket back in her hotel room.

She found a phone booth and called her contact at Marks & Spencer to postpone her two o'clock appointment until the following morning. Then she took a taxi back to her hotel. She wanted to make certain the knife was still in her coat before phoning the police. It was. She handled it with a handkerchief to avoid smudging fingerprints more than she already had. Placing it on the desk by the telephone, she called Scotland Yard and asked for the detective assigned to the Ellis killing. She gave her name and said she might have information about the murder weapon.

After much switching around, a deep masculine voice identifying itself as Inspector Cheever came on the line. "You're calling about the murder at the Princess of Wales Hotel, Miss Holt?"

"That's correct. Around twelve-fifteen this morning I witnessed a knife attack on a young woman outside the Princess of Wales. The man ran away but he dropped his knife and I picked it up. I have it here in my hotel room."

"Was the attack reported to the police?"

"No. The young woman was uninjured and she did not wish to report it."

"And where is your room?"

"The Grosvenor House, Room Three fifty-nine."

"Please remain in your room, Miss. Someone will be there shortly."

"Thank you." She hung up and sat staring at the knife, wondering what she had gotten herself into.

There was a knock at the door ten minutes later but it wasn't the police. A bellman was delivering a vase of flowers. Susan's first thought was Abidine, but they were from Yolanda. The note read simply: "Thank you again! Yolanda." She placed the vase on a table near the window, remembering that the singer had noted her name and room number.

The next knock at the door was indeed the police, in the person of Inspector Cheever himself, accompanied by a woman constable. "Here's the knife," Susan said.

The constable handled the weapon carefully, placing it in an evidence bag. Then she took out a small tape recorder and, with Susan's permission, began recording the conversation. "Did you close the blade?" Cheever asked. He was a gray-haired man with cold blue eyes and a square jaw, not at all friendly.

"I'm afraid so," Susan admitted. "I wasn't thinking."

"Don't worry. This may not be the murder weapon. But I need to know exactly what happened outside the hotel last night."

She recounted it in detail, beginning with her business dinner at the hotel. The only things she left out were the overheard telephone conversation and Yolanda's beeper. "She knew this man who attacked her?" Cheever asked, making a note of the singer's name.

Susan nodded. "She said he was called 'Cargo.' It was a nickname because he'd been a merchant seaman. Was this man Ellis killed with a similar knife?"

"We don't know. The preliminary autopsy report indicates the stab wounds were inflicted by a left-handed killer who took the weapon with him." He glanced around the room.

"Yolanda Delgado stayed here overnight?"

"She was afraid to return to her apartment. She sent these flowers to thank me."

He walked over to the flowers and examined the card. "She's a singer at the Princess of Wales Hotel?"

"At the roof restaurant."

"Had you ever seen her before last night?"

"No."

He went over her story in more detail and said they'd probably want to speak with her again. "How long will you be in the country?"

"I fly back on Friday."

Inspector Cheever got to his feet. "I hope we won't need to delay your return, Miss Holt. I'll be in touch."

"I know nothing more than I've told you."

"This killing might have far-reaching implications. Crimes involving government officials are always messy in this country, especially when the tabloids start talking of love nests. I hope you won't add to the clamor by speaking with the press."

She assured him she had no intention of doing so, but he left her wondering if she'd done the wisest thing by calling the police. Suddenly it became very important that she speak to Yolanda again before the inspector got to her. She phoned the dining room at the Princess of Wales and asked how she might contact the singer.

"The band plays from seven till midnight," a bored woman responded. "You can see her then."

"No, I mean now—this afternoon. What's her home number?"

"I'm sorry. We don't give out that information."

Susan hung up, certain they'd have given it out to Inspector Cheever. Then she remembered the vase of flowers. The card with Yolanda's message also bore the name of the florist. The address was in Chelsea, probably a neighborhood place near where she lived. Susan decided to go there rather than call.

She took a taxi from the front of her hotel and reached the florist shop shortly after three o'clock. The woman clerk was friendly and chatted while she arranged fresh flowers in a basket. "The vase to Grosvenor House? Certainly I remember it. Did the order myself, just this morning."

"I want to call Yolanda and thank her but I've mislaid her number. Would you happen to have it?"

"Don't have her phone number but we have her billing address in the files. She's a regular customer."

"That would be fine," Susan assured her.

The address proved to be on Old Church Street, two blocks away.

She walked up to the second-floor apartment and rang the bell somehow confident that Yolanda would answer. Of course she didn't. If she was in there, she wasn't about to admit it.

Susan went back downstairs. The building had once been a private house, converted to apartments sometime in the distant past. Hallways led off the main corridor toward rooms in the back. As she walked past one of them, a hand shot out to grab her.

It was Yolanda.

"You gave me a fright," Susan told her, recovering from the verge of a scream.

"Never mind that. What are you doing here?"

"We have to talk. There was a murder at the Princess of Wales Hotel last night."

"I saw the papers," the woman said. "How did you find me?"

"Through your florist. Thanks for the flowers."

"What are you doing here?" she asked again.

"I still had the knife Cargo used to attack you. I called the police and told them about it. Maybe Cargo killed that man Ellis."

"Come in here," Yolanda ordered, grasping Susan's arm as she propelled her down the side corridor and into a room. She closed and locked the door behind them.

Susan glanced around, seeing a modestly decorated flat with inexpensive furniture. "I thought you lived upstairs."

"That's an apartment I maintain for entertaining. I like to stay down here when I'm trying to avoid people."

"Like Cargo?"

"Him and others." She lit a cigarette. Susan had noticed that more people smoked over here than at home. "What did you tell the police?"

"That he tried to attack you with the knife and maybe it was the same weapon used in the murder."

Yolanda looked unhappy. "They'll come looking for me, nosing around."

"Maybe that'll keep Cargo away. You've got nothing to hide, have you?"

She gave a snort. "Everyone's got something to hide. Before I started getting regular singing jobs I worked for an escort service. Cargo was my boss."

Susan simply stared at her. "You mean he was your pimp."

"I don't like that word, but I suppose it's true."

"That was Cargo on the phone with you last night, wasn't it?"

She ground out her cigarette in the ashtray and gave a reluctant nod. "He wanted me for a special client. I refused to go. I told him I had a good singing job and I was out of the game."

"I overheard you say peacocks."

"You have good ears." She started to smile but then her face grew somber, as if she was remembering something better left forgotten. "They called it the Peacock Parliament because many of them were young parliamentary aides. Some of the girls said members of Parliament themselves sometimes took part, but one could never be sure. They all wore these fancy masks made of peacock feathers so we could never see their faces. We'd pair off and go to separate rooms. Sometimes one of the members would request a favorite girl."

"That's what happened last night?"

Yolanda nodded. "Cargo rang my beeper and when I called back he said I'd been requested by one of the Peacocks. I told him no, that I wasn't doing it anymore. He said I'd be sorry, that he'd cut my face. I didn't believe him then."

"Was Jonathan Ellis one of the Peacocks?"

"I never knew any of their names."

"His picture was in the afternoon papers."

"I told you we didn't see their faces."

"Not even by accident?"

"Sometimes, sure. But I didn't know him."

"He was the one who was stabbed at the hotel. Cargo might have killed him and then come after you."

She shook her head. "Cargo would never kill a cash customer."

"But he'll probably come after you again."

Yolanda opened her purse to show Susan a silver-plated .25 caliber automatic. It had a pink pearl handle. "I'll be carrying this with me now. I call it my ladygun."

They both tensed at the sound of footsteps on the stairs to the upper floor. "Police," Susan guessed. "Is there a back way out of here?"

"This way."

At the door Susan paused. "Will you be singing tonight?"

Yolanda gave her a smile. "If I'm alive."

When Susan returned to her hotel she was surprised to find Abidine Tekin waiting for her. "What are you doing here, Abidine? How did you find me?" She seemed to be echoing Yolanda's words to her.

"The people at Marks & Spencer knew where you were staying. When you postponed your appointment I thought you might be ill."

"No, I'm fine. I just had some business to tend to."

"There was a murder at the hotel where we dined last night."

Susan nodded. "I read about it."

"It seems to be causing quite a scandal." He glanced at his watch. "Are you free for dinner tonight?"

"I—" She really didn't want to become involved with this Turkish gentleman who no doubt collected women on every business trip. Still, she could take care of herself. And she wanted to make certain Yolanda could too. "You know, this sounds crazy with all the restaurants in the city, but I wouldn't mind going back to the top of the Princess of Wales again. The food was fine, the music was pleasant, and I'd like to really enjoy it without the pressure of a business dinner."

"I agree completely. Shall we make it eight o'clock?"

"That would be fine."

"I'll pick you up here." He took her hand in both of his and gave her a smile.

Upstairs in her room, Susan wondered why she had agreed so readily. But she knew the answer. She wanted to see Yolanda again, to make certain she was safe from Cargo, and the Princess of Wales was not the sort of place where one dined alone. She could endure another evening with Abidine, who was, after all, a pleasant enough companion.

The phone rang and she answered it at once, resigned to another call from Inspector Cheever. Instead she heard an unfamiliar Cockney voice ask, "Is this Susan Holt?"

"It is."

"Name's George Cox. I write for the *Daily Telegraph*. Could you spare me just a few minutes of your time?"

"What's this about?" she asked cautiously.

"The death of Jonathan Ellis."

"I know nothing about that."

"All I ask is five minutes. I'm in the lounge."

"It's a waste of your time, but I'll come down."

Her curiosity had the better of her. What did the reporter want, and how had he managed to link her to the Ellis killing? She took the elevator to the lobby, peering into the lounge at the only man seated alone. He was short and bald, and looked reasonably respectable.

"Good afternoon, Mr. Cox. What can I do for you?"

He jumped to his feet, perhaps surprised at how quickly she'd appeared. "I don't want to take much of your time. I believe Inspector Cheever questioned you earlier today."

"You make it sound as if I'm a suspect," she answered with a smile, sitting down on the sofa next to him. "I was having dinner at the hotel's roof restaurant last evening, and I assure you all of my time is accounted for."

"Certainly you're not a suspect, Miss Holt. In fact, my queries to New York indicate you've been helpful to the police on previous occasions. Perhaps Cheever consulted you for some advice."

She had to laugh at the suggestion. "No, as a matter of fact I called him. I had a bit of information I thought might be useful,"

"What information was that?"

"You'll have to ask the inspector,"

George Cox smiled, trying to seem friendly. "This story is getting bigger by the hour. This morning I received a sealed envelope from Jonathan Ellis, mailed by his solicitor as soon as the news of his murder broke." He passed her a note handwritten in purple ink and signed with Ellis's name: "If anything happens to me, this will be the reason."

"What was enclosed?" Susan asked.

"He belonged to a group called the Peacock Parliament. They engaged in sexual activities with highly paid prostitutes. Apparently Jonathan Ellis was attempting to blackmail other members of the group. Along with this note was an extortion demand he'd apparently faxed to certain members of the House of Commons and their aides."

"A good motive for murder."

"Ellis wore a hearing aid behind his left ear. I understand the police found a feather caught on it when they examined the body."

"Don't tell me. It was a peacock feather."

"Smart girl! Now you tell me what you know."

"Very little. Certainly nothing about the Peacock Parliament. The sex in my country is a bit more straightforward than that."

"Did you ever meet or speak with Jonathan Ellis?"

"Certainly not! Now I believe your five minutes are up." She stood and held out her hand.

Cox took it with a smile. "They'll be after you. The press won't let this rest. You'll be sorry you weren't more forthcoming with me."

"I'll phone you if I am."

The smile widened. Perhaps he believed her. "Here's my card. I have voice mail if I'm away from my desk."

Susan went back upstairs to shower and change, pleased that she'd learned more from Cox than he had from her.

"Are Turkish men always this prompt?" she asked as Abidine Tekin ushered her out the hotel's Park Lane entrance.

He smiled. "We are when a charming young woman awaits us. It's such a lovely night I thought we might stroll down to the hotel rather than take a taxi, if that's agreeable with you."

"Certainly. Tell me about your day at Marks & Spencer."

By the time they reached the hotel he had her completely at ease with his funny stories of the afternoon's activities. They took the elevator to the top floor and found a window table awaiting them. "At least it's a different view tonight," he remarked.

"You must be bored with this place," Susan said, aware that Yolanda was on the bandstand with her group, launching into the refrain from a Gershwin standard. The sight of her, alive and well, was reassuring.

"Not at all. I have only begun to sample their menu, and the music is pleasant. I enjoy your American tunes."

They'd had a drink and studied the menu by the time the band took its nine o'clock break. Yolanda, wearing a slinky green gown that reached to her ankles, walked off the stage without a glance in Susan's direction. The room was crowded and perhaps she didn't notice them at the window table.

Susan ordered Dover sole while her Turkish friend chose a steak. Their conversation was pleasant and the wine was good. She was thoroughly enjoying herself, even as the business with masked men and dead bodies and knife attacks continued to churn around at the back of her mind. They ate leisurely and were just finishing when the band returned from its ten o'clock break. Yolanda had changed into a red cocktail dress that showed off her legs. She sang some Duke Ellington jazz numbers from the forties and then settled down to a more danceable tempo. "Would you like to dance?" Abidine asked. Susan smiled, emboldened by the wine. "Sure." This time Yolanda saw her and smiled as they danced in front of the band. As they returned to their table she thought she saw the reporter, Cox, speaking with the head waiter near the entrance. She wondered if he'd come to spy on her, and realized she was becoming more deeply involved in the scandal.

"What are you thinking?" Abidine asked.

"That I've been here two days and haven't accomplished a great deal for Mayfield's."

He laughed. "You're spreading good will. What more could they want?"

She glanced toward the headwaiter's station again. He and Cox were both gone, but standing in the entrance, staring fixedly at Yolanda, was Cargo. Susan shivered involuntarily and Abidine asked what was wrong.

"Someone walking on my grave, I guess. Isn't that what they say?" When she looked again Cargo was gone, but she knew it had been him. She still remembered her first sight of him, his knife raised above Yolanda's head.

She remembered it—

"Excuse me for a moment," she told Abidine. I'll be back."

She hurried toward the ladies' room near the elevators, keeping an eye out for Cargo, but now there was no sign of him. When she emerged a few moments later a couple of women were just getting off the elevator. She had started toward the dining room when suddenly the elevator doors on her left slid open and there was Cargo.

They stared at each other in surprise for just a moment. Susan opened her mouth to speak, but the short man was faster. His hand fastened on her like a claw and he yanked her into the elevator. She had time for the beginning of a scream and then his hand clamped onto her mouth. The doors slid shut just as one of the women outside, seeing what was happening, shouted for help.

Cargo's hands were all over her, pinning her to the wall, tightening on her throat. She gasped for breath and flailed out, hitting the red emergency button as the elevator began its descent. Somewhere a bell began to ring and the elevator stopped, but by now he had both hands on her throat. As his grip tightened she saw spots before her eyes. The emergency bell was still ringing and she thought she heard voices from the other side of the door.

Then, as consciousness was about to leave her, the doors slid open and there was Yolanda holding the ladygun at her side and she raised it and put a bullet through the back of Cargo's head.

"Now we're even," she told Susan.

Somehow Inspector Cheever was there even before Susan had fully recovered herself. They'd taken her to a couch in the ladies' room, and when she finally got to her feet and inspected her bruised throat and torn dress in the mirror, she knew she wanted to see Yolanda. In the corridor a folding screen had been put up to shield the death scene from diners. Police technicians were at work and Susan suspected Cargo's body was still on the floor of the elevator car.

She found Yolanda with Cheever and a police stenographer in the restaurant manager's office. The singer smiled at Susan and said, "I'm just telling them how you saved my life last night."

"You more than made up for it just now."

"I'd seen Cargo lurking around out there, and then when you went out and I heard the screams I grabbed my purse and came off the bandstand. When they got that door open and I saw him strangling you I just shot him." The little pearl-handled pistol lay on the desk between the inspector and her.

Susan sat down in the only empty chair. "It's not every day I'm almost strangled. I'm still trying to recover."

Cheever smiled gently but resumed his questioning of Yolanda. "You say you never knew Cargo's real name?"

She shook her head. "He was just Cargo. I—I worked for him once."

"As a call girl?"

She moistened her lips before replying. "Yes. That was why he tried to cut my face last night, because I disobeyed him."

He turned his attention to Susan Holt. "I'd like to hear your version of how you saved Miss Delgado's life."

Susan described what had happened, including the part about the overheard phone call. She could see Cheever was annoyed that she hadn't told the whole story earlier. When she'd finished, Yolanda added, "He'd paged me while I was singing and when I called him back he wanted me to go to a hotel room. He didn't say where, but it was probably the one where Ellis was killed later. I wouldn't do it; that's why he attacked me as I was leaving."

Susan stared at her. She felt a real fondness for the young woman, but she knew that the truth had to come out now. "Yolanda, Cargo didn't attack you because you disobeyed him. He wanted you dead because you obeyed him completely."

"What?" she asked, almost in a daze.

"You killed Jonathan Ellis."

The blood drained from Yolanda's face. "That's impossible. I was on the bandstand singing at eleven-thirty. It was our final set."

"You killed him during the eleven o'clock break, then set his watch ahead twenty minutes before smashing it. Killers have been using that trick for a long time."

"Why would Cargo have wanted him dead?" Cheever asked.

"As you know, Ellis had faxed blackmail demands to several MPs and their aides, threatening to tell the press about the Peacock Parliament. Cargo and the people who paid him decided that Ellis had to die. When Ellis called for a girl last night, Cargo saw his chance. Yolanda was singing upstairs at the same hotel. He paged her and when she phoned him during her break he told her what she had to do. She refused at first—that was the part I overheard—but he finally convinced her, probably with more money. Maybe she'd done things like that before. Anyway, after she'd done it he tried to kill her, to shut her up. It often happens in America that hit men are silenced by the people who hired them."

"How do you know he was trying to kill her? She claims he wanted to scar her for disobeying him."

"I saw that knife, Inspector. Cargo had it upraised in his right hand, bringing it down toward her body. It wasn't a cutting motion but a stabbing one. He was trying to kill her, to silence her."

"There's nothing to link her with Ellis's murder."

"But there is! A reporter told me the police found a peacock feather behind his ear, caught on his hearing aid. These men wore peacock masks during their sex games to conceal their identities. That feather shows he was wearing his mask at the time of his death or just before it. He would have worn the mask for only one reason—not to hide his face from Cargo or any of the other men but only to hide it from one of the women. A woman was with him when he died, and probably yanked the mask from his face afterward to hide that very fact."

"The woman might have let Cargo into the room to do the actual killing," Cheever suggested.

Susan shook her head. "Cargo was right-handed. I saw that last night when he had his knife. You told me the killer was left-handed."

The inspector turned toward Yolanda. "Are you left-handed?"

Susan already knew the answer. "This morning in my hotel room I was looking in the mirror and saw her jot down my name and room number on a slip of paper, to send me flowers later. She seemed to be using her right hand in the mirror, which means it was really her left. And there's more. That slip of paper was from a Princess of Wales notepad, the sort hotels keep next to their room phones. It also had the notation Y 11, written in purple ink like Ellis used to write that reporter. I think it indicated Yolanda at eleven, the time Cargo said she'd visit Ellis's room."

"That doesn't prove she went there, though."

"Then how did the note get into her purse? She took it with her after she killed him, because it would have implicated her."

Yolanda sat frozen to the spot. Cheever casually moved the little pistol out of her reach and asked, "Is there anything else?"

"Yes. Are we to believe that a singer in a fancy dining room like this would wear a beeper strapped to her thigh just so she wouldn't miss a casual phone call? If she needed a beeper that urgently she was either dealing drugs or still working as a call girl. The only thing she briefly resisted was Cargo's hiring her for a killing, and he overcame that quickly enough. I can tell you too that last evening she changed her gown just before the last set. Tonight she changed earlier. I think she waited till after the murder to change, in case she got blood on her dress."

Yolanda scoffed at that. "I had a fifteen-minute break. Is that time enough to take an elevator down to the ninth floor, stab Ellis, come back up here, and change my gown?"

Inspector Ellis blinked his eyes and asked, very quietly, "How did you know it was on the ninth floor? None of the press accounts gave the room number and you said Cargo didn't give it to you."

"I—one of the waiters told me."

"Which one, Miss Delgado?"

The spirit seemed to go out of her then. "What do you want me to say?" she whispered.

"You have the right to remain silent, and to have your lawyer present."

"Never mind that," she said with a wave of her hand.

"Then tell us what you did with the knife."

Her eyes were dull and unfeeling as she answered. "It was a steak knife I took from the kitchen. I dropped it through that little space between the elevator floor and the hallway. I suppose it's at the bottom of the shaft."

"I'm afraid you'll have to accompany us, Miss Delgado."

"Can I tell my band I won't be back?"

"We'll tell them."

She gazed at Susan for just a moment, then said to the inspector, "If it's names you want, I can give you names. Everyone involved—Cargo's bosses, a dozen or more of our customers. I'm ready to deal."

"We'll see."

Susan left the room and walked back across the dance floor to the window table where Abidine still waited. "They said you were with the police. You were gone a long time."

She looked across at the band, playing a slow blues number. "Not so long as Yolanda will be gone."

A SHIPMENT OF SNOW

Susan Holt stepped out of the Fort Myers airport wheeling her floral-patterned suitcase, a wave of Florida heat hit her like a hammer. The temperature had been hovering around the freezing mark a few hours earlier in Manhattan. The change had been a bit sudden for her, and the air conditioning in the rental car felt especially good. It was also a treat driving with an uncluttered windshield after the registration and inspection stickers required on New York cars.

Her position in store promotions for Mayfield's of Manhattan often took her to other cities. South Florida was not as exotic as Japan or Iceland or even London, but it was a nice change from the crowds of Fifth Avenue shoppers bundled against the first flurries of winter. Heading south on route 75, bound for a big shopping mall near Naples, she tried to convince herself that the two-night stay was really necessary. Certainly the type of Christmas shopping promotion planned by Gulfpalm would be out of place in New York. A shipment of snow from the north was hardly needed there, even in a mild winter, and there'd be no space near the store to dump it anyway. Gulfpalm's facility, surrounded by a sea of mall parking lots, was another matter entirely.

Susan checked into her Naples hotel by midafternoon and called her contact at the store. Marci Chester sounded young and perky over the phone, urging her to come right out for a look around before the big snow event the following morning. "Sounds good," Susan decided. "I'll be there shortly."

She'd seen photographs of the Gulfpalm store, but it was even more impressive as she drove up and parked in the massive lot. Two stories high, it swept around in a gentle curve to connect with one end of a gigantic shopping mall. Approaching the main entrance, past dancing fountains and groves of palm trees, Susan could almost imagine herself at a first-class Vegas casino. Inside, all was brightness and glass, with wide aisles in the cosmetics department that signaled luxury in both product and price tag.

Marci Chester was as perky as her voice. Still in her twenties, she had the sort of big blond hair and perfect skin that was fashionable these days. "Great to meet you at last, Susan!" she enthused. "Seems like we've been writing and talking to each other for months. I want you to meet Mr. Vangridge, our store manager, before I show you around."

Susan glanced at her watch. "It's going on five, I don't want to keep you if that's your quitting time."

"I'll be here late tonight making sure everything's lined up for the promotion. We did this last year and had a real mob of people. All these transplanted northerners brought the kids to see the first snow of their young lives."

They rode up on the gleaming glass-sided escalator to the second floor. Benjamin Vangridge's office was over in one corner with promotions, art, advertising, purchasing, and the other departments. "Everything is right here," Susan noted, thinking of the scattered offices in her own Manhattan store.

"Everything but billing. That's handled by the home office in Atlanta."

Obviously they were expected, and the secretary waved them through while pushing a buzzer. Vangridge was a tall, silver-haired man who looked exactly like the pictures Susan had seen in the trade magazines. He smiled and shook hands and welcomed her to the Gulfpalm store. She took a chair opposite his desk and found herself surprised by his southern drawl, something the magazine photographs couldn't reveal.

"It's a pleasure to be here," she assured him. "It's not every day I fly four hours to see a truckload of snow."

Marci lifted a black scrapbook that occupied a corner of the president's desk. "Here's what we have so far, just from this year. I think we're going to top last Christmas, at least for publicity."

"The first item was from yesterday's *Buffalo Evening News*, a three-column captioned photo from page one of the second section. It showed workmen using shovels and a bulldozer to fill a truck with snow: *Flakes to Florida! A large refrigerated truck is loaded with some of Buffalo's recent snowfall, starting a 1,500-mile journey to a shopping mall near Naples, Florida. The Gulfpalm department store rented the truck and will use the snow to launch its Christmas shopping season this Saturday morning.*

Susan turned the page and found a folded full-page ad from the Naples paper: *It'll be snowing bargains at Gulfpalm this Saturday! Bring the whole family—especially those who've never seen snow before! Souvenirs, prizes, snowman contests! Fun for all!* On the opposite page were news articles about the event. The truck from Buffalo was scheduled to pull in at ten o'clock, and the pile of snow was expected to last throughout the day, despite temperatures in the seventies.

Vangridge smiled. "I don't have to tell you the object is to generate traffic in the store. Last year's event was extremely popular and got the holiday season off to a fine start. Unfortunately, the early winter weather was so mild we had to settle for shaved ice from a plant in north Florida. It looks pretty much like snow."

"Did you go up to Buffalo yourself this year?"

"No, no. Our ad manager, Hank Burnside, makes the trip. Not in the truck—he flies up and back. Marci keeps the publicity flowing at this end."

"I have plenty of help," she assured Susan.

"Mr. Vangridge, can you tell me something about the population base you draw upon here?"

"Please call me Ben." He was every inch the southern gentleman, flirting just a bit with this carpetbagger from Manhattan. She wouldn't be surprised if he invited her to dinner before she flew back north. "Most of our customers come from Naples and North Naples, though our location near the route 75 highway makes us accessible from Fort Myers and points north. Naples itself has grown tremendously in recent years." He had the sort of pleasant, flowing voice Susan enjoyed listening to, and she was almost sorry when Marci Chester suggested a few moments later that they should get on with the tour. "Is there anything here you can take back to Manhattan?" he asked as she was leaving.

"I hope so. Perhaps our two stores could run a joint event next Christmas—Snow Day at Gulfpalm and Sun Day at Mayfield's. It's worth thinking about."

Ben Vangridge shook hands again, giving her a particularly warm smile. "I'll be downstairs in the morning when the truck from Buffalo rolls in. I'm sure we'll see each other then."

Though the Gulfpalm store hardly compared to Mayfield's, Susan was impressed with many modern features that added comfort and convenience to the shopping experience. She even found herself complimenting Marci about the spacious ladies' room where they paused near the end of the tour. They finished up at the young woman's second-floor office, where Susan was introduced to the advertising manager, Hank Burnside.

"Susan Holt from Mayfield's of Manhattan," Marci announced. "Susan, this is Hank Burnside." He was good-looking, thirty or so, with rumpled brown hair and a bit of a squint. A pencil was stuck behind his ear.

"Pleased to meet you," he said, letting his eyes roam quickly down her body in its fashionable gray suit. "Is that what they're wearing in New York this winter?"

"I didn't bring my winter clothes, to Florida," she replied. "Should I have?"

His eyes came back to her face. "A bathing suit is fine, if you've got one."

Susan dismissed the topic with a shrug. "I'm only here two days. Hardly enough time to get all sandy."

"You could have brought us some New York City snow."

She shook her head. "Just rain so far this season."

He seemed to lose interest in their banter and suddenly turned to the telephone. "I have to call the TV station, schedule two more spots for tonight. 'Bye for now. See you later."

"He's a nice guy," Marci said after he'd left, "but you may want to be busy if he asks you out to dinner."

"Susan grinned. 'Thanks for the tip. Is this personal experience speaking?"

"You bet! Come on. I'll walk you to your car and show you where we're dumping the snow."

The parking lot at Gulfpalm's end of the mall was actually divided into two sections split by a landscaped strip."That's for the Christmas overflow," Marci explained, waving toward the farthest area. "The Lincoln you see there belongs to Mr. Vangridge. For tomorrow the lot becomes a winter wonderland with tons of snow all the way from Buffalo. The kids will be climbing on it and throwing snowballs and even making snowmen, all right here in sunny Florida with the temperature in the seventies."

"I'll see you then," Susan promised. "It sounds great!"

As she got into her car she was aware of a middle-aged man with a dark complexion, perhaps a Cuban. He stood by his car in the next row, openly watching her, though he made no attempt to approach. She thought no more about him as she pulled out of the parking lot and headed back to the hotel.

Susan Holt read the morning paper over breakfast and saw the two-page spread announcing Snow Day at Gulfpalm. The features for children and adults, including the presence of Santa Claus and a high-school band, were boxed and printed in bold type on the left-hand page. An illustration of romping youngsters dominated the opposite page. Hank Burnside and the advertising department had done a nice job. She wasn't surprised when she pulled into the mall parking lot at nine-thirty to see several dozen cars already there, awaiting the truckload of Buffalo's snow. It was a sunny morning with the temperature, already over seventy.

Susan spotted Marci Chester at once, clutching a clipboard as she hurried back and forth between various groups. As yet there was no sign of Ben Vangridge, but his car was in its parking space. Hank Burnside came over as soon as he saw her. "Good to see you again, Susan. I'll bet they don't do things like this on Fifth Avenue"

"Our big treat is when they cart the snow away, not bring it in." She happened to scan the crowd and saw again the dark man she'd noticed as she left the store the previous afternoon. "Do you know that fellow over there?" she asked Burnside.

"That's Jimmy Garcia, our security chief. Don't worry, he stares at everyone like that."

"He looks like he might be Cuban."

"He is. Born and raised there. He fought Castro for a long time, then took a boat across about ten years ago. Most of the Cubans settle around the Miami area, and I met him there through some Cuban friends. He came over to our Gulf Coast and Vangridge gave him a job. I'll introduce you later."

Their conversation was interrupted by a cheer from the crowd as a big silver truck with New York plates turned into the parking lot. Across its side was strung a banner, no doubt repeated on the opposite side: *A Shipment of Snow, from Buffalo to Gulfpalm with Love!* The high-school band struck up a lively rendition of "Winter Wonderland."

Hank Burnside left Susan's side to greet the two drivers, who were responding to the cheers. Susan moved over behind a young mother with three children who were about to witness their first snow. "It's white and it's very, very cold! Your father and I moved south to get away from it."

"Will it hurt us?" a small child wanted to know.

"It can freeze your little fingers, but I'll make sure it doesn't. Come on! They're dumping it now!"

The truck had tipped its cargo section and the huge mound of snow slid out easily, forming an impressive pile in the parking lot. As the children broke free and ran toward the snow, it was Garcia, the security chief, who first noticed something wrong. He held up both hands and shouted, "Back! Everyone stay back!"

Susan ran up to the other side of the snow pile, where Marci stood still clutching her clipboard. "What is it? What's wrong?"

"I don't know, but I'm sure going to find out." Marci ignored the warning to stay back and hurried over to Garcia. "Why did you stop them?" she asked. "What's the trouble?"

Then, edging forward a bit, Susan saw it too. An arm clad in a dark suit coat was protruding from the snow. The security chief shouted at the drivers. "What's this? Help me here!"

Mothers covered their youngsters' eyes, and one woman screamed. Garcia and the drivers brushed some snow away and they saw that it was indeed a body. Benjamin Vangridge, president of Gulfpalm, was impossibly dead in the snow that had just arrived from Buffalo.

It was Marci Chester's quick wits that saved the day. Seeing that body surrounded by horrified mothers and gaping children, she ran over to the band and ordered them to lead a march away from the scene. She pulled some mothers and children into line behind the band and within minutes a parade was snaking its way across the parking lot.

Many of the children turned to look back at the mound of snow, where Vangridge's body appeared from a distance like a great black bird tumbled from the sky. But their mothers urged them on and soon the parade had worked its way to the far end of the mall, with Santa Claus keeping pace all the, way. "Don't worry," she heard Marci shout to the children. "We'll be back to play in the snow before long. You'll have the whole day there."

Susan had followed the parade for a time, leaving the death scene to the store employees. She'd noticed Hank Burnside on his cellular phone almost at once, calling the police. Within minutes a patrol car was on the scene, quickly followed by an ambulance and an unmarked car with a roof flasher. Never one to shy away from the police, she headed back toward the action.

Garcia was explaining what he knew to a tall detective with small, piercing eyes and thin blond hair. He noticed her as soon as she came up, and when she started edging away he reached out to touch her arm. "Did you see all this too, miss?"

"Yes, I did."

"I'll be with you in just a minute," he said, winding up his conversation with the security chief. "Stay right there."

Burnside hurried up with one of his young women assistants. "Can you tell us how soon the body will be out of there so we can resume our Snow Day event? Time is pretty important with that sun beating down."

"You're—?"

"Hank Burnside, the store's advertising manager."

The detective tried a smile, but it didn't fit with his face. "I'm Sergeant Appleton. I guess it'll take us some time."

"An hour, two hours? Don't you just photograph the body and take it away?"

Appleton's attempt at a smile faded. "The dead man is Gulfpalm's manager, right? His body is over there with a chest wound. It looks very much as if he was murdered. Your security chief tells me he was in the store yesterday. So what's he doing in a truck full of snow that left Buffalo two days ago?"

"I—I don't know," Burnside admitted.

"Neither do I. And we're going to have to search through every bit of that snow for some sort of clue. When we're finished, you can have what's left." He turned on Susan as Burnside beat a hasty retreat. "Now what about you?"

"I don't know. You said you wanted to talk to me."

"Yeah. I'm Sergeant Appleton. Are you a store employee?"

"Not this store. My name is Susan Holt. I'm in the promotions department at Mayfield's in New York. I flew down for two days to see how their Snow Day came off."

"I'd say it's come off poorly so far. Did you know Ben Vangridge?"

"I just met him yesterday."

"Then he was here in the store."

"Oh yes. We had a nice chat."

"Any idea how his body got into that truck with the snow?"

"None whatsoever. Can you tell how long he's been dead?"

"Not with the body packed in snow like that. Maybe the medical examiner can take a guess."

A detective came over with one of the drivers. "This is Walt Creasey. He was driving when the truck pulled in."

Creasey was a bearded man in plaid shirt and jeans, wearing a baseball cap backward on his head. With the beard it was difficult to estimate his age, though there were a few gray strands visible in it. "Hey," he said, I don't know anything about this body. The truck was already loaded when I took over."

"Where was that, sir?" the detective asked. Susan had the feeling it wasn't good when he called someone "sir."

"Buffalo, New York, where the snow is!"

"You drove it alone?"

"Hell, no! It's over fifteen hundred miles and they wanted it here quick. This is my partner, Pierre Rivage."

Sergeant Appleton eyed a short dark man with a thin moustache and glasses, who'd come up to join them. 'You French?" he asked.

"French-Canadian," the man answered with a slight accent. "We often team up on these long trips."

The detective shifted his attention back to Creasey. "Where'd you stop overnight?"

"We didn't. One of us drove while the other slept. We left Buffalo right after dinner on Thursday and drove through two nights. Ate at truck stops on the way."

"You must have stopped somewhere else."

"Didn't," Rivage confirmed. "We stayed on the road. Would have made better time except for a storm in West Virginia."

"What about this morning?"

"Got to Naples a bit after eight. We lingered over breakfast so there'd be a crowd here to greet us. I was driving and then after breakfast Walt took over."

"So how did Vangridge's body get in your truck?"

"Beats me," Walt Creasey said. "Maybe it got put in with the snow up in Buffalo."

"Several people saw him here yesterday afternoon, after you were already on the way," Appleton said. Susan could see that his patience was wearing thin. He was a detective who thrived on the routine of robberies, drug busts, and domestic violence. A bizarre case like this was beyond his comprehension. He wanted easy answers and there weren't any.

Creasey looked frightened. "Do me and my buddy need a lawyer?"

"Not if you have nothing to hide. I want a list of all the places you two stopped on the way here, what you ate, how long it took. I want times, addresses, everything you can give me."

Marci had come over to see what was happening. Appleton confiscated her clipboard and gave it to the drivers for their list. "You should just concentrate on the Florida stops," Susan advised him. "Vangridge couldn't have intercepted them any further north."

"You think he went off to meet the truck?" Marci asked.

"How else could it have happened?" Susan reasoned. "Maybe he intended to arrive with it as a surprise to everyone. Then something happened and he was killed. They foolishly put him in the truck rather than leaving him by the side of the road."

"That's a nice theory," the detective said. "Any proof for it?"

"Not yet," Susan admitted. "But I've been lucky in the past, helping the police."

"You do this sort of thing regular?"

"It's not my job. Things just happen to me."

"Well, you two ladies better run along now. This is my job and I'd better get at it."

Susan shook her head and moved away with Marci. "Is he always like that?"

"Don't ask me, I only met him once before, when he investigated a break-in at the store."

"That's more in his line. Was anything taken?"

"Some rifles from our sporting goods department. Nothing big."

Susan could hear the high-school band still playing from around the back of the mall. She noticed that a couple of patrolmen were shoveling the small mountain of snow, really just tossing it from one pile to another. It didn't seem that they'd found anything yet. Meanwhile, the body was being photographed and videotaped from all angles. When the photographer finished with the body he took several shots of the truck. Susan opened the door and peered into the cab. Behind the seats was a cramped-looking mattress for sleeping. She studied the instruments and the clear windshield, unmarked except for a few splattered highway bugs. Then she closed the door and returned to Marci.

She was chewing at her lipstick, sneaking an occasional peek at her watch. "I've gotta get those kids back to the snow pile before the whole thing melts. Won't they ever finish?"

"It looks as if they're finishing up with the body. And those two with the shovels sure aren't finding anything."

More cars were arriving, bringing more children to play in the snow. Marci went back over to Sergeant Appleton as soon as the body had been removed. "Can't you give us back our snow pile?" she pleaded.

He walked over and spoke quietly to the two officers who had just about finished their shovel work. "All right," he said, turning to her. "It's all yours."

Marci grinned and ran over to tell Jimmy Garcia; "Signal the band to start back this way with the kids. It's Snow Day at last!"

Susan spent much of the next hour circulating among the parents and children, some of whom were experiencing snow for the first time. She heard one mother warn her children against throwing snowballs because they were too icy, and indeed the snow seemed icy to Susan's touch. A day and a half in the truck had not helped its consistency.

A bit later, joining Susan for a late lunch in the store's cafe, Marci sat back and sighed. "I think it's going well, all things considered. How does it look from your New York viewpoint?"

Susan took a bite of her club sandwich to give herself a moment in phrasing a reply. "I suppose if Mayfield's manager was found murdered outside the store we might have closed the place and canceled all events for the day."

"That wasn't my decision," Marci hastened to explain. "Hank phoned the owners in Atlanta and they said as long as the snow was here we should go ahead rather than disappoint the children."

"Doesn't Vangridge have a wife?"

"Divorced, and she moved to California."

"No rumors about affairs with employees? It happens at Mayfield's all the time."

Marci shrugged. "A few jokes about the assistant manager."

"Who's that?"

"Ann O'Toole. She's head of purchasing. I don't think you've met her. But nobody takes the jokes seriously."

"This whole thing isn't any of my business, but I've had some experience investigating crime. If you'd like me to look into this—"

Marci was obviously uncertain what to do. Finally she said, "Come on, I'll see if we can find Ann." She paid the check and they went back outside.

When they located Ann O'Toole she was talking to Garcia, trying to work out the details of what had happened. "I just got here," she told Marci. "This is terrible!" She was slender and tanned, around forty, fairly attractive but with a take-charge attitude that would turn some men off. Susan decided she could have been a schoolteacher. "Has Atlanta been notified?"

"Hank Burnside phoned them. They told us to go ahead with Snow Day."

"They would." She looked exasperated. "Their store manager is dead, for God's sake!"

"This is Susan Holt from Mayfield's of Manhattan. Remember? I mentioned she wanted to come down and study our promotion."

Ann O'Toole tried to smile. "I'm afraid you're not seeing us at our best, Susan."

"I wonder if I might help in some way. I was telling Marci I've had some experience with criminal investigations."

"Thank you, but I'm sure the police can handle it."

"Did Mr. Vangridge say anything about going out to meet the snow truck?" Susan asked, as if she hadn't heard the woman decline her offer of help.

"Not to me, and I was talking to him just last night."

Jimmy Garcia had started walking away during their conversation, but Susan wanted to speak to him. She caught up with him and said, "I guess we haven't been formally introduced."

"I know who you are," he replied.

"I saw you watching me yesterday when I got into my car."

"I watch everyone. It's my job." He flexed the fingers of his right hand as he spoke, as if keeping his gun hand limber. On second thought, she wondered if he even carried a gun. At Mayfield's the security men usually didn't.

"Were you working last night?" she asked.

"I was here till the store closed. Ten o'clock. Friday nights are busy, so I'm usually here."

"Did Mr. Vangridge work late?"

"The detective asked me that too. A lot of them were here till ten because of Snow Day this morning. Vangridge and Burnside and Marci. Miss O'Toole, too. They were going over last-minute details, I guess."

The man seemed reasonably friendly now and Susan decided he was her best chance of learning more about the police investigation. "Look, I think I can help locate the killer but I need a list of the stops the truck drivers made. Could you ask Sergeant Appleton for it?"

"I got a copy already," he told her. "The sergeant asked me to run some off on my copier so his men could start checking the truck stops right away. Appleton knows what he's doing."

"I guess he does," Susan agreed. "Do you think I could just have a peek at it?"

"It's confidential."

"Then how come you have a copy?"

"I made an extra for myself."

"Does Appleton know about it?"

He sighed and reached into his breast pocket. "It won't tell you much."

At first glance she was ready to believe him. They'd stopped for breakfast in North Naples around eight o'clock. The previous stop had been after midnight somewhere outside Tampa, at a truck stop with a neon dolphin jumping from the water. They didn't remember the name. Walt Creasey had gone in for coffee and the rest room, staying about fifteen minutes in all. The Canadian, Pierre Rivage, had remained in the truck sleeping. Creasey brought him some coffee, and after drinking it Rivage took over the driving while Creasey slept.

"Would you like to take a run up there?" she asked the security man, pointing to the stop north of Tampa.

"What for? The police are checking it. Couldn't have happened there anyway. The Canadian was asleep in the truck. The sound of the shot, or the truck doors being pushed up, would have wakened him."

Susan smiled. "Don't you remember Sherlock Holmes? When you've excluded the impossible, whatever remains, however improbable, must be the truth. I think the killer left something there, and I think he'll be back for it."

"We don't even know the name of the truck stop, except that it has a neon dolphin on its sign."

'That should be easy to find."

"Hell, it's a three-hour drive from here, probably more. And what's there to see after you get there?"

She didn't have any answer to that, and couldn't really blame him for declining her offer. What was there to see after she got there, except the uncertain scene of the crime? She needed more than a wild idea that was bouncing around in her head.

It was Sergeant Appleton who finally decided her. She was watching the snowman judging when he intercepted her. "Been asking lots of questions, haven't you?"

"My store in Manhattan expects a full report on Gulfpalm's Snow Day, and that includes all the glitches. I'm just trying to figure out how to word it. I could use some help."

"It's far too soon for me to comment on the case. We're just now beginning our investigation."

"But he was shot, wasn't he?"

"Yes," he admitted.

And the drivers must be your primary suspects. No one else would have had the key to open the truck."

"Certainly they're under suspicion. Finding a motive is the difficult part. Apparently Vangridge wasn't robbed. Why was he killed? How and where was he placed in the truck? And if it happened north of here, what was he doing up there in the first place?"

"I can answer some of those questions for you," she said, with a bit more confidence than she really felt. All she had at the moment was a vague hunch.

"But first tell me if your men have learned anything. Have they checked out the last few places the truck stopped on its trip down?"

"There was nothing at the North Naples place. We asked the Tampa police to check the truck stop in that area and they just notified me there's nothing suspicious at that scene either. No one remembers the truck with the banners on it, but the night crew would be home sleeping how. They promised to have someone check again after midnight."

"I'd like to go up there."

He smiled like a father humoring a child. "Why, Miss Holt? Do you think you can find something the police missed?"

"I may know what to look for."

He turned away, not about to get involved with amateur sleuths: "Let me know if you find anything interesting."

"What's the name of that truck stop in Tampa?" she called after him."The one with the neon dolphin."

"The Neon Dolphin. How's that for a name?"

The last of the snow was melting in the Florida heat when she found Marci Chester bidding goodbye to the family responsible for the best snowman."You've put in a long day."

The perky young woman hardly had a hair out of place. "I thrive on it." She smiled.

"Even with your boss being found dead?"

"Not that, of course. But the hustle and bustle of an event like this. I can't imagine working anywhere else."

"Look, Marci, I've got a crazy idea about where Ben Vangridge might have been killed. It's a truck stop near Tampa, about three hours from here."

"Why do you think it was there?"

"Because nowhere else makes sense at all. And I think the killer left something up there."

"But the body and the truck and the snow are all down here," Marci insisted. "What else is there? Even if Ben was killed up there, the murderer isn't still hanging around."

"I have to go. Want to come with me?"

Marci's face turned serious. I have a sort of date tonight, with Hank Burnside. We wanted to unwind together, after all that's happened. You know how it is."

"Sure. Go ahead. I didn't realize you two were an item."

"We're not, really."

"Have a good time."

Susan went back to her car and took out the map the rental agency had given her. Tampa was a clear shot up route 75. Maybe she could make it in less than three hours if the traffic was light.

"I'll go with you," a voice behind her said. She turned to see Jimmy Garcia standing there. The security man was carrying his jacket and she could see the holster on his belt. "Get in. I'll drive. I can make better time."

"Are you sure you want—?"

"Get in."

The highway unwound before them as Garcia drove north toward Tampa. At first he said very little, but finally Susan decided some conversation was necessary. "What made you change your mind about coming with me?"

At first he didn't answer. Finally, perhaps to fill the silence between them, he said, "Vangridge was a good man. He gave me a job when I needed one. I guess I owe him this much."

"Do you know who killed him?"

"It had to be one of those drivers. I can't figure out why, though."

"That's what we're going to find out. Sergeant Appleton says the place we want is called the Neon Dolphin. Ever hear of it?"

He shook his head, speeding up to pass a van. "Those truck stop places are pretty much alike."

"Some are different," Susan said."

"How do you mean?"

"Sometimes they have a parking lot where drivers can leave their rigs overnight to be picked up by a relief driver. Sort of a transfer point."

"But the truck is at Gulfpalm. There was no transfer."

Susan said no more about it, shifting the conversation to the weather. "It must be great living down here, never having to worry about winter clothes or snow shovels."

"Do you live in Manhattan?"

"Yes."

"Married?"

"No. I was living with someone but we're having a trial separation at the moment. With the amount I travel each year it's difficult to maintain a relationship. What about you?"

Garcia smiled. "I have a wife and three kids. The only thing we ever argue about is politics. She thinks I should be more active in the Cuban community. I tell her I moved to this side of the state to get away from the Cuban community."

They reached Tampa around dinnertime and found, the Neon Dolphin without difficulty. Susan was pleased to see the parking lot filled with a dozen or so trucks behind the restaurant. At least the trip hadn't been in vain. She parked her rental car and they strolled along the line of parked trucks until she stopped at one that might have been a twin of the snow truck from Buffalo.

"This is it," she announced. "Now all we have to do is open the padlock on the back doors."

"Do you mind telling me what we're looking for? Is it drugs?"

"Not drugs. They head north from here. This cargo came south." She walked to the back of the truck, and took a look at the lock. "Think you could open this?"

It was almost dark and a spotlight on the roof of the truck stop illuminated only the front of the vehicles. Garcia used a small flashlight to study the padlock at the bottom of the door. "I'll give it a try." He slipped a small tool from his pocket and went at it like an expert. In a moment she heard a gentle click as the lock came open. Quickly removing the padlock, he pushed the door up far enough for them to peer inside with the aid of the flashlight.

"Boxes!" Susan said. "It's full of boxes."

"Crates, to be exact. Wooden crates."

"Give me a boost up."

She took his flashlight and moved closer. The crates were too heavy to move. "What is it?" Garcia asked.

"The motive for Ben Vangridge's murder."

Garcia climbed into the back of the truck after her, and she saw him reach for his revolver. She felt a familiar chill, and for a split second wondered if she'd made a terrible mistake. Then he opened the cylinder and emptied the cartridges into the palm of his hand. "Here, maybe I can pry it open with this."

He inserted the revolver barrel under one of the wooden slats and pushed down while Susan held the flashlight. The nails were pulled loose and the slat came up easily. She turned the light down, into the crate.

"Guns! It's full of assault weapons!"

Jimmy Garcia nodded. "For sale to Cuban exiles. That's what this is all about. There are always Cubans ready to buy weapons for the next invasion, and arms dealers willing to sell them."

Suddenly they were blinded by a powerful light. "Don't move!" a familiar voice commanded from outside the truck. "I have a gun aimed at both of you."

Garcia raised his empty pistol. "And I have one aimed at you."

In another instant the man outside the truck might have fired, but he never had the chance. With the light in her eyes Susan couldn't see what was happening, but she heard the shouts and the scuffling. Then the light disappeared, replaced by another, less blinding, and Sergeant Appleton was climbing into the truck. "We've got him, Jimmy. Is she all right?"

Garcia snorted. "Let her tell you."

Susan took a deep breath. "It's Hank Burnside, isn't it? I recognized his voice."

"That's him, Miss Holt. Now suppose you tell us how you knew about this truck."

Somebody went into the truck stop for coffee and Appleton took time to introduce a couple of Tampa detectives, explaining what he was doing there. "Jimmy Garcia believed you were on to something. He told me he'd drive up here with you if I could be here too. So I flew up in a police helicopter and got here ahead of you."

Garcia seemed pleased with himself. "If you were right about the killer leaving something here, I figured he'd be coming back for it. I wanted to catch him just as bad as you."

She took her cup of coffee and walked over to the police car where Hank Burnside, Gulfpalm's ad manager, sat in handcuffs. "You should hear this too, so you'll know what you did wrong."

"I didn't do anything wrong. There's no way you could have known about that truck."

Appleton interrupted the exchange. "Perhaps you'd better tell us what happened first, Miss Holt, and why Vangridge was killed."

"Burnside here was earning some extra money selling illegal guns to Cuban exiles in south Florida. That earlier theft of rifles from the store was probably his doing. I guess police surveillance had gotten a little tight lately, and with Gulfpalm about to repeat its Snow Day, he decided the perfect way to bring a shipment of weapons into the area from the north was in a truck proudly announcing it was carrying snow to Florida. He dumped the snow outside Buffalo and filled the truck with the guns."

Already Appleton was shaking his head. "If the truck was full of guns, how did they deliver snow to the parking lot this morning?"

Susan gestured at the truck. "That answer was obvious to me almost from the beginning. There were two almost identical trucks. The switch was made here. The two drivers were switched and the truck's license plates were switched. When the truck arrived today it needed to have the New York plates it started with, and that's where you made your mistake, Hank. New York vehicles carry registration and inspection stickers on their front windshields. Florida vehicles don't. The truck that pulled in with its New York plates and cargo of snow had a bare windshield. When I had a chance to examine the snow itself I realized it was shaved ice. It came from the same Florida plant as last year's so-called snow. That got me thinking. If the snow was loaded in Florida, what had the original truck carried this far? What had the killer left at this truck stop, which was the only possible transfer point? When we got here it was easy to spot the truck because it had Florida plates but New York stickers on its windshield."

"Did you know Burnside was involved?"

"Almost certainly. Vangridge must have planned to meet the truck here and ride the rest of the way with them. That was strange in itself. He could have accomplished the same dramatic effect getting on a few blocks from the store. I think he suspected something. Maybe the ice company phoned him about the order. In any event, he drove up here after the store closed at ten o'clock. And he didn't come alone."

"How do you know that?"

"Because his Lincoln was still in its parking space this morning. That could mean only one thing. He drove with someone else, and that person had to be the killer. Otherwise, why didn't he report the crime to the police? Either he went in the killer's car or they took his car and the killer brought it back. I don't believe you planned to kill him, Hank, unless you had to. But he was suspicious of something and you convinced him you should go along." She turned back to the detective. "If the killer left the Gulfpalm store with Vangridge, it was almost certainly one of the four people working late with him—Garcia, Hank Burnside, Marci Chester, or Ann O'Toole. Of the four, Burnside was the most likely, simply because he'd been in Buffalo arranging for the shipment of snow. And he told me he met Garcia through Cuban friends in Miami. That gave him the connections for selling the guns to the right group. When I started asking people about this truck stop he heard about it and panicked. He followed us up here, hoping to move the guns before we found them."

"What about the drivers?"

"One of them, the Canadian Pierre Rivage, had to be involved. He claimed he was sleeping in the truck when the switch must have taken place. Once the license plates were changed, the other driver, Creasey, might not have realized it was a different truck. Rivage drove the rest of the way into Naples while he slept."

"Why do you think Vangridge was shot?" Appleton asked.

"I think Burnside and Vangridge drove up together and Vangridge spotted the two identical trucks. Maybe the driver opened one to show him the snow and then something happened. Burnside shot him and they put his body in with the snow because they had nowhere else to put it. They couldn't just leave it there with the guns the Cubans were buying and I don't suppose Burnside wanted it in the car with him."

"Rivage shot him!" the ad manager shouted from the back of the police car. "I didn't have anything to do with that part!"

"I think your gun will tell the story," Appleton said.

Burnside was in a panic. Perhaps he was remembering they had a death penalty in Florida. "The gun was Rivage's. He gave it to me to get rid of!"

"I'll have both drivers picked up," Appleton decided. "It seems to me Creasey might know more than he's admitting."

On Sunday morning Marci Chester phoned Susan's hotel as she was packing. "What's this about Hank being arrested for the murder? He never showed up for our date."

"Garcia can tell you all about it, Marci. I've been up half the night with the police and I'm all talked out. Besides, I have a plane to catch."

"Do you think something like this would go over at Mayfield's?"

"What? A truckload of snow, illegal weapons, and a murdered store manager? Not a chance! That's too much excitement for New York!"

Susan Holt awoke with a start, wondering why her bed felt so hard. Then memory flooded back in a blinding instant of terror and she knew she was in a jail cell, accused of murder. She opened her eyes and saw a woman in the next holding cell staring at her through the bars. "You're awake," the woman said.

"What? Yes. Yes, I'm awake. What time is it, please?"

"Barely daylight. Quarter to seven."

Susan groaned. She'd slept less than three hours and her mouth felt as if it was full of cobwebs. She glanced at the lidless toilet in one corner of the cell. "Do they give you anything to eat here?"

"Pretty soon now. They'll bring something around seven o'clock. What you in for?"

"Murder, I guess. I haven't been charged yet." The other woman gave a low whistle of appreciation and Susan hastened to add, "I didn't do it."

"Have you called a lawyer?"

"Not exactly. I called someone who'll get me a lawyer." She had called Mike Brentnor, her coworker in promotions at Mayfield's, Manhattan's largest department store. He was hardly a friend but in the middle of the night in a strange city she was feeling desperate. Considering that she'd awakened him from a sound sleep, he'd been both concerned and reassuring, promising to be on the first morning plane out of LaGuardia, a flight that would take less than an hour.

Presently a guard brought her a breakfast tray with some juice, coffee, and a hard roll. "You'll be brought before the judge at ten o'clock," he said, not unkindly. "Have you seen your lawyer yet?"

"No. I think someone's on the way."

Mike Brentnor arrived a few minutes before nine, looking just a bit flustered. He was slim and slyly handsome, around thirty, the sort of man Susan used to see by the dozen in Manhattan singles bars. She met with him now in one of the interrogation rooms. "I phoned Marx from the airport and he gave me the name of a good criminal lawyer up here," he told her.

For an instant she was dismayed that he'd reported to their superior, but of course Saul Marx would have to know about it. She wouldn't be flying back as planned this afternoon. She'd be in a jail cell in upstate New York. "What did he say?"

"That it must be a mistake. Who is this person you're supposed to have killed?"

"Betty Quint. It's a long story. I'd rather just go over it once when the lawyer's here."

"I left word at his office. They were going to try catching him at home so he could come directly here. Mayfield's name carries some weight, I guess."

"I'm glad of that!" The coffee had revived her and she was feeling a little more human.

"I'm pleased you phoned me, Susan. I heard you broke up with Russell and I can't say I'm sorry about that. You know I've always had a fondness for you."

"Fondness? Is that what you call it?" She decided to make things clear from the beginning. A night in a jail cell had intensified the anger she sometimes felt toward Brentnor, though she knew none of what had happened was his fault. "I phoned you because I didn't want to wake Saul in the middle of the night, and yours was the only other Mayfield's home phone number I had with me. I do appreciate your flying up here, but let's not get the wrong idea."

"All right," he agreed, flushing at her harsh words. "Now tell me what—"

A guard came to announce that her lawyer had arrived. He bustled in looking like an upstate version of Mike Brentnor, though with more style. She had a sudden vision of him in a courtroom defending her on the murder charge.

"Hello, Miss Holt," he said, holding out his hand. "I'm Irving Farber from the firm of Freeman and Farber. That's my father in the firm name, not me." A smile flashed across his face, then was gone. He was all business. "What happened here?"

"I've been arrested for murder is what happened," Susan said, her anger rising again.

"Have you made a statement to the police?"

"I told them what happened. They questioned me for hours until I demanded a lawyer."

"That's good." He took a yellow legal pad from his briefcase and started to make notes. "What about the assistant D.A.? Was he in to see you?"

She nodded. "After they photographed and fingerprinted me. I told him I wanted to phone a coworker to get me a lawyer. By that time all I wanted was some sleep."

"All right, Susan. May I call you Susan? Suppose you tell me your story from the beginning."

He glanced questioningly at Mike Brentnor and Susan said, "It's all right if he stays. I have nothing to hide."

"Let's start at the beginning. What brought you to our city?'

Susan took a deep breath, as if she was about to dive into a swimming pool. "I work for Mayfield's, the Manhattan department store. We're open-ing our first location in western New York at your new shopping mall in Pembroke and I flew up to work out the details of some special promotions, Betty Quint was my contact here."

More notes. "How long had you known Miss Quint?"

"I'd met her once at our New York office about six months ago. She stayed overnight at my apartment. We'd been in constant touch by phone, fax, and E-mail since then. This is my first trip up here because there was no point in coming until the store was almost ready to open."

"When does it open?"

"Next Tuesday. A week from today."

"Go on. Describe everything that happened."

I took the Monday afternoon flight up from LaGuardia (Susan continued), arriving at midafternoon. Betty met me at the airport and drove me to the new store. She was a friendly, uninhibited young woman of about my age, around thirty. Seeing her again confirmed my impression of her from our initial meeting at the New York store. She was a good worker, perfect for this store, but perhaps lacking the cool sophistication needed for the Manhattan retail scene. She liked jokes and didn't mind attracting attention to herself. I wasn't surprised when she mentioned she was active in a local theater group.

We toured the completed Mayfield's store, where clerks were busy unpack-ing merchandise for the shelves and racks. Betty consulted her notebook frequently as she led the way through the store, pointing out special features of interest. A small cafe was already open for the employees and we took advantage of it for coffee and a snack.

"I'm so excited to be part of the Mayfield's team!" Betty gushed. "Have you been with them long?"

"About nine years. Ever since college."

"I thought Manhattan was very exciting when I was there in the spring."

"It is, but most of my excitement has come from traveling for the store. I've been to Tokyo, Iceland, Switzerland, London, and all over America."

"Do you meet lots of men on the job?"

"Not too many," I said. "I told you about Russell."

"Are you back living with him?"

"No." I felt like, saying it was none of her business. Instead, I shifted the conversation back to the new store. "Do you have anyone helping you on promotions?"

"Sadie Shepherd, she's my secretary." Her face brightened. "There she is now! I'll introduce you." She called out to a slender dark-haired woman in her twenties who was already headed in our direction. "Sadie, this is Susan Holt, the promotions coordinator at Mayfield's flagship store in Manhattan."

The young woman had a pleasant smile and seemed eager to please. "So glad to meet you! Betty told me about the great time she had in New York."

"It was fun for me too. Perhaps you can come down and see our store sometime."

"I'd love that," Sadie said, then turned her attention briefly to Betty. "I wanted to catch you before you left. Here are a couple of phone messages."

"Thanks, Sadie." She glanced at them and slipped them into a pocket of her notebook. When we were alone again she turned back to me. "It would be great if you could stay and help me through next Tuesday's opening."

"I'm afraid that's impossible, Betty. I have to fly back tomorrow afternoon. But we can go over lots of things while I'm here. If you're free we can have dinner tonight. My expense account is fairly generous."

"That would be great! We have a wonderful new French restaurant down by the harbor."

"I'll have to check in at my hotel first. I don't want to inconvenience you. I should rent a car."

"Why bother, for just one night? I'll drive you to the hotel and then we can go to my place while I change."

It wasn't quite as simple as it sounded. Just as we pulled up at my hotel Betty received a call on her cell phone. She seemed annoyed at the caller, someone named Roger, and tried to get rid of him. "Look, I'm working right now, Roger. Sadie gave me your messages, but I was too busy to get back to you. Can't we talk about this later?" She listened for a moment and then said, "I'm with someone from the New York office and we'll be going back to my apartment." When he said something else she uttered an obscenity and pushed the Off button on the phone.

I gave a grunt of approval. "Is Roger an old boyfriend?"

"Worse than that," she said, but explained no further.

It took me a few minutes to check in and she accompanied me to my room.

"I just want to slip into a dress and we can be on our way," I told her.

"It's not a fancy place."

"I've gotten a bit rumpled from traveling. I'll only be a minute." She sat down on the bed. "Do you smoke?"

"Tried it. Gave it up."

She'd opened her purse to take out a cigarette but then thought better of it. Meanwhile, I'd unzipped my overnight bag and removed this simple print dress I'd brought with me for early fall wear. I didn't bother retreating to the bathroom for a modest change of clothes. We'd seen pretty much all of each other the night Betty stayed over at my Manhattan apartment. That was also the night she'd startled me by suggesting we stop for after-dinner drinks at the Plaza bar and then paying for them with a hundred-dollar bill.

"Can I use your phone?" she asked as I was freshening my makeup.

"Go ahead." I motioned toward the nightstand.

She got an outside line and punched in a local number. When the party answered she started right in. "Roger phoned me awhile ago." A pause and then, "Well, I don't like it."

I tried to keep busy with my makeup to avoid being too obvious about my eavesdropping. "I'm at the hotel now," she said, "but I'll be back to my apartment shortly. What'll I do if he comes up and wants the money?"

She listened intently after that, finally said, "All right," and hung up with a sigh.

"Is anything wrong?" I asked casually, finishing with my makeup.

"No, no. Just man trouble. You know how it is."

We started out for her apartment but she was openly nervous, keeping an eye on the rearview mirror as if fearful of being followed. I wondered about that but asked no further questions, even when she seemed to double back on her route and take the long way through a number of narrow residential streets. "Less traffic this way," she muttered, sensing my questioning gaze.

Presently we entered a neighborhood of large older homes, many of which had been split into apartments and needed ugly second- and third-floor fire escapes to comply with housing codes for multiple dwellings. Betty Quint parked in front of one of these. "Come on up. I want to take a quick shower and then we'll be on our way."

It was already after six and starting to get dark. Thick gray clouds had rolled in, threatening rain. She led the way to a side door which she quickly unlocked. I noticed there were two mailboxes, one with her name and the other with Mr. & Mrs. R. James Liction. "The landlord," she said by way of explanation. "A retired couple. They live downstairs. Come on up." She led the way to her second-floor apartment.

"It's so large!" I marveled.

"I have the entire second floor," she answered with pride. "These old houses are great bargains." She dropped her things on the coffee table and walked to the front window, gazing down at the street. "Damn!"

"What's the matter?"

"He's down there in a car. I think we were followed."

"Roger?"

"I'm going to shower," she said, walking into the bedroom as she shed her outer garments. I hesitated to follow but then she called to me. "Here's something you might like even if you did quit smoking."

I walked into the bedroom and found her holding out a cigarette, with crimped ends. "What is it, pot?' I asked.

"Sure! It's good stuff. Helps you unwind after a day's work."

"No thanks. But go ahead if you want one."

She shrugged and tossed the joint on the bedside table. "I don't like to smoke alone."

Wearing only a bra and panties she went into the bathroom and turned on the shower, rummaging in a cabinet for a bath towel. "Come on in, Susan. Talk to me while I shower." She handed me the towel to hold.

I sat on the closed toilet seat, feeling uncomfortable as she shed her underwear and tossed it into a laundry hamper. Then she felt the spray of water with her hand and stepped into the shower, pulling the curtain closed behind her. "Tell me about the Manhattan store," she called out over the rush of water. "Is it true a homeless man lived there for days before he was discovered?"

"I've heard stories like that, but I—"

Betty Quint screamed, just once, chilling my spine. Then there was a thump as her body went down in the tub. "Betty!" I yanked open the shower curtain and stared at her body, drenched in the pounding spray of hot water.

She'd been stabbed once in the back with a slender dagger that still protruded from the bloody wound. A second, identical dagger lay in the tub near her foot. Otherwise the tub was empty.

I was alone in the steamy bathroom with her body.

Irving Farber scratched his nose and stared at Susan. "That story is impossible, you know. It couldn't have happened the way you told it."

"But it did!" she insisted. "I called 911 and the police were there within minutes."

"And they arrested you."

"Not right away. They questioned me for hours, trying to make me change my story. They accused me of all sorts of wild things, especially after they found the pot. I told them neither of us had smoked it but they kept pounding at it. One of the detectives suggested we'd been high on pot and made love to each other, and then I killed her to hush it up. That's when I demanded a lawyer."

Farber's face was grim. "What was the detective's name?"

"Sergeant Razerwell."

He made a note of it. "Tell me, Susan, what's your explanation for Betty Quint's death?'

"I have none. I agree it's impossible."

"Did you touch anything in the apartment after you phoned the police?"

"No. I didn't even turn off the shower. I couldn't go back in there and see her again. I just sat in the bedroom and shivered until I had to open the door for the police."

Farber glanced at Mike Brentnor. "Will the store go bail for her?"

The question startled him. "I—I don't know. Depends on how much it is, I suppose." He wasn't about to admit he had no authority in the matter.

"Who's your boss?'

"Saul Marx."

Irving Farber glanced at his watch. "Is he in the office by now? It's nearly ten."

"He should be."

"Get on the phone and ask him about bail. Meanwhile, I'll talk to the assistant D.A. and find out how much they'll be wanting."

"Is there a chance I'll get out of here?" Susan asked, her hopes soaring at the thought of it.

"Depends on the D.A.'s office. Don't get your hopes up." He put the yellow pad in his attaché case and snapped it shut.

Susan glanced at her watch. "I'm supposed to be in court in ten minutes."

"They'll come for you when they're ready. Sometimes these things are a bit loose. If they don't get you there, it's their fault, not yours."

The attorney and Mike Brentnor departed, leaving Susan to wonder just where she stood. She'd investigated a few murders in the past, during her travels for Mayfield's, but she'd never been accused of committing one herself. The killing of Betty Quint while she was alone in the shower seemed so impossible that, paradoxically, Susan felt the solution must be a simple thing she could easily discover once she was free.

Presently one of the guards came for her. "Am I going before the judge?" she asked.

"Not yet. They want to question you some more."

Susan was immediately on guard. "My attorney—"

"He's been notified."

She was ushered into one of the interrogation rooms, where she sat down at the bare table to wait. Presently the door opened and a stocky red-haired man she'd never seen before entered. He was carrying a briefcase and Irving Farber was right behind him. "Good morning, Miss Holt," the redhead said, flashing a smile that was quickly gone. "I'm Adam Dullea, U.S. Secret Service." He flashed an ID that looked like miniature currency with its finely engraved borders.

Susan panicked, imagining some labyrinthian plot against the president. What had she gotten herself into? "What do you want?"

"I just have a few questions regarding your relationship with Betty Quint." He opened his briefcase and took out a clear plastic envelope with a hundred-dollar bill inside. "Have you ever seen one of these?"

"A hundred dollars? I guess I've seen a few."

"Did Betty Quint ever show you one?"

"No." Then she remembered something. "She came to New York for a meeting about six months ago. We went out for dinner and drinks later and I remember she paid for the drinks with a hundred-dollar bill. I was a bit startled, but some people like to use big bills when they travel."

"This one is counterfeit," he said.

Susan peered at it more closely. It looked fine to her, "What's its connection with Betty?"

"She passed it at a local restaurant. There've been a few other incidents too. We've had her under surveillance."

"Is it true you can do these on a good color copier?" she asked.

"Not of this quality. We think it was printed overseas."

"How—"

"I'm asking the questions, Miss Holt. Did Betty Quint ever show you or give you a hundred-dollar bill?"

"Just that one time when she paid for the drinks. And she gave it to the waiter, not to me."

"I understand from your statement to the police that she received a phone call from someone named Roger while driving you to your hotel."

"That's correct."

"Did she identify him further?"

"Not to me, no."

"And she made a call from your hotel room?"

"Yes. I'm sure you could trace that. Most hotels keep a record of phone charges for billing purposes."

Adam Dullea looked at her sadly. "The call was made to the local Mayfield's store, Miss Holt."

That surprised Susan and she must have shown it. "We'd just left there. Why would she—?"

He took a deep breath. "Look, Miss Holt, we're inclined to accept your story for the moment, and so are the local police. If you had killed her, you would certainly have come up with a better story than you did—a burglar on the fire escape or a prowler under the bed, for example. Also, your coworker Mike Brentnor has informed the police that you've been helpful with other murder cases in the past. You'll be released on your own recognizance, but you're to remain in the city for at least forty-eight hours pending another court appearance on Thursday, when charges may be dismissed. Is that agreeable?"

"I suppose it'll have to be." What were they doing, giving her two days to find the real killer?

The Secret Service agent departed and Farber smiled encouragement. "Come on, Susan. You're on your way out of here."

In the courtroom it went exactly as predicted. The preliminary hearing was adjourned until Thursday morning at ten and she was released on her own recognizance. Mike Brentnor was waiting in the back of the courtroom. "Let's go celebrate!"

"I've nothing to celebrate, Mike. A woman's been murdered and I'm the only one who could have killed her."

That was when Adam Dullea reappeared, his smile a bit more sincere this time. "Now that you're released from custody, I wonder if we could talk."

"About the murder?"

He nodded. "If you'll excuse us, Mr. Brentnor—"

Susan was happy to escape from Mike's eager clutches. She allowed herself to be guided out of the courthouse and into Dullea's car. "Where are we going?" she asked.

"Back to the scene of the crime. Isn't that how these things are done?"

She laughed. "I'm no psychic, you know. I don't pick up the killer's thoughts or visions. Sometimes I notice things that others have missed."

'That's what I'm hoping for."

This time as the car pulled up to the house a white-haired man came onto the front porch to greet them. He introduced himself as James Liction. "I own the place. You folks more police?"

Dullea showed his identification. "Secret Service. The victim was part of an ongoing investigation into counterfeit currency. Could I ask you if she paid her rent in cash?"

He shook his head. "Always a check, first of the month. My wife Mona was just saying what a nice tenant she was. Never any trouble. I can't believe she was involved with counterfeiters."

His wife, a stocky woman who moved slowly, came out to join them. "Tell 'em about that suspicious-looking guy across the street, James."

"Well, I already told Sergeant Razerwell."

"Tell me too," Dullea requested.

Liction shifted his gaze to Susan. "I happened to see the two of you drive in. After that a fellow parked across the street. He just sat there in his car for a long time. It was too dark to get a good look at him. When he heard the sirens coming he left quick."

Susan remembered that Betty Quint had glanced out the front window and become upset when she saw the car. "We're going to take another look upstairs," Dullea told him.

James Liction shrugged. "Go ahead." He and his wife went back inside.

The apartment was much the same as the day before, except that the door was sealed by yellow police crime-scene tape. Dullea pulled it away and used a key to enter. Inside Susan noticed signs that the drawers and closets had been searched by the police or Dullea's people. "What are you looking for?" she asked. "More counterfeit money?"

He nodded. "A great deal of it. Before she went to work for your store, Quint was employed on the reservations desk of a major airline. Her boy-friend, a copilot on international flights, brought back several small pack-ages of counterfeit money, all hundreds like this one. They're often printed overseas and used as bulk payoffs for drugs." He brought out the bill he'd shown her earlier, in its clear plastic envelope. He pointed to the lower right of the portrait where it read "Series 1996" in small print. "Notice anything wrong with it?"

She shook her head. "There's Ben Franklin, looking the same as ever."

"That's what's wrong. Beginning in 1996 the hundred-dollar bills changed significantly. The portrait is larger and off-center. There's a new watermark and other safety features. Skillful as this job is, the counterfeiters made a fatal mistake in using the old design and dating it 1996. These bills couldn't be passed in bulk overseas, where a suitcase full of drug money would be care-fully examined by the seller, so they were smuggled into this country to be passed individually."

"You think Susan's boyfriend hid them here?"

"Yes."

"And then killed her?"

Dullea shook his head, "His name was Lloyd Baker. He was found shot to death last week in the parking lot at Kennedy Airport."

Susan sat down on the couch. "You think the same person killed Betty?'

"No, as a matter of fact, Baker's killer is in custody. We were moving in on Betty Quint and obtaining a search warrant for this apartment. The easy answer is that she feared being caught with the counterfeit money and com-mitted suicide."

"She stabbed herself in the back? And where did she get the knife? She didn't take it with her when she stepped into the shower. I was right there."

"All right, then. If it wasn't suicide, what happened?"

Susan recalled the scene vividly. "I don't know. It was almost as if a shower of daggers hit her, instead of water."

"Daggers? There was only one."

Susan had gotten up and gone into the bathroom. She opened the cabinet that held the towels, then turned her attention to the shower itself. It was made of molded plastic, recessed into the wall. The plastic was solid and there was no clear sight line to the room's only window, which had been closed in any event. The ceiling was smooth and unmarked, with the room's only lights arranged on the wall above the mirror. The showerhead was normal. It had not dispensed daggers. The shower curtain was ordinary white opaque vinyl. "There were two daggers," she called out to Dullea. "One in her back and another in the bottom of the tub."

Susan turned on the water and couldn't hear Dullea's reply. Something caught her eye. She reached down and peeled it away from the bottom of the tub. It was a piece of Scotch tape, several inches long. Stuck fast near the drain, it had been all but invisible, "Look at this," she called to him.

He came into the bathroom. "Tape. Where was it?"

"Stuck to the bottom of the bathtub. They could have overlooked it in their crime scene search."

"What does it tell us?"

"I don't know." She stared around the bathroom. "You mentioned a search warrant. When were you planning to use it?"

"Last evening."

Susan thought about it. "Someone named Roger phoned her in the car, before we arrived at my hotel."

"I read that in your statement."

"Maybe he was going to take the counterfeit money off her hands. With her boyfriend dead she'd need to do something."

"You don't just get a friend to deal in counterfeit."

"Maybe it's the same friend who was selling her pot. He might have been interested."

"Roger?"

"Roger," Susan agreed. 'When she made the call from my hotel room she sounded a bit frightened of him. And she'd had other messages from him earlier. Maybe she was afraid he'd kill her for those counterfeit hundreds. Maybe he did kill her, but I'm damned if I know how."

Susan still didn't have a car of her own, and after Dullea left her off at the hotel she asked the room clerk where she could rent one. He directed her to a place just a few blocks away. As she was turning from the desk another thought struck her. "Do you keep a record of guests' outgoing phone calls, with the numbers called?"

"Yes, ma'am, we do."

"Could I see mine, please? I've mislaid a local number that I need."

He brought it up on the computer and jotted it down for her. "This is the only call from your room."

Susan glanced at it, a bit puzzled. "Yes, that's the one. Thank you." Dullea had told her that Betty Quint phoned Mayfield's from her room, but the number at Mayfield's new store ended in 6700. This number ended in 6743. Susan went up to her room and dialed it.

A woman's voice answered with, "Store promotions."

"Whose office is this?" she asked.

"I—it was Betty Quint's office."

"Sadie? Is this Sadie Shepherd?"

"Yes. Betty is—"

"I know. This is Susan Holt."

"Oh! Miss Holt!"

Susan made a snap decision. "I'd like to speak with you after work today. Could we have a drink together?"

"I don't know. I'm busy tonight."

"I have to rent a car. What time do you finish up?"

"Usually five, but until the opening I can pretty much leave any time. Since Miss Quint's death—"

"I'll pick you up at five, Sadie. If you don't want to go anywhere we can talk in the car."

She was outside the store in a new Chevy when the young woman emerged, exactly on the hour. Sadie heard her beep the horn and headed over to join her in the front seat. "It's good to see you again, Miss Holt. That was terrible news about poor Betty."

"How do you think I felt, being right on the scene?' Susan left the motor off since Sadie had indicated she had no time for a drink.

"How did it happen?" the young woman asked.

"I was hoping you could tell me."

Her face froze into a mask of ice. It could have been fright or defiance. "I don't know what you mean."

"How was Betty Quint killed in that shower, Sadie? You know, don't you?"

"Why do you say that?"

"Because I think you were responsible for her death."

Sadie Shepherd exploded into fury. "That's a damned lie! I know nothing about it!"

"Calm down and listen. This is what I know so far. Betty's boyfriend was killed after smuggling a large quantity of counterfeit hundred-dollar bills into this country from overseas. They had a flaw in them that made it necessary to pass them individually rather than in bulk, where they'd be closely examined. After her boyfriend's death, Betty tried to find a buyer for the money and she went to a man named Roger who was supplying her with pot and maybe other drugs. You two became friendly and she confided all of this to you. Somehow Roger frightened her, perhaps by demanding the counterfeit hundreds for less money than she wanted. He phoned her yesterday and made more threats. Back at my hotel, she phoned you at the store to tell you what was happening. She phoned her own direct number, but of course you answered. At the store yesterday you gave her some messages you'd taken in her absence, so I knew you answered her phone. Just as you did when I called that number earlier."

"You think you know everything, don't you? We didn't become friendly only recently, as you say. We've been friends for two years, since we were in a local theater production together. She got me the job as her assistant at Mayfield's. I liked her. She was lots of fun, always joking and doing crazy things."

"What about her drug problem?"

"She smoked a little pot, sure, but nothing more than that."

"Roger was her supplier?"

She nodded. "I told her not to go to him about the money, but she had all these hundreds and she was afraid to pass them herself. She'd tried a few here and in New York, but it made her too nervous."

"Her boyfriend had hidden the counterfeit money with her?"

"Sure. He thought it was the safest place, but it didn't keep him from getting killed."

"Roger followed us back to her apartment last night. He was parked across the street."

Sadie turned away. "I told her what to do on the phone earlier."

"What was your advice?"

"I said if he was at the apartment she should manage to make her escape somehow. If he went after her, I'd go up there and take the money before he got it. She'd given me a duplicate key."

"She made her escape all right, by getting killed. Did you go there last night?"

"God, no! When I heard about her death on the news I knew there'd be cops all over the place."

"Where was the money hidden?" Susan asked.

"Inside a folded towel in the bathroom cabinet."

"If it was still, there, the police certainly found it. They were all over that bathroom."

She touched the door handle. "Look, I've got to go. I've told you everything I know."

"Not quite everything. Where can I find Roger?"

"I don't know. He was just a name to me. Betty never told me anything about him."

She left the car quickly, walking across the paved lot to her own little white Neon. Susan sat where she was until Sadie Shepherd had pulled out and vanished down the highway. She wanted to make certain she wasn't being followed.

Back at her hotel she found the Secret Service waiting for her. Adam Dullea intercepted her on the way to the elevator. "You're a tough one to keep up with. I leave you alone for a few hours and you're off on your own."

"I thought I had to clear myself by Thursday morning. I can't do that sitting in a hotel room."

"Where did you go?"

"You mean you didn't have me followed?'

He laughed. "That was my job."

Susan just stood there in the lobby, wondering how much she could safely tell him. Finally she said, "All right, come on up and I'll tell you what I learned."

In the room she opened the minibar and offered him a drink which he declined, "Maybe a Coke, if you're having something." She joined him in one and he said, "Your friend Brentnor's been worried about you."

"I shouldn't be so hard on Mike. He did fly right up here and help rescue me from a jail cell. I just always have the feeling he's waiting for a chance to paw me."

"Has he tried it before?'

"Once or twice. But he backs off when he sees I don't like it."

He sipped his drink. "Where were you this afternoon?"

"Out at the store. I still work for a living."

"So do I. Who did you see there?"

"Betty's assistant, a young woman named Sadie Shepherd."

"Does she know anything about the killing?"

"Betty was an old friend. She told Sadie about the counterfeit money. She was afraid this Roger fellow wanted to take it without paying her price."

"That's about what we figured."

"The money was hidden in the bathroom cabinet with her towels."

"It was?" The news seemed to startle Dullea. "Sergeant Razerwell told me he personally searched the entire bathroom, including the toilet tank."

Susan looked up. A sudden thought struck her. "What's Razerwell's first name?"

"Eric. Don't let your imagination run wild."

She brooded about it for a moment, then remembered something else. "While I was in her bathroom earlier, you said something about the dagger that killed her and I told you there were two daggers."

He shook his head. "Only one."

"There was a second dagger at the bottom of the tub."

"No, just the weapon that killed her. It was still in her back."

She held her breath, eyes closed, and asked one more question. "Were you parked across the street at the time of the murder, watching the apartment?"

"Sure. I told you we were going to use the search warrant last night. I had to make sure she didn't remove the money before my men arrived. When the police came I drove away until I could find out what was going on."

Susan opened her eyes and smiled. "Then I know how it was done."

It was back to Betty Quint's apartment once more. Darkness had settled in and a strong breeze was blowing a few dead leaves down the center of the street. White-haired James Liction opened the door in answer to their ring and seemed more resigned than surprised at seeing them. "What is it? You want to examine the apartment again?"

"I don't think that'll be necessary right now," Susan told him. "I just want to ask you one question."

"Well, you might as well come in. You too, Mr. Dullea. Now what's the question?"

The answer came before she had a chance to ask it. From the kitchen, his wife called out, "Who is it, Roger?"

"It's just—" Liction began. Then he must have seen the expression on Susan's face and realized what had happened. He tried to twist away as Dullea reached out to grab him.

When the Secret Service man had him under control, Mrs. Liction came into the room. "Hey, what's going on?"

"We just have a few questions for your husband, that's all."

She seemed resigned to it. "About the drugs, I suppose."

"That and other things."

Then Susan spoke. "I was going to ask you what the 'R' stood for in R. James Liction, the name on your mailbox. I thought maybe it was Roger. That's what Betty Quint called you, wasn't it?"

"I guess so," he mumbled. "I might have sold her a little pot. Nothing wrong with that."

"Are you growing it in the basement?" Dullea asked. "Some people do."

"Can I call you Roger?" Susan asked, then went on. "Roger, we know Betty offered to sell you a quantity of counterfeit hundred-dollar bills from overseas. She was frightened that you might try to steal them from her."

"I didn't kill her," Liction insisted. He could see where the conversation was leading. "I couldn't have killed her. You were alone with her when it happened."

"How did you know that?' Susan asked. "By looking in the bathroom window from your perch on the fire escape? Yes, I know there's a fire escape outside that window even though I didn't actually look at it. I saw the fire escape to the second floor when I drove up with Betty yesterday, and Mr. Dullea here even commented on the unlikely prospect of a burglar coming through the bathroom window from the fire escape."

Liction moistened his lips. "I think I want a lawyer."

"You'll get one," Adam Dullea said, formally stating his rights. "First thing, we're going to get Sergeant Razerwell down here to make the formal arrest. The murder is his job. I'm just interested in the money."

Mrs. Liction spoke from the doorway. "If we give you the money, will you forget about the killing?'

"Shut up, Mona!" he nearly screamed.

"You see," Susan continued, "I made a big mistake. Betty had seen someone in a car across the street and that frightened her. I thought it was Roger, but she knew it was Mr. Dullea here. She was caught between the two of them, with no way out. Maybe she'd even spotted you on the fire escape, Roger. Anyway, she decided to fake an attack on herself in the shower and escape by being taken to the hospital in an ambulance. She'd done some community theater work and had a fake dagger with one of those collapsible blades, the sort that ejects imitation blood when the blade retracts. It has adhesive to stick to the skin. While she was rummaging for a towel, she took the fake dagger and a real one and attached them to her body with Scotch tape, probably under her arm where I couldn't see it. Her secretary Sadie said she was a great joker. Maybe she'd even pulled this stunt before."

Dullea was shaking his head. "Are you saying she accidentally killed herself?"

"No, no! She meant to tell me she was wounded and to call an ambulance. Then she'd give herself a flesh wound with the real dagger before they arrived, and she'd be rushed to the hospital, escaping both Roger and the Secret Service. But after sticking the collapsing dagger to her back, she let herself fall in the shower and accidentally hit her head, knocking her out for a moment. The real dagger, still taped to her body, came loose and fell in the tub. I saw the daggers and thought she was dead. Roger here had heard her scream, and while I was phoning 911 he came in the window of the bathroom to get the package of money. He must have seen her hide it there earlier. She was beginning to stir in the tub and he stabbed her with the real dagger. He saw that the first one was a fake, so he pulled it off her back and took it with him, along with the money. He went back out the window and closed it behind him."

"How long would that have taken?"

"Not more than thirty seconds, and any sounds would have been covered by the water from the shower, which I hadn't turned off. I stayed out of the bathroom completely after I called the police."

"What would she have told you and the doctors after the hoax was discovered?" Dullea asked.

Susan shrugged. "She'd have had a slight flesh wound to show the doctors, and she'd have thought up some story to explain the knife. She'd have told me it was meant to be a joke and it back-fired. At least she'd be safe from both Roger and you. That was the important thing."

Dullea allowed a brief nod of agreement. "How did you know it was Liction? That first initial wasn't much evidence to go on."

"There was something else. When Betty called Sadie from my hotel room, she said she was going back to her apartment and what should she do if Roger came up and demanded the money. She was saying that Roger lived downstairs, if I'd only known how to interpret her words. And once I knew Roger was so close, the method of murder wasn't so hard to work out. One of the daggers had disappeared, and that meant someone had entered the bathroom before the police arrived. No one came through the door and the window was the only other entrance. If I hadn't killed Betty, the person who entered through the window must have done it. Roger was too likely to be ignored."

It was Mona Liction who returned with the package of counterfeit money while they waited for the police. "Here! Take it! I told him not to get involved in this. Take it and leave us alone."

Adam Dullea reached out a hand as a police car pulled up in front. "I'll take it, but I'm afraid we won't be leaving you alone for quite some time."

Susan Holt's plane from New York landed in Phoenix at 5:45 and Mike Brentnor was there to meet her, having driven his rental car down from the bed-and-bath trade show in Las Vegas a few days earlier. Brentnor was tall and sandy-haired, a few years older than Susan but still in his early thirties. As a buyer for Mayfield's, Manhattan's largest and most prestigious department store, he often worked closely with Susan's promotions department.

"Right on time!" he greeted her, starting to give her a hug until her no-nonsense expression warned him off. "Long flight, huh? Tired out?"

"I'm just all business, Mike, as you know. Save your hugs for the secretaries in the office."

"Aw, Susan! Give a guy a break."

She ignored it and asked, "Have you been out to the training camp."

He nodded as they headed out of the terminal toward his car. She was puling along her small suitcase on wheels, compact enough to fit in the plane's overhead bin. "I drove out yesterday, after I checked in. Roitler wasn't around, though. He's the big cheese who has to approve any exclusive merchandising deals."

"So what do we do now?'

"Get you settled in at the hotel. He's due back in the morning. They've got some nice-looking stuff and you've seen the logo. I think it'll take off."

"If the Tri-City Comets take off." The Comets were one of major league baseball's new expansion teams, just six weeks away from playing their first game. Mayfield's was hoping to land an exclusive contract to handle some of their newer items of merchandise in New York City.

On the drive into the city he said, "A lot of kids will want the jackets just because they're new. That red comet with the three gold stars is a winner. We should talk about it over dinner."

Susan sighed, pushing back the wisp of hair that had a habit of falling over her face. "I think I'll eat in my room and turn in early. I'm still on Manhattan time." Then, trying to end on a friendlier note, she asked, "How was Vegas?"

"You know what those trade shows are like. Even the sight of models wrapped in bath towels can get boring after the first day. I did a little gambling to perk myself up."

"Win anything?"

"The first day. Lost most of it the second day."

He parked in the underground garage at their hotel near the state capitol. She checked in and agreed to meet him for breakfast at eight-thirty in the morning. "The spring-training camp at Bank One Ballpark is right downtown, only ten minutes away, he said, "but we should be there by ten."

"Bank One Ballpark?"

"The locals call it Bob."

Alone in her-room, Susan sat by the telephone trying to think of someone she could call back in New York. Since her breakup with Russell there were only a few friends who might really care that she'd arrived safely. She called one of them and and got an answering machine, hanging up without leaving a message. Could an evening with Mike Brentnor be any worse than this?

Yes, it could, she decided, and went to bed early.

Over breakfast he showed her the Comets' new gold-colored baseball cap with the Tri-City logo. "They're going to be wearing this at all Sunday games, at home and on the road," he told her. "Later on they might adopt a whole different uniform for Sunday games."

Susan put the cap on Mike's head and studied the result. "The kids'll like them," she decided.

After breakfast they drove out to the training camp the team shared with two other teams. It was south of the Phoenix Civic Plaza, near the railroad tracks that bisected the central city, in a sun-baked area of old warehouses just now beginning to change from wasteland to wonderland. A new hotel and a science center had recently opened, Mike told her, along with a retail and restaurant complex with a twenty-four-screen movie theater.

"Their training camp isn't exactly off the beaten path."

"They have to go where the people are, even for non-season games. They're using the new stadium here. It's only been open a year."

Soon they came upon a sign that read: Bank One Ballpark: Winter Home of the Arizona Diamondbacks, the San Diego Padres and the Tri-City Comets. Rather than the small field she'd expected, there was a brick and glass stadium with large full-color, live-feed monitors and a metal retractable roof. The building blended into the area nicely, yet still presented a modern look. Mike pulled into one of the parking areas and they walked to the clubhouse entrance. Their meeting was with Larry Freedman, whom Susan instantly identified as an eastern jock gone to middle-aged flab. He and Mike had talked the previous day.

"It's a pleasure to meet you at last," he said, pulling out a chair for Susan. "We've accomplished a great deal by fax and phone but there's nothing like a face-to-face meeting."

"It must be very exciting to be in on the ground floor of a new major-league baseball team," she said with a smile.

"It is," Freedman answered, probably repeating something he'd said a hundred times before. "The Tri-City folks are great. They're big boosters of the team and they'll be packing our new stadium on opening day."

Mike Brentnor grinned. "All wearing your logo jackets and sweat-shirts."

"You bet!"

Susan unzipped her briefcase. "Here are rough layouts of some of the newspaper ads our art department came up with, Mr. Freedman. As you can see, we'll rely heavily on our exclusive line of the higher-priced Tri-City merchandise."

"Did Mike show you the new Sunday cap?" he asked as he glanced over the layouts.

"He did."

"What do you think?"

"It might be more of a children's item, but that's not my decision."

Freedman lifted a warm-up jacket in the same gold color. "What about this?"

"Nice!" Mike told him. "I have the contracts right here if you're ready to sign."

"This is for the exclusive deal?"

"Exclusive in New York City for two years, with an option to renew. We'll guarantee a major advertising campaign using print ads and TV spots."

Freedman picked up the contract, pretending to read it. "Mr. Roitler will have to approve this. He should be here momentarily."

As if on cue, the door opened and they were joined by a gray-haired man with a moustache to match. Hans Roitler, one of the owners of the Tri-City Comets, was a German-born businessman who'd been brought to America by his parents at the age of eight, just before World War II. He shook hands with Mike and Susan, listening intently while Mike outlined their marketing strategy.

"We've already settled most of the points," Mike told him. "It's just these new high-end items. We think Mayfield's could do very well with these if we had them on an exclusive basis for the first two years, with an option for more." He passed the contract over to the club owner. "Frankly, Mr. Roitler, we don't make much profit selling baseball caps. These higher-priced jackets are another matter entirely." Roitler took out a cigar but didn't light it. He pondered the contract at some length before saying, "A one-year exclusive and no option. That's the best I can do."

"Mr. Roitler—"

He held up a hand to end the discussion. "No, no. Who knows where the Comets will be a year from now? We may have won the World Series. Look at the Marlins. They won it in their fifth season."

Susan knew that Brentnor was pleased with even a one-year exclusive on the items, but he went through the motions before finally agreeing and passing his pen across the table for Hans Roitler's signature. "Let's get this wrapped up today. It's only six weeks till your opening game."

"My attorney will have to vet it first."

Susan could see the frustration on Mike's face. "We need to order the merchandise and—"

"All right. I'll have it faxed back East to him today. We should have his opinion by tomorrow. Can you both stay an extra day?"

"I think so," Susan answered for them.

Larry Freedman was all smiles. "I can show you around the training camp if you'd like. You can watch some batting practice."

Roitler snorted. "If the bats ever arrive."

"They're here, sir. They were delivered to the hotel where the team is staying by mistake and I'm having them sent out on the team bus."

"You had no bats?" Susan asked. "Doesn't everyone have his own?"

"The veteran players often do, but we need bats for practice and replacement when one breaks. We need them for the rookies and the pitchers too. A major league team can go through hundreds in one season. We ordered a gross of them in different sizes and weights."

While the owner went off to fax the contract to his attorney, Freedman took them into the big dome. "Of course, it's not as large as Toronto or Houston or our new stadium back home, but it holds forty-eight thousand people. It's got a retractable roof, air conditioning, and natural turf. There are picnic areas, a children's playground, and even a swimming pool behind the outfield fence. San Diego and Arizona are holding their spring training here, and, of course, our Comets. They have the training and exhibition schedules all worked out to accommodate three teams, and we expect big crowds." He smiled ruefully. "If we don't get 'em, we may be in the old minor-league ballpark for next spring's practice. We might be back there anyway if the Diamondbacks decide we're too disruptive to their own opening-day planning."

Susan watched the workmen repairing the natural turf along the dugouts. Suddenly the loudspeaker squawked and a harsh voice asked, "Larry, have you seen Willa around?"

Freedman lifted his head toward the announcer's booth. "She rode the bus into town to collect the bats, Chet. Anything I can do for you?"

"No, I was just looking for her."

He showed them the team locker rooms and then took them on the elevator to the top of the dome. These are the sky boxes. There are around forty of them here and that's where the real money is, with corporations willing to pay extra for luxury. We have them in the new Comets stadium too." Susan had never been in a sky box before and she was intrigued that the bar and partying area seemed larger than the seating area for actually watching the game.

When they came back to ground level and went outside, Freedman glanced at his watch. "The bus should have been back by now. It's only ten minutes each way, plus time to load the bats. I hope the hotel didn't misplace them."

"Are they in boxes?" Mike asked.

Freedman nodded. "Usually a dozen to a box, though some suppliers pack differently. Willa doesn't have to lift them. She's our front-office manager, Willa Bright. She just went along to supervise and make sure the hotel people loaded all the boxes on the bus."

He pointed out the animated scoreboard that could show replays and crowd scenes as well as graphics, then took them back outside into the morning heat. "How long before Roitler hears back from his attorney?" Mike asked.

"Probably tomorrow morning. If we get an answer today I'll leave a message at your hotel. Meanwhile, take a look around Phoenix. There's a lot to see."

Mike and Susan headed back toward their hotels. Do you think the lawyer will find some reason to change the contract?" she asked.

"I hope not. We've got little enough time now if we want the items on sale for opening day. I'll have to phone Saul." Saul Marx was their boss back in New York.

Susan was more practical. "So long as we have them by the time the Comets come to New York in June, there's no great harm done."

"I suppose not," he grudgingly agreed.

As they pulled out of the parking lot Susan noticed a large green bus at the entrance to another lot across the street. "What's that, Mike?"

"Looks like a bus."

They pulled up beside it and she saw the Comets logo on a large adhesive strip affixed to the side. "This must be the bus they've been waiting for. It may have broken down."

"I don't see any sign of an accident."

Susan got out and went up to the bus door, with Mike reluctantly following.

There was no driver visible and the doors were closed. Mike noticed the driver's window was open slightly and stood on tiptoe to reach through it. "Sometimes this works," he said, feeling around for the right lever to pull. There was a sudden whoosh of compressed air as the passenger door opened.

Susan led the way onto the bus, seeing the empty driver's seat with a pack of cigarettes and stack of hard-rock tapes next to the audio system. Long boxes of bats were piled in the aisle. One box had been opened, and she noticed that the bats were neatly packed, six in each direction.

Except that one was missing.

"My God, Mike!"

"What is it?"

Near the back of the bus, drooped across the seats with her bloodied head dangling in the aisle, was the body of a young woman.

Mike used the missing driver's cellular phone to call the police and then Susan notified Larry Freedman back at the training camp, using the number jotted down on the driver's pad. It took Freedman a moment to realize what she was saying. "A dead woman? Is it Willa?"

"I don't know. Woman in her twenties, short, with brown hair. Wearing a Comets T-shirt and jeans."

"It sounds like her. What happened?"

"Someone hit her with one of the bats. Possibly the driver, since he's not here."

"I'll come right down. Exactly where are you?"

"Not far. A parking lot across the street, near the brew pub."

A police car arrived as she finished talking, and another followed soon after. By the time Larry Freedman reached the scene, along with a man she didn't know, the bus had been searched and a crowd was gathering. Larry introduced his companion as Chet Elton, and as soon as she heard his deep voice she recognized it as the one that had called to Freedman over the stadium's loudspeaker. "Willa works for me in the front office," Elton explained. "What happened here?"

"If that's her on the bus, she's dead," Mike told him. "Killed with a baseball bat. No sign of the driver. Susan and I stopped when we saw the logo on the side of the bus. We knew you were waiting for your bats."

The detective investigating the case was named Cena. He gazed at Susan with dark Latin eyes and asked, "Did you know, the victim?"

"No. Mike and I are here on business from New York. We never met her."

"She was killed with one of the baseball bats. Someone had to open a box and take it out."

Susan shrugged. "She might have done that herself, to make sure it was the correct shipment."

Detective Cena turned back to the others. "Where's the driver?"

Nobody knew. "This bus is used for intercity travel," Chet Elton observed. "Did you check the lavatory in back?"

"Empty," Cena said. "Can you give me the driver's name and address?"

"John Nez. He lives in the mobile-home park out at the Salt River Indian Community. I'd have to look up the actual address."

"You do that. We'll want to talk with him as soon as we can."

"Do you think he killed her?" Freedman asked.

"He's missing. That tells us something. And another thing bothers me too."

"What's that?"

"Like all intercity buses, this one has a large baggage compartment. It's empty."

"It wasn't needed. The bus had no passengers." Freedman showed his exasperation.

Detective Cena remained calm. "Exactly my point. If the baggage compartment was empty, why did they go to the trouble of loading twelve boxes of baseball bats onto the bus itself, in the aisles? Could that have been John Nez's idea, so he'd have a weapon available for the murder?"

Chet Elton was on his cell phone trying to reach Roitler, the team's owner. Police technicians were still taking photographs and measurements. Mike was standing by helplessly, talking in a low voice to Freedman, probably wondering if this event might somehow delay the signing of the contract. Susan decided they didn't need her anymore, and when Cena gave her permission to leave she asked Mike for the keys to the rental car.

"What for? Where you going?"

"I want to run back to the hotel for a bit. You should probably return to the stadium with these people anyway, to see if this will delay the contract. I'll pick you up there later, or you can get a cab back to the hotel."

He nodded absently, handing over the keys. "I'll take a cab. See you back there."

With a road map of Phoenix open on the seat beside her, Susan headed for the freeway that would carry her to the reservation just east of the city. The mobile-home park was shown on the map, and she had no trouble finding it. Hopefully she would arrive ahead of Cena's men.

A couple of Native American men were seated by one of the mobile homes as she drove up. "I'm looking for John Nez."

One of the men motioned down the street. "Last trailer on the left."

"Thanks."

She pulled up in front of the mobile home, already hearing the beat of rock music and remembering the tapes on the bus. There was a little black Toyota parked in the driveway but the music was coming from inside the home. A slender woman in her thirties came to the screen door when Susan rang the bell. "Is John Nez at home?" she asked.

The woman, whose features appeared more Mexican than Native American, eyed her suspiciously. "Are you from the Indian Agency? Is it about my Toyota?"

"No, I'm working over at the new ballpark." Not exactly a lie, she decided. "Are you Mrs. Nez?"

"That's me. Delores." She glanced back over her shoulder. "John's getting ready to leave, I don't know if he has time to talk."

"Where is he going?" Susan asked, but before the woman could answer a man appeared behind her.

"I'm John Nez. Who wants me?" There was no doubt that he was a Native American, with the weathered skin and chiseled features so familiar to Susan from the movies and television. He wore a workshirt and jeans that seemed about to burst.

"Susan Holt. There's been an accident with the bus you were hired to drive. The police will be here soon to question you."

"John, what's she talking about?" his wife asked.

"Be quiet, Delores. What do you want, Miss Holt?"

"Is there a place we can talk?"

"You can talk right here," the woman insisted.

Nez ignored her. "The park across the street," he suggested to Susan, motioning toward a little square of grass with a single bench and a few pieces of playground equipment. When they'd gone over there he asked, "What's this all about?"

"I think you know, Mr. Nez. A woman was killed on the bus you were driving. Willa Bright, the Comets' office manager. Don't pretend you weren't there. The police already think you killed her."

"You're a cop, aren't you?"

"No. I work for a department store back in New York. I just want to help get to the bottom of this so it doesn't interfere with a business deal."

"Why do they think it was me?"

"Probably because you ran away from the scene."

"I didn't kill that woman."

"Then why did you run?"

He kicked at a loose stone by his feet. "Reservation folks don't get a fair shake from the law. They'd listen to my story and lock me up for life."

She stared into John Nez's sad brown eyes. "Why don't you try out the story on me? What happened on the bus?"

"I picked her up at the stadium this morning. We drove to the hotel and I waited while they loaded those bats. I guess the company got mixed up and sent them there instead of the stadium."

"Louisville Sluggers?"

"Nah, they were cheap bats from across the border. They don't use 'em in real games, just for practice."

"I never heard of such a thing!"

"All I know is what they tell me."

"The police think the loading of the bats onto the bus itself rather than in the baggage compartment might have been done to provide you with a handy weapon."

"No, no!" he insisted. "That's not what happened at all."

"Then tell me."

"She wanted the bats inside."

"Willa did?"

He nodded. "She told me she wanted to check them over to make sure they were the ones she'd ordered."

"The drive only takes about ten minutes. She couldn't wait that long?"

"You'd have to ask her."

"I can't. She's dead."

He thought about that for a moment and then started talking. "I couldn't see her. She was behind me in the back of the bus, opening one of the boxes. I was playing a loud tape and couldn't hear very well." Susan nodded, remembering the tapes of rock music. "I did hear a noise of some sort, maybe a bat dropping, and I looked around. I saw her body hanging over the seat and all that blood, and I pulled off the road into one of the empty parking lots by the stadium. I went back to look at her and she was dead I don't know how it happened. Maybe I hit a bump and the bat—"

"That was no bump," Susan assured him. "She was deliberately hit with a bat, very hard. If you didn't do it, who did? Who else was on the bus with you?"

He moistened his lips with a nervous tongue. "No one. There was just the two of us. I swear!"

"Could one of the people from the hotel have stayed on the bus after they got the bats loaded?"

Nez shook his head. "I sat there in the driver's seat the whole time. Two of the bellmen loaded the boxes while Willa supervised. I saw them both get off."

"All right. What did you do after she was killed?"

"I ran away," he admitted. "I got off the bus and started running. I cut through the Civic Plaza and found a taxi to bring me home. I knew the city cops and the tribal police would be after me."

"A taxi? Where was your car?"

"It's not running. The company lets me drive the bus home at night till I get it fixed."

"Do you have a police record, John?"

"Little things, way back. Drugs, mostly. But I didn't want to be arrested again."

His story was so unbelievable that she believed it. Any killer could make up a better story than that. "Take my advice and wait for the police to come, John. Anyone can understand panic. If you run away now they'll come after you, convinced you're the killer. When they find you, out there in the desert or wherever, they might shoot first."

Perhaps he might have agreed to her suggestion. She never had an opportunity to find out. A tribal-police car came into view, traveling fast. A Phoenix police car was right behind it in a cloud of dust. John Nez's options had run out.

Mike Brentnor was angry. Pacing back and forth across the hotel room, he directed his fury at Susan. "Damn it, you can't keep doing this, meddling in police work all the time! Mayfield'll have you out on the street, and I'll be right behind you!

"They've never complained before," she murmured.

"Well, they're complaining now. Saul Marx is furious at both of us. The police think you were encouraging John Nez to run away, and Roitler has put the entire contract matter aside till this is resolved."

It was early evening and they were at the hotel, following hours of police questioning and phone calls back to New York. Nez was in jail, held on suspicion of murder, though he hadn't yet been formally charged. "What motive did he have for killing her?' Susan wanted to know. "The police say she wasn't sexually assaulted."

"But he admitted to you that he was alone on the bus with her. Who else could have done it?"

Susan didn't answer. Instead she asked, "Just what did Roitler say about the merchandising contract?"

"That he was too upset to go into that now. Apparently he was very close to Willa Bright and her death was quite a blow to him."

"I have to get back there in the morning," she said.

"Right now, I don't think they want to see either of us."

But by morning, things had changed again. Susan was awakened at seven-thirty by the buzzing of the telephone next to her bed. "Hello?" she answered sleepily, about to be angry with Mike for awakening her.

"Miss Holt, this is Larry Freedman at the ballpark. Sorry to bother you so early."

She was instantly awake. "That's all right, Mr. Freedman. What's up?"

"Mr. Roitler has heard from his attorney back East. He just called to give his approval to the contract."

"That's good news. I was afraid things might be delayed."

"Mr. Roitler would like to see you before he signs. Without Mike Brentnor, if that's possible."

"Certainly."

"Could you come over now? You can have breakfast here if you haven't eaten yet."

"I'll be there in a half-hour," she promised and hung up. She knew it would mean more trouble with Mike, but she had little choice.

Freedman escorted her to the office Hans Roitler was using during spring training, then left them alone. The team owner waved his hand. "Isn't this luxurious, Miss Holt? My office back home at the Comets' new stadium won't be nearly so plush."

"It's very nice," she agreed. After a few words of regret about the previous day's tragedy, she got right to business. "I understand your attorney has approved our contract calling for exclusive New York City rights to the merchandise we listed."

He nodded. "With the proviso it be limited to one year, with any additional periods to be negotiated. Here, they drew up this revised contract and faxed it to me. There are two copies."

This was where it got awkward. She skimmed through the words without really seeing them and finally said, "Mike Brentnor is the one who'd have to sign this for the store. I'm just along to handle the promotional aspects."

"That's why I wanted to speak to you alone, Miss Holt, to discuss our joint interest in promotion, though I'll tell you that in any case I always prefer dealing with an attractive young woman. You must realize that anything which reflects badly on the Tri-City Comets is certain to hurt sales of our merchandise, in Mayfield's and every other store."

"Of course."

"I understand that when the police went to that bus driver's trailer on the reservation yesterday, they found you with him."

"We were talking, yes."

"About what, may I ask?"

"About the killing of your office manager. I've had some success helping the police in the past. I thought I might lend a hand."

"I believe Detective Cena is in charge of the investigation."

"He used some bad reasoning yesterday in casting suspicion on John Nez, the bus driver. Because the boxes of bats were stored inside the bus rather than in the baggage compartment, he thought it meant that Nez had wanted a weapon handy to kill Willa. But if he'd planned to kill her he certainly would have brought a weapon with him. He wouldn't have found it necessary to load twelve heavy boxes of baseball bats into the bus so he could use one of them. When I asked Nez about it, he told me it was Willa who'd wanted the boxes inside the bus so she could check the order. He also told me the bats were cheap ones from across the border."

"What does that prove?"

"Nothing in itself, but I'd like to examine them."

"Do you really think we're smuggling cocaine or something inside baseball bats?"

Susan smiled. "I know it sounds ridiculous, but I do read occasional stories of players corking their bats to add distance to their hits. If a cylinder of cork can be inserted into a bat, I suppose something else could too."

"Need I remind you once again that anything hurting the Comets hurts Mayfield's as well?"

Susan folded the revised contract and put it in her purse. "I'll show this to Mike. But there's no way we can be part of a cover-up, especially since an innocent man could be charged with a crime he didn't commit."

"Don't be too certain of John Nez's innocence," Roitler said. "He may not have told you that he was having an extra-marital affair with the victim."

"With Willa Bright?" She knew the surprise showed on her face. "But the team just arrived here."

"Willa was part of the advance guard. She'd been here for three weeks, making arrangements for everything, including the team bus to run between the hotel and the stadium. She's the one who hired Nez."

"And you think he killed her?"

"It may have been a lovers' quarrel. Let it go at that, Miss Holt."

She left the office not knowing what to think. The stadium roof was open to the morning sun and she paused for a few minutes, watching some players tossing a ball back and forth. Another was swinging a bat. On the plane out from New York she'd read newspaper accounts of the new expansion teams. She knew they liked to build their stadiums downtown rather than on the outskirts of a city, to make a trip to the game an event which could include dinner before and a drink after. It brought new business to the entire area. The expansion teams acquired their players by first hiring some free-agent amateurs and then picking from a special expansion-team pro draft. After a few trades with existing teams, they were ready for spring training, where the final choices would be made. Then it was on to opening day.

She realized with a jolt that she had the power to change that scenario for the Tri-City Comets.

Back at the hotel Susan found Mike Brentnor pacing the lobby waiting for her. "Where've you been, for God's sake? When I saw the car was missing I figured you'd gone off someplace."

She told him where she'd been and what Hans Roitler had to say about her activities: "He really didn't like me going out to the reservation to talk with that bus driver. I think he's hiding something, Mike. He takes the position that what's bad for the Comets is bad for Mayfield's."

"Well, he's right in a sense. The whole deal depends on the success of his new team."

She handed over the contract Roitler had signed. "Then you'd better sign this."

"You've got it! Good!" He started reading through it for the changes.

"I'll see you later."

"Now where are you going? We should get an afternoon plane back to New York."

"There's something I have to do first."

She didn't tell him that she was on her way to see Detective Cena. The Police and Public Safety Building was on South Third Street and she drove directly there.

Cena didn't seem surprised to see her. "You have something to add to yesterday's statement, Miss Holt."

"I have. Are those bats still here?"

"The bus was towed in as evidence, along with the bats. We'd planned on returning them to the team today, all but the murder weapon."

"You'd better look inside one of them. Cut it open, or whatever you have to do."

Cena allowed himself a slight smile. "We've already done that, miss. My men X-rayed one and it looked suspicious."

"Cocaine?"

He shook his head. "Anabolic steroids, the sort sometimes used by athletes. Only this is a new stronger type being made in Latin America. They're illegal in this country. I believe Mr. Roitler wanted to ensure a winning team in his first year. We're checking to see what laws were violated. Now tell me what you know about all this."

Susan took a deep breath and told him.

There was no rock music playing at John Nez's mobile home this time. Though the Toyota was still in the driveway and Nez had been let out on bail, she knew he wasn't home. His wife came to the door and confirmed it. "The police came for him a few minutes ago. They want to question him further. Something about those bats."

"Can I come in, Mrs. Nez."

"Sure!" She held open the screen door and Susan entered.

"The place is a mess. I've got to get some cleaning done."

Susan took a seat. "Your husband is in trouble," she began at once. "The police have found illegal steroids inside those bats, apparently smuggled across the border."

The news seemed to surprise her. "He wasn't involved in anything like that, was he?"

"They're not sure. Since Willa Bright wanted the bats inside the bus so she could check them, it seems likely that she knew. One problem is that the way your husband tells it, only he could have killed her. He insists he was alone on the bus with her when it happened. That's why he panicked and ran away."

"Do you believe that?"

Susan looked into the woman's eyes. "No, I don't. They say he was having an affair with her, one that started some weeks back when she rented the team bus and got him as a driver." Delores Nez's expression never changed. "If he'd planned to kill her, he'd have had some other weapon with him. And I don't see it as a spur-of-the-moment thing. I think someone else did it."

"Without John seeing or hearing them?"

"He was driving the bus, playing loud rock music, and there is one place where the killer could have hidden."

"Where's that?"

"In the lavatory at the back of the bus. The killer emerged, picked up one of the bats, hit Willa Bright with it, and returned to the hiding place. When the police searched, it was empty. But of course the killer would have left the bus right after your husband."

Delores Nez smiled slightly. "You're forgetting one thing. The killer had no opportunity to board the bus in the first place. John would never have left his bus unguarded. And if he did, Willa would have been there."

"Exactly," Susan agreed. "The killer had no opportunity aboard the bus and hide in the lavatory, once he began the trip. The killer had to hide there before the trip began."

"That shows how wrong you are! He didn't pick up the bus at the garage. It was parked in our driveway overnight."

"I know that," said Susan quietly. "He told me earlier."

"So no one could have hidden in it before he drove to the stadium to pick up that woman."

"You could have, Delores. You could have slipped onto the bus just before he left."

"Why would I do that?"

"To catch Willa and your husband together, to confirm what you already suspected. After you heard the talking, after John turned up the music, you came out of the lavatory, hit her while she checked them over. You killed her, Delores, and hid in the lavatory until John left the bus. Then made your own escape and took a cab right home, arriving here before he did."

"I'd have been a fool to do that," she argued. "For all I know, he might have driven the bus to the police station instead of abandoning it."

"You were married to him. You knew about his past record. It was a good guess that he'd run. Besides, you hadn't planned to kill her until you heard them talking. Isn't that true?"

There was a moment's silence and then she spoke up angrily. "I hadn't planned it but I'm glad I killed her! She came here for a few weeks and stole my husband away. John was a good man until she came to town. She didn't care about him, not really. She'd be back home in April. He was only another conquest, and I couldn't let that happen. We may live out here in a trailer, but I don't let women like her treat me like dirt!"

"You have to tell the police, Delores."

She snorted at that. "Police? You think they can prove anything? There's no evidence against me."

"They'll find the cab that picked you up and brought you back here."

"That proves nothing."

Then Susan told her. "You know why the police took your husband away just before I arrived, Delores? It was so he wouldn't be playing his loud rock music. It was so this wire I'm wearing could pick up every word you said."

She dove for Susan in a sudden blind fury. If there'd been a baseball bat handy she'd have swung it before Detective Cena ever got through the door. As it was, he had to yank her off Susan and quickly handcuff her.

The Mayfield's contract was never signed. Hans Roitler was too busy trying to explain the smuggled steroids to the authorities, the baseball commissioner, and the press. Mike and Susan flew back to an unhappy Saul Marx.

Six weeks later the Tri-City Comets lost their opening game.

A CONVERGENCE OF CLERICS

The first thing that struck her as odd was the number of Catholic priests who seemed to have booked passage on the maiden transatlantic voyage of the *Dawn Neptune*, one of the largest and most luxurious cruise ships afloat. Susan Holt stood on the upper deck watching them board and realized there must be fifty or more of them.

Of course, for a ship carrying twenty-five hundred passengers, that wasn't a large percentage, but it was still worth noting for Susan. She was on board as director of promotions for Manhattan's largest and most prestigious department store, and her job was to gauge public reaction to the opening of the very first Mayfield's branch on a cruise ship.

She was one of those who'd pushed for the seagoing store at board meetings a year or more ago, when the ship was still being built. "Where else can you find a captive audience this large, in one place for seven days, or fourteen days if they do the round trip? Every one of those twenty-five hundred people is going to walk past our shop a couple of times a day, and chances are every one of them will come in to look around at least once during the voyage. The shops were arranged around an atrium three stories high that wouldn't have seemed out of place in New York's newest luxury hotel. The space allotted to Mayfield's shop, some two thousand square feet, was almost as large as the ship's casino. Following the customary life-jacket drill upon sailing, Susan was standing outside the shop, admiring the look of the place, when Sid Cromwell, the ship's security officer, came along behind her. "Thinking of buying something?"

"Hi, Sid. It's impressive, isn't it?" She'd known Sid when he worked security at Mayfield's years ago.

"This your first store on a cruise ship?"

"The first, but maybe not the last. What are all the priests doing onboard?"

"We're sailing to Italy, remember? There's a big papal conference scheduled for next week and we offered discounts to any clergy attending it. We have fifty-six, I believe. They were hoping for more, but even with the discounts I guess it's cheaper to fly."

They were departing from New York and sailing across the Atlantic with stops at the Azores and Gibraltar before going on to Naples and then to Greece. The cruise line had chartered buses to take the clergymen from Naples to Rome, about a three-hour trip. "You taking the round trip with us?" he asked.

She shook her head. "Flying home from Italy. Just wanted to see how the shop managed on its maiden voyage and how we can improve it next time."

She left him and entered the shop. Lisa Mandrake, the manager, was ringing up a sale. "That your first one?" Susan asked as the customer departed with a familiar Mayfield's shopping bag on her arm.

Lisa was younger than Susan, a chipper girl in her twenties who'd come to New York to be an actress and ended up at Mayfield's. She was a good choice to manage their first floating store. "Third so far, and we're barely out of port." She was all smiles, as were her two assistants.

"I'll check with you periodically, to get a fix on what's selling best."

One of the priests had entered while they talked and he interrupted to ask if they had any men's sport shirts. "Right over here, Father," Lisa directed him.

He glanced at Susan, somewhat embarrassed, apparently feeling an explanation was called for. "I knew we'd be wearing our black suits and collars in Rome. It didn't occur to me that my fellow clergymen would wear more casual attire aboard ship."

Susan thought she should introduce herself. "I'm Susan Holt, Mayfield's director of promotions. This is our first shipboard shop and we're interested in customer reactions."

He beamed at her, looking younger than he probably was. "Father John Ullman from Omaha. This is a first for me, too, my first cruise. So far I'm enjoying it immensely." She guessed him to be in his mid thirties, with a friendly, youthful face and dark hair showing the first strands of gray at the temples.

"Is this your first trip to Rome?"

"I flew over for the Holy Year Jubilee in 2000, and I've wanted to go back ever since. It's a wonderful city, especially for Catholics."

Lisa helped him pick out a dark blue sport shirt with a pattern of small, subtle palm trees and he left quite pleased. "We should run a special on sportswear for priests," she said with a chuckle.

An older priest came in, introducing himself as Father Broderick. He already had a sport shirt, but was looking for some socks. "Any color but black," he told Lisa. "I think I'm the eldest in our flock and I don't want to look it."

Susan chatted with him for a few minutes and then went off.

She was at the first seating for dinner, and she joined more than a thousand other passengers in a huge dining room that ran the width of the ship. Sid Cromwell had been assigned to the same table, and he arranged to sit next to her. "So what have you been doing with your life, Susan? Are you still living with Russell?"

"Not for nearly eight years. You're really behind the times, Sid. I'm a full-time career woman now, in charge of Mayfield promotions."

He reached over and tucked in a loose strand of her hair. "You must do something besides work all the time."

"Sure. I lie awake nights thinking of more work I can take on."

"You won't have much to do on this crossing, just check in at the shop a couple of times a day. We could relax and enjoy ourselves."

"Aren't you working security?"

"I get time off. Are you sharing a cabin with someone?"

She shook her head. "All to myself. It's one of the perks of the job."

"Suppose I come by your stateroom tonight around ten when I'm off duty. We could go up to the Crow's Nest on the top deck for a nightcap."

She considered the offer. "Ring my room when you're off. If I'm free I'll meet you up there. I'm in 556."

Father Ullman wasn't the only priest who'd come aboard the *Dawn Neptune* without casual clothes. After dinner Susan saw a second one, about the same age as Father Ullman but with thinner hair and more of a paunch. She approached him as he was leaving the dining room. "Pardon me, Father."

He turned toward her with a smile. "Yes, my dear?"

"I'm Susan Holt from the Mayfield's shop here on board. We've had some priests stop in to look over our sport shirts. I thought I'd mention it in case you wanted to be a bit more casual on shipboard."

"Well, thank you, young lady. I'm Father Dempsey from Little Rock. I might take you up on that suggestion."

"You've got quite a group going to Rome."

"This is just a small contingent. We have another couple hundred flying over. I preferred this more leisurely method of travel, even if it is more expensive."

"The *Dawn Neptune* is quite a ship," Susan said.

"That it is! I already had the tour of the ship's bridge and met the captain."

"Captain Mason. We had some meetings with him last month about opening our shop. You'll see him again at tomorrow night's dinner. It's more of a dress-up affair and he'll be greeting everyone at the door. They'll even take your picture with him, if you like. That's the way these things usually work."

Father Dempsey smiled at her. "This isn't your first cruise."

"I've been on a couple for pleasure, but this is a working one. I have to write a report on Mayfield's first shipboard shop."

They chatted awhile longer and then Father Dempsey went off with one of the other priests who wore a sport shirt with his black trousers. Susan checked in at the Mayfield's shop and found that business was still brisk. Lisa Mandrake was waiting on customers while one of her assistants was restocking the selection of bathing suits. There'd already been a crowd at the ship's pool.

She was back in her stateroom well before ten and when Sid Cromwell phoned about that drink she was more than willing to join him. The Crow's Nest was on the very top passenger deck, just below the ship's bridge. It afforded a spectacular forward view of the ship's progress. Even at night there was often something to see. "Look there!" Sid said while they waited for their drinks. "That's lightning."

It was indeed, and for the next twenty minutes, over their drinks, they were treated to a rare view of a thunderstorm at sea, growing constantly closer until it veered off to the south and out of sight. "You don't see those every day," Susan commented.

"I arranged it just for your first night," Sid told her with a grin.

"How about you? Are you keeping busy on security matters?"

"Not yet. That usually comes around the third or fourth day, when the close environment of the ship starts fraying nerves and causing altercations. Of course, this is the *Dawn Neptune's* first transatlantic voyage and things might be different."

"What about robberies?"

"Ships usually have them, but no more so than a big Manhattan hotel. I know your Mayfield's shop has closed-circuit TV to discourage shoplifters."

Susan nodded. "I suspect shoplifting might be less of a problem on cruise ships. All they could do with their loot would be to take it back to their stateroom where a search might uncover it. And just about everyone shares a cabin with a friend or relative who might become suspicious."

Cromwell nodded. "I have my own room in the crew quarters on the lower deck, but it's pretty small. Yours is probably larger."

"Umm," Susan replied, sipping her drink. She wasn't about to invite Sid Cromwell to her room for any reason. He was a casual acquaintance, a nice guy but nothing more. She wondered if agreeing to this drink had been a mistake.

At that moment the beeper on his belt came to life. He glanced at the text message and stood up. "They need me for something. Sorry to cut this short. I was enjoying it."

"Another time," she said with a smile.

In the morning, on her way down to breakfast, Susan stopped to check on the shop. Lisa Mandrake and the other girls were already there, an hour before opening, restocking the shelves and changing the displays around. It was Lisa who said, "Did you hear the news? One of the priests got killed last night!"

"What?"

"Yes. The priest he was sharing the room with found his body."

"Are you saying someone killed him? Murdered him?"

"That's what I hear."

Susan hurried down to breakfast, hoping to learn more. Across the room Sid Cromwell was deep in conversation with Captain Mason and two other ship's officers. When he left them, she caught up with him as he headed for the door. "What's this I hear about a priest being killed?"

"Hi, Susan. It's true. That was the page that interrupted our drink last night. His cabin mate came back to their room around ten-thirty and found him stabbed to death on the bed. This is a terrible thing for the cruise line. They're trying to hush it up, but the word is spreading fast."

He kept walking as he spoke and she hurried to keep up with him. "Who's in charge of the investigation?"

"I guess I am, for the moment. Crimes on the high seas fall under admiralty law. If we were in port, the local police would be summoned, but for the moment it's up to me to investigate and take statements. Since the victim is an American citizen, we've notified the FBI. They'll have an agent meet the ship in the Azores, but that's still two days away." He was walking a few steps ahead of her but suddenly he stopped. "Come to think of it, maybe you should have a look at the stateroom. The body's been removed."

"Why should I—?"

"You may have met him. We found a Mayfield's bag in the room. Looks like he was one of your customers."

Susan felt a chill run through her. "What was his name?" Cromwell consulted his notepad. "Father John Ullman from Omaha."

She nodded. "I was there yesterday when he came in for a sport shirt."

"Come along. Maybe when you see his things you'll remember something about him that could help us."

The staterooms for the priests had been grouped more or less together in the 600 numbers. She remembered Father Ullman saying he was in 675. When they reached it, another man wearing black pants and a sport shirt was standing outside.

"Are you finished with the room now?" he asked. "I spent the rest of the night sleeping on deck."

"Sorry, Father. Susan, this is Father Stillwell. He found the body."

She introduced herself and asked, "Did you share the room with Father Ullman?"

"That's right. We just met yesterday. I have a parish in Spokane."

Sid Cromwell unlocked the stateroom door. "I had the room dusted for fingerprints, but I expect the FBI will want to check it over in the Azores. I'll arrange another room for you, Father."

"I hope so," he muttered. "I don't think I'd want to sleep in there."

"What did you do when you found him?" Susan asked.

"I—I phoned for help and gave him the last rites. It was terrible. I'd only known him a few hours, but it was terrible."

"Don't touch anything," the security man cautioned. "Susan, that's your store bag in the corner, isn't it?"

It was indeed the very bag Lisa Mandrake had used for the sport shirt he bought. Susan could see a splatter of dried blood half obscuring the Mayfield's name. "Was he wearing our shirt when he died?" she asked.

Cromwell shook his head. "Just an undershirt and pants."

"So his visitor was probably male. A priest would have slipped on a proper shirt to receive a female guest."

"Maybe, maybe not." He'd donned a pair of latex gloves and was carefully opening the dresser drawers. The roommate, Father Stillwell, was standing in the doorway, afraid to come all the way in. Sid Cromwell lifted a large manila envelope from one of the drawers and asked, "Is this yours, Father?"

"No. It must have been his."

He opened it and slid out a thick sheaf of paper. After a moment's inspection he closed the envelope. "I'd better take this with me," he said.

They left the room and Sid locked the door, placing a seal over the slot for the key card. "When this is over I still owe you a drink," he told Susan.

She dined that night with Lisa Mandrake from the shop, who was assigned to a nearby table and easily made the switch. The conversation was about the murder, as it was throughout the ship. No announcement had been made, but the word had traveled fast. "They say the FBI will be coming aboard at the Azores," Lisa told Susan.

"I understand that's routine on the high seas when an American citizen is involved. You know, he was one of your customers—the young priest who bought a sport shirt yesterday."

"Yes, his roommate, Father Stillwell, told me. He was just wandering around without a room, but I guess they found one for him."

"Have any of the other priests stopped in?"

"None that I recognized. We're attracting a lot of women, though."

Susan let her gaze travel across the large dining room. Since dress was more formal tonight, she spotted the tables of priests quite easily. They'd all worn their black suits and clerical collars for their photographs with Captain Mason. Between courses, Susan went over to see how Father Stillwell was doing.

"Did they find another stateroom for you?" she asked.

"They have me right up next to Captain Mason," he said with a smile. "He'll have me steering the ship next."

She glanced around for anyone else she knew. "I don't see Father Dempsey."

"His stomach was a bit off. He said it was nothing serious." Sid Cromwell saw her standing by the priests' table and came over to her. "Could I see you after dinner? Up in the Crow's Nest?"

"Sure."

She assumed he was going to buy her that drink, but when she joined him at the table an hour later he had something else in mind. "Captain Mason is concerned about this killing, especially since the victim was a priest on his way to Rome. He says it's terrible publicity and bad luck for something like this to happen on a ship's maiden voyage. To him it's like the *Titanic* sinking. He says if we don't have the killer in a cell by the time we hit the Azores it might mean his job. And by implication it might mean my job, too."

"In a cell?"

"We've got an actual cell, with bars, down below in case it's needed. Most big cruise ships have them these days." He took a sip of his drink. "I remembered when I worked security for Mayfield's you were involved in some crime investigations. You were quite successful in solving a few puzzles."

"That was years ago, Sid. Believe me, my job as director of store promotions has nothing to do with solving crimes."

"This job means a lot to me, Susan. If you could help out—"

She sighed. "What can I do?"

For the first time she noticed the large manila envelope on the seat next to him. It looked like the one he'd found in the dead man's drawer. He opened it and said, "Look at these."

There were several dozen copies of a one-page form giving details of some sort of investment opportunity for clergymen, aimed at supplying extra income for their retirement years. At the bottom were spaces for a signature, address, phone number, and social-security number. "Interesting," Susan commented, glancing through the stack of identical forms. "I'll bet you counted them."

He nodded. "Fifty-five. Father Ullman had fifty-five fellow priests on the voyage."

"You suspect this is some sort of swindle?"

"I wouldn't be surprised."

"But a priest swindling fellow priests?" Susan protested.

"Who's to say he was a real priest? I've sent a message to the Omaha archdiocese to check up on him."

"I can talk to some of the others," she volunteered, "to see if he approached any of them. But it was the first day of the voyage and there are no completed forms in here."

"See what you can find out. We'll be in the Azores by Thursday morning and I need to have something before that."

After breakfast on a sunny Wednesday Susan walked past the photo gallery where passengers could purchase pictures of themselves with Captain Mason, then sought out the company of the priests. They were easy to spot beside the pool on the upper deck because Father Dempsey was with them in his usual black suit and Roman collar. "Are you feeling better?" Susan asked him.

"Fine. I wasn't really sick, just a brief bit of diarrhea. I'll have to eat twice as much at dinner tonight."

She settled down in the deck chair next to him. "I thought you'd be in the pool with the rest of the clergy."

He chuckled at that. "Dear lady, no one would want to see this paunch in bathing trunks."

Father Stillwell, the victim's roommate, came out of the pool with dripping hair and walked over to join them. "Any news on the killing yet?"

Susan shook her head. "Nothing I've heard."

"I just thought of something," he said. "You know that shirt he bought at your shop? When he tried it on it was a bit snug and he phoned the shop to see if they had a larger size."

"Oh?"

"I think the woman there was going to drop it off at our stateroom and pick up the other one. I remember thinking Mayfield's was very accommodating to do that."

"We like to be accommodating," Susan murmured, wondering if she was missing something here.

She left them at the pool and took the elevator down to the atrium floors. Lisa Mandrake was bagging a customer's purchase and returning her credit card as Susan entered. When she'd finished, Susan motioned toward the small stockroom at the back of the store. "Could I see you for a minute, Lisa?"

"Sure. What's up?"

She closed the door so the other clerks wouldn't overhear their conversation. "Did you go to Father Ullman's cabin Monday night?"

Lisa avoided her gaze. "He needed a larger size shirt and I took it to him after we closed. Nothing wrong with that."

"What was wrong was your not mentioning it. What time was this?"

"I closed the shop at ten and went to his room then. But I didn't even go inside. I think he had someone with him."

"Perhaps the killer. You should have told Sid Cromwell about it. His roommate found Ullman's body around ten-thirty. You were probably the last person to see him alive."

"Except the killer," she corrected. "You certainly can't think that I had anything to do with his death."

"It would have looked better if you'd revealed this at the beginning. You're sure you weren't in his room? I don't want Sid thinking he tried to molest you and you stabbed him."

"My God, Susan! The man was a priest! I know you read about those things sometimes, but Father Ullman was just a young innocent guy. He didn't try to molest me and I didn't stab him!"

"All right, keep your voice down. I believe you."

They exited the stockroom and Lisa returned to waiting on customers. Susan took the escalator down to the lobby floor, searching for Sid Cromwell, who was nowhere in sight. She asked at the desk for the security office and was directed down the corridor, where she found him at his desk. "I was going to come looking for you," he told her. "Here's a reply from my query to the Omaha archdiocese."

She took it and read quickly: *Rev. John Ullman, 34, native of Little Rock, AR; ordained 1999, served in St. Michael's and Sacred Heart parishes in Omaha. Intelligent; highly regarded.* A photograph had been faxed along with the message and it clearly showed the dead man.

"Well, there's no doubt it's him," Susan admitted. "So much for that theory."

"I also checked that manila envelope for fingerprints. There were none. I wore gloves when I handled it, and apparently it had been wiped clean before that."

She thought about it. "Well, what do we have? A possible scheme to swindle priests out of their money. The only evidence is that envelope of forms. Maybe it didn't belong to the victim. Maybe it belonged to Father Stillwell, his roommate. Naturally when you asked him, he would have denied any knowledge of it."

"I'm going to hold a meeting of all the priests on board. It's probably something I should have done yesterday. This individual questioning is getting us nowhere."

"Some of them are on the upper deck right now. They could probably spread the word to the others."

Sid got to his feet. "Let's go see if we can get them all together this afternoon. The captain really wants us to have something for the FBI tomorrow."

It wasn't hard to do. Most of the clergymen were in the pool or the gym, while others were playing shuffleboard or Ping-Pong. Susan found Father

Dempsey on the putting green. "They have everything here," he said. "I may skip Rome and stay on for the return trip."

"The Pope wouldn't approve of that," she said.

"No, I suppose he wouldn't."

"The ship's security officer has asked me to gather all the clergy together at two this afternoon."

"It's about Father Ullman, of course."

Susan nodded. "We're meeting in the small auditorium, where you all say Mass in the mornings."

"I'll be there."

Next she sought out Father Broderick, the senior priest on board. She found him at a more sedate bingo game on a lower deck. "You're not wearing your colored socks, Father," she said.

He shook his head sadly. "It's not a time for frivolity after what happened to Father Ullman. I'll be saying Mass for him in the morning."

"Mr. Cromwell, the ship's security officer, wants all the clergy assembled where you have Mass. Be there at two this afternoon. We're trying to determine if anyone might have seen Father Ullman speaking with other passengers."

"A good idea. I'll tell the others when I see them."

Then Susan hurried through the atrium to Mayfield's. She spoke to Lisa and arranged for her to be at the meeting, too. Time was running out. The FBI would be taking over in another twenty-four hours. She spoke to Sid again just before the meeting with the clergy began, then stood in the back of the small auditorium with Lisa while the priests filed in.

"Fifty-five," she said, doing a quick count. "The word got around to everyone."

Sid Cromwell opened the meeting with a few words about the killing and his investigation so far. "An FBI agent will be coming aboard tomorrow in the Azores, but I hope to have everything cleared up by then. We're investigating two possible motives for Father Ullman's murder. One involves the possibility that someone was trying to swindle the clergy with a questionable retirement scheme. Have any of you been approached while you were on board?"

The priests glanced around at each other, shaking their heads. Father Broderick stood up so he could see them all, but no one raised his hand to offer any information. "How about Monday night?" Sid continued. "Did you see anyone with Father Ullman, especially around nine or ten o'clock?"

Only his roommate, Father Stillwell, raised his hand. "I ate with him and we stopped at the bar for a bit of sherry. That was the last I saw of him."

Susan knew Sid had heard all that before. There was nothing new to be had from these priests. "All right," he said grimly."I want to move on to the second possibility. I have information that Father Ullman purchased a sport shirt at the Mayfield's shop shortly after we sailed on Monday afternoon. He needed a larger size, and the shop's manager brought him one when she closed up at ten o'clock. There's a possibility that something happened between them in the cabin and Lisa Mandrake stabbed—"

"*No!*" Lisa shouted, springing away from Susan's side. "You're not pinning this on me! He had a visitor with him when I brought the shirt and I know who it was!"

"Then please tell me," Cromwell said, "and we can put an end *to* this business."

"I'll tell the FBI tomorrow, and no one else."

"Miss Mandrake, I'm afraid I'll have to insist."

She ignored him and started out of the room. "Hold her!" Sid yelled.

Susan grabbed her arm and pulled her around. Lisa aimed a punch at her but missed. She was in tears, half hysterical now, and Susan held her until Sid reached them with a pair of handcuffs.

"I'll have to hold you, Miss Mandrake," he said. "Maybe a night in our cell will shake some sense into you."

Susan accompanied Sid and Lisa to the cell on the lower deck. "I'd better tell the other clerks they'll have to cover your shift," she told the girl. "I'll be back to see you later."

Father Broderick was waiting near the shop when Susan returned. "Do you think she did it?" he asked. "We don't need any sort of scandal before we see the Pope."

"We should know tomorrow when the federal agent comes on board. If she has anything to say, she'll say it to him."

The lower deck where the ship's holding cell was located was a dreary place, lit only by dim ceiling bulbs along the corridor. Past midnight there was no one on duty and the prisoner was left alone on the cell's single cot, up against the white bars that made up two of the cell's four walls. Susan had visited Lisa earlier, but now, in the post-midnight hours, all was quiet.

It was sometime after one when the elevator down the corridor descended to that level and the doors glided open silently. The visitor moved softly, barely breathing, until he reached the cell with its dimly seen shape wrapped in blankets on the cot. For a moment he merely stared at the shape, then he took out a five-inch knife that flicked open at the touch of a button. He reached through the bars and drove it into the blanketed shape, once, twice—

Suddenly the corridor was bright as day and Sid Cromwell dove across the room at the intruder. They rolled over on the floor and Sid knocked the knife free. "I've got him," he said.

Susan and Lisa came out of the storeroom where they'd been hiding. "You can be thankful you weren't under those blankets," Susan told the girl.

Sid snapped the cuffs on Father Dempsey and raised the stout man to his feet. "I'll clear those life jackets off the cot and you can take their place till morning."

"Not a shred of evidence," Susan said a little later, "but it worked."

"You suspected it was Dempsey. How'd you know?" Sid Cromwell was sitting with Susan and Lisa in his office, drinking coffee till five o'clock, when he knew the captain would be up and eager to hear the good news.

She laughed. "I should say it was a woman's intuition. The only priest who insisted on wearing his black suit and collar all the time was the one who wasn't a priest at all. But there were a few facts, too. There were no fingerprints on that envelope containing the clergy retirement forms. That told me two things—that the forms were important enough for the killer to have wiped his prints off the envelope before abandoning it, and that they belonged to neither the dead man nor his roommate. Certainly Father Stillwell's prints on an envelope in their drawer wouldn't have been suspicious. No, the killer came on board to swindle the priests, posing as a priest himself. It was his bad luck to start with Father Ullman."

"Why was that?" Lisa wondered.

"Because the fax Sid showed me about Ullman said he was originally from Little Rock, the same city Dempsey claimed to be from. Somewhere during their conversation Ullman tripped him up and realized he wasn't from Little Rock, maybe wasn't a priest at all. That was when Dempsey killed him. He had to abandon his con scheme after that, of course, so he left those forms in Ullman's room rather than be caught with them. It might have been better to throw them overboard, but at that point he was afraid even to leave the cabin with them. He had to be very careful after that. He even faked an illness to avoid being photographed with Captain Mason and having his picture on file. That was how I knew he couldn't risk letting Lisa talk to the FBI after what she said this afternoon. He was there when she brought the shirt to Ullman's room, and maybe she'd caught a glimpse of him."

"You thought up this whole scheme to force his hand?" Sid marveled. "How did you know she could bring it off?"

Susan smiled and hugged Lisa Mandrake. "I remembered she came to New York to be an actress. This afternoon was her first starring role."

It had been a long time since Susan Holt had thought of Mike Brentnor, who used to work with her in the promotions section of Mayfield's Department Store. Susan was director of promotions now and Mike had fallen off her radar years ago. That was why it was such a surprise hearing his voice on the phone that balmy May evening.

"Susan? How are you? It's Mike."

She hesitated, thumbing through the index of her memory before asking, "Mike who?"

"Mike Brentnor! Don't tell me you've forgotten me!"

"Of course not, Mike. But it's been a lot of years. What are you doing now?"

"This and that. Right now I'm promoting the new racetrack they're building near the Catskills. I was wondering if I could buy you a drink."

There was a time when they'd been friends, but that was long over. "I don't think that would be a good idea, Mike. I'm pretty tired after a day at work."

"It's nothing personal. I want to talk about a business deal."

"Mike—"

"How about lunch tomorrow? At that place across from Mayfield's?"

She smiled into the phone. "You've been away too long, Mike. That place, Sandra's, is long gone. It's a drugstore now."

"Where do you eat lunch?"

"Most days I skip it, or send out for a sandwich."

"You're missing a good opportunity, Susan."

For what? she wondered. "*A roll in the hay?*" But she relented and said, "I could meet you for a quick drink tomorrow after work, but I'd have to leave by six-thirty."

"Fine! Whereabouts?"

"Nathan's is as good as any place. Five-thirty?"

"Swell! I'll see you then."

The following day was filled with the usual Wednesday staff meetings, plus a brief office party for one of Susan's assistants who was leaving. By the time five o'clock rolled around she still hadn't caught up with the work she'd planned. For a moment she considered skipping the drink with Mike Brentnor, but then decided she had to show up. She was not one to break her promises.

Nathan's was crowded with the usual five-o'clock faces and she noticed a couple of young administrative assistants looking surprised to see her there. She almost regretted her choice of meeting places, but then she spotted Mike holding down a booth in the far corner. It took her an instant to recognize his face behind the dark moustache and neatly trimmed beard, but the familiar lopsided grin was still there.

"What's with all the hair?" she asked, giving him a formal handshake in greeting.

"It's my new, more mature self. How've you been, Susan?"

"Fine. I had a nice cruise on the *Dawn Neptune* awhile back. We opened a Mayfield's branch on board."

"Hey, I read about that!" He signaled to the waitress. "What are you drinking?"

"Just a Corona for me. It's a bit early in the evening."

He ordered the same, and when the beers arrived he ceased the casual chatter and came to the point. "It's about this new racetrack near the Catskills. It's going to be a really class place, with Gateway resort hotel and casino already open. They were forever trying to get state approval. You know how those things are, owned by Native Americans but operated by professionals." He took a sip of beer, collecting foam on his moustache. "I have two things I wanted to ask you about. First, might Mayfield's be interested in opening a branch in the hotel? They're developing a little street of luxury shops."

Susan smiled and shook her head. "That's out of my hands. New branches are a top management decision. It took them months of meetings to approve the *Dawn Neptune* branch."

"All right," he said. "It was worth a try. Here's the second thing. I don't know how you're fixed financially, but there's a great opportunity for new investors in this place."

She simply stared at him. "You're asking me to invest my money in it?"

"Look, Susan, you've got a top job at Mayfield's now, earning big bucks. You get in on the ground floor here and you'll be set for life."

"Sorry, Mike, I can't do it."

He lowered his voice a notch. "I've got the inside dope on this track. I can't go into detail, but once this place is up and running it'll be a gold mine for bettors with the right information."

"And when will that be?"

"The hotel is open now, and they're putting the finishing touches on the track and grandstand. We hope to have racing by the end of next month. The track itself was designed by a Chinese expert, Lam Kow Loon. He's done a number of tracks in China and one in Hong Kong."

Somehow the entire thing struck her as funny. He wasn't trying to seduce her after all, just persuade her to invest in a racetrack. Susan downed the rest of her beer. "I'm sorry Mike, but I'm not the person you want. I've no loose change for investments of that sort."

He wasn't quite ready to give up. "Look, the Memorial Day weekend is coming. Can I drive you up there to look the place over? We could stay at the new hotel.... Separate rooms, of course."

Then she had to laugh. "I can't. You're a nice guy, but I guess we're on different wavelengths. Have a good holiday."

"I have to get going now."

"Susan—"

She stood up. "Thanks for the beer. Good seeing you again, Mike."

The Memorial Day weekend started out on the cool side, but Susan didn't care. Her closest friend was out of town and she looked forward to just relaxing. She went for a run in Central Park on Saturday morning and returned to her apartment invigorated just after noon. The phone was ringing as she walked in the door. She recognized Mike Brentnor's voice at once.

"Susan, I need help! I'm in big trouble up here." She could hear noise in the background, perhaps a television.

"What's going on? Where are you?"

"I'm with some people. They left me alone for a minute so I'm taking a chance and calling you. They're dangerous. They've got guns."

"You should call the police instead of me."

"No! Listen, Susan, you have to come up here today."

"I can't—"

"Please, I'm begging you. I have no one else to ask. I'm staying at the Big Bear Inn near Middletown on route 86, but I'm not there now."

"What do you want of me, Mike?" she asked.

"It's that racetrack thing I was telling you about. These people need some plans that I have. I want you to get them for me."

"Mike, this is crazy. I'm calling the police."

"If you do that, they might kill me. Listen, all you have to do is go to the Big Bear Inn and pick up a portfolio being held for me at the front desk."

"Why can't you do it yourself?"

"They won't let me go. I'll explain later, but right now I need your help. You can drive up here in a couple of hours and it'll all be over."

For anyone else it would have been an easy decision to hang up the phone and call the police. Or else simply forget the whole thing. If Mike Brentnor had gotten himself into a jam he'd have to get himself out or suffer the consequences. She couldn't imagine why he would reappear in her life now, with this crazy story about a racetrack.

And then something clicked in her memory. Mike knew that she'd been involved in several crime investigations in the past, and thought of herself as something of a detective. Maybe that's why he'd turned to her for help.

"All right," she heard herself say. "I'll do it. I'll just ask for your portfolio at the desk?"

"That's right. I'll call them and describe you, tell them it's all right."

"Look, Mike, why couldn't one of these people you're involved with do the same thing?"

"I can't let them get the portfolio. It's the only evidence I have against them."

"If I get this thing, where'll I bring it?"

"I'm at One Twenty-four Summit Street, but keep the portfolio hidden after you get it. Someone at the hotel can give you directions here. I'm hoping they'll let me go without having the portfolio, but I'll trade it for my life if I have to."

"All right," she told him, hoping she wouldn't regret her decision. "I can start out in about a half-hour."

"They're coming back!" he said quickly, breaking the connection.

Susan expected the traffic to be fierce on Saturday afternoon of Memorial Day weekend, but most travelers must have gotten a Friday head start. Once she crossed the Tappan Zee Bridge things moved right along and she found the Big Bear Inn along the new route 86 without difficulty. The room clerk was an attractive brunette woman with pale skin and a nametag that read Rita.

"I'm here to pick up a portfolio for Mike Brentnor," she said.

"What's your name?"

"Susan Holt."

Rita nodded. "He called to say you'd be coming by." Reaching under the desk she produced a brown leatherette case of the sort artists or architects might carry.

"Thanks," Susan said. "Can you give me directions to Summit Street?"

"Turn right at the next stoplight. That's Summit."

She put the portfolio in the trunk of her car, under a blanket, and tried calling Mike, but there was no answer. The address was easy to find, a gray two-story house in need of repair. She pulled in the driveway and rang the doorbell. From somewhere inside she heard Mike yelling. She tried the door and it was unlocked. Carefully opening it, she found a sparsely furnished living room. Mike was seated on the floor, handcuffed to a radiator pipe.

"My God, Mike! What happened?"

"I think someone's been shot. The killer might still be here. Do you have your phone?"

"Right there."

"Call nine-one-one and get the police here."

She called as instructed and then turned to Mike. "Tell me what happened."

"Do you have the portfolio?"

"In my car trunk."

"Don't mention that to the police."

"Where's the key to these cuffs?"

"Lam Kow has it. I came here to meet him, but there was someone in the kitchen that I never saw. Lam Kow caught me phoning you, took my cell phone, and handcuffed me to this radiator. Then he went back in the kitchen and seemed to be arguing with someone. I heard a shot, then nothing. I thought I'd be a dead man any minute, but no one came back through the kitchen door. After a few minutes I heard a thumping, as if a body was being dragged downstairs."

Already two state police cars were pulling up in front of the house. She opened the door for them. "Are you the one who called?" a trooper asked.

"That's me, Susan Holt." She told them what she knew, omitting mention of the portfolio. "The killer might still be here."

They quickly searched the house, guns drawn, and reported finding a body at the foot of the basement stairs. "I'm Corporal DeGeorgio," one trooper said. "We found this key in the dead man's pocket. It might fit those cuffs. The rest of the place is empty, but a back door is unlocked. This cell phone was on the kitchen table. Is it yours?"

"Yeah," Mike told him. "He took it from me when he handcuffed me."

The key unlocked the cuffs and Mike relaxed a little, happy to be free. His familiar lopsided grin returned. "I really got myself into a mess this time," he told Susan. "I think you saved my life."

Another police vehicle arrived, and two more troopers entered with cameras and crime-scene equipment. DeGeorgio directed them to the basement, then said, "We'll need a preliminary statement from you, Mr. Brentnor."

Mike repeated his story. "I've been doing some promotion work for the new racetrack and Gateway casino up here. This Chinese architect, Lam Kow Loon, is designing the racetrack part. He's done some tracks in China and Hong Kong. Anyway, he was looking for investors to help pay for some additional features not covered in the original budget."

"What sort of features?" DeGeorgio asked, making notes.

"I don't know exactly. He never told me." Mike avoided Susan's eyes as he spoke.

"Go on. What happened here today?"

"He asked me to come up and talk over my promotion plans for the track."

"Was he alone?"

"There was someone else in the kitchen that I didn't see."

"How did you happen to phone Miss Holt here?"

"He wanted me to suggest investors. I'd spoken to Susan about it earlier so I called her. Lam Kow thought I was trying to make trouble for him. He took out a gun and searched me for a weapon. Then he handcuffed my wrist to that pipe."

She noticed he'd been careful not to mention the portfolio, which was what Lam Kow Loon must have been after. "Did you witness the shooting?" DeGeorgio asked.

"No. Lam Kow left me here and went into the kitchen to talk with this other person. I could hear the murmur of voices. Next thing I knew, there was a shot. I was really scared then. I could hear noise, probably the body being dragged down the basement stairs, then there was just silence. I didn't know what to do because I was afraid he'd kill me next. For a long time I was afraid to do anything but keep silent. He'd taken my cell phone so I couldn't call the police."

The trooper nodded. "The back door was unlocked. That's how the killer left. We found a pistol in the trash barrel, probably the murder weapon. You'd better come look at the body."

"Do I have to?"

"He's Asian, but we need to know whether he's Lam Kow Loon or the other guy."

Mike followed them down the basement stairs while Susan tentatively brought up the rear. The body was at the bottom, faceup, and the bloody steps showed it had been dragged down. Mike gasped and managed to say, "That's him. That's Lam Kow Loon."

"And you don't know the name of the other man, the one who shot him."

"I never saw him."

Corporal DeGeorgio nodded again and closed his notebook. "I'll have to ask you both to give us your home addresses."

"We're not from here," Susan told him. "I work for Mayfield's Department Store in New York. Here's my card."

"All right. Both of you come along with me and we'll try to get to the bottom of this."

Susan was beginning to regret that she hadn't stayed in New York.

It was almost evening before they were finally free of the state police, having made and signed official statements. As they walked out to their cars, the first thing Mike asked was, "Do you have the portfolio?"

"It's in my trunk. What's this all about?"

"Let's go back to my hotel room and I'll show you."

"I don't want to see your etchings, Mike. I only want to know what you've gotten yourself—and me—involved in."

"Trust me, I'll show you."

Susan had already decided to spend the night at the Big Bear rather than drive back to the city so late. When they got there, Rita was still on the desk and checked her in. "You're lucky to get a room here on a holiday weekend," she said. "And I see you found Mike Brentnor, too."

"I sure did!"

"Room Sixteen. It's right down the hall from his room."

Susan grunted noncommittally and accepted the key. She followed Mike to his room, realizing for the first time that she'd brought no extra clothes or toilet articles with her for an overnight stay. When she mentioned this to him, he assured her they could purchase whatever she needed. "There's a drugstore down the road that's more like a general store. They even sell T-shirts."

"We'll try that later," she said as they entered his room. "Now let's see your etchings or whatever you have in that portfolio."

"It's not mine. Lam Kow Loon loaned it to me to study his proposal. He was upset when I didn't return it right away. Look at this. He unzipped the leatherette case and opened it, revealing architect's renderings of the racetrack and clubhouse, together with a detailed diagram of the racecourse itself, with distances and grading carefully marked. At one point, where the finish line was indicated, a row of dots had been carefully marked across the track, with Chinese symbols next to them.

"He's the one who tried to sell you shares in this?"

"That's right."

"But—but he didn't own the track, did he? How could he be selling shares in it?"

"He wasn't selling shares in the track, but in his invention. Look here." He opened a manila envelope beneath the drawings. It contained press clippings in Chinese and English. One of the English clippings was from a Hong Kong daily newspaper, the other from the *New York Times*. Both told of the discovery of a remote-controlled device buried in the turf at the starting gate of Hong Kong's Happy Valley Racecourse."

"What is this?" she asked, still unable to make sense of it.

"They found a mechanism with a dozen launching tubes buried at the starting gate. It could use compressed air to fire tiny darts into the bellies of the racehorses. The darts were filled with poison or a tranquilizer in an attempt to fix the outcome of the races."

"And you're part of this?"

"Not of poisoning horses. Lam Kow knew of the Hong Kong plan and claimed to have worked on the device. He said it could also be used to deliver stimulants to horses we want to win."

"And you asked me to invest in this? They test racehorses for drugs, you know."

"He claimed these would be undetected."

"Mike, this is the craziest scheme I ever heard of! Do you think the horses will just stand there quietly when the darts hit their bellies?"

"He claimed the mechanism was already in place at the new track. The starting gate is often moved at tracks, but the tubes are buried at the most frequent gate location."

"Did you give him any money?

He averted his eyes. "Two thousand dollars. He said he had to have more. That's why I asked you to go in with me."

"I don't believe any of it. They may have tried that stunt in Hong Kong, but it would never work here. I'll tell you the sort of bet I like. I'll bet you ten bucks this device isn't buried at the new track at all."

He thought about that. "It's a bet. Look, as long as you're staying over, let's grab dinner somewhere and then go out there and look around."

"Out there?"

"The track. Are you game?"

Susan took a deep breath: "Sure, why not?" If he had other things in mind, she was probably as safe out there as in his hotel room. Safer, maybe. "I still have to stop at that drugstore, remember."

They decided to try dinner at the new Gateway casino hotel next to the track. It was an almost lavish place, with much of the glitter of Vegas and Atlantic City casinos, but done on the cheap. The fancy Roman columns at the entrance had a hollow sound to them, and gold wallpaper in the gaming room was already beginning to peel in one or two spots. The dining room food was passable, not great, and the drinks were on the watery side. Still, the place was crowded with folks obviously enjoying themselves. The ringing of slot-machine wins seemed almost constant.

"You folks need help?" a handsome man in a tux asked them. "I'm Ron Meyer, the room manager. This your first visit to the Gateway?"

"It is," Susan told him. "We just ate in the dining room. When does the track open?"

"Not till next month. We wanted to have it running for the holiday, but we couldn't quite make it."

"Well, we'll be back," Mike told him.

It had grown dark while they ate and as they left the hotel they headed for the parking lot, then cut across toward the gate to the racetrack. "How do we get in?" she asked him.

"I've got a key. Lam Kow gave me one when he hired me to promote the track." He had the padlock open in seconds and they walked out in front of the darkened grandstand. "The clubhouse is on this end, with its own dining room and betting windows. The track is arranged so the finish line is opposite the clubhouse. The track is one mile around, and that's the length of most major races, so the starting gate is at the finish line. For a shorter race of seven furlongs or less, the gate is moved to the other side of the track. For the occasional race a mile and one-sixteenth or longer, it's moved back a bit."

"So Lam Kow's scheme could only fix mile-long races."

"Correct but that's most of the important ones." He used a penlight to guide her onto the track itself. "We should look for evidence of digging, but the system may have been in place since construction started last summer. Take my flashlight and—"

He was interrupted by the crack of a gunshot as a clot of dirt kicked up at their feet. "Someone's shooting at us!" Susan shouted, dropping flat on the ground.

"Damn!" Mike doused the light and was beside her in an instant as a second shot cracked in the night air. "It's Lam Row's partner, the one who killed him!"

She grabbed the penlight from him and turned it back on, covering the bulb with the palm of her hand. Then she hurled it as far as she could, close to the ground. Two more shots were fired at the light. The second one nicked it, sending it spinning off course.

"He's a good shot," Susan whispered.

"We've got to get out of here."

"How?"

"They have a watchman here day and night. He must have heard the shots."

"Unless he's dead too."

They stayed there hugging the dirt for a quarter of an hour, until Mike started a slow crawl back the way they had come. Susan reluctantly followed. They reached the gate without incident and found a burly watchman at the opening. He was a Native American, the first they'd seen at this supposed Indian casino site.

"Was that you fired those shots?" he asked

"No indeed," Mike told him. "Someone was shooting at us."

"This here's private property."

"My name is Mike Brentnor. I'm handling promotions for the track. I have a key."

"Your name's not on my list."

"I'm working with Lam Kow Loon, the track designer. We're staying at the Big Bear."

"I just heard on the news he got killed. You'd better come into my office so I can check you out."

They followed him into a construction trailer parked nearby. "My name's Fred Chatow," he told them. "Now let's see some ID."

"Right here," Mike said. "How late are you on duty?"

"Noon to midnight, then the other guy comes on. Long hours, but easy work."

He seemed satisfied by what they showed him and he allowed them to go on their way. Susan stopped at the drugstore for some toothpaste, a toothbrush, and a T-shirt. When they got back to the Big Bear, it was almost midnight.

"That starting gate could be a gateway to heaven for some of those horses," Mike remarked. "We were shot at because they feared we'd find out that device was really there."

"Or else because we'd find out it wasn't there."

They stopped in the hotel bar for a late-night drink, talking over what had transpired that day. "All I know is that someone tried to kill us tonight," she told him. I'm heading back in the morning. You can do what you want."

"Susan, I shouldn't have involved you in all this."

"No, you shouldn't have."

"I'm beginning to think that Lam Kow Loon was nothing but a clever con man. He took those newspaper clippings and a few sketches of the track and built them into a major swindle."

She wasn't about to argue with him. "In the future, choose your business acquaintances more carefully," she advised.

They paid their tab and got up to go. "Who do you think was shooting at us?" he asked. "Who was Lam Kow's partner in this?"

They were walking along the hall to their rooms when it began to come clear to Susan. "I think I know the answer to that, but it doesn't explain—"

He'd slipped his key card into the slot and was opening the door as she spoke. As he started into the room, three quick shots lit up the darkness. He gasped and fell back, pulling Susan to the floor with him.

"Mike!" she screamed.

"The gunman leaped over their fallen bodies and into the hall. She saw Corporal DeGeorgio appear from somewhere and bring him down with a quick chop to the neck. It was the track watchman, Fred Chatow, of course, but that didn't matter just then. "Get an ambulance!" she cried out. "Mike's still alive."

She insisted on riding with him in the ambulance, holding off the intern with his needle. "Just a minute," she pleaded. "I have to tell him something."

Mike Brentnor opened his eyes and stared at her, perhaps unseeing. "Who was it?" he managed to whisper his mouth filling with blood.

"Chatow, the watchman. He had to be in on it, or how could they ever have dug that trench and buried the device? It had to be after dark, before he went off duty at midnight. The troopers got him. DeGeorgio had been following us after a report of gunshots at the track."

"It hurts, Susan," he managed to say.

"I know. We're almost to the hospital."

"Chatow must have killed Lam Kow so he'd have the whole thing for himself." More blood, and she knew she'd have to speak faster.

"No, Mike Chatow couldn't have killed Lam Kow this afternoon because he told us he worked from noon to midnight. It had to be you."

His lids were starting to close. "What? What are you saying?" he asked, his words slurring.

"You said Lam Kow handcuffed you and took your cell phone as soon as you finished talking to me. If that were true, how could you have phoned the Big Bear and told Rita I was coming for the portfolio?"

"I—"

"You killed him, Mike. There was never anyone else at that house. You wanted this racetrack scheme for yourself, crazy as it was. You killed him, dragged his body to the basement, and dumped the gun in the rubbish barrel. You'd brought the handcuffs along yourself, and you planted the key in the dead man's pocket, then went back upstairs and cuffed yourself to the radiator. You had to leave the front door unlocked for me, of course, something Kow would never have done. You knew I'd come, relying on my reputation for never breaking my promises. But he did have a partner, the track watchman, Fred Chatow. When he heard Lam Kow was dead, he knew you'd done it to get the track plans for yourself. He shot at us at the track, then after midnight he got into your hotel room and waited to kill you."

She realized his eyes were closed and he was no longer listening. "I'm afraid he's gone, miss," the intern told her.

They tried to revive him at the hospital but it was too late. She took the portfolio from the trunk of her car and gave it to Corporal DeGeorgio. He listened to her shaking his head. "That's the craziest thing I ever heard. This Chinese fellow must have been a supreme confidence man to convince anyone it was true."

"Maybe not," Susan said. "If Chatow was in on the scheme, it must have been more than a con game. Something must really be buried out there." She remembered Mike Brentnor's phrase. "Sort of a gateway to heaven. For the bettors and maybe for the horses."

That was when she remembered the bet she'd made with Mike. If the mechanism was really there, she'd lost the bet. But Mike had lost more than that.

It was the sort of smoky, crowded singles bar Libby Knowles had always detested, and as she leaned back to study the man across the table she wondered what she was doing here.

"I'm frightened," the man told her. His name was Bryan Metzger and he was a meteorologist for Sunny Days, a private weather-forecasting service. "I want to hire you."

"That's what I'm for," Libby agreed readily. "My rates are by the day and expenses are extra."

"Sergeant O'Bannion recommended you," Metzger said, moistening his lips with a nervous tongue. "He said you're the best bodyguard in the business."

"Well," she replied, not knowing whether to curse or thank O'Bannion for sending her this one, "I'm the only one in town who makes a specialty of it. Detective agencies and private security firms are generally more interested in guarding property than people. And when they do take on bodyguard work, they generally send out a burly tough-guy type with a bulging shoulder holster that can be spotted a mile away. I like to think I'm a bit more subtle than that."

"You're certainly not the burly tough-guy type," he agreed.

"So what are you afraid of?" she asked.

"Being killed."

"By whom?"

It took him a long time to answer. She became aware of a couple dancing near the bar in time to a throbbing beat from a trio of amplified instruments at the far end of the room. "Me," he answered finally, in a voice she could barely hear above the music. "I'm afraid I'll kill myself."

Libby had started out as a policewoman, assigned mainly to the guarding of visiting dignitaries and their families. In an age when any famous person was fair game, it was a job that demanded instant reflexes and the wisdom to make the right snap decision. Libby had had a boy friend in those days—only two years ago but it seemed a lifetime. They'd talked of getting married. He was a vice-squad detective named Phil Proudy, and he had been caught in a messy internal investigation holding a pound of pure cocaine he'd taken off an East Side pimp. He had tried to outrun two police cruisers on the Crosstown Expressway and smashed into a bridge abutment. He died three hours later and Libby Knowles resigned from the force the next day.

O'Bannion had been one of those who urged her to stay. Nobody thought she was involved, after all, and her police career was just beginning. But for Libby the whole thing had a different point of view. If she wasn't guilty, she was dumb, and no one would ever forget that she'd been in love with a crooked cop. In a job where judgment was all-important, she'd made a bad call.

So she had taken her mother's small inheritance and rented an office in a moderately priced downtown building. The simple name *Libby Knowles Protection Service* didn't attract much business, but with some help from O'Bannion she began to get occasional assignments. Mostly it was guarding visitors—often well heeled out-of-town businessmen who liked the idea of shepherding a lovely young woman around town, especially a young woman who carried a snub-nosed Cobra revolver in her purse and knew how to use it.

During the past year she'd helped guard a man running for United States Senator, and another who was waging a proxy battle for control of a local corporation. She'd dined with a famous rock star and even flown to Miami with a television actress who was worried about traveling alone. In all that time Libby had fired her revolver just once, when a mugger armed with a knife had made the mistake of coming after an elderly black educator who was in town to accept an honorary degree at the university. Libby had shot the mugger in the leg and phoned the police.

But Bryan Metzger was something different.

She should have known that from the moment he phoned her and requested that they meet in a singles bar. Clients usually came to her office or made arrangements by long-distance phone and were met at the airport. Not in singles bars. And she'd never before been hired to protect anyone from themselves.

"I'm not sure I can keep you from committing suicide if you want to," she said. "After all, my fee doesn't include sleeping with you. I can camp by the bathroom door and make sure nobody interrupts while you're shaving, but I won't be in there with you to keep you from cutting your throat with the razor."

"I use an electric."

"You know what I mean. You need a psychiatrist, not a bodyguard. Why do you think you might try to kill yourself?"

"Because a good friend of mine did, just last week. And because I tried to do it once already."

"Tell me about the friend first."

"Horace Fox shared the office with me at Sunny Days. Last Saturday night a little before midnight, he jumped out of the window." Bryan shook his head with a look of incomprehension Libby understood. "He didn't have a reason in the world to kill himself, yet that's exactly what he did."

"Was he alone at the time?"

"All alone. I'd gone down the hall to get a cup of coffee out of the machine."

"Did you two always work that late on a Saturday night?"

"No. We were getting out the five-day forecasts for the West Coast. There are a great many businesses, especially in the California wine country, whose livelihood depends on private weather forecasts. They need something more detailed for their area than the National Weather Service can provide. Sunny Days is especially good on five-day forecasts. Our accuracy rate is a full ten percent better than the weather bureau."

"Tell me more about Mr. Fox."

"When I came back with the coffee he was gone and the window was open. He'd jumped. The office is on the seventh floor."

"And this was just before midnight?"

He nodded. "About a quarter to. We were due to knock off at twelve, but I wanted some coffee before I drove home."

"And he'd said nothing to indicate he was about to take his own life?"

"Not a word, but I'd noticed he seemed unusually somber. Generally he joked and chatted with me, but not that night. We pretty much went about our work in silence."

"No one else was in the office?"

Metzger shook his head. "Julie Wade, our secretary, went home around ten. And Chris Romeo, the chief meteorologist, hadn't been in at all."

Libby said, "Now what about you? Why do you think you might kill yourself, too?"

"Horace jumped on Saturday night. On Monday morning, when I was working the day shift, I found myself being drawn to the window behind his desk. I stared out of it, and for just an instant I thought about jumping, too."

"That's common enough," Libby tried to reassure him. "I think everyone has had those feelings in a high building or on a bridge. It doesn't make sense to hire me for something like that."

"I've got the money right here," he said, slipping the wallet from his pocket. "Look, today is Wednesday. Suppose I pay you for five days in advance, through the weekend. Maybe by that time I'll have snapped out of this."

Under any other circumstances Libby would have turned him down. But when he slid the money across the table she accepted it, hoping no one noticed it and took her for a high-class call girl. She accepted it because she knew he was lying. He wasn't afraid of suicide—he was afraid of being murdered by the same person who had murdered Horace Fox.

Libby had developed a regular routine in her job. In the case of female clients, she often shared a bedroom with them. Her male clients required techniques that were both more circumspect and more intensive. She began by checking out Bryan Metzger's apartment. It was a moderately priced third-floor walkup in a remodeled building near downtown. There was a sofa bed in the living room, and she decided at once that she'd be sleeping there.

"You mean you're actually going to spend the night?" he asked.

"You're paying for five days of protection and that's what you're going to get. I'll be sticking to you like glue, Mr. Metzger."

"In that case you'd better start calling me Bryan."

"All right, Bryan. But before you get any ideas, I never get personally involved with my clients."

"Of course not."

"Just so we understand each other."

Libby passed an uneventful night on the pullout bed, her fingers close to the Cobra pistol under her pillow. In the morning she got up early, checked her client, who was snoring on his back, and started to prepare breakfast. He joined her just as the toast popped up.

"Say, couldn't we make this a permanent arrangement?"

Libby smiled. "Not a chance. Do you like your toast buttered or plain?"

"Buttered. But let me do it. I'm used to making my own breakfast."

"Maybe that's what's driving you to suicide."

"Don't joke about it."

Libby emptied frozen orange juice into a pitcher. "If you're suicidal, I'm a monkey. You're one of the most normal guys I've ever met."

Metzger grinned. "If I was all that normal I'd have made a pass at you last night." Libby measured water into the pitcher without answering. "O'Bannion told me you were a policewoman. How come you quit the force?"

Libby set the orange juice on the table and sat down. "That's a long story for dinner some night, not now."

"You're the boss," he said, sitting across from her and taking a bite of toast.

"What time do you start work?" she asked.

"I'm working nine to five this week."

"We'd better hurry."

"You're not staying around all day, are you?"

"I'll see how it goes," Libby told him.

Sunny Days occupied several adjoining offices on the seventh floor of the Midway Bank Building. Libby rode up in the elevator with Bryan and was introduced to some of his co-workers. The chief meteorologist, Chris Romeo, was tall and dark-haired, with a special smile Libby suspected he reserved for young women. Bryan introduced her as a visiting cousin who wanted to see the office and Romeo didn't question the story.

The secretary, Julie Wade, was another matter. She was a good-natured blonde who joked with Bryan but eyed Libby with a distinctly suspicious gaze. "It's the first of May," she reminded Bryan. "You should have the thirty-day forecasts ready to go."

"Don't worry, I will. I just want to show Libby around a bit."

Libby followed him into his office, leaving Julie Wade looking unhappy. "I don't think she likes me," Libby said.

"Julie? She has her possessive moments, but I try to ignore it."

"Have you ever been married?"

He shook his head while he glanced through the mail on his desk. "I lived with a girl for three years but we broke up."

Libby looked around the large office with its weather gauges and computer terminals. There were two identical desks set before two large windows, separated from each other only by a short wood-and-glass partition. Metzger was at the right-hand desk—the top of the one at the left had been cleared. "Well, you each had a window to help you determine if it was raining out. But how do you go about the task of weather forecasting for the West Coast from here?" Libby asked.

He answered by turning to the computer by his desk and punching a series of numbers. Immediately the large video screen came to life. "It's really quite simple. You see, the Weather Bureau's radar pictures of dozens of cities around the country are available on the computer. You're looking at the San Francisco area right now. See the rain pattern moving in from the ocean? This is just one tool we use, of course, but it's an important one. It gives us an instant, constantly changing look at weather anywhere in the country. We also have a string of spotters all over the country to feed us information—"

"And people pay for this service because it's that much superior to regular weather forecasts?"

"You bet. Florida fruit growers, California vineyard owners, even long-distance truckers need to know the specifics of weather for a particular area, and that area is often far removed from the large metropolitan centers serviced by the weather bureau."

Libby ventured to the other side of the partition. "This was Horace Fox's area?"

"Yes." Metzger brooded. "When I came back with my coffee, his window was wide open. Even then I didn't realize he'd jumped until they came up from the street."

"How did they know he jumped from here?"

"This was the only office with a light on."

Libby opened the window and very carefully leaned out. "It's too bad the building doesn't have those modern windows that don't open."

She stared straight down at the striped canopy over the building's entrance, then quickly withdrew her head.

"I suppose he'd have found another way," Metzger said, "if he wanted to do it that badly."

"Look, Bryan, I want to check up on a few things. Do you think you can stay away from these windows for an hour or so until I get back?"

"I'm feeling better now. I think so. Having you around has been a big help."

"That's my specialty, providing confidence."

"My specialty is providing the weather."

Libby smiled. "I guess it's the age of the specialist..."

Sergeant O'Bannion was just finishing the morning lineup, shepherding a tearful rape victim away from the one-way mirror where she'd viewed a half dozen young men in jeans and T-shirts before finally identifying one of them as her assailant.

"Hi, Libby," he said when they were alone in the hallway. "How're things?"

"Thanks to you, I have a new client."

"Good. Who is it?"

"Bryan Metzger—a meteorologist at Sunny Days, the weather-forecasting service."

"Where the guy killed himself last weekend."

She nodded. "I was wondering if you could give me a little help with it, since you recommended me to him."

His big face crinkled into a familiar frown. O'Bannion liked her, Libby knew, but there were times when he tried to be overly protective, like a loving uncle. "I don't know about this bodyguard business, Libby. Why can't you open a nice dog-walking service instead?"

"Sergeant."

"Okay, okay, how can I help you?"

"Is there any chance Horace Fox was murdered?"

"There's always a chance, but there's no evidence. Why do you ask?"

"Because my client is afraid of something. He claims he's afraid he'll kill himself just like Fox did, but I think there's more to it. Maybe he fears the killer will come after him next."

"Well, if it *was* murder the killer covered his tracks pretty well. As near as we could tell, no one was in the building at the time except your client and Fox."

"What about Chris Romeo, the chief meteorologist for Sunny Days? And Julie Wade, the secretary? Metzger said she had been there earlier that evening."

"She signed out downstairs at 10:08. There's no record of Romeo having been in the building at all, though I'll admit these building security people can be easy to slip past. They go off to the John or someplace and an elephant could walk through the lobby."

"Was there anything in the dead man's pockets?"

"Nothing unusual. I'll show you if you'd like. The family hasn't claimed the stuff yet."

"What sort of family did Fox have?"

"Just an ex-wife out in Las Vegas. I understand she's a showgirl." He led Libby up to his office and then went out to a filing cabinet in the squad room. When he returned, he had a manila envelope with Horace Fox's name on it.

"Doesn't the coroner usually keep these things?"

"Suspicious death," he muttered.

"Then there was something for you to investigate."

"Libby—you know the routine! Metzger insists the man had no reason to kill himself. That alone is cause for investigation."

"He didn't live to make a statement?"

"After a seven-floor fall? No way. He hit right in front, just to the left of the canopy over the entrance." O'Bannion opened the envelope as he spoke and let the contents of the dead man's pockets slide out onto his desk.

Libby saw at once that there was nothing unusual: a handkerchief, keys, a wallet containing credit cards and a few bills, some loose change, and a wristwatch. Then she noticed something. "The watch is stopped at ten minutes to one."

The sergeant shrugged. "I suppose it stopped when he hit the ground."

"But that was before midnight."

He consulted the police report. "You're right. The first call came in at 11:51. I guess his watch was wrong."

"Why?"

"Libby—" O'Bannion said impatiently. "All right, I know. I was just asking. It seems strange."

"Libby, Metzger didn't hire you to solve a mystery. He simply wants to be protected."

"I know," she answered reluctantly.

"You're not on the force any more, Libby."

"I know that, too."

It was on Friday evening as she was preparing for her third night on the sofa bed at Bryan Metzger's apartment after they'd dined together at a French restaurant nearby that he said, "You know, I think I'm really over it, Libby. After these couple of days with you I'm not afraid any more."

"Good," Libby said.

"Are all your jobs as boring as this one?"

"You're paying me to keep it boring, if you know what I mean."

"Let's add a little excitement. Come to bed with me."

"No."

"I suppose you've got a guy."

"No, not right now, but that's not the point. I'm working."

"You asked me if I'd ever been married. How about you?"

"I was engaged to a cop once, when I was on the force. He was killed in an auto accident. Now you know my life story."

"There must be more to it than that."

"Maybe after our five days are up I'll tell you about it. Now I think I'll go to bed."

"You're a hard one to figure, Libby."

"Not so hard when you know me. Goodnight, Bryan."

She had been sleeping for a few hours when she came awake suddenly, her reflexes alert, knowing at once it wasn't any usual night noise that had awakened her. She lay perfectly still and listened until it came again.

A footstep.

Someone was moving very quietly across the floor, toward the bedroom door.

Libby gripped her revolver and tensed for a spring. Her eyes functioned well in the near-darkness and she could make out the shape of a man wearing dark pants and a dark pullover sweater. He was holding something long in his right hand, possibly a pistol with a silencer on the barrel.

She moved all at once, springing from the bed with a yell meant to startle the intruder. He whirled, and she saw the flash from the pistol in his hand. Then she was on him, pinning his arm against the wall before he could fire again and trying to stun him with a glancing blow to the temple.

Metzger was up and out of the bedroom. He turned on the overhead light. Libby relaxed her grip on the intruder for just a second and he scrambled free. She still had a grip on his gun but he abandoned it and dove for the open window by which he'd entered.

"Are you all right?" Metzger demanded as she raced to the window. She wanted to pursue the gunman, but she knew her responsibility was to her client. There may have been more than one of them and she couldn't risk leaving him alone.

"Yes, except that he got away. Did you recognize him?"

He shook his head. "I never saw him before."

"He used a silencer. That means he was probably a professional hit man. Is there any reason somebody might want you dead?"

He turned away from her. "Of course not."

"You haven't been leveling with me, Bryan. You weren't afraid of committing suicide. You were afraid of being murdered like Horace Fox."

"Who says Horace was murdered?"

"I do, and I can prove it—at least to my own satisfaction."

Metzger walked over to examine the window. "He came over the adjoining roof and used a glass-cutter. Do you think we should call the police?"

"That depends on what you're prepared to tell them." He sighed and walked out to the kitchen. "Let's have some coffee and talk. Neither of us will be able to sleep for a while anyway."

"All right."

Boiling water for instant coffee, he asked, "What makes you think Fox was murdered?"

"I went to Headquarters and looked over his possessions. His wrist-watch was stopped at ten minutes to one, an hour after the police report says he jumped. I puzzled about that for a while, until I remembered the date. Saturday was the last weekend in April—the start of Daylight Savings Time. He had moved his watch ahead an hour for the start of Daylight Savings at 2 a.m. If he'd been about to kill himself, I don't think he'd have done that."

"No, probably not," he agreed, looking thoughtful.

"So are you going to tell me about it?" Libby said, measuring the powdered coffee into two cups.

"You're quite a detective, aren't you?"

"I observe odd details, that's all."

"Have you observed anything odd at the office?"

Libby shrugged. "Julie Wade and Chris Romeo—are they an item?"

Metzger frowned. "What makes you think that?"

She laughed. "Maybe their names suggested it. Romeo and Juliet, you know? It just crossed my mind. —She was there the night Fox was killed, wasn't she?"

"She'd left earlier."

"But she could have come back. Or Romeo could have slipped past the guard downstairs."

The kettle whistled and Bryan poured boiling water into the cups. "You're full of ideas, aren't you?"

"But I don't like any of them. I want you to tell me who killed Fox, and why they want to kill you."

"Honestly, I don't know." He sat at the table with his coffee and helped himself to sugar.

Libby shook her head. "Fox had an ex-wife in Las Vegas, a showgirl who just might have mob connections. Maybe she had him killed and you saw too much, so they want you out of the way, too."

"It might explain a few things," he said thoughtfully. "But if I did see anything I'm not aware of it."

Libby started for the telephone. "We'd better call the police about tonight."

"That won't get us anywhere. The police will just drive them undercover. Maybe they'll try again soon and you'll get them next time. I can't afford your rates forever, you know."

"I know. You hired me for five days, and half that time is gone already."

"Will you stick it out?"

"Of course," she said. "Now let's finish our coffee and get some sleep."

"Won't it keep you awake?"

"It never has yet," she told him serenely.

They stuck close to the apartment all day Saturday, then toward evening she called Sergeant O'Bannion at home. Briefly she told him what had happened the previous night. Bryan was in the shower with the door closed and she could speak freely.

"You didn't report it?" O'Bannion growled into the phone. "What's the matter with you, Libby?"

"Bryan may be right that we need to lure them into trying again. But I wanted to tell you about it just in case there's a slip-up."

"A slip-up. Terrific. Meaning if we find both of you dead somewhere."

"That won't happen," she answered confidently.

"As long as you called, there's something else."

"What?"

"I shouldn't be telling you this, but it might tie in. The Coast Guard seized a big shipment of heroin off the California coast three nights ago—close to five million dollars' worth."

"What would that have to do with—?"

"On the boat they found weather reports from Sunny Days."

Libby was silent for a moment. Then she said, "Thanks, Sergeant."

"Funny thing—the most recent five-day forecast from Sunny Days was way off. It failed to mention a spring storm that came up suddenly in the Gulf of California. The storm caused the drug-runners' boat to founder on the rocks where the Coast Guard picked it up."

"That might explain a great deal," Libby said. The shower shut off behind the bathroom door. "I have to go now. I'll talk to you later."

"Be careful."

A few minutes later, Byran came out of the bathroom, a towel wrapped around his waist. "I think we should go out to dinner tonight."

"That might be tempting fate," Libby said. "We have plenty of food in. Let's wait till tomorrow."

They played cards and watched the eleven o'clock news before retiring. The night passed uneventfully, though Libby did not sleep as soundly as on past nights. She found herself prowling the living room and the kitchen, checking the windows and listening for unexpected noises. But the intruder did not return.

In the morning, as they were leaving the apartment for Sunday brunch at a nearby hotel, Chris Romeo arrived unexpectedly. "Sorry to bother you on your weekend off, Bryan, but something's come up."

"That's all right," Bryan said. "Come on in. You remember my cousin, Libby."

"Of course. Still enjoying our city?"

"Very much," Libby replied, wondering if Romeo had really bought the cousin story.

"I hope you'll excuse us for a few minutes," he apologized. "Bryan, the police have been checking into Fox's suicide, and that prompted Julie and me to do some checking of our own. We've discovered a number of secret accounts, mainly on the West Coast and in Florida. They were being serviced by Fox without our knowledge."

Bryan looked blank. "I don't understand."

"Neither do we, completely. I was hoping you could help. Did you ever hear Fox talking business to anyone you didn't know on the phone? Did you ever see him making up maps and five-day forecasts for areas in which we had no known clients?"

Bryan thought about it and shook his head. "No, I don't remember anything like that."

"This is very important, Bryan," Romeo insisted. "The police are nosing around. A scandal could put Sunny Days out of business."

Libby decided to join in. "What sort of scandal could involve a weather-forecasting firm? Using synthetic isobars instead of the real thing?"

Romeo ignored her but answered the question, addressing his reply to Metzger. "We think he was providing weather information for all sorts of illegal activities, including drug shipments to the California and Florida coasts and night-flights across the Mexican border with both drugs and aliens."

Bryan shook his head. "It could explain a great deal, but I knew nothing of it till now."

"What could it explain?"

"Why he was killed, for one thing. Libby has just about convinced me it was murder."

"Libby?" Romeo shifted his attention back to her. "You'd be wise to stay out of this, you know."

"I'm trying to."

Romeo headed for the door. "If you think of anything that will help with this, give me a call, Bryan. I'll either be at my apartment or Julie's."

When he was gone, Metzger said, "I guess you were right about Romeo and Julie."

"I guess so," Libby agreed.

"I still can't believe it about Fox, though. I—"

The doorbell rang and Metzger went to open it. "That's probably Romeo back about something he forgot."

Libby started to warn him, but she wasn't in time. The ring was different this time, more hesitant. It wasn't Romeo again. Bryan opened the door and stepped back at once, raising his hands. There were two of them this time, the one from the other night and a partner who could have been his brother. Both had guns.

"Get her gun," the familiar one said.

Libby cursed herself for being off guard. The second man grabbed her purse and pulled the Cobra out of it.

Metzger looked sick. "Libby—"

"Don't worry, Bryan. I'll think of something."

The first man laughed. "A real liberated woman, eh? Kill him first, Joe. I want her for myself."

"No! Don't—" Libby started to fall sideways onto the still-open sofa bed where she'd spent the night.

"Get her!" the second men cried, and the other swung his gun to aim at her.

Libby hit the rumpled bedclothes and found her target, fastening on the other pistol under the pillow. She fired two shots through the blanket and the first man went down. "Drop it or you're dead!" she warned the other one.

"My God!" Metzger said. "You shot him!"

"Not fatally, I hope. Call the police and ask for Sergeant O'Bannion. He should be on duty now. Tell him to send an ambulance."

A half hour later, still at the apartment, O'Bannion told her, "That was good shooting. You got him in his gun arm and side, but he'll live. You think these are the ones who tossed Fox out the window?"

She turned to Metzger. "What do you think, Bryan?"

"I suppose it makes sense, especially after what Romeo told us. Fox was supplying weather data to organized crime. His information went wrong and they lost a ship that was running drugs. So they killed Fox, not knowing if the misinformation was intentional, and tried to kill me in case I knew something about any of it."

O'Bannion nodded. "We'll check Fox's bank accounts tomorrow. If he was getting regular payments, we should be able to trace them." He went downstairs with the stretcher, promising to return.

"I guess I did the right thing hiring you," Metzger told Libby. "You sure came through when I needed it. Where did you get the second gun?"

"Like you, they forgot I wrestled the silenced pistol away from that guy the other night. I had it in bed with me, and when they took my purse I knew I had to make a dive for it."

"You saved my life."

Libby shook her head. "No, perhaps I just prolonged it. You could get the death penalty in this state for killing Horace Fox."

"What?"

"I'm no dope, Bryan. You just mentioned the drug ship being lost because of the bad weather forecast, but that's something O'Bannion told me on the phone and I didn't repeat to you. And the ship wasn't lost until some days after Fox's death, so it couldn't have caused it. You found out about Fox's little arrangement and it seemed like a great way to make safe and easy money. So you killed him and took over the illegal side of Sunny Days' business. The only trouble was that Fox managed to get his revenge, even from the grave. A ship foundered in a storm and fell into the hands of the Coast Guard. After that, you knew they'd be coming to kill you. It wasn't the sort of story you could tell the police, so you hired me to protect you."

Bryan Metzger turned away. "You're right about me wanting to take over his business. Why should he get all that extra money for supplying forecasts to smugglers and organized crime when I could do it just as easily. He tricked me on that California one, though. He gave me the wrong information and when I sent out the five-day forecast after he was dead it caused the heroin shipment to run aground."

"Why didn't they simply hire the services of Sunny Days in the normal way?"

"That would mean pinpointing the section of coastline or western desert where the ship or plane would be landing. They couldn't risk the authorities learning that they wanted that information. It was worth what they paid to keep the whole business secret. But, Libby, just because I took advantage of Horace's death doesn't mean I killed him. He jumped out of that window."

Libby shook her head. "No, Bryan. The building's entrance canopy is directly below his window. If he'd jumped from it, he'd have hit that canopy and gone through it. But O'Bannion told me he hit to the left of the canopy. He went out the window by your desk, which is on the right-hand side facing the street—that's the left of the canopy from O'Bannion's point of view. You got him to your window on some pretext, pushed him out, closed that window, and opened his, because a suicide would more likely choose his own window to jump from."

O'Bannion was in the doorway, listening. "I hired you to protect me," Metzger pleaded, "not to try to convict me of murder!"

"And I did protect you from those hoods. I couldn't protect you from yourself."

"Then let me go," he said, and broke toward the window. It wasn't the one to the roof the gunman had used but a front one three stories up, facing the street.

"Stop him!" O'Bannion shouted from the doorway. Libby hesitated only an instant. Metzger had, after all, paid her for five days' protection, to keep him from killing himself. And the five days weren't up yet. She tackled him just as he reached the window.

THE INVISIBLE INTRUDER

Clients of the Libby Knowles Protection Service sometimes proved to be a bit paranoid, and at first Libby would have placed Frederick Warfer in that category. He was a balding man of around fifty who glanced over his shoulder even as he entered her outer office.

Libby's new secretary, Janice, was out to lunch at the time, and when he saw Libby at the reception-desk, he jumped to the wrong conclusion. "I—I don't have an appointment. Do you suppose Miss Knowles could see me?"

Libby straightened up. "I'm Libby Knowles. My secretary is at lunch."

"Maybe I should come back later," he muttered. "I didn't realize it was lunchtime."

"No, come in. I've already had some yogurt."

He followed her into the inner office, a big square room with a wide window overlooking the busy traffic on Madison Street. The building was old, but the rent was reasonable, and that was what mattered to Libby in her first year of being in business on her own.

"Now what can I do for you, Mr.—?" She glanced at the card he'd handed her. "Warfer."

"Frederick Warfer. I'm an industrial consultant—an inventor of sorts. Companies come to me with technical problems and I try to find solutions for them."

"You want me to protect an invention of yours?"

"No, I want you to protect me. Someone's trying to kill me."

"Why do you think that?" Libby asked, sitting down behind her desk and indicating that he sit, too.

"Someone's been getting into my house at night," he said, perching on the one visitor's chair. "It sets off the alarms, but by the time the police arrive no one's there. There's never any sign of forced entry."

"Perhaps the alarm system's defective," Libby suggested.

"I've checked it completely and it's working perfectly." He hesitated "I want you to come out and stay at the house with me."

"All right. That's my job, of course. But I don't share a room with male clients. Do you have a spare room?"

"Yes."

"Are you married, Mr. Warfer?" She'd started making notes on a yellow legal pad.

"I—no, not at present. My wife left me two years ago."

"I see. Are you alone in the house? Do you have any children?"

"No, no children. I'm alone. My address is on my card there."

Libby studied it, then asked, "Who do you think might want to kill you?"

"A business competitor, maybe. I don't know. I just need protection. The police don't believe me any more. After a full week of that alarm going off, they're starting to think I'm doing it myself."

"Are you, Mr. Warfer?"

"No, of course not! But I'm afraid the police are going to stop coming out when the alarm goes off. Or else they'll take their time about it. And that's when he'll do it."

"He'll?"

"She'll! Whoever!"

"Do what?"

"Kill me."

"I see. All right, Mr. Warfer, I'll be there this evening."

"Will you be armed?"

"Yes. I'm a former policewoman. I know how to use a handgun responsibly."

Libby had arranged to meet Sergeant O'Bannion for a drink late that afternoon. He was a bulky man with a big face that seemed to crease itself into a gloomy expression at the least opportunity. People who didn't know him well thought he was perpetually unhappy but Libby knew better. O'Bannion had been the one person who'd urged her to remain on the force after her lover, a vice-squad detective had been caught in a cocaine scandal and killed himself in an auto crash while fleeing his fellow cops. She hadn't followed O'Bannion's advice, but he'd been good to her—and good for her—ever since, often sending business her way that the department couldn't handle on an official basis.

"I have a new client," she told him over drinks. "A man named Frederick Warfer. Do you know him?"

O'Bannion shook his head. "Should I?"

"His alarm's been ringing every night for a week. He's afraid the police will start ignoring him."

"I'll check the reports in the morning. Where does he live?"

"Maple Shade Drive. I'll be out there tonight."

"Take care of yourself, Libby. Lady bodyguards are hard to replace."

She smiled. "The biggest threat to my health so far has been starvation."

Warfer's home proved to be an expensive Moorish-looking place with a long curving driveway. Libby guessed it had probably been built back in the 1930s when the popularity of Moorish architecture had reached this part of the country. She'd expected to find her client alone in a darkened house, but the window showed plenty of light and he opened the door with an attractive blonde woman at his side.

"Come in, Miss Knowles. This is Helen Rodney, my neighbor from across the street."

Helen Rodney appeared to be in her late thirties, with the sort of eyes that stayed hard even when she smiled. "This is your bodyguard?" she asked him with a laugh. "What will she protect you from?"

"I'd like to have a look around the house," Libby told Warfer. The June night had been warm and she'd worn only a light jacket over her blouse and slacks. She dropped it on top of her overnight bag in the entryway and followed after her client, turning her back decisively on the blonde neighbor. They stepped down into a large living room, dominated on its far end by a massive fieldstone fireplace "That's lovely," Libby said, going and peering into it. "I never use it. It's too much trouble."

"It's almost big enough for a man to hide in," Libby said, peering up into the chimney.

Warfer shook his head. "Not really. I checked it out."

The dining room was almost as large, with a table and ten chairs, and the kitchen was spacious and lavishly equipped. It was a house obviously designed for entertaining and Libby said as much.

"We did a great deal of entertaining before my wife left," Warfer said quietly.

He showed her the highly sophisticated burglar-alarm system that not only wired the doors and windows but also threw a pattern of invisible beams across rooms and doorways. "Once it's switched on, any movement in here, no matter how slight, triggers the alarm," he explained.

"I've seen only one alarm system this elaborate in my life," Libby told him "and that was in a museum. What do you have here that's so valuable, anyway?"

"I told you, I'm an inventor. There are times when a small fortune in ideas, notes, and mock-ups can be found in this house."

Helen Rodney had followed along a few steps behind them, but when Warfer led Libby to the stairs to the second floor she said, "I think I'd better be going. If you get frightened of anything during the night, Frederick, just give me a call."

When she'd gone, Libby remarked, "I feel as if I'm coming between you two."

"No. Helen's just an old friend. A friend of my wife's, really. She's been trying to take care of me ever since Betty left."

"Your wife?"

He nodded, leading her into the master bedroom and indicating a framed color photograph on a bedside table. "Betty and I were married for twenty-one years. And then she just left."

"I'm sorry." The woman was smiling at the camera, but the picture was overexposed and she was squinting slightly into the sun. Her eyes were a stunning blue. The photo had obviously been blown up from a much smaller candid shot. "She's very attractive."

"She was."

When he added no more, she said, "Tell me about this intruder. What time does he usually arrive?"

"Shortly after I retire. Sometimes I'm still awake when the alarm goes off. See—" he showed her the mechanism "—it buzzes next to the bed, too."

"Midnight? One o'clock?"

"It varies. Closer to one, usually, but that may be because I go to bed late. The police have come and searched every inch of the house, but they've found no one. The intruder is invisible by night and non-existent by day. But I have a terrible feeling he's getting closer to me every time."

"We'll see what happens tonight," Libby said.

Warfer showed her the guest room and she brought her bag up and unpacked what she needed. The .38-caliber snub nosed revolver went under her pillow.

Warfer rapped at her door a few minutes after one, waking her. "The alarm just went off!" he told her anxiously

Libby, who slept fully clothed when on a job, grabbed her gun from under the pillow and ran down the stairs ahead of him. Her left hand hit the living-room light switch as she went into a crouch in the doorway. "Hands up!" she shouted. "I have a gun!"

The room was empty, and so was the dining room. The entire first floor was empty.

"You can see for yourself that the doors and windows haven't been tampered with," Warfer said after they had both checked them "It's just like the other times."

"Maybe you've got mice."

"Mice four feet tall? That's the height of these alarm beams that were broken."

A flashing red light suddenly lit up the wall opposite the front windows. "That'll be the police," Libby said. "I'll go out and talk to them."

There was a single officer in the squad car a slim young man whose name tag read David Oakes. He was new since Libby's days on the force and she introduced herself.

"I know," the officer said wearily. "The alarm went off again and no one was here." His deep-set brown eyes took in the scene.

"Well, I was here this time, but I didn't set it off."

Oakes sighed and recorded the time on his call sheet. "They're talking about fining people with defective alarm systems. It wastes one hell of a lot of our time."

"He claims it's not defective. He's an inventor and he's checked all the wiring."

Frederick Warfer joined them. "I'm sorry, Officer. I had hoped that hiring Miss Knowles might solve the problem."

"Give me a chance," Libby countered. "It's only my first night."

A light went on in the house across the street and she saw Helen Rodney appear in the doorway. "Are you all right, Frederick?" she called.

"I'm fine, Helen," he called back. "Just another false alarm." She wrapped her robe more tightly around her, waved, and went back inside.

"You'd better disconnect the alarm for tonight," Oakes suggested after taking a quick walk around the house, shining his flashlight at the windows and trying the doors.

"All right," Warfer told him. "I'll disconnect the call-in alarm that flashes at the police station, but I'll leave on the house alarm."

Somehow she didn't think their unseen visitor would be back that night and she was right. They spent the rest of the time till dawn in undisturbed slumber.

Since the bodyguard assignment was only for nighttime, Libby left Warfer's house and drove to her office in the morning as usual. She was going through the mail, dictating some replies to her secretary, when Sergeant O'Bannion phoned. "How'd it go last night, Libby?"

"The alarm went off but there was no one in the house. The same as before."

"I dug out the complaint file and checked on this guy Warfer. He's had a string of false alarms lately."

"I know. That's why he hired me."

"But there's more. Somebody flagged his file with a cross-index to Missing Persons."

"How come?"

"He had a wife named Monica Warfer."

"He told me she walked out on him." But he'd called her Betty.

"Maybe it's true. It was eleven years ago and she just disappeared one day. He said she went downtown to shop and never came back. We never found a trace of her. Some of the smart guys in the Bureau thought maybe he buried her in the back yard, but there was never any evidence of it."

"How old would she have been at the time?" Libby asked him. Warfer had told her Betty left him just two years ago.

"Somewhat younger than her husband. Only thirty-five. A good age for running off, I suppose."

"Any relatives?"

"A brother who still lives in town. Ralph Forrest. Want his address?"

"I think so, yes."

After lunch she tracked down Ralph Forrest at work. He was a used-car salesman at a lot near downtown. When she told him what she wanted, his manner turned into something resembling annoyance. "Monica's gone," he said. "She's been gone for eleven years. Why are you bothering me now?"

"You must have heard from her during that time—a postcard or something."

He shook his head. "We weren't very close toward the end."

"The end of what?"

"I mean before she went away. I'd be the last one she'd write to."

"Who'd be the first one?"

"Her husband, I suppose."

"Are you friendly with Frederick Warfer?"

"Not so's you'd notice. He came raving to me a few times after she left, but I haven't seen him in years."

"You think she ran away from him?"

"You met Warfer? What do you think? Me, I always thought she was crazy to marry him in the first place. Anything might have happened."

"He believes someone has been breaking into his house, trying to harm him."

"Who'd bother?"

"You don't think your sister could be back in the city, do you?"

The very idea seemed to startle him. He thought about it, but only for a moment. "No, she's not back. She's never coming back."

"Would you happen to have a picture of your sister?"

"I might have an old snapshot in my desk. Let me see."

Libby followed him into an office at the center of the lot. He rummaged through the drawers of a cluttered desk before coming up with a photograph of a solemn woman in her thirties with dark hair and eyes. It wasn't the same woman as the one in the photograph by Frederick Warfer's bed.

"Was your sister ever called Betty?"

"Betty? No—her name was Monica." He seemed about to say more, but Libby was in a hurry now. "May I keep this picture for a bit?"

"Take it," he told her tiredly. "I don't need it."

Libby arrived promptly at eight o'clock to begin another night of guard duty This time Warfer was alone and there was no sign of his neighbor from across the street.

"I'm going to sleep down here in the living room tonight," she told him.

His eyes widened a bit but he said nothing to dissuade her. Once more she searched the ground floor of the house and made certain the doors and windows were locked. It was a warm night, but she didn't want to risk opening a window. "Don't you have air-conditioning?" she asked.

"It's bad for your health," he said with conviction. "I leave the windows open upstairs. Do you want to change your mind and—"

Libby shook her head. "I'm more likely to hear someone trying to break in if I'm down here," she told him.

After he went up to bed, Libby read a little, then, before she turned out the lights, she switched on the alarm system so that a small red light would go on in the house but no signal would be transmitted to the police. It just might be that the arrival of the squad car was scaring away the invisible intruder.

Taking care to keep below the four-foot height of the electronic beams that criss-crossed the first floor, she settled down with a blanket, a flashlight and her revolver close at hand on the coffee table. She could hear Warfer moving around upstairs for a time and then there was silence. It was about midnight.

For the next half hour, nothing happened.

Remembering how quickly the alarm had sounded the previous night. Libby began to grow uneasy. She kept glancing at the alarm switch in the hallway but no red light glowed. Then she remembered they hadn't retired until twelve-thirty last night and it had been a good half hour after that before the alarm had sounded.

She must have dozed momentarily. She awoke with a start, certain she'd felt something brush the air near her head. It was just before one by the glowing digits of her watch. She glanced toward the hallway and froze. The alarm light was showing red!

She rolled over on her back and quickly reached for the flashlight on the table. Holding it in her left hand, she picked up the revolver with her right. Then she felt it again, the feather-light rush of air. She snapped on the flashlight.

It was a bat, swooping and soaring about the room as if seeking an exit. Libby jumped to her feet and hit the light switch. Turning back, she saw the bat fly into the fieldstone fireplace and disappear.

The fireplace! Of course! It had gotten in there somehow a week ago and was unable to find its way back up the chimney! Every night, after the lights were turned out, it flew around the ground floor of the house seeking its freedom, then retreated up the chimney again when the lights went back on. It was as simple as that.

Libby was grinning as she ran up the stairs to break the good news to Frederick Warfer. The light was on in his room, as she knew it would be once the alarm light had shown. "It's all over," she announced, knocking at his half closed door, "I found our intruder."

The silence that greeted her was so ominous, she pushed the door open cautiously.

Frederick Warfer was slumped against the bed by the window. His throat had been cut and he was dead.

Libby had to steady herself against a chair as she looked down at the bloody sight. Then the wave of nausea passed and she looked around the room to make certain the killer wasn't hiding there. She checked the closet and under the bed. The window was open, but it was a good fifteen-foot drop to the ground.

The red alarm light on Warfer's bedside panel was still on. It reminded her of the police and she went to the phone to call them. In almost no time, she heard a squad car pull up.

There were two cars, actually, and Officer Oakes emerged from one. "We figured we'd hear from you tonight," he said.

"Mr. Warfer's been murdered," she told him. "He's upstairs, in his bedroom."

"What?"

"Someone cut his throat."

The young policeman ran up the stairs ahead of her with the two officers from the second car behind him. "So the intruder finally got to him," Oakes said after checking out the body for signs of life.

"No, the intruder who set off the alarm was a bat."

"Then who—?" He stared at her.

"I don't know. I was downstairs. He was alone up here."

There were other cars pulling up outside and she was thankful to see Sergeant O'Bannion climbing the stairs, followed by some other detectives. "What happened?" he asked.

She told him about the bat and about finding Warfer dead. "He was my client," she heard herself saying. "And now he's dead."

"We lose clients all the time, Libby. Every time a taxpayer is mugged or killed, it's a client we've failed."

"This is a first for me."

"Any ideas about it?" he asked as the lab technicians set about their business.

She glanced at the photograph of Warfer's wife. "Not right now."

"It looks as if the killer either came up the stairs or through the window. Go home and get some rest, Libby. We'll handle it from here."

"Don't you want a statement from me?"

"Come down to the office in the morning."

Still she felt she had to remain until they took the body away. Frederick Warfer had paid her for the week and she hadn't earned it. Maybe she wouldn't really earn it if she found his killer, either, but it was the least she could try to do now.

On the way out to her car later, she saw Helen Rodney watching from behind her picture window across the street.

Libby stopped by the office in the morning before going to police headquarters. She wanted to look through the mail and tell her secretary what had happened, but instead she found a familiar-looking middle-aged woman waiting in the reception room.

"This is Mrs. Coxe," Janice said from behind her desk. "She'd like to talk with you."

Libby glanced at her watch. It wasn't yet ten and she had a few minutes. If only she could remember where she'd seen the woman before. "Come in, Mrs. Coxe. I have to go out again in ten minutes, but perhaps I can help you."

"I heard on the morning news that Frederick Warfer was killed last night while you were guarding him."

Then it clicked. ""The photo in his bedroom! You're Betty Warfer!" The woman smiled slightly. "Not any more," she said, taking the seat opposite Libby's desk. "That was over two years ago. In fact, I'm not really sure I ever was Mrs. Warfer legally. That's why I wanted to see you before I went to the police."

Libby took out the photograph of Monica Forrest. "I think you can help me clear something up. Frederick Warfer told me he'd been married to you for twenty-one years when you left him two years ago. But eleven years ago he had a wife whose maiden name was Monica Forrest—this woman—who disappeared and was never seen again."

Betty Coxe nodded. "I can explain it in one word—bigamy. Frederick had two wives at the same time."

"How did he manage that?"

"He and I lived in the house on Maple Shade Drive. He had another house well out in the suburbs where he lived with Monica. His consultant's business involved a great deal of travel—or so I was always led to believe. He kept up this double life for twenty years or more. I suspect he might have had a child by her. It was never clear which of us he married first, so I don't even know if my marriage was legal. My divorce was, though."

"How did you find out about his other marriage?"

"One day eleven years ago I wanted to use one of his credit cards for some shopping. We needed some yard equipment—a pruning hook for the trees and some shovels to dig up the rose garden and put in some new things. In his wallet I found a credit card in his name but with a different address out in Shady Heights I asked him about it and he went to pieces. He confessed to a double life and begged me to forgive him. He promised he'd get rid of this other woman, Monica, and be faithful to me. A short time later he told me she'd run off, disappeared. He even filed a missing-persons report with the police but she never turned up."

"What happened to this child you mentioned?"

"Fred never admitted the boy was his. He said it happened about the same time we were married and she used her pregnancy to trap him into marrying her, too. After she disappeared, her brother raised him. I had believed everything Fred said, but about two years ago the brother, Ralph Forrest, came to see me. He told me for the first time that the police suspected Fred of murdering Monica. But they hadn't known about his double life and they never found her body. I was horrified."

"Why did her brother come to you at that late date?"

"He'd only just found out about me himself. He was clinging to the hope that Monica was still alive and might have contacted Fred. When I couldn't help him, he told me the police theory. Once he put it into words, I realized it might be true. That's when I decided to leave Fred. I got a divorce and have since remarried."

"You say you're going to the police now. For what reason?"

"To tell them what I know. If Monica's brother really suspected Fred of causing her death, he might have had a motive for killing him."

She hesitated. "I just wondered—"

"What?" Libby asked.

"Well, Fred was never one to be without a woman. I wanted to make certain there wasn't another one around who might have had a reason to kill him. I don't want to get the police after Ralph Forrest without cause."

"There was no other woman that I know of," Libby answered. Then she remembered Helen Rodney across the street.

Sergeant O'Bannion listened to Betty Coxe's story and when she had gone he called Libby into his office. "What do you think about this, Libby?"

"I'm not on the force any more," she reminded him. "I don't have to think anything about it."

"Come on, Libby. Give me a break."

"All right—have you questioned the woman who lives across the street? Her name is Helen Rodney. She was at Frederick Warfer's house when I arrived two nights ago. He said she'd been trying to take care of him since Betty left him—"

"Rodney." He shuffled through the reports on his desk. "Sure—young Oakes talked to her last night. I'll read you his report: 'Arrived at Warfer home at one A.M. in response to burglar alarm. All seemed, quiet outside the house but noted a neighbor, Helen Rodney, crossing her front yard at number 34. The Rodney woman reported she'd been walking her dog and thought she saw a light in the Warfer garage. Before I could investigate further, patrol car arrived in response to telephone call reporting dead man at Warfer home.'"

"So she was on the prowl last night," Libby said.

"Walking her dog. People do walk their dogs at night."

"A woman alone, at one in the morning?"

"Maybe it's a big attack dog."

"And maybe we should have a look at Warfer's garage."

O'Bannion grinned at her as he got to his feet. "I'll get you back on the force yet, Libby. Let's go ..."

When they reached the Warfer home, they found Oakes and a police officer named Skefski just coming out the front door with a large butterfly net. "We caught your bat," Oakes said. "It was in the chimney, all right."

Libby peered at it and made a face. "I hate those things."

She followed O'Bannion into the attached garage and watched while he looked over the accumulation of garden tools, automotive parts, and just plain junk. "The side door was unlocked," O'Bannion pointed out. "Anyone could have come in here. Maybe that woman across the street did see something."

Libby nodded. "The killer could have picked up a pair of garden shears, slipped up the stairs somehow, and killed Warfer."

"Except that the door to the kitchen and the rest of the house was locked on the inside. We need a better theory than that, Libby."

She'd walked over and was examining the long pruning hook leaning against one wall of the garage. It was in two sections that fastened together. Each was six feet long or more and the top section had a curved, saw-toothed blade at the top for cutting high limbs. Looking up at it now, the blade appeared a bit rusty from disuse. Ironic, Libby thought, remembering that it was the pruning hook Betty had been going to buy when she discovered her husband's double life.

"What is it?" O'Bannion asked, following her gaze.

"The garden," she said. "Betty Coxe was buying gardening supplies. They were digging, putting in new things. This was eleven years ago, remember, when she discovered the truth and Warfer promised to break it off. And then the other one, Monica, disappeared. Your officers thought he might have buried her in the back yard but there was no evidence of that. But suppose he put her body in the trunk of his car and drove back over here? Suppose he buried her in this back yard?"

O'Bannion was unconvinced. "Why would he do that?"

"They were digging here anyway. Betty told us that. And he'd have been renting or selling the other house after Monica was gone. Much safer to have the unmarked grave here, where he could watch it."

"It makes sense, I suppose." He groaned wearily. "This is a big back yard."

"Not that big when you know what you're looking for." Libby led the way into the yard and headed for the back. "They were digging up the rose garden," she said.

O'Bannion stood staring at it for a full two minutes, then he gave a yell. "Skefski! Oakes! Grab a couple of shovels from the garage and come back here—we've got some digging to do!"

The two officers shed their Sam Browne belts and started digging up Frederick Warfer's rose garden. They'd been at it about ten minutes when Skefski's shovel encountered something besides roots. "A piece of canvas," he said, peering down into the excavation. "Pretty well rotted away."

"Go easy now," O'Bannion cautioned. "Use your hands."

Libby hated herself for what she was about to do.

"There are bones here," Officer Oakes said, his voice breaking.

"They belong to Monica Forrest," Libby said quite clearly. "They belong to your mother, Mr. Oakes. You thought all along that he killed her. That's why you murdered Frederick Warfer."

She was ready for him to come charging out of the newly uncovered grave in a murderous rage, swinging his shovel at her. Instead, he sank slowly to his knees and wept. "What is all this?" O'Bannion asked, bewildered.

Libby felt drained of emotion. "David Oakes is Monica Forrest's son. Maybe he's Warfer's son, too, but we'll probably never know that for sure. He looks very much like the picture of Monica that her brother gave me, especially his eyes. After his mother disappeared David was brought up by his uncle, Ralph Forrest, and he changed his name before becoming a police officer. Maybe Forrest suggested Oakes to him. Warfer's double life began at least twenty years ago and Betty told me she thought Monica had a child by him early on. That would make the child in his or her early twenties."

While she spoke, Oakes remained kneeling. Skefski stood by him. Neither man spoke. "How do you know he killed Warfer?" O'Bannion asked quietly.

"In his written report about seeing Helen Rodney walking her dog he said he came here in response to the burglar alarm. But no alarm sounded because I turned it off myself. The second car came in response to my call.

He came here earlier for another reason, and when Helen Rodney saw him prowling around the house moments after he'd killed Warfer, he had to avoid suspicion by questioning her."

"How could he have entered the house?"

"He didn't enter it. Remember that pruning hook in the garage? The blade at the end seemed to me at first to have rust spots, but now I think they may be traces of dried blood. Officer Oakes must have noticed it when he searched the house for intruders earlier in the week—and he probably noticed Betty's picture upstairs, too, rather than his mother's. He would remember Warfer after eleven years even if Warfer didn't recognize him. He came here last night, assembled the two sections of the pruning hook in the garage, and went around to the back of the house. The thing is at least twelve feet long with a saw-toothed blade at the end. Held by a man, it could easily reach a second-floor window fifteen feet off the ground. He probably tapped on the window with the blade or threw pebbles at it. Warfer looked out and saw a police officer he knew standing in the yard, opened the window wider, stuck his head out—and got his throat ripped open with that saw-toothed blade."

"I always knew he'd killed her," Oakes said dreamily, still kneeling by the grave. "I was asleep that night but I woke up and heard them fighting. He was going to break it off and leave her. They fought a lot and I went back to sleep. Later he said she left him, but I knew it wasn't true. She'd never have left him without taking me along. My uncle Ralph thought so, too. I joined the police force thinking someday I could find the evidence against him, and when I got called out here this week and saw him, I—"

"I must caution you," O'Bannion interrupted, "that you're entitled to an attorney before making a statement."

"That's all right, Sergeant. I did it and I'd do it again."

O'Bannion motioned to Skefski. "Take him into custody. I'll get that pruning hook from the garage, then—"

"I think I'll go now," Libby said.

"Thanks to you," O'Bannion told her, "we've wrapped up two murders."

"But I wasn't successful in protecting my client's life," Libby said. "He's dead and I don't feel any triumph about finding his killer."

O'Bannion took her arm. "It was probably fate that brought Warfer and Oakes together again after eleven years."

"Fate," said Libby. "Or a bat caught in a chimney."

It was a man named Matt Milton who telephoned the Libby Knowles Protection Service on a hot Monday morning in August. Libby's secretary Janice said he sounded like a client and Libby took the call.

"What can I do for you, Mr. Milton?"

"Am I speaking to Libby Knowles?"

"That's correct."

"I'm calling about an extremely confidential matter involving one of my clients."

"Are you a private investigator, Mr. Milton?"

"I'm a personal manager. An agent. You must have heard of my client, Krista Steele, the rock singer?"

"I don't follow the contemporary music scene as closely as I should," Libby admitted. "Is your client in need of protection?"

"She is."

"From fans, or from some specific person?"

"From herself. She's been using cocaine and other drugs lately, and she's finally agreed to my suggestion she hire a bodyguard to keep her off the stuff. Is it the sort of thing you could do?"

"It's not what I'm in business to do," Libby said, "but if your client is willing to cooperate, I could give it a try."

"Good. Could you meet with Krista and me this afternoon at my office? We'll discuss your duties and your fees."

Matt Milton was a fatherly looking man in his fifties who wore a string tie of the sort Libby remembered from movies of the Old South. He was a bit chubby around the middle and smoked expensive-looking cigars. He was the last person in the world one might expect to be promoting the career of Krista Steele.

Krista was slender and tall—close to Libby's own five-foot-eight. She wore a dangling earring in her right ear. Her hair was all on the left, hiding that ear, and her pale-blue eyes were almost lost in a maze of harsh black eyeliner.

Her silk dress looked expensive. She pouted at Libby from her chair. "You're going to be my nursemaid?" she asked in a cold voice.

"If you need one. But what you'll be hiring is a bodyguard, and I don't come cheap."

"I thought bodyguards were male," Krista said, fidgeting with the clasp of her little purse.

Matt Milton cleared his throat. "I thought Miss Knowles could do the job better, without distractions. She's highly recommended."

Krista studied Libby for another moment and then asked, "You know what you're supposed to do?"

"Tell me."

"Keep me off drugs—cocaine, speed, grass, LSD. If you see me buying any-thing or taking something from a stash someplace, take it away from me."

"All right. Will you be cooperative?"

When Krista didn't answer, Matt Milton did. "Yes, she'll cooperate. But if she resists you, be as firm as necessary. That's what you're being paid for. We'll pay you a thousand dollars a week. Is that satisfactory?"

It was more money than Libby had ever made before. "Plus expenses?"

"Plus expenses."

"For how long?"

"Week to week, till we see how it goes."

"How much travel is involved?"

Krista Steele shifted in her chair. She stopped playing with the clasp on her purse and said, "I have a concert tour next month, but for the next few weeks there are only recording dates here in town, and rehearsals."

"Will I be living with you?"

"We'd expect full-time service," Milton said. "Is that a problem?"

"No, I'm used to it."

"How soon can you start?"

"As soon as I phone my office."

Matt Milton smiled. "I believe tomorrow morning will be satisfactory. Krista has a recording date then. This is her address."

As he wrote it on a card, Krista stood up. "You'd better be worth the money," she told Libby and walked out of the office.

Libby turned to the agent, "One thing I don't quite understand, Mr. Milton. Do I get fired for doing a poor job, or for doing a good job?"

Krista Steele lived in a fourteenth-floor condominium near the center of the city. The doorman looked like an ex-wrestler and there was a television camera in the elevator. It was obviously a place for people who worried about security. Her apartment was large and well furnished, with a fine view of the river, but Libby's first impression when she entered was the sweetish odor of marijuana smoke that accompanied the leather-jacketed young man who was just leaving.

He passed her without speaking and Libby asked, "Who was that?"

"Sonny Ritz, an old pal from before I hit the big time. I figured I needed one last night of kicks before I went on the wagon."

"Did he supply the pot?"

"Yeah."

"Is he your pusher?"

"I told you, he's an old friend." She hadn't yet gotten around to making up her eyes and the rest of her face, and Libby saw something sweet and almost innocent about her face.

"Is there any more pot around?" Libby asked her.

Krista shook her head. "Search the place if you don't believe me. Want some breakfast?"

"I already ate, but I'll take another cup of coffee."

Krista was wearing a lounging robe that had started to come open, and she seemed to have nothing on beneath it. "So tell me about yourself," she said in the kitchen. "If we're going to be together all the time I guess I should know what I hired."

"I used to be a policewoman," Libby said. "Now I run this protection business."

"Are you married?" Krista opened a can of food for a large aggressive white cat that seemed to appear out of nowhere.

Libby shook her head. "My boyfriend was killed. He was a cop, too. He was involved in a cocaine scandal and smashed up his car."

"Why are you telling me this?" Krista asked, pouring some coffee.

"Because you asked me. Because I thought maybe you'd be interested in knowing that cocaine almost ruined my life, too."

"I get all the lectures I need from Matt." Krista went into the bedroom and started to dress.

Libby followed her. "How old are you, Krista?"

"Twenty-four. I started out in a Greenwich Village club and hit it big with the theme from *August Heat*. They did a neat video of me dancing around a fireman while he squirted his hose at me. The kids went wild with it and the album sold a couple of million copies. Now I'm doing more albums and I've got the concerts coming up. Maybe you saw me on that late-night show last Friday."

"No, I've never seen you. But I'm sure you're good."

"Fox wants me to star in a movie after my tour. I'm thinking about it. That's one reason why Matt wants me off the stuff. He says it's ruining my career. God, he's worse than my father!"

"Where are your folks?"

"They live outside Chicago. I haven't seen them in a year, but I send money home once in a while. You grow away from them in this business, you know?"

She had pulled on tight jeans and a blouse, which Libby supposed must be her recording costume. "What time are you due at the studio?"

"Whenever I get there." She started combing her hair. The earring had apparently stayed in her right ear all night. "Do you carry a gun?"

"Sure," Libby said.

"Where?"

"In my purse. Sometimes under my clothes."

"Where under your clothes?"

"Strapped to my thigh."

"That must be a real kick."

"It's damned uncomfortable, if you want to know," Libby said.

They rode down in the elevator to the basement and walked directly to an underground parking garage for tenants. Libby saw no sign of a parking attendant and decided the security wasn't that great after all.

Krista insisted on driving and took the wheel of the little white sportscar as if she'd been born with it in her hands. Weaving in and out of the morning traffic, they arrived at the suburban recording studio in fifteen minutes. "Matt keeps telling me I should record in Nashville, and I'm going to after this record," she said as they entered the building. "But Shawn Gibbs has been good to me. His setup's the best in town. Here are a couple of full-sized-studios and behind this blank wall is another one he rarely uses."

Gibbs, a tense, balding man with hornrimmed glasses, was pacing the corridor awaiting Krista's arrival. "The musicians have been tuning up for an hour," he told her. "We have to pay them, you know."

Krista kissed him lightly on the cheek. "This is Libby Knowles. She's my bodyguard."

He shook Libby's hand limply, not giving her a second look.

Inside the studio, Matt Milton seemed relieved to see Libby. "You're late. I was worried," he said.

Krista dropped her purse and sunglasses on a chair and accepted some sheet music from a bearded young man with an electric guitar.

"Fill me in on some of these people," Libby said to Matt.

"The beard with the guitar is Zap Richards. He's Krista's arranger and composes some of her songs, too. He did the *August Heat* theme. They've been friends for years. The rest are local musicians Shawn hires for the sessions."

Libby glanced around at the expensive equipment. "He seems to be really big time."

"He is now, since Krista hit the top. He'd be lost without her."

"Do you know someone named Sonny Ritz?"

The agent frowned. "That crud! Has he been around?"

"He was at her apartment when I arrived this morning."

"Don't let him near her again," Milton said firmly, "or sure as hell he'll slip her something she shouldn't have."

They started recording the first number and Libby settled back to enjoy it. Krista Steele's voice was a surprise, deep and mellow and assured. She needed very few tricks to put across the song. She built to a climax that brought enthusiastic applause from Matt and Shawn outside the recording booth, and Zap Richards put aside his guitar to give her a hug. But she wasn't satisfied and insisted that they run through it once more before it sounded right to her.

The second number was just as good, but on the third one she started having trouble. Twice she stopped in the middle, and the third time she still wasn't satisfied. Finally, she called for a break and picked up her purse, heading for the ladies' room.

"Go with her." Milton told Libby. "Make sure she doesn't take anything."

Libby was following Krista when Zap Richards emerged from the studio to block her path. "She just needs to freshen up," he said. "She won't be a minute." His long slender fingers caught Libby's arm but she brushed them away.

"Neither will I," she said.

Krista was standing on one of the toilet seats, reaching up through a ceiling panel. Her hand reappeared with a plastic envelope full of white powder. Libby quickly crossed the tiled floor and grabbed it from her. "I'll take that."

"No! I need it to get me started for this next number!" Krista tried to claw the envelope out of Libby's hand, but Libby ripped it open and poured the cocaine into the toilet.

"I'm just doing what you hired me for, Krista. Is there any more hidden up there?"

"No!"

Libby climbed up beside her to take a look. She pulled two more plastic envelopes from where Krista was reaching for them and emptied the contents down the toilet. "I'm not kidding, Krista, and it's time you realized it. You can have your agent fire me, but you can't con me into not doing my job. You hired a bodyguard and that's what you've got."

Krista returned to the recording studio, pouting and unhappy. Her first attempt at the song was again off-key, but she took a few minutes' break and did better the second time. Shawn Gibbs applauded on the third try and told her they'd use that one. She nodded nervously and said, "That's it. We'll have to do the rest tomorrow."

Zap Richards unplugged his guitar and came over to her. "You all right, Krista?"

"I'll make it." She gave him a halfhearted smile.

He dug around in his pocket and produced a hand-rolled cigarette. "This is all I've got on me."

Libby stepped between them and Krista said, "Put it away, Zap. I don't want it."

"This is some watchdog you hired for yourself."

"I've been called worse," Libby said.

They had a late lunch with Shawn Gibbs and Matt Milton. Gibbs was either pleased at the way the session had gone or he was putting a good face on it for Krista's benefit. He talked about his plans for the album and Matt tried to sell him on merchandising ideas connected with the upcoming concert tour. By the time they left the restaurant, the afternoon had pretty much ended and Krista had to go to her dressmaker's for a fitting.

Afterward, they headed back to the apartment. "We'll eat in tonight," Krista said. "Something light."

"Is this a fairly typical day?"

"Sometimes it's a little more exciting. There are a couple of parties this weekend. But I'm afraid next week you're going to have to sit through five days of dance class. I'm adding some dance numbers to my show."

"How long do you think you'll need me?"

"Maybe through the concert tour. If I can stay clean that long I should be okay." She hesitated and then added, "You did good work today, Libby. On that third number I was sure I needed a snort, but when you wouldn't let me have it I managed without it, didn't I?"

"You sure did."

Libby played with the cat for a while before they ate, but Krista's habit of allowing it to roam at will over chairs and tabletops turned her off. She had to race to finish her coffee before Tabby licked up his share. But the real challenge of the evening began with the return of Sonny Ritz, still wearing his leather jacket, shortly after ten o'clock. It seemed obvious to Libby that he intended to spend the night with Krista, and she didn't know how she could prevent a drug exchange from taking place without sharing the bed with them.

"This is your nursemaid, eh?" Sonny asked, looking Libby up and down with a smirk. "Do I have to wrestle her for you?"

"You're welcome to if you think you can," Libby said.

He made a grab for her and Libby sidestepped, catching his arm and twisting it behind him until he dropped to his knees. When she let him up, the color had drained from his face.

Krista loved it. "Sonny," she said, "you've finally met your match."

Sonny seemed not about to quit that easily, but the intercom buzzed and the doorman announced that Shawn Gibbs was on his way up to see Krista.

"What does he want this time of the night?" she complained. She turned to Sonny. "You'd better go. I'll call you in a few days."

"What is this, the brushoff?"

"Just go, Sonny. I'll call you, I promise."

He left just as Shawn Gibbs reached the door. Libby noticed they didn't speak.

"Is he still hanging around?" Gibbs asked Krista. "I thought you got rid of him."

Libby was checking out the area of the room Sonny had occupied, making certain he hadn't left any little envelopes for Krista.

"Sorry to come by so late," Gibbs said, "but something's come up at the studio."

"What's that?"

"Somebody stole the master tape of the three songs we recorded this morning."

"*What?*"

"At least I think it's been stolen. It could have been misfiled—I'm going to tear the place apart in the morning. But I wanted you to know we may have to do the whole thing over again."

Krista took the news in good humor. "It's not even in the stores yet and my public is clamoring for it. You'll make a mint on this one, Shawn."

"I'm glad you can take it so lightly. How about a drink to settle my nerves?"

"Be my guest," Krista said.

He poured three shots of bourbon and passed one to Libby without asking if she wanted it. After a sip, she left the rest on the table unfinished. She was a Scotch drinker, when she drank at all. "So was the studio broken into?" Krista wanted to know.

"No sign of it." Shawn Gibbs was nervous, sitting at the kitchen table with them for a time and then pacing back and forth. "I suspect an inside job, but I can't figure out who would have done it. If they wanted to steal the tape, why not wait until tomorrow when we were planning to finish it?"

"Maybe Libby here can find it for you."

Libby held up her hands. "Protection, not detection, that's my business. Just because I was with the police people always think I can solve crimes. Have you reported the theft to the police?"

"Not yet," Shawn said. "I thought I'd wait until morning when I can make a more careful search."

He finished his drink and declined a second, saying he had to go. Krista saw him out and he promised to phone in the morning if the tape reappeared before her recording session at ten.

When they went to bed around midnight, Libby insisted on leaving the door between her room and Krista's open. She had trained herself to be a light sleeper when she was on a case and she knew any unusual movements by Krista would awaken her.

The telephone in Krista's bedroom rang somewhere toward dawn. The first bits of daylight were beginning to show through the closed blinds as Libby opened her eyes and listened. She heard Krista's voice, briefly, and then silence. She hadn't been able to make out her words, and decided it wasn't important until some minutes later, almost asleep again, she heard the apartment door close. The clock read 6:55.

She jumped out of bed and hurried barefoot into Krista's room. The bed was rumpled and empty. With a growing sense of panic, Libby checked the rest of the apartment and then the outer hall. Krista was gone and Libby had no idea where. She saw little point in phoning Matt Milton to report it. She was sitting on her bed, thinking about what to do, when Krista's telephone rang again. She glanced instinctively at the clock and saw that it was 7:22. Running to answer the phone, she prayed it was Krista.

It wasn't.

"Is this the residence of Krista Steele?" a male voice asked. He was reading the name off something and Libby knew at once it was a police officer.

"Yes. What is it?"

"Are you a relative, ma'am?"

"No. I work for Miss Steele," Libby replied.

"I'm afraid I've got some bad news, ma'am. There's been an automobile accident. Could you tell me how to reach the next of kin?"

"Next of—?"

"I'm awfully sorry, ma'am. Miss Steele was killed instantly."

Libby found her old friend, Sergeant O'Bannion, in his office when she reached police headquarters less than an hour later. He glanced up and gave her a grin. "A bit early for you, isn't it?" He was a large man with a big face that was more often gloomy than smiling.

"There was a fatal car accident an hour or so ago, O'Bannion. Krista Steele, the singer, was killed. Do you have a report on it yet?"

"An hour ago? I doubt it. The investigating officers are probably still at the scene."

He got up to check a pile of forms on one of the other squadroom desks and she followed him.

"The officer said it happened on Dakota Street, near Windsor. The car hit a tree."

"Nothing here yet," he started to say, and then stopped. "What time did you say?"

"A little after seven."

"There's a report here of a fatal on Dakota Street, one car, driver killed, time about six-forty-five."

"That would have been too early," Libby said. "I was at her apartment and she didn't leave until at least ten minutes after that. It would have taken her another ten minutes to get her car and drive to Dakota Street."

"What's your connection with this, Libby?"

"She was a client."

"You were protecting her from a death threat?"

Libby shook her head. "She was on drugs and her agent convinced her to hire a bodyguard to keep her away from them."

"Odd sort of assignment. Okay, come along and we'll look into this."

They went first to check out the death car, which had been towed to a city lot nearby. There was no doubt it was the white sportscar Libby had ridden in the previous day, though now the interior was scorched and blackened by flames.

"According to the report, the body was burned beyond recognition," Libby heard O'Bannion say. "They identified her from the license number and the contents of her purse, which was thrown clear."

"Convenient."

"What?"

"If the accident happened at 6:45, it was someone else," Libby insisted. Quickly she went over the events of the previous day and that morning.

"You might have been wrong about the time," O'Bannion said.

"I was fully awake when I looked at that clock."

"Then maybe it wasn't Krista Steele you heard leaving at 6:55. Maybe this guy Ritz came back and spent the night, after all."

"I'd have heard him. It was Krista who answered the phone and it was Krista who left at 6:55."

They went back to O'Bannion's office and read the report of the investigating officers. Both swore the accident happened no later than 6:45. They came upon the burning car while on routine patrol. Some nearby neighbors were already on the scene, awakened by the crash a few minutes earlier.

"Then it wasn't Krista," Libby said again.

They had to wait an hour for the preliminary report of the medical examiner. The body was that of a female in her early twenties, about the same height and weight as Krista Steele. Fingerprints were of no use since Krista's were not on file and the impact of the crash had caused such extensive damage in the area of the mouth that a comparison with Krista's dental records would be difficult if not impossible.

"I'll still lay you odds it's her," the sergeant said.

"Then how do you explain the time discrepancy?"

"Simple," he said with a shrug. "The clock you looked at was running fast."

Returning to Krista's condominium, Libby used her key to let them in. The white cat, Tabby, had awakened and was purring near the door as if expecting his mistress. Libby ignored him and went immediately to the bedroom she'd been using. "Here it is. Check it for yourself."

The clock was actually a couple of minutes slow.

"Somebody might have changed it," O'Bannion said rather lamely.

"If someone were going to change it, wouldn't they have changed it the other way, to discredit my story?"

O'Bannion sat down on the unmade bed. The cat jumped up beside him and the policeman stroked him absently under the chin. "You've got a point there," he admitted. "Let's check the downstairs garage."

The attendant didn't come on duty until eight o'clock and, as Libby had observed the previous day, even then security was not very tight. No one had been there to see Krista or her car leave. Though the garage door opened only from the inside, it wasn't impossible to suppose that someone had entered the garage through a fire door and stolen the car sometime before six-thirty.

"Why?" O'Bannion asked. "You think she's trying to pull an insurance fraud?"

"That's what I intend to find out," Libby said. "Whoever's behind this, they had to arrange for that crash. And somebody died in that car. Somebody was *murdered* in that car."

Matt Milton took the news of Krista's apparent death very hard. Even after Libby told him she had reason to believe the body was not Krista's the agent remained close to tears. "It's her all right," he said. "I always figured she'd end up this way. The drugs and—" He wiped his eyes with a handkerchief. "God knows I did my best to help her."

"Mr. Milton, I have to ask you this and I hope you'll forgive me. Could this whole thing be some sort of publicity stunt on Krista's part, to promote her new album?"

He stared at Libby as if she was out of her mind. "Publicity stunt! Why would she have allowed me to hire you if she was planning something like that?"

"To have a witness on the scene. After the funeral she could reappear, claiming it was a hitchhiker who died in the car and she wandered off after the crash with temporary amnesia."

"You're saying she'd cause someone's death for a publicity stunt," Milton said. "Krista would never do anything like that."

"Did you know the master tape from yesterday's session was stolen from Shawn Gibbs' studio last night?"

"Really? Who would do a thing like that?"

"Perhaps someone who knew it would be her last recording. I suppose that would give it some extra value."

"Now you're saying she's dead. Make up your mind, Miss Knowles."

But Libby couldn't make up her mind. She felt certain Krista hadn't died in the fiery crash, but that conclusion only opened a whole new barrel of questions. O'Bannion had promised to keep her informed of the police investigation, but when she left Milton's office and tried phoning him. He was out.

She drove to the recording studio, where the gloom was even thicker than at Milton's office. Zap Richards met her just inside the door, looking naked and alone without his guitar. "One of the cops says you don't think she's dead. Is that true?"

"I don't know what to think," Libby admitted. "But I'm certainly not convinced she's dead."

She went on down the hall to Shawn Gibbs' office. The door was open. "I was hoping you'd come by," he said, looking up from his desk.

"How's it going?"

"The place has been a madhouse. We've had two television crews and I don't know how many reporters here."

"Anything new on the missing tape?"

"That's what I wanted to tell you. We found it. Zap was helping me search this morning, before we heard about Krista, and he found it in among some blank tapes."

"Could it have gotten there by accident?"

"I suppose so," he admitted, "but it's unlikely."

"What do you think happened to Krista?" Libby asked.

"I can't imagine."

She met O'Bannion for a drink at a bar across from headquarters. She occasionally liked to go there because it had been a hangout while she was on the force, but tonight it brought back unexpectedly painful memories of the man she'd loved—who'd died in a single-car accident. She'd always wondered if it was suicide, and now she found herself asking the same question about Krista. Maybe she had decided she couldn't go on living without drugs.

But there had been the phone call that had lured her out before seven. Someone had made that call.

"Case got you down?" O'Bannion asked, reading her silence.

"I can't get a grip on it," she admitted. "A tape is stolen and then reappears. Krista might be dead but maybe she isn't."

"The papers sure think she's dead. There are bigger headlines than she ever got alive."

"Anything more from the autopsy?"

"Yeah, but you're not going to like it. The body showed traces of heroin."

"Krista Steele wasn't on heroin!"

"Who knows what she was on, Libby?"

She played with her glass in silence for a moment, then asked, "Could the accident have been faked?"

"Sure. She could have been beaten to death and her teeth messed up earlier, then the killer could have spilled gasoline around the inside of the car, tied down the accelerator and the steering wheel, and aimed it at the tree. The fire would have burned any string or rope that was used."

"And if the body isn't Krista's, whose is it?"

"From the approximate age and traces of heroin, along with the fact that we have no new missing-person report, it could be some prostitute or drifter, chosen because she was about the same size and age."

"Then you're willing to accept that as a possibility?"

O'Bannion thought about it. "I've been a cop long enough to know that the most likely explanation is usually the true one, Libby. Your idea is pretty far-fetched. Bring me some more evidence and I'll listen."

"If the body is that of some prostitute or even a runaway, maybe her fingerprints are on file even if Krista's aren't."

"That's an idea," he admitted. "I'll see how badly the fingers were burned."

After leaving O'Bannion at the bar, Libby went back to Krista's apartment to gather up her things. The place still looked the same, even to the empty glasses on the table from the previous night, but Libby didn't stop to wash them. She was on her way out the door when the whole thing came to her in a flash.

She went back inside, unpacked her other gun, and changed from slacks to a full skirt.

Libby parked across the street from the recording studio and slipped out of the car, moving silently around the side of the building. The figure by the back door heard her just as he popped the lock. He whirled, but she had him covered with the revolver from her purse. "A little breaking and entering, Sonny?"

Sonny Ritz dropped the crowbar and took a step backward.

"Are you after Krista's tape, too?"

"I don't know anything about it."

"Then what are you doing breaking in here?"

"She kept a stash hidden in the ceiling of the ladies' john. I figure it won't do her any good now—I might as well have it."

"I beat you to it, Sonny. Now get lost."

"What?"

"Get lost before I call the cops."

He didn't need to be told again. He hurried down the alley, disappearing from view.

Libby waited another few seconds and then stepped inside through the jimmied door. A pen light from her purse helped guide her along the corridor. She avoided the recording studio Krista had used the previous day and went instead to the smaller, windowless studio that was rarely used. It was locked, of course. Libby fired a single shot into the lock area. The wood splintered but held, and she had to give it a sharp tug before the door finally came open.

A muffled groan reached her ears at once and she knew she'd guessed right. Her searching fingers found the light switch and in the sudden glare of brightness she saw Krista Steele bound and gagged on the leather couch.

Libby put down her pistol and quickly untied her, pulling the gag from her mouth.

"Thank God!" Krista gasped. "How did you find me?"

"I'd have been a hell of a bodyguard if I hadn't. Your cat—"

There was a sudden gasp from Krista, and Libby turned to see Shawn Gibbs standing in the doorway. He had a .45 automatic aimed at them. "Don't touch your gun," he warned Libby, "or I'll kill you both!"

"I'm not moving," Libby assured him.

"Raise your hands above your head!" he commanded. "Krista, you stay on that couch."

"Shawn, this is—"

"Shut up!" He motioned toward Libby.

"How did you find her here? When I heard the shot I thought it was the police."

"They're on the way," Libby bluffed.

"Not likely. You'd have waited for them. But tell me what I did wrong."

Libby saw the madness in his eyes now and knew she had to keep talking. "I was convinced Krista didn't die in that crash. Once I knew that, there were two things to implicate you—her purse and her cat. Krista didn't leave the apartment until 6:55, ten minutes or more after the accident. It couldn't have been her body in the car, yet the police identified her from the purse near the wreckage. If Krista couldn't have been there, how could her purse be there? Only if someone took it from the apartment earlier. She'd had it with her yesterday while she was recording. Two people visited us last night—you and Sonny Ritz. Sonny stayed only briefly and I watched him every second. You stayed longer, and you walked around nervously. You had plenty of opportunity to pick up that small purse and hide it under your shirt."

"You're a smart girl," Gibbs admitted.

"You know someone or found someone who resembled Krista in a general way and killed her this morning. You wanted to make sure the crash and the fire worked as planned before you kidnapped Krista, so you waited until after the crash to phone her—"

"He said it was something important about the stolen tape," Krista told Libby. "He said he'd pick me up in ten minutes."

"But of course the whole scheme wouldn't work if I was awake and heard the phone. I might have insisted on coming along. At the very least I'd know who called. How could you be sure I wouldn't wake up, Shawn? Only if you drugged my drink while you were stealing the purse. You were the one who suggested we have a drink. I only took a sip of mine and left the rest on the table, but tonight the glasses were all empty. If I didn't finish it, who did? Then I remembered how Tabby likes to climb up on tables and how he licked up my coffee. This morning he slept through two phone calls and Krista's departure—highly unusual behavior for a cat, unless he was drugged instead of me."

"You figured it all, didn't you?"

"Only you could have stolen the purse, only you could have drugged the drink. Stealing the car itself was no problem. You probably took the elevator straight to the garage after you left Krista's with the purse and used her own key to drive it away. You'd arranged the early-morning appointment with your victim and after killing her you phoned Krista from the crash scene. You picked her up by seven o'clock, drugged her, and brought her here before Zap and the others arrived.

"Figuring she was still alive, I asked myself where you could hide her. Then I remembered this windowless recording studio. These places are all sound-proof—where better to hide her? She was going to leave you after this album and record in Nashville—she told me that—and you couldn't bear to lose her."

Krista spoke again from the couch. "He said they'd think I was dead and nobody would be looking for me. He'd keep me a prisoner and I'd record just for him. After six months or a year he'd pretend to find the recordings and say they were made before my death. He said they'd be worth a fortune."

"You can't keep her here," Libby told Gibbs, starting to lower her hands.

"Keep them up!" he barked, waving the gun.

Libby stepped back until her legs touched the couch. "No one stole that tape. It was an excuse to visit Krista last night and lure her from the apartment this morning."

"Time for you to shut up," Gibbs said.

He was aiming the .45 when Krista's hand crept beneath Libby's skirt and found the second gun. She fired once and the bullet struck Shawn Gibbs in the right shoulder, spinning him around.

Libby crossed the room quickly and knocked the gun from his hand.

"Good work!" she told Krista.

"I remembered what you told me about your other gun."

"I should hire you for my bodyguard," Libby said. "Now get out to a phone and call the police."

Annie Sears was driving west, hoping to cover the 750-mile distance from El Paso to San Diego in two days. She didn't like driving in remote areas after dark and by the time she'd crossed the Arizona border she was looking for a town where she might spend the night. About an hour into the state on I-10, still a long way east of Tucson, she spotted a hand-lettered sign that read: CACTUS VALLEY DAYS NEXT EXIT.

Well, she reasoned, if they were trying to attract tourists they must have motel accommodations for them. She took the indicated exit and followed the infrequent signs south a few miles toward the Mexican border. Cactus Valley, when she reached it, was little more than a small town with a main street that seemed left over from the back lot of a Hollywood Western. But it did have lots of cactuses, not even counting the giant plastic one that dominated the grassy square and temporary crafts booths at the center of town.

Annie decided to get a room before pursuing the delights of Cactus Valley Days, and she settled on a low-priced motel just past the plastic cactus. The room clerk, a dour young man wearing glasses and an aggressive brush cut, managed to say, "Welcome to Cactus Valley," without smiling or even looking at her. "How long you staying?"

"Just one night. I'm driving through to San Diego."

He raised his eyes to take her in. "Going to school out there?"

That brought a little laugh from Annie. "I've been out of school quite a few years. I'm taking a job there. That's why I decided to drive. I'll need my car."

"Too bad you won't be staying longer. This is our summer festival time. Cactus Valley Days is held every June."

"You certainly have lots of cactuses around. On the hillsides they looked like an army of tall green men, waving their arms at me."

"Arizona is noted for its cactuses. Our state flower is the blossom of the Saguaro cactus. It appears in May and June, blooms during the cool desert nights, and closes again by midday. It's a special time of the year around here."

She filled out a registration card and paid in advance for the room. "After I shower I might take a walk over to the festival. It looks like fun."

He handed her a key. "Room 28 on the second floor. If you need anything, just call me. My name is Bill Symons."

"Thanks, Bill. I'll do that." She went up the stairs carrying her overnight bag. At least he'd grown a bit friendlier. Maybe she wouldn't have to worry about him stabbing her in the shower.

A Mexican band was on a makeshift stage playing a lively song Annie remembered from the El Paso bars, though she couldn't come up with its name. She'd changed into a T-shirt and jeans, with her long hair pulled into a ponytail. It was still daylight and a good crowd was wandering around to the various food and craft booths, A few people were even dancing to the Latin rhythms. Next to the stage was the plastic cactus, nearly twenty feet tall. She went up and felt the realistic two-inch spines clustered on the cactus ribs. Artificial blossoms adorned the ends of the branches.

"It's just like the real thing," a young woman next to her said. "We used to have a ten-footer until three years ago, but Russ Jewitt replaced it with this bigger one. He keeps it in his warehouse the rest of the year."

"I'm just passing through," Annie confessed. "Who's Russ Jewitt?"

"He has a lumberyard and dabbles in real estate. Stay around and you'll hear him give a speech. Are you here overnight?"

Annie focused on the young woman. Brown hair, fairly attractive in a blouse and jeans, probably a bit younger than her, maybe mid twenties. "I'm at the motel till morning. Then I'm off to San Diego."

"Great city. I visited it when I was in high school." She stuck out her hand. "I'm Marci McGreggor."

"Annie Sears. Pleased to meet you."

"We don't get many visitors to Cactus Valley, except during the festival. It's every year around this time, when the cactuses blossom. Have you met Bill Symons at the motel?"

"He checked me in."

"Bit of an odd bird, but he's harmless."

A boy was wandering through the crowd distributing a small tabloid newspaper and Annie took one. "What's this?"

"Our weekly paper with a schedule of festival activities. Too bad you won't be here longer."

A boxed item at the bottom of page one caught her eye: CACTUS KILLER STRIKES AGAIN. "What's this?"

"Don't worry, he's not killing people, just cactuses."

"Is it some sort of local joke?"

Marci smiled ruefully. "I wish it were! Some of the cactuses out there are over a hundred years old, and this guy's been going around with a high-powered rifle drilling them full of holes."

Something stirred in Annie's memory. "Wasn't there someone who shot at a cactus and it fell over and killed him?"

"Yeah I think that was over near Tucson somewhere. No such luck here. The sheriff thinks he sits in his car and fires from the road. We've had a lot of rain and the cactuses are plump this year."

Their conversation was interrupted by a voice on the loudspeaker. The Mexican music had ended and a well-built man in his forties, with graying hair and cowboy boots, had taken the microphone. "That's Russ Jewitt," Marci whispered in her ear. "He'll talk forever."

Jewitt began with the usual greeting, and then launched into a history of the area that residents had probably heard many times before. He spoke of plans for the town's future, which seemed to include a large discount store that would bring shoppers from a hundred miles away. "Naturally it'll be built on property he owns," Marci whispered again. "Come on! Let's get a beer."

That sounded like a good idea, so Annie followed along. A bar with the unimaginative name of Oasis was closest, and they settled at an outdoor table just far enough from the loudspeakers so they could ignore Jewitt's ramblings. "Do you have a job here in town?" Annie asked her new acquaintance.

"If you could call it that," the brown-haired woman answered. "I work at the county motor pool, checking vehicles in and out all day."

"Do you have a family?"

She shook her head. "I'm between husbands at the moment. How about you?"

Annie shrugged. "I lived with a cowboy back in El Paso for three years. When we broke up I decided to try San Diego. How are the men around here?"

"Stiff as cactuses and just as prickly. You can see how desperate we are when I tell you Bill Symons at the motel is considered one of our most eligible bachelors."

"He can't be more than twenty-five. How'd he manage to get a motel of his own?"

"He's twenty-seven actually. The motel belonged to his folks, but his mother died and three years ago his father, Pete Symons, just ran away. Hasn't been seen since."

"Was it a woman?"

"That was everyone's guess, maybe somebody passing through, like you are. It happened during the Cactus Valley Days festival. Jewitt saw him talking to a woman and then they were both gone. His car was still at the motel, so he must have gone off with somebody."

Russ Jewitt had ended his speech without their noticing, and the crowd was flowing down the paths to the various refreshment stands. A man wearing a uniform shirt and sheriff's badge wandered over to join them at their table. "Hi, Marci. How's it going?"

"Fine. Sheriff Redmont, this is Annie Sears. She stopped to see our festival on the way to California."

"Nice to have you, Annie. Don't let Marci here lead you astray. She's one of Cactus Valley's wild girls." He said it in a way that might have hinted at some past relationship. Certainly the sheriff was handsome, with a lazy smile that would have looked good in a Hollywood Western.

"Sure, I'm wild," Marci agreed, with a wink at Annie. "Think I'll go out and shoot me some cactuses tonight."

"What is all this cactus killing business?" Annie asked Sheriff Redmont. "Can you really kill one with a bullet?"

"Probably not with one bullet, but we think this guy fires several shots from an automatic rifle. Cactuses collect water and when they're fat and bulging with it, a few well-placed shots can split their skin and the water comes pouring out. There've been instances of cactuses exploding if they're hit by lightning. The cactus just collapses and that's the end of it."

"How long has this shooting been going on?"

This is the third year, though for some reason it's mostly in May and June. My deputies keep an eye out when they're on patrol, but there's a lot of land out here. At first he just seemed to hit targets within sight of the road, as if he was firing from his car, but lately we've found some collapsed cactuses up in the hills. There are plenty of dirt roads through there. It's probably some kid with a rifle and a pickup. He's causing lots of damage, though."

Russ Jewitt was edging through the crowd with a smile and a handshake, working his way toward the sheriff. When he reached their table he took the empty chair and smiled at Annie, waiting to be introduced. Marci obliged and he shook hands with a gentlemanly nod. "Just passing through? That's a shame. We're friendly folk here in Cactus Valley. Where you staying?"

She shrugged. "The motel." Somewhat defensively she added, "It's only for one night."

"That's one night too many to be under the same roof with Bill Symons. That young man is a bit creepy. Wouldn't you say so, Tom?"

Sheriff Redmont hedged his reply. "Well, he was under his father's thumb for all those years. His mother died when he was only ten, and then a few years back Pete ran off. Young Bill was left with a motel to run, and no one in town he could call a real friend."

"I don't know about that," Jewitt said. "You went out with him a few times, didn't you, Marci?"

She gave a snort. "That was back in high school, ten years ago."

"I keep thinking Pete will return one of these days," Sheriff Redmont said. "I find myself searching the crowds for him every year at the festival."

But Russ Jewitt simply shook his head. "I saw the woman he was with that night. She looked like a keeper. Even if they split up, he'd probably be too ashamed to show his face around here again."

"I don't think so," Marci disagreed. "I think he really cared about his son. He'd want to know how Bill was doing with the motel."

"If he cared about him, he wouldn't have run off in the first place," Jewitt said. "I offered to buy the motel from Bill, but he won't sell. I'm hoping he'll change his mind once his father is declared legally dead."

"What would you put up there?" Marci asked. "A discount store? Or maybe you'd get one of the tribes to build a casino."

"Maybe. Stranger things have happened."

Annie finished her drink and stood up. All this local banter had made her sleepy. "I think I'll turn in early," she told them. "I want to be on the road by eight in the morning. Nice to have met you all."

"We've got fireworks planned for ten thirty," the sheriff told her. "Hope they don't keep you awake."

Back at the motel, a night clerk had taken over for Bill Symons. Annie saw Symons across the narrow lobby, filling the soft drink machine, and walked over to say good night. "I thought I might see you at the festival."

"I stay away from them," he told her. "Too much work to be done around here."

"I met Marci McGreggor. She's very friendly. She said she knew you."

Symons grunted "In a place like Cactus Valley everybody knows everybody."

"The sheriff said there'll be fireworks at ten thirty, but I'm a bit tired."

"They last for ten minutes tops. It's not the fancy stuff you see on TV."

He was right about that. From her window she saw a few sparklers and bursting skyrockets, climaxed by a fiery display in the shape of a big green cactus. As the last of it faded and died, she was about to pull down the blinds and go to bed when a movement in the motel parking lot caught her eye. Someone was walking toward a dark pickup truck parked a bit away from the other vehicles. It looked like Bill Symons and he was carrying a long cloth bag over his shoulder. Golf clubs, she thought.

Or maybe a rifle.

Annie was still dressed and she went quickly down the stairs to the parking lot, reaching it in time to see the pickup turn right on the highway, heading away from town. She slipped behind the wheel of her car and followed.

Symons stayed on the main highway for about five miles, and then turned off to the left Annie had doused her headlights, relying on moonlight to show the way. There was virtually no traffic on this stretch of highway, and she could follow the pickup's lights easily as it made its bumpy way up a slight hill. Then suddenly the truck stopped and the lights went dark. If he was looking back he might have seen her in the moonlight, so she kept driving for another quarter mile before making a U-turn on the highway. Then, as she approached the turnoff, she pulled off the highway and killed her engine.

She opened the window to the cool night air and sat there for a few moments, waiting. For all she knew, he might be up there driving golf balls. Then, with the suddenness of a summer storm, the shots came—four of them bunched together. Annie left her car and started up the hill on foot, past the fat, rain-swollen cactuses. She heard four more shots in the distance and presently came upon a partly collapsed cactus, still leaking water through its side

"Bill Symons!" she shouted. "I know you're up there! Come down here and talk to me!"

There was only silence for a moment and then his voice shouted back. "Who is it?"

"Annie Sears. I followed you from the motel."

More silence. She waited. Presently she heard him approaching and made out his silhouette against the night sky. "It's not wise to sneak up on someone with a rifle in his hands," he told her.

"I knew you wouldn't shoot me. You only shoot cactuses."

He pointed the rifle at the ground as he came closer. "How did you know that? Why did you follow me?"

Close up, even in the semidarkness, he did not seem as dour and brooding as he'd first appeared. "I think I know why you've been killing those cactuses. I just wanted to see if I was right." She felt the chill of the desert night air. "Can we talk in your truck where it's a bit warmer?"

He hesitated, and then said, "All right." She followed him over to the truck.

He slipped the rifle back into its case and slid it behind the seats. Then he stood with his hand on the door handle, waiting for her to speak.

"When I registered at your motel you happened to mention that the blossoms of the Saguaro Cactus bloom in May and June. Later the sheriff told me that cactus shootings have occurred mostly in those months. I got to thinking about that. Could there be a tie-in between the shootings and the blossoms? Could this so-called cactus killer be firing at cactuses with blossoms? That hardly seemed likely. The blossoms open at night and only last till midday. Besides, if the shooter were aiming at the blossoms at the top of the branches, he wouldn't be hitting the middle of the cactus where it could split and collapse. That made me wonder if the opposite might be true. If he was shooting mainly during the blossom season, but not aiming at the blossoms, was it possible he was aiming at cactuses that didn't have blossoms?"

"Why would he do that?" Symons asked uneasily.

"Well, what did he accomplish by drilling cactuses with several bullets until they burst open? He established at a distance, by moonlight, that they were really cactuses and not a plastic fake, like the one standing in the town square right now."

He moistened his lips nervously. "How do you know all this?"

"A kid shooting at cactuses probably would have moved on to other amusements after the first year. I was looking for another motive. This is the third year of the shootings so they started two years ago, and the artificial cactus in the square replaced a shorter one three years ago. What if someone had placed that ten-foot-tall artificial cactus out in the desert among all the others, weighted down inside so it wouldn't blow away? What if someone like you suspected this and went hunting for the fake cactus?" Before he could answer they both saw the lights from a car driving slowly along the highway. Annie remembered she'd parked her own vehicle just off the road, and the new arrival stopped behind it. "That's not a sheriff's car," he told her, and she detected the alarm in his voice.

She slipped the cell phone from the pocket of her jeans. "Do you have a 911 system here?"

He nodded. "But it might be faster to call the sheriff direct I know his number by heart after running that motel for three years."

"That's when your dad disappeared, wasn't it?" She punched in the number he gave her and waited. "Sheriff Redmont," a voice answered.

"This is Annie Sears. I'm with Bill Symons on the hill off Route—" She glanced at Symons for help.

"One eighty-six," he told her. "Just before the turn-off for Fort Bowie."

She repeated what he'd said. "We may be in trouble, Sheriff. It's the cactus killer"

"I'm on my way."

She turned off the phone and waited with Symons in the darkness, crouched low so as not to be visible in the moonlight. Soon they heard someone approaching. "It's Russ Jewitt, isn't it?" she whispered.

"It has to be. I must have picked the right area this time. But how did he know?"

Before she could answer they heard Jewitt's voice call out, "I know you're here, Symons. Let's talk about this."

"All right," he called back, but Annie placed a restraining hand on his arm before he could stand up.

"Who's with you? That's not your car on the highway."

She answered for him. "Annie Sears, from the motel. I followed him out here."

"Well, Miss Sears, then you must know he's our cactus killer."

"I know that."

She could see him then, less than twenty feet away, moving toward them between the cactuses. He was carrying something in his hand and in the darkness she thought it was a long stick. Then as he got closer she saw it was a double-barreled shotgun, pointed at the ground. "Tell me something, Symons," he said, stopping about ten feet away. "Why have you been destroying our cactuses like this?"

"You know why. And I must be getting close if you came out here with a gun. What'd you do, attach one of those global positioning gadgets to my truck?"

"Maybe I did. Maybe I suspected you and wanted to catch you in the act."

"That's no good, Jewitt," Annie told him. "He started shooting cactuses after his father disappeared, which was the same year that you replaced your ten-foot plastic cactus with one twice as big. You know he's searching for his father's body, hidden out here inside your original plastic cactus."

"That cactus is back at my lumberyard," Jewitt told them.

But Bill Symons was ready for that. "No, it isn't. You were the only one who saw my father with this woman he supposedly ran off with. I never believed that for a minute. You killed him, didn't you? And hid his body inside that plastic cactus. Your lumberyard was the first place I checked, and the original cactus isn't there."

"Are you accusing me of killing your father?"

"Damned right I am! You've wanted that motel property for years, probably to build the discount store you were touting. When he wouldn't sell it, you killed him expecting I would sell it to you with him gone."

"You'll need a body to prove that," he said.

"The sheriff will find it," Annie assured him. "It'll be in this area and it won't have a blossom on top. You could hardly take a chance coming out here to attach a fake blossom that only lasts one day anyway. That's why Bill has been shooting at cactuses without blossoms."

As she mentioned the sheriff they saw his car speeding along the highway toward them. The siren was off but his red lights were blinking. Jewitt raised the shotgun. "You've brought this on yourselves. At this distance I can blow you both away!"

Annie and Symons had been backing up until they felt the needles of a cactus pricking them. Now, with a sudden motion, Annie shoved Symons aside and hurled herself after him just as the double-barreled shotgun roared. The giant cactus shredded as the water gushed out and it toppled forward, catching Jewitt before he could jump aside.

Sheriff Redmont and his deputies located the false cactus within ten minutes, not far from where Russ Jewitt had been fatally injured. Inside they found the body of Pete Symons, wrapped tightly in plastic sheets to help preserve it against the desert heat.

"Why did he do it?" Marci McGreggor asked Annie the next morning, as she was checking out of her room.

"For this property," Annie replied. "He thought Bill Symons would sell it to him after his father was gone."

"No, I mean why did he hide the body inside a fake cactus instead of just burying it out there someplace?"

"I had to think about that, but I finally figured it out. Jewitt had spread the story about Pete Symons running off with some woman. If Bill had been willing to sell the property, Jewitt would have had to wait seven years until the state declared Pete Symons legally dead and ownership passed to his son. In that case, he could have unwrapped the body and left it along the highway to be found and identified sooner. Since Pete's son wouldn't sell, he left the body in the cactus. It was probably a safer place than in the ground, where it might have been found or dug up by animals."

Marci simply shook her head in wonder. "You know, you should have been a detective."

Annie Sears smiled. "I am. I was with the El Paso police force, and now I'm on my way to take a better job with the San Diego force. If you're ever out that way, look me up."

FIRST BLOOD

If the cactus forest of Arizona had impressed Annie Sears on her drive from El Paso to San Diego, she was almost as impressed with the line of giant wind turbines atop a hill where cattle grazed. Somehow they seemed to symbolize this new megacity, already the seventh largest in the country and almost twice the size of San Francisco.

"You know, we have a much larger department than El Paso," Chief Williams told her the first day she reported for duty.

"Of course." She'd dressed conservatively for their first meeting, deciding on a white blouse and gray cotton suit for this warm June morning. Her long hair was pulled back in a neat ponytail, and she'd kept her makeup to a bare minimum.

"We do have some of the same problems, though, with illegal border crossings that add to the crime statistics. I need all the help I can get."

She shifted uneasily in her chair, hoping they hadn't hired her away from the El Paso department merely to chase illegals across the desert. "I've been wanting a chance on a big-city force," she told him. "I hope I've found it here."

"Your record speaks very well for you, Ms. Sears." He pressed a button on his desk. "I'm going to assign you to work with Sergeant Reynolds in Homicide. I think you'll find him to be a good teacher."

Annie wasn't really looking for a teacher, just a partner who knew his way around the city until she got her bearings. But the door opened and there was Sergeant Reynolds extending his hand. "Call me Josh," he suggested with a wry smile. He was a good decade older than her, probably around forty, with dark hair and a strong jaw line. "Good to have you aboard, Annie."

He showed her around the squad room and took her down to the forensic lab. Along the way, she met over a dozen people whose names became a blur in her memory. She guessed she'd sort them all out eventually. Reynolds assigned her an empty desk just outside his own cubicle and handed her the badge and holstered pistol he'd picked up from the captain.

"You're one of us now," he said. "You'll want to put in some time on the range with the weapon, just to familiarize yourself with it. You should carry it even when you're off duty." Over coffee he explained the workings of the department and the geography of the city. "City Hall, the courthouses, and the Metro Correction Center are all here within an area of a few blocks. Unfortunately, police headquarters is a dozen blocks to the east."

He showed her the map on one wall. "This is all San Diego?" she asked.

He laughed. "It's a big city. Some people call it the birthplace of California. Most of our work will be downtown." As if on cue, the phone on his desk rang. He answered it with a brusque "Reynolds, Homicide." When he hung up, he reached in a drawer for his service automatic. "Your first case, sooner than I expected."

"What is it?"

"Robbery and shooting at the Essex Jewelers in Emerald Plaza. Let's go." The time was 11:25.

Emerald Plaza, Reynolds explained as they drove west on Broadway, was barely ten years old. It consisted of three hexagonal towers topped with emerald neon rings, with a hundred-foot-high atrium featuring a huge chandelier made of emerald green panels. Essex Jewelers had offices high up in one of the towers. "They're not looking for walk-in business. They buy gold and diamonds from estates and sell it to wealthy buyers in Beverly Hills or Miami Beach."

He pulled up behind an ambulance and police car already on the scene. "The chandelier is impressive," Annie admitted as they hurried across the atrium to a waiting elevator.

"Pin your badge on," he told her. "These guys won't know you."

"Right."

They took the elevator to the twentieth floor, where a uniformed patrolman was awaiting them. "What's the story, Rodriguez?"

"Attempted robbery. One man dead. In here."

They followed him through an open door into a small reception area. There was no desk for a receptionist, only a leather sofa with two matching chairs. On the wall was a sign calling attention to an intercom speaker. Another officer was inside, directing them to a small, windowless office with a thick wooden door. Two empty chairs faced a desk where a man was slumped facedown in a welter of blood.

A grayhaired man in a conservative pinstriped suit and blue tie followed them in from an adjoining office. "I'm Matthew Kirk, president of Essex

Jewelers. The dead man is our vice president, Perry Valencia. I don't know what happened."

Sergeant Reynolds introduced himself and Annie. "Suppose you tell us what you do know, Mr. Kirk"

The forensic people were arriving on the scene, so they moved into Matthew Kirk's somewhat larger office. This one had a window, with a magnificent view of downtown San Diego.

"I was here in my office, going over some figures. None of us heard a thing."

"Who else was here at the time?" Annie asked, making notes. He seemed remarkably calm for someone who'd just had an employee killed in his office.

"There are usually five of us: myself, Perry, Jenny Presburg, Chris Fox, and Ashley Cooper. Ashley is out ill today. For business reasons, our offices are soundproofed, with thick doors." He motioned toward a corner of the ceiling where Annie had already observed the tiny eye of a security camera. "We have cameras in every room, and each of us has a small monitor to observe the entrance. You understand, we don't sell jewelry here. Our business is buying gold, silver, diamonds, and other precious stones, mainly from estates. These are resold to dealers around the country."

"We're more interested right now in the killing of Perry Valencia," Reynolds told him, trying to mask his impatience. "If you didn't hear the shot, you must have at least seen who was in the room with him."

"I didn't, but the monitors for the rooms are in Chris's office. He's our treasurer. He's the one who spread the alarm."

"I guess we'd better talk to him," Reynolds decided.

Kirk called him in from the next office. He was a blond man in his thirties, with frown lines already deeply etched around his eyes. A small goatee seemed out of place on his face. "Tell them what you saw," Matthew Kirk said.

Chris Fox was a bundle of nerves, taking a seat and then immediately standing up. "Have you caught him yet?" he wanted to know.

"Just tell us what you saw."

"Well, first I saw someone entering the office on the door monitor. We need magnetic key cards to get to the inner offices. Outside of us, the only other cardholder is Miguel, on the cleaning crew. He personally comes in each morning and empties our trash. I only caught a glimpse, but I knew it was him."

"Could anyone have come in with him?" Annie asked.

"I don't think so, but I wouldn't swear to it. Usually when someone enters the waiting room, whoever's free greets them on the speaker, asks their business, and then comes out to escort them inside. I don't do appraisals, which is why the monitors are in my office away from visitors." He sat down again. "God, this is awful! I can't believe it happened."

"What did you see?"

"I'm not often watching the screens. They're out of my line of vision. But I suddenly became aware that Perry was slumped over his desk. I never heard the gunshot, but that's not surprising, with the soundproofing and the thick doors."

"Don't you have sound on the security cameras?" Annie asked.

"It's against the law unless there's a sign advising people they're being recorded."

"Had Miguel left by this time?"

"I don't know. I was more concerned about Perry. I called to the others, and we ran in."

"Knowing a killer with a gun was somewhere in the office?"

"We didn't know it then. We'd didn't even realize he'd been shot until we saw all the blood and looked at the tape."

"That's what we'd all better do right now," Reynolds decided. "Where's this woman, Jenny Presburg?"

"She was sick at the sight of it. She's still in the restroom."

He turned to Annie. "See if she's all right, Sears."

The single restroom was next to the mailroom with its fax and copy machines. Annie knocked and tried the door. It was locked, but a voice called out, "Who is it?"

"Detective Sears, Ms. Presburg. Are you all right?"

She flushed the toilet, unlocked the door, and showed Annie an ashen face. "I'm sorry. It's not every day I see a friend with his brains splattered—" She turned back to the toilet, and Annie went in to offer whatever help she could. But the worst seemed to be over. The young woman flushed the toilet one more time and straightened up, washing her hands and face before retrieving her purse and brushing off the front of her blouse and pants. "I'm all right now," she told Annie. "Let's go into my office."

Her office was much like the one the dead man occupied, fairly small and windowless, with a phone, computer, and a monitor to view the office entrance. On a shelf next to the desk were a high-powered microscope and a flat-topped scale, which she explained was for accurate weighing of gold and silver items. "You can usually tell if a piece of jewelry is pure gold simply by weighing it," she explained. "The microscope is for close examination of diamonds and other precious stones."

"All the offices have these?" Annie asked.

"Just mine, Perry's, and Ashley's. We do the appraisals. Of course we check with Mr. Kirk on items of special value."

"What about Chris Fox?"

"He writes the checks. He's our treasurer. We have a policy of immediate payment when we make a purchase. Usually it's by check, but we keep a supply of cash on hand, too, for clients who prefer it."

"So this was probably an attempted robbery."

"It must have been."

"Was Valencia here when you arrived this morning?"

She shook her head. "I was the first one in, around eight thirty. I had to finish up some work from yesterday. The others drifted in around nine, except for Ashley. She phoned to say she was sick."

Sergeant Reynolds entered just then. "The security camera caught it all," he told us. "We have the murder on tape. Want a look?"

While the medical examiner completed his work and preparations were made to remove the body, they went into Chris Fox's office, where a bank of television monitors showed views of each office and the waiting room. Matthew Kirk had taken Fox's seat behind the desk. It was he who spoke first.

"Go on. Let's see it."

Chris Fox had rewound the tape, and he pressed the play button. The camera was peering over the shoulder of a slender man with a receding hairline whom Kirk identified as the victim, Perry Valencia. He was on the phone, and the time at the top of the photo showed 10:00, when the office opened for business. Then he was seen reading from a sheet of stiff red paper. "That's a weekly report we receive on the price of gold, silver, and various precious gems," Matthew Kirk explained. "It's invaluable in this business."

Fox fastforwarded the tape, then went back to play. "Here it is. Here's something just before eleven. See the door opening just a crack, and somebody says something." On the tape, Valencia glanced up and waved them away.

Annie's eyes were glued to the monitor. "They have these cameras running all day?"

"They can have me shut them off, but no one ever does. I keep the tapes for a week and then record over them."

Annie kept watching the monitor. She saw the heavy wooden door open and a figure in a long black coat and gloves enter. His or her head was completely covered by a rubber Batman mask. Valencia looked up, startled. The Batman figure never spoke but simply raised a long-barreled target pistol and fired two quick silent shots. The screen flared for an instant, then cleared to show the masked figure exiting the office, pausing only long enough to drop the weapon. The time was 11:09.

"The gun!" she exclaimed, pointing to the screen. "He dropped it!"

Sergeant Reynolds nodded, "We found it in the wastebasket next to the desk. He didn't want to be caught with it on his person."

"That seems like a gang killing," Annie ventured. "An execution. Did it have a silencer? We couldn't hear the shots."

"The cameras don't record sound," Chris Fox verified.

Annie turned toward Matthew Kirk. "Have you had any dealings with organized crime?"

"Certainly not!"

"Drugs? Illegal immigration?"

"I run a respectable business here!"

"I'm sure you do," Reynolds acknowledged, taking over Annie's line of questioning. "But that doesn't mean your employees might not be into something shady. What about Valencia? Does he have a wife, family?"

Jenny Presburg answered. "He's unmarried. I always thought he might be gay."

"Why's that?"

She shrugged. "Just a feeling I had."

The sergeant turned back to Chris Fox. "What about the rest of the tapes? What do they show?"

"Not much. We had no clients in yet this morning."

"You mean you four were the only ones in the office?"

"Miguel came in to empty the trash, like he does every morning."

"Let's take a look."

"I usually don't turn the security cameras on till we open at ten o'clock, but we have him when he came back after that." The tape of the reception area showed a shapeless person in green work clothes using a key card to open the inner office door. The timer at the top of the screen showed it to be 10:56. "Is that Miguel?" Reynolds asked.

"It sure looks like him," Jenny said.

"Why doesn't he come at night?"

"We don't allow anyone in here when the office is closed," Kirk explained. "His key card only works during regular office hours. The offices are cleaned between nine and ten each morning, before we start receiving clients."

"Are you certain Miguel came in earlier?"

Chris Fox nodded. "He emptied my wastebasket." Kirk and Jenny Presburg agreed. He'd been in all their offices shortly after nine. "We don't allow the cleaning people in unless one of us is in the office." He motioned toward a closet door. "We have a vault in there that often contains jewelry and large sums of money. Even with all the security devices we can't take any chances."

"What makes you think the killing was part of a robbery attempt?" Annie asked. "On that tape the killer never said a word about money or anything else."

Matthew Kirk was growing impatient. "Of course it was robbery! What else could it be? If some enemy wanted to kill him they'd have done it at his home or on the street, not in this office with security cameras everywhere."

"But the security cameras prove one thing," Reynolds reminded him. "You three were in the office when he was shot. No one else was here. Therefore, one of you must have killed him."

"What about Miguel?" Chris said. "He came in at 10:56."

Reynolds turned to Annie. "Find this Miguel and bring him up here if he knows anything."

She took the elevator to the lobby, now cluttered with news people and TV cameras. The word had traveled fast. One young man about her age headed for her at once. "Pardon me, Detective—" She realized he'd spotted her badge. "Pardon me, I'm Paul Goodhue from the *Union Tribune.* Can you tell me what's happening here?"

"An ongoing criminal investigation. We'll issue a statement in due course."

"We saw them take a body out—"

"Sorry, no comment."

She hurried over to the lobby reception desk. "Where can I find Miguel? He's on the cleaning crew."

"I'll page him," the woman said.

He came off the elevator a few minutes later, a short, somewhat overweight man in his forties. "You looking for me, lady? I'm Miguel Fernandez."

"Detective Annie Sears. I just want to ask you some questions."

He was immediately on the defensive. "I'm legal. I got my papers."

"It's not about that. There's been a killing at Essex Jewelers on the twentieth floor. You clean and empty their wastebaskets, don't you?"

"I know nothing about a killing!" he insisted.

"You entered their office around eleven this morning."

"No!" He shook his head violently. "I clean between nine and ten, always between nine and ten. I don't go there again."

"I saw the tape from the security camera. It looked like you."

"Not me!" he insisted, and Annie had to admit that she hadn't seen the man's face clearly on the black and white tape.

"Where were you around eleven o'clock?"

"On my lunch break. We start early."

"Where did you go for lunch?"

"We have a room in the sub-basement. My wife, she fixes a sandwich for me. And there's vending machines for us."

"Anyone see you there?"

"Sure, there were people around."

Annie opened her notebook. "I need their names, Miguel."

He shrugged. "I don't know names. I know I didn't kill anybody."

"You have a key card to open the Essex office door. Did you loan it to anyone?"

"No. I got it right here." He showed her the plastic card with the Emerald Plaza logo.

"All right, Miguel. We'll want to talk with you again later."

"I got nothing to hide."

She left him there and took the elevator back upstairs. Kirk, Fox, and Jenny Presburg were seated in the reception area with Rodriguez, the patrolman who'd been first on the scene. "What's up?" she asked him.

"The sergeant and two officers are searching the offices," he told her.

Reynolds came out and asked about Miguel. "He insists it wasn't him," she reported. "He was taking a lunch break then."

He nodded without comment. "We're searching this place top to bottom. We found that black coat the killer probably wore."

"It's Ashley's raincoat," Kirk explained. "She wore it one day months ago when it rained, then forgot about it. She decided to leave it here in the closet. The gloves were in the pocket."

"Ashley?"

"That would be Ashley Cooper," the sergeant told her. "The woman who's out sick today"

"It points to an inside job," Annie said. "Someone had to know the coat was here."

Chris Fox stirred in his chair. "Miguel would have seen it when he cleaned the office."

"What about the Batman mask?"

"That's what we're searching for," Reynolds explained. "Our onscreen killer had four items. He dropped the gun in the wastebasket. We found the coat and gloves in the closet. But the mask isn't here. We've searched every desk drawer, filing cabinet, and closet. The ceiling and walls are solid. The windows can't be opened. I'm going to request that you three submit to a body search. Annie, please take Ms. Presburg into the bathroom and check her out."

Jenny shrugged. "I have nothing to hide."

"Bring your purse too," Annie told her. "I'll have to search that."

She had no Batman mask or anything else hidden beneath her blouse and pants. Her purse yielded only a handkerchief, lipstick, nail file, manicure scissors, wallet, and key chain. "All right," Annie said. "I guess you're clean."

"Nothing on the men," Reynolds told her when she returned to the treasurer's office while the others waited outside.

"She's clean too. Could we test their hands for nitrate, see if they fired a gun lately?"

He shook his head. "You're forgetting the killer wore gloves."

"Then where are we?"

"The Batman mask is missing. It's nowhere in this office and none of these three left the office. If I can play Sherlock for a moment—"

She smiled slightly. "Do you frequently?"

"—if the mask is gone, the killer had to remove it. Therefore, the killer is the only person we know left the office—Miguel Fernandez or someone posing as him."

"Maybe we think differently in El Paso, Sergeant. There's one place in this office that hasn't been searched, and that's where you'll find the missing mask."

"Where's that?" he asked with a frown.

"The vault."

In the best of all possible worlds, Annie Sears would have solved her first murder case with the San Diego force in a matter of two hours. The missing mask would have been in the vault, and Chris Fox would have confessed to the killing.

But there was nothing in the vault except currency, carefully wrapped diamonds, several pieces of gold jewelry, and a few contracts with buyers and sellers.

No mask.

"Go out and talk to this Ashley Cooper," Reynolds suggested, aware of her disappointment. "It was her raincoat. Find out if she's really sick. Meanwhile, I'll collect the videotapes from the security cameras and take them back to headquarters."

She didn't argue, feeling a bit foolish over her failed solution. She got the woman's address from Matthew Kirk and set off for an apartment on Grape Street, eight blocks away on the north side of downtown.

Ashley Cooper answered the door in a pink bathrobe, holding a tissue to her nose. "It's not a cold," she assured Annie. "Just a bad asthma attack. My doctor can't see me till morning." She was an attractive blond woman, perhaps in her mid-thirties, who was a bit shorter than Annie in her bare feet. "Come on in."

"I'm Detective Sears, the one who phoned you. Mr. Kirk told you what happened this morning?"

She nodded, curling up in an armchair across the room from Annie. "I couldn't believe it. That office has every sort of high-tech security device there is!"

"How well did you know Perry Valencia?"

"Well, only five of us work there, so naturally we're close. I had lunch with him a few times."

"Ever date him?"

"No. He didn't seem attracted to women. But he knew his job. He was probably the best appraiser in the place."

"Did he have any enemies?"

"I suppose everyone has enemies, but I didn't know anyone in the office who disliked him."

"What about the other woman, Jenny Presburg? Did he have lunch with her too?"

"Sometimes. There's a nice restaurant in our building, and occasionally all three of us would go there."

"But not Mr. Kirk or Chris Fox?"

She shook her head. "I think Mr. Kirk likes to go over the books with Chris when we're not around to interrupt. They sometimes lunched together later."

"Do you know Miguel Fernandez?"

"I don't think so." She paused a moment and then said, "Oh! Do you mean Miguel on the cleaning crew?"

"That's right."

"He was usually in our office early, cleaning up before any clients arrived. Mr. Kirk didn't like it done at night."

"Miss Cooper—"

"You can call me Ashley."

"Ashley, the security camera in Valencia's office recorded the killing. It appears that the killer was wearing a mask along with your raincoat and gloves from the office closet."

"My God! What does that mean?"

"It indicates the killer was someone in the office, or someone who has access to it. He or she knew the raincoat would be in there and could be used."

"None of us could have killed him. It's just not possible."

"How long had your raincoat been there?"

"Oh, since last winter sometime—March, I think. We don't get much rain, but there was a nasty morning in March when I wore the coat. By afternoon it was sunny and warm so I left it in the office."

"Was Miguel ever in the office after ten o'clock?"

"Only if someone paged him. You know, if there was damage of some sort that needed to be cleaned up. That hardly ever happened."

"When do you think you'll be able to work?"

Ashley shrugged. "Depends what the doctor says. Maybe she can give me a different prescription. The office will probably be closed till after Perry's funeral anyway."

Annie left the apartment and walked back along Grape Street to her car. As she was unlocking the door, she heard her name. "Detective Sears, isn't it?"

She turned and recognized Paul Goodhue, the reporter from the *Union Tribune*. "That's right," she admitted with a smile. "You wouldn't have followed me here, would you?"

"Pure coincidence." He was a bit older than she'd thought at first, with fine lines beginning to form across his forehead and around his eyes. She noticed he wasn't wearing a wedding ring. "I came here to see Ashley Cooper, one of the Essex employees."

"I just saw her, as you no doubt know. She's a bit under the weather. I doubt if she'd welcome another visitor."

He glanced at his watch. "What time does your shift end? Could I buy you a drink?"

All she could do was laugh. "Is this the way it's done in San Diego? You buy the detective a drink to get an inside track on the story?"

"Only if they're as attractive as you."

"Sorry, Paul. You picked the wrong one."

'You're new to the city, aren't you? I could show you around, take you on a boat ride around the harbor, or a trip to the zoo."

She got into her car. "I have to get back now. I'll promise you a scoop if there is one. Nice talking to you." She drove away before he could say anything else.

Back at the squad room, Josh Reynolds told her to go home. "Your shift ends in fifteen minutes. You've done enough for your first day."

"I did nothing. We've got an unsolved murder on our hands."

"Relax, Annie. It's a rare case that gets closed the first day. If you're not ready to go home, fire off a few clips on the pistol range. Get the feel of your weapon."

She followed his advice and went down to the range. Her aim was as good as ever, and after three clips she became aware that Sergeant Reynolds was standing off to one side watching her. "How'd I do?" she asked him.

"I guess you didn't need the practice," he told her with a smile. "Here, I'll buy you a cup of coffee."

They sat at a picnic table in what served as a lounge adjoining the pistol range. "Do you know a reporter named Paul Goodhue?" she asked, taking a sip of coffee from the Styrofoam cup.

"Yeah. He been bothering you?"

"Not really. I think he asked me for a date."

Reynolds snorted. "Your first day. He doesn't waste any time."

"What's his story? Is he a good reporter?"

"He's helped us out a couple of times. He knows his way around the city."

"He offered to show me the zoo."

"I'll bet he did."

"What's next?" she asked, changing the subject.

"I'm bringing Matthew Kirk in for an interview in a half hour. I'll have the other two in the morning. And then probably Miss Cooper and that Miguel

Fernandez after I read your reports on them. Your shift is over, but do you want to sit in on my interview with Kirk?"

"I wouldn't miss it."

He arrived promptly at five o'clock, accompanied by his lawyer, a stodgy man who might have been Kirk's brother but turned out to be his nephew. "There's no need for you to be present," Reynolds told him. "We just want a statement from Mr. Kirk about what happened this morning."

"Wait out here," Kirk told him. "I'll call you in if we need you."

Annie sat to one side, letting Reynolds do the questioning. "As you told us earlier, you were in your office at the time Perry Valencia was shot."

"That's correct. We don't have a great deal of walk-in business. Generally, someone phones for an appointment. Chris Fox handles our finances and writes the checks when necessary. Perry, Jenny, and Ashley did the actual appraising and purchased the items from our clients. Anything above ten thousand dollars has to be cleared with me."

"Were there any problems with Perry?"

Matthew Kirk hesitated. "Not—not really."

"What does that mean?"

"Last week Chris noticed something odd with a purchase he made. We receive regular fliers from your department regarding jewelry thefts, in case someone tries to sell us stolen goods. There was a diamond ring in one lot that seemed familiar to him. It had been purchased by Perry the day before, and Chris asked him about it. He told me later that Perry seemed flustered by his question and said he'd look into it. He claimed to know the person who sold him the jewelry, though the name wasn't familiar to me."

"Do you suspect Valencia was acting as a fence for stolen goods?"

He shook his head. "It hadn't gotten that far yet, but I was a bit concerned."

"Was he a Mexican-American?"

"Well, yes. But I don't see what that has to do with it. He'd lived here over twenty years, since he was a child."

"I'm wondering if he might have been friendly with Miguel Fernandez, one of the crew that cleans your office. The security video indicates that Miguel or someone dressed like him entered your office shortly before the murder."

"You think Perry was involved with Miguel just because they're both Mexican-Americans? We've got a million and a quarter people in this city, and more than a quarter of them are Hispanic"

"I'm trying to touch all the bases, Mr. Kirk. It just seems odd that Miguel came up to the office at that time."

Annie felt she had to interrupt. "When I questioned him he denied he was there. It's possible someone impersonated him."

"He had a key card to unlock the inner door, Detective," Reynolds answered, and she knew he was displeased at her interruption. "If it wasn't Miguel, he had to obtain the key from Miguel."

She knew she should keep quiet then, but she had to speak. "There's one other possibility. Ashley Cooper must have a key card too."

"Ashley?" Kirk repeated with a frown. "She's home ill."

"I interviewed her this afternoon," Annie said. "She had an asthma attack, that's all. She wasn't in bed or anything."

Sergeant Reynolds sighed. 'We have the tapes from your security cameras here. Suppose we look at Miguel again." He chose a tape from the pile on his desk and popped it into the tape player. After a moment's fast-forward they again came to the spot where the figure of a man in work clothes entered the waiting room and used his key card on the inner door.

"That's Miguel," Kirk insisted. "It's no one else."

"It looks like him," Annie had to agree. "But why did he lie to me about being there?"

"Perhaps because he killed Perry," Kirk said. "And that's how the Batman mask left the office."

They advanced the tape further and saw Miguel leaving at 11:01. He'd been in the office for exactly five minutes. "Let's see the tape of the killing again," Annie suggested.

They watched it once more and froze it at the instant of the shooting. "Look at the time!" Annie said, rising from her chair. "It's 11:09, eight minutes after Miguel left the office. Why didn't we notice that before?"

Reynolds nodded. "Whether or not that was Miguel, he was gone before the killing. We're back to just three suspects."

Annie had another thought. "Look, you have tapes there showing each of the offices. Let's see who wasn't in their office at the time of the killing."

They played the tapes one at a time, with Matthew Kirk's first. In each case the camera was positioned to look over their shoulder, focusing on the visitor. Kirk seemed to be alone, but all they could see was his left elbow. It did move from time to time, and at 11:16 they saw Chris Fox burst into the office and both of them went out. The tape of Jenny showed her more clearly, opening her mail and taking a thick reference book from the shelf. She left the office at 11:17. Chris Fox was also moving around, though the angle of the camera in his office didn't show the bank of TV monitors. He muttered a soft curse and left the office quickly at 11:15.

"Nobody could have done it," Annie concluded.

Reynolds shut off the monitor and thanked Kirk for coming in. "What happens now?" the jeweler asked.

"We sleep on it. And in the morning we find out what Miguel was doing in your office and why he lied about being there."

Annie went along with Reynolds in the morning. Somehow, she felt responsible for Miguel since she'd interviewed him, and if he'd lied she wanted to know why. Arriving at the building, they were directed to eighteen, where they found him using an electric polisher on the floor by the elevators.

He smiled at Annie. "The lady with the questions."

"That's right. This is Sergeant Reynolds. He has questions too."

"Is there someplace we can talk?" Reynolds asked.

"I've got to finish polishing the floor."

"All right, just stop for a minute. I have only one question. Why did you go to the Essex office just before eleven yesterday morning?"

"I told the lady it wasn't me!"

"You've been positively identified on the security tape. You entered the office at 10:56 and left five minutes later."

Miguel shifted his gaze from Reynolds to Annie and back again. "I didn't kill him," he insisted. "Someone left a message for me to check with Valencia about some problem in his office, but when I got up there everything was fine."

"You spoke to Valencia?"

"Sure. I poked my head in his office, and he said everything was fine there. Said he hadn't called, that it must be a mistake."

"Did you talk to the person that called?" Annie asked.

He shook his head. "It was a text message on my pager." He showed it to them. "It just said, 'See Perry V. at Essex.' But when I went up there, he said he hadn't paged me."

"Were those his exact words?"

Miguel thought a bit. "He said there was nothing for me. I figured he'd taken care of whatever there was, so I left."

"Did anyone else see you?"

"No. They all had their doors closed."

Josh Reynolds took over the questioning. "Did you at any time remove a Batman mask from that office?"

"No sir! And I didn't remove a thing when I went back yesterday."

When they were in the elevator, Reynolds asked, "Can we believe him?"

"We can about the mask. The security camera shows him leaving the office at 11:01, and the murder didn't happen till 11:09."

"There's something not quite right here," Reynolds decided. "I can almost sense it."

"Do you think they're all in it together?"

He gave a low snort. "I may feel like a master detective sometimes, but not Agatha Christie. If they were in it together they could have devised any number of methods better than this one. But I do think the key to it is what Kirk told us about Valencia buying a stolen diamond ring. If someone else there arranged for him to act as a fence, that would provide a motive for killing him before he talked and the whole operation went down the drain."

"Yeah." She was still thinking about his words when the elevator reached the lobby. "Look, Josh, I've got an idea about that Batman mask. I'm going to check out neighborhood stores that might have sold it."

"Good luck. It was probably left over from Halloween. It might mean the killer has children."

"I'm working on another angle. I'll see you back at the squad room."

There were no costume shops in the upper-class neighborhood, but she found a large toy store a few blocks away in Horton Plaza Shopping Center. Yes, they had several superhero costumes for sale, the sales clerk said. Wouldn't she prefer Wonder Woman?

"No, all I really need is one of these rubber Batman masks that covers the whole head."

She bought it and headed back to the squad room, wondering what her new boss would think of the idea.

The Essex office was still closed for business the following day, but Sergeant Reynolds had asked Kirk to assemble his staff for further questioning. Ashley Cooper was feeling better and agreed to come in too. They gathered in Kirk's office where there were seats for everyone. Reynolds and Annie had arrived with another detective in overalls carrying a toolbox. He went into the restroom and closed the door.

It was Reynolds who did most of the talking, and Annie could see he was enjoying it, facing the suspects like Charlie Chan at the end of one of those old movies. "We've developed a theory that the shooting of Perry Valencia was connected with an earlier incident in which a stolen ring was discovered in a group of items he'd supposedly purchased from an estate. If someone in this office supplied it to him, that person might have killed him to silence him."

"But who would be brazen enough to commit the murder in front of our security cameras?" Kirk asked.

"The killer used those cameras to advantage, hiding face and shape. And a text message sent to Miguel brought him to the office within minutes of the killing, as a possible suspect. Unfortunately for the killer, he came and went minutes too soon."

It was Ashley Cooper who interrupted at this point. "I wasn't here myself, but Chris says the security tapes show everyone in their offices at the time of the shooting. If that's true, and if Miguel was already gone, who could have don't it?"

"Exactly!" Reynolds said, glancing in Ashley's directions as he followed the reasoning she'd outlined to him. "The only possible explanation is that the killer arrived in the office early and changed the digital clock that records the time for one of the security cameras."

Chris Fox was out of his seat. "Look here, if you think I—"

That was when Annie pressed the pager in her pocket, summoning the detective in overalls waiting outside. He entered with a triumphant flourish, holding several small pieces of wet rubber. "I found them in the toilet trap," he announced, "just like you thought, Sergeant."

It was Jenny Presburg who jumped up then, trying for the door. But Annie grabbed her by the waist. "All the time you were being sick in the restroom you were in there cutting up your Batman mask with manicure scissors and flushing it down the toilet."

Sergeant Reynolds made it official by arresting her and reading her rights. She just shook her head, looking dazed. "How could you have known?"

"If anyone changed the time on their security camera, it almost had to be you. You told us you were the first one in the office that morning. It was Annie here who figured out what happened to the mask."

Later, after she'd been taken away and booked, Reynolds turned to Annie Sears. "We could have looked in the toilet trap for some real pieces of rubber, you know, rather than cutting up the mask you bought."

She merely smiled. "Why risk it? I knew she'd crack when she saw them."

"You did pretty well for your first case. First blood's not always that easy."

"I've had practice," she said. Then, "Do you have the phone number for the *Union Tribune*? There's a reporter I promised a scoop."

Annie Sears had been a detective with the San Diego Police Department only a few months when she received an unexpected assignment. She was to accompany one of the veteran detectives to La Paz near the tip of Baja California to bring back a prisoner being extradited to the United States. Frank Munson, the detective sergeant she'd be traveling with, was middle aged and a bit stocky wearing a belt in its last notch that told Annie he'd been putting on weight.

"This is one bad guy," he told Annie in the squad room, handing her the plane ticket for the following day's flight. "Dunstan Quentis is his name." He passed over a photograph, apparently a mug shot, showing a scruffy-looking man with a shiny shaved head. "His parents were Mexican Americans, very religious. He and his older brother both started out studying for the priesthood. After that he graduated from passing bad checks to stealing jewelry. He served a stretch in prison, and when he came out he turned to armed robbery. Last month while fleeing from a jewelry store holdup on Broadway, he hit a police officer with his car and killed him."

Annie studied the picture. "And they arrested him in La Paz?"

Munson nodded. "The store owner here ID'd him, but by that time he'd made it across the border and kept going south."

"Till there was no more south," she mused. "It was that way back east too. Sometimes people on the run get as far as Provincetown or Key West and discover there's no place else to go."

"Oh, he had reason enough to head for La Paz. His brother lives down there and for a long time it was said to be the pearl center of the world. That's changed now, but there is still an active trade in pearls."

"Is that what he stole from the jeweler?"

Munson nodded. "Pearl necklaces are his specialty. He contacted a fence there who would have bought the pearls, reset them, and sold them, but it turned out he was a police informer. The Mexican authorities arrested Quentis and he waived extradition. We get the job of bringing him back. It's a wonder the cops made the arrest. Mexican police aren't above a bit of bribery at times."

"We're bringing him by air, I hope."

"Certainly. I wouldn't want to drive the length of Baja with a cop killer."

The following morning was a Tuesday, and Annie met Frank Munson at the San Diego airport at eight o'clock. They were booked with their prisoner on a late afternoon return flight, so it would be a fast back-and-forth trip. Munson explained that the only problem was the airport, actually at San Jose del Cabo, nearly sixty miles south of La Paz. "That's the resort complex where most tourists go, so that's where the airport is. We'll rent a car, but it's probably about an hour's drive."

"How long is the flight?"

"Over six hundred miles, close to two hours."

Their plane was a small regional jet filled with a few businessmen and assorted tourists. They had to check their weapons through, and when Munson objected, the woman at the desk explained that a couple had been arrested recently for trying to get guns on board by impersonating police officers escorting a prisoner.

Once on board, Annie strapped herself in and said, "My first case with your department involved a jeweler, the Essex killing a few months back."

He nodded. "I was on vacation then, but I heard you did a fine job."

"The jewelry business seems to be a hazardous trade." He laughed. "I'm sure banks get robbed more often than jewelry stores."

Flying high over Baja California, it was sometimes possible to see both coasts of the narrow peninsula at once. The calm waters of the Gulf of California, once called the more colorful Sea of Cortez, contrasted sharply with the livelier waves of the Pacific Ocean. "From up here the land seems to be all desert," she remarked.

"Desert and cactuses, but there are some nice beaches. Many Californians have second homes down here."

"Have you been to La Paz before?"

"A few times. Steinbeck once wrote that you can get anything in the world there."

She smiled. "You're a literary man." Munson shrugged.

"Off and on."

"Is it true? Can you get anything in the world in La Paz?"

"We won't be there long enough to find out, will we?"

They rented a four-door sedan for transporting the prisoner. The drive north from the airport was dull and dusty, but as they approached La Paz, Annie became fascinated with the iron-shuttered colonial houses they passed on the way. Once in the city itself, luxury tourist hotels took over. In the main square, vendors did a brisk business selling lottery tickets and tacos to the visitors.

"Do you know where the jail is?" she asked.

"If my directions are correct, it should be that building on the left."

"I'll buy that. There are bars on some of the windows."

"We'd better have lunch first, so we don't have to stop once we have Quentis in tow."

It sounded good to her, so they stopped in one of the hotel restaurants that catered to tourists. The food was good and it would go on their expense account for the trip. Munson drove to the jail and parked the rental car around the back of the building, in a dusty lot near the rear entrance.

"I don't like the looks of this place," he said, nodding toward a group of youths playing ball in an adjoining field. "You'd better stay with the car and I'll go in for Quentis."

"You can't do that alone," she objected.

"One of their men can accompany us to the car. It'll be all right."

Annie waited by the car with growing unease until she saw Munson reappear with the handcuffed prisoner. She recognized the bald Dunstan Quentis at once from his photograph and held open the rear door. Munson introduced the Mexican officer, Miguel Paseo, who'd accompanied them. He wished them a safe trip back. "Be careful of him," Paseo warned, gesturing toward the prisoner. "He's a mean one."

"We'll get him back in one piece," Munson promised.

Annie made certain their prisoner's handcuffs were attached to a security belt and then got in the back seat with him, sitting behind Munson. "We're taking you to the airport at San Jose del Cabo," she told him. "Then we'll have you back in San Diego in two hours."

He looked at her and grinned, showing two gold teeth. "I'm not back yet," he said.

Munson spoke up from the front seat. "We have to warn you that anything you say during the trip may be used against you in a court of law. And if you act up we'll put leg irons on you too."

"What about the pearls?" Annie asked her partner.

"The authorities recovered them, but we just came for the prisoner. Transferring the pearls will be handled separately. There'd be too much risk sending them back with us and the prisoner."

"Makes sense," Annie agreed.

Dunstan Quentis said very little on the drive south to the airport, commenting once on the city he was leaving. "I'll miss La Paz. They have beautiful beaches and beautiful ladies. I could have stayed here the rest of my life, gazing at the sunsets."

"And the pearls?" Munson asked him.

Quentis didn't answer. He just kept gazing out the window at the passing scene.

As they neared the airport, Annie tried to make some conversation. "We're nearly there. You'll be on the plane in no time." But her words brought no reply.

Frank Munson pulled into the rental car return area, and Annie went around to the other back door to help Quentis out. That was when it happened. Their prisoner slid out fast, bumping Annie as if by accident and knocking her off balance. Then in a flash he was gone, sprinting across the asphalt toward a chain-link fence.

"Stop or I'll shoot?" Munson shouted, his service pistol already in hand. He raised it to fire, an easy shot at that range.

Annie hit his arm just as he fired, the bullet going harmlessly off target. "Don't shoot!" she yelled. "I'll get him!"

She couldn't let the man die because of her bungle, and she was sure she could beat him to the fence. He'd never get over it anyway, cuffed to that belt. She took off running before her partner could fire again. Quentis was at the fence, with Annie not ten feet behind, when suddenly he whirled and threw the handcuffs at her face. She dodged and went down on one knee, and before she knew it, Quentis was over the fence. The car rental employees had scattered when Munson fired, and as he came running, trying to get a bead through the fence on the running man, they stayed hidden.

He fired another useless shot and turned on Annie in a fury. "Christ, Sears, don't ever do that again! You let him escape!"

"He got the handcuffs off somehow. I didn't—"

"Get in the car!"

They spun around through the rental car gate, with Munson showing his badge, and took off across the rutted field in pursuit of the running fugitive. But she could see that he'd make it to another fence and the highway before they were close enough to risk another shot.

"Frank," she managed to say as he slowed to a stop. "I'm sorry I messed up. I just didn't want you to shoot him if it wasn't necessary."

"It was necessary, Sears, believe me." He pounded on the steering wheel in frustration. "Damn!"

"What do we do now?"

"I'll tell you what we don't do. We don't go back to San Diego without him!"

Annie could imagine her whole career going out the window as they drove along the highway trying to spot him. Of course he was long gone, either on foot or after hitching a ride. "He'll head north, back to La Paz," she guessed. "He must have friends there. And a brother."

"What am I supposed to tell them back home?" His voice was still angry, and she really couldn't blame him. "That I had an easy shot at him and you bumped my arm to save a cop killer's life?"

"No," she said quietly. "Can't you tell them there was a paperwork delay with the local police?"

"That might work for a day," he admitted. "No longer."

They drove in silence for a time, past the resort hotels and golf courses, scanning the highway without much hope. Finally she said, "We have to go back to that police officer, Paseo. He must know where Quentis was living when they arrested him. And what about that older brother?"

Frank Munson nodded. "I'll call Paseo on my cell phone."

Paseo answered at once on the other end. "We had some trouble," he began. "Quentis got away from us. . . . I don't know how it happened. He got loose from the handcuffs and made a run for it. . . . Look, I need to know where he hangs out, who his brother and his friends are. . . . No, we can't go back without him. Call the SDPD and tell them there's been a paperwork delay, and you can't release him till tomorrow. . . . I know, I know. Listen, do this for me and I'll make it worth your while."

He snapped the cell phone shut and Annie asked, "Did you just offer him a bribe to lie for us?"

"It's no big deal. I'll give him a liter of rum."

"That's still a bribe."

"I'm trying to save your skin, Sears, in case you didn't notice."

That silenced her for a few minutes. When she'd finally gotten up courage to speak, she asked, "Did he give you an address?"

"Where they arrested him, yeah. Don't know if that'll do us much good. It's the last place in the world he'd head for. A man named Kurt Striker lives there. Don't know what his connection with Quentis could be."

But they had to start someplace. The address was near the docks, and that gave Munson an idea. "There's a ferry runs across the Gulf to Los Mochis on the Mexican mainland. That would be his best way out of here if he wanted to get away fast." When they reached the harbor area they checked the schedule and found the next trip wasn't until six thirty that evening.

They found Striker's address easily enough. It was one of those iron-shuttered colonial houses Annie had admired earlier, with a line of trees separating it from the beach. A bandstand stood near the water's edge, an afternoon plaything for a half dozen small boys romping around on it. A police car was parked in front of the house and the officer, Miguel Paseo, was just coming out the door. Munson cursed under his breath and got out of the car with Annie behind him.

"He's not here," Paseo told them. "I checked."

"Not likely to come here either with a cop car out in front," Munson told him. "Who's inside?"

"Fellow named Kurt Striker and his girl."

"I want to see them."

"What's the use? Quentis hasn't been back here since we arrested him."

"I want to see them," Munson repeated.

The Mexican police officer shrugged and led the way back to the door. He rang the bell, and after a moment it was opened by a Mexican girl wearing a T-shirt and jeans. She appeared to be still in her teens. "What? You back again?"

"We need to see Striker," Munson said, forcing his way into the house. It was a shabby place, about what Annie expected along the docks, with the curtained windows admitting only dim light.

A man in an undershirt and pants came in from the kitchen. He was smoking a cigarette and had a tattoo of a harp on his upper left arm. "What is it now?" he asked, annoyed at the interruption.

"These are the San Diego police," Paseo explained. "They insisted on speaking to you personally."

"I told Officer Paseo everything I know," Striker said.

"Dunstan Quentis has escaped from our custody. It's urgent that we apprehend him," Frank said.

Striker gave him a smirk. "And how did that happen, Sergeant Munson?"

"He got free of his handcuffs somehow. We thought he might head back here."

"No chance of that."

"What was your relationship with him?"

"I met him in a bar. He was a fellow American and we struck up a friendship. He wanted to know where he could sell some pearls. I sent him to Papa Belota's, a pawn shop I visit sometimes. I don't know what happened there, but the police came and arrested him here that night."

"He'd given this as his address?"

A shrug. "I suppose so."

"Was he living here?"

Striker glanced at the girl, who said nothing. "I gave him a bed. He promised me a cut of the money when he sold the pearls."

"Did you know they were stolen?"

"Of course not! He said they belonged to his grandmother."

"All right," Munson said finally. "I need to find our missing prisoner. If he should come here or contact you, let us know."

"Will do."

As they were leaving, the girl followed them to the door. When she was closing it she whispered in Annie's ear, "Quentis here!"

At first Annie wasn't sure she'd heard her correctly, but by the time they reached their cars she repeated the words to Munson and Paseo. "She says he's in there! Right now!"

Munson doubted that. "She probably just meant he was there earlier, before he was arrested, but we already knew that."

She turned to Officer Paseo. "Can't we go back in and search the place?"

He shook his head. "We'd need a search warrant, just like in your country."

"How long would it take to get one?" Munson wanted to know.

"Depends on the judge. Probably tomorrow at the earliest, the way things move down here. It's late in the day already."

"All right," Munson told him. "Get it as fast as you can and ring me on my cell phone when you do. Can you get a patrol car to drive past here a few times? If they think we're watching the house he may stay put, if he's in there at all."

"Maybe we should stay here," Annie suggested.

Munson shook his head. "I've got one other place we might try—Papa Belota's, where Dunstan Quentis tried to sell his pearls."

The pawnshop was in an older part of the city, away from the glitter of the resort hotels. It had a large sign announcing Papa Belota's, with a crude painting of three gold balls. Steel shutters rolled down at night, and when

Annie and Munson reached it a lumbering old man was pulling them down. Annie was surprised when she glanced at her watch and saw it was already after five.

"Hold up there!" Munson called to the man. "We're police. We have some questions to ask."

"I have no answers. It is after five o'clock." Munson showed his badge and the man laughed. "That's the San Diego police. You have no authority here."

"Look," Annie said, "we only have a few questions. Can't we come in for five minutes?"

"No."

"You're American, aren't you? Down here hiding from the police. Why else would you be helping the local authorities?"

He glanced around nervously and waved them inside, under the half lowered shutter. The place was a litter of objects, pawned for a fraction of their value. Violins and saxophones competed with cameras and jewelry. Annie even saw a portable typewriter from another era, reminding her of the one a character pawned in *The Lost Weekend*. Munson pointed out a German Luger, someone's relic from World War II.

"What do you want?" Papa Belota asked.

"We're looking for Dunstan Quentis," she told him. "We know he brought you some stolen pearl necklaces to sell, and you reported him to the police."

"Am I to be hounded for obeying the law?"

"We just wondered what your relationship is with Quentis."

"There is no relationship. I never saw him before he walked in here with those pearls."

"You must get many pearls in this city."

"Not so many. Folks are more likely to sell them to jewelers. But the police had issued an alert about these stolen necklaces. As soon as I saw them I reported it, and they arrested him at the address he'd given me."

There was no more to be learned at Papa Belota's. As they went back to the car Annie had another idea. "What about that older brother Quentis had down here? Wouldn't Quentis have contacted him?"

"It's worth a try," Munson agreed. He called Officer Paseo on his cell phone and asked about the brother. He made a few notes and then hung up. "Brother's name is Benedict Quentis. He's in the wholesale fish business. Runs a company that sends a boat out to buy fish as soon as they're caught. The fishermen sell to him and don't need to come into port to unload their catch."

"Do you have his address?"

"Yeah. He might still be around the docks. It's not the sort of job where there are regular office hours."

They found the brother without difficulty at the dock where his boat was anchored. He was obviously older than Dunstan but bore little resemblance to him. For one thing, he had a thick head of dark hair, handsome features, and a suave manner that seemed more capable of obtaining pearls by persuasion than by robbing jewelry stores. He was laughing and joking with his men.

"I know nothing about my brother," he insisted after they introduced themselves. "The last I heard he was serving time in a California prison. If he was on the run, he'd never come to me." As he spoke he watched his men unloading the day's catch into a wheeled cart to take inside.

"A good day?" Annie asked.

"Average." The cart bore the name of Benedict Quentis and a symbol of a cup and a coiled serpent.

"What's that?" she asked. "Do you catch snakes too?" He smiled at the question. "It is a symbol of Saint Benedict. I come from a Catholic family."

"You and your brother studied to be priests," she remembered.

"It didn't take for either of us, especially Dunstan. I think that broke my mother's heart. It's a blessing she or my father didn't live to see what became of him."

"He's wanted in the States for killing a police officer," Munson told him.

"Nothing about him would surprise me."

He had to leave then to help with the fish.

"There's nothing more for us here," Munson decided.

"You don't think he could be lying?" Annie wondered.

The detective smiled. "Think Quentis is hiding here under a pile of fish? Want to go searching for him?"

"Then where do we go?"

"There's still the ferry to Los Mochis for us to check out. It's almost six thirty."

The ship proved to be a large car ferry capable of transporting scores of vehicles and several hundred passengers across the hundred and forty miles to Lechuguilla Bay and Los Mochis. The journey took almost three hours, but a good crowd was lined up for the evening trip.

"If he is here we'll never find him in this mob," Annie said.

"They all have to pass through that gate. We'll spot him if he's here."

They scrutinized the boarding passengers and even checked the cars in line, but Quentis was not to be seen. "If he's wearing a wig over that bald head we might never spot him," she said.

"You're right about that. I've been looking for baldies."

The last of the passengers hurried on just before sailing time, and Munson turned away. "Another good idea gone sour," he decided. "Maybe he stayed near the airport after all."

But then suddenly she gripped his arm. "Is that him? The man running for the gate?"

"It sure is! Stay away from me this time, Sears. I've got him."

Quentis saw them at the last moment. He seemed to skid to a stop and change direction, but Munson already had his weapon out. "Freeze, Quentis, or you're a dead man!"

The fugitive turned suddenly toward them. It was unclear whether he meant to surrender or attack them, but Munson didn't wait to find out. He fired three quick shots, all three catching the bald man in the chest.

"You had to shoot him three times?" Annie asked later.

"I wasn't taking any chances this time."

"He wasn't even armed."

"Don't worry so much, Sears. Nobody asks many questions south of the border. He's a cop killer, remember?"

Officer Paseo had come at once following Munson's call to his cell phone. Unlike Annie, he saw no problem with the shooting of a cop-killing fugitive. "They'll probably give you a medal back in San Diego. Saves them the cost of a trial. You going to take the body back with you?"

Frank Munson thought about it. "No point in that. His parents are dead and his only sibling is down here. Maybe Benedict Quentis will even pay for the funeral, though I doubt it."

"We have to tell him about it anyway, before he sees it in the paper," Annie insisted. "I'll go if you don't want to, Frank."

Munson shrugged. "It's all yours."

Quentis's body had been removed. Munson accompanied Paseo back to the police station to give them an official statement, while Annie Sears took the rental car and drove back to the dock where they'd interviewed Benedict Quentis. He was nowhere around, and the fishing operation seemed to be closed down for the day. Finally she spotted one of the men who'd been loading fish into the cart.

"I'm looking for Benedict Quentis. Is he around?"

"Gone," the man replied. "Gone home."

"Where?"

"Or maybe to the Corridor for a beer. Who knows?"

"Where is the Corridor?"

He gave her directions to a restaurant and bar a few blocks away. At first Annie didn't see him in the dim light and decided she'd have to get his home address. Then she heard his distinctive laughter and spotted him in a corner booth with a woman.

She made her way over there and asked, "Could I see you alone, Mr. Quentis? It's very important."

He glared at her, squeezing the woman's shoulder and promising to be right back. They went off to a corner near the restrooms, and she told him his brother was dead. "My partner shot him as he was getting on the ferry to Los Mochis. He wouldn't surrender."

"Dunstan always was a stubborn fool," he said.

"Will you bury him here?"

He thought about that. "He doesn't deserve a funeral. Bury him where you like. If there's an expense, I will pay it. That's all. He was dead to me long ago."

"All right," she told him, not surprised at his decision. But something was still bothering her, something she couldn't quite put her finger on.

In the morning, she sought out a library that had English-language books. It took her some time to find what she wanted, and then she phoned Benedict Quentis from the police station. "We need you to identify the body," she told him. "Can you meet me at the morgue in the morning?"

"What is this? Can't you check his fingerprints? I haven't laid eyes on him in nearly twenty years."

"I'm sorry, sir, but as next of kin the local police say you must identify the body."

When she hung up, Frank Munson was standing over her. "What's that all about? We've got plane reservations for this afternoon."

"It won't take long, Frank. It's just something I want to check on. I messed this up at the start and I don't want to mess up again."

"Was that Quentis's brother you were talking to?"

She nodded. "I'm meeting him at the morgue in an hour."

"We don't need any identification. Paseo already sent the dead man's prints on to San Diego. That'll prove who he is."

"Just humor me. I want to make up for letting him get away yesterday."

"All right. Just make sure you're at the airport by one o'clock."

While she waited for Benedict, she spoke with the chief of detectives and phoned her office in San Diego. She had to make sure she was right this time. An hour later she was at the morgue, awaiting Benedict Quentis's arrival. When he came in he was hurried and nervous. "I don't want to see his body," he told her. "Not with bullet wounds in it."

"The wounds were in his chest. His face was untouched. He had a shaved head, so he's sure to look different from when you last saw him." She led the way in to the morgue supervisor, who pointed at one of the examining tables.

"That's the one from the ferry boat shooting," he told them.

Annie pulled back the sheet, revealing Dunstan Quentis's shaved head.

Benedict peered at the body. "I don't know. He looks so different now." He bent over and pulled the sheet down a bit further, revealing his left arm, and took a deep breath. "This isn't my brother," he said quietly. "This isn't Dunstan."

Annie allowed herself a slight smile. "Because there's no tattoo, right?"

She found Munson with Officer Paseo in the police squad room. "It's all over, Frank," she told him.

"What? What are you talking about?"

"Dunstan Quentis is still alive. You shot the wrong man."

He stood up, shaking his head. "That's crazy. Paseo here already sent the dead man's fingerprints to San Diego."

"Then I guess you've both got a lot of explaining to do."

Two local detectives had entered the room behind her. One of them said, "You'd better surrender your weapons."

"What is this?" Munson yelled. "Has everyone gone crazy?"

"Only you, Frank. How did you ever expect to get away with this?"

"Do you mind telling me what you're talking about?"

"Two things struck me as odd when we called at Striker's house yesterday. First, he called you by name—Sergeant Munson—though no one had mentioned your name or rank. Then as we were leaving, the teenage girl with him whispered 'Quentis here' in my ear. I didn't realize she was trying to tell me that Striker was really Quentis. But I remembered the tattoo of a harp on his upper arm. When his brother Benedict told us he used the serpent and cup as his logo because it was a symbol of Saint Benedict, I remembered that harp. I spent some time at a library this morning and discovered that a harp is a symbol of Saint Dunstan. It was a religious family, as Benedict told me. I checked with the SD police and learned that Quentis had a harp tattoo."

"I know nothing about this," Officer Paseo muttered without much passion.

"I think you know everything about it. Quentis had money from his robberies. Once he was arrested it wasn't too difficult for him to bribe you and arrange for Frank to handle the supposed extradition. You picked me as your partner, Frank, because I was new to the force and you figured I wouldn't ask questions. You showed me a mug shot of Quentis, which was really a shot of Striker, already set up to take his place. Once down here, you found an excuse to enter the jail alone to pick up Quentis. Paseo came downstairs with you both and in the lobby the switch was made. Quentis became Striker and Striker became Quentis. You brought the bald Striker out in handcuffs while the real Quentis escaped out another door. It might never have worked in a San Diego jail, but down here it was easy."

"If I knew he wasn't really Quentis, why did I shoot him?"

"Supposedly you'd arranged for him to escape, slipping him a key to the handcuffs. But in truth killing him was always part of the plan. He'd be buried here, and Quentis's real fingerprints would be sent to San Diego as proof of his death. Quentis would start a new life as Striker. But I hit your gun arm and saved his life the first time, which complicated everything. We met the phony Striker and we met Benedict Quentis. I put a few ideas together and asked Benedict to identify his brother's body. The tattoo was missing, of course, and I knew the truth."

One of the detectives took over the story then. "We arrested the real Quentis at Striker's home an hour ago. It looks as if you'll be flying home alone, Miss Sears. Quentis and these two will all face charges here—everything from bribery and prison escape to murder."

"I think I'll enjoy the trip." She turned to Munson. "I'm sorry I didn't work out as your partner, Frank. I guess you should have picked a man for this job."

A Traffic in Webs. *Ellery Queen's Mystery Magazine*, mid-December 1993
A Fondness for Steam. *Ellery Queen's Mystery Magazine*, July1994
A Parcel of Deerstalkers. *Ellery Queen's Mystery Magazine*, January 1995
An Abundance of Airbags. *Ellery Queen's Mystery Magazine*, July1995
A Craving for Chinese. *Ellery Queen's Mystery Magazine*, December 1995
A Parliament of Peacocks. *Ellery Queen's Mystery Magazine*, June 1996
A Shipment of Snow. *Ellery Queen's Mystery Magazine*, December 1996
A Shower of Daggers. *Ellery Queen's Mystery Magazine*, June 1997
A Busload of Bats. *Ellery Queen's Mystery Magazine*, November 1998
A Convergence of Clerics. *Ellery Queen's Mystery Magazine*, December 2006
A Gateway to Heaven. *Ellery Queen's Mystery Magazine*, January 2008
Five-Day Forecast. *Ellery Queen's Anthology #48* 1983
The Invisible Intruder. *Ellery Queen's Mystery Magazine*, mid-December 1984
Wait Until Morning. *Ellery Queen's Mystery Magazine*, December 1985
The Cactus Killer. *Alfred Hitchcock's Mystery Magazine*, October 2005
First Blood. *Alfred Hitchcock's Mystery Magazine*, March 2007
Baja. *Alfred Hitchcock's Mystery Magazine*, September 2008

Hoch's Ladies

Hoch's Ladies by Edward D. Hoch is printed on 60-pound Natures recycled acid-free stock, from 12-point Goudy Old Style, a font devised by Frederick W. Goudy in 1915. The cover design is by Gail Cross. The first printing is in two forms: trade softcover and one hundred fifty copies sewn in cloth. Each of the clothbound copies includes a separate pamphlet, *The Cases of Nancy Trentino* by Edward D. Hoch. The book was printed by Southern Ohio Printers and bound by Cincinnati Bindery. It was published in November 2019 by Crippen & Landru Publishers, Cincinnati, Ohio.

Subscriptions

Subscribers agree to purchase each forthcoming publication, either the Regular Series or the Lost Classics or (preferably) both. Collectors can thereby guarantee receiving limited editions, and readers won't miss any favorite stories.

Subscribers receive a discount of 20% off the list price (and the same discount on our backlist) and a specially commissioned short story by a major writer in a deluxe edition as a gift at the end of the year.

The point for us is that, since customers don't pick and choose which books they want, we have a guaranteed sale even before the book is published, and that allows us to be more imaginative in choosing short story collections to issue.

That's worth the 20% discount for us. Sign up now and start saving. Email us at info@crippenlandru.com or visit our website at www.crippenlandru.com on our subscription page.